Chris Thorndyke was born in Totnes in South Devon and lived in what he describes as the most beautiful coastal resort in Britain, Torbay. A father of three grown-up sons and five grandchildren, he now lives in Sweden with his wife and their two pet dogs – Alice, a sweet little King Charles spaniel, and Sally, an adorable woolly Australian labradoodle.

For Sheila, my mother, who is never too busy for a good story.

For Sheila, my mother, who is never too busy for a good story.

Chris Thorndyke

EBENEZER DUNN

A Charlatan, Traitor and Spy

AUSTIN MACAULEY PUBLISHERS™

LONDON * CAMBRIDGE * NEW YORK * SHARJAH

A CIP catalogue record for this title is available from the British Library.

ISBN 9781528978552 (Paperback)
ISBN 9781528978576 (ePub e-book)

www.austinmacauley.com

First Published (2021)
Austin Macauley Publishers Ltd
25 Canada Square
Canary Wharf
London
E14 5LQ

My thanks to the people of Ashprington village in Devon whose help and assistance enabled me to visualise Sharpham Estate and their lovely village in the eighteenth century. Also, to the National Trust whose information and guidance allowed me through the door of the resplendent Saltram House in Plymouth in the year 1775. Not forgetting a big thank you to my wife, Anki, whose never-ending patience saw me through to the last chapter of my tale.

Synopsis

Devon, 1775. A temporary rector arrives in the Devon village of Ashprington, but he is certainly not what he seems to be to his parishioners.

The church of St David in the village of Ashprington, sees the arrival of the Reverend Ebenezer Dunn, who has instructions from the French to spy on the bustling harbour of Dartmouth and to create instability amongst the inhabitants in the villages and hamlets along the River Dart. He embraces his mission with fervour, seeing it also as a means of fulfilling his desires to follow a life of self-indulgence and affluence.

Establishing links with Squire Roger Maddock of Darton Hall, a ruthless smuggling baron, Ebenezer forms a syndicate of smugglers from the village to undertake the hazardous smuggling contracts proposed by the Squire.

The drums of war are beating in the American colonies, and a treacherous member of the village pressures Ebenezer to gather more information for his spymaster in Plymouth.

Hearing of a secret plan to bring King George III to the stately home of Saltram House in Plymouth, Ebenezer conspires with his spymaster to bring about a disaster that would deliver a catastrophic blow to England and fuel plans for an imminent invasion by the French.

Chapter 1

Devon

1775

The shoal of wild brown trout flittered through the limpid waters of the River Dart, riding the current as it flowed through the lush Devonshire countryside of Dartington, to pass under the old stone bridge at Totnes and then on to meander its way around the evergreen pastures of Sharpham Estate.

Here, the river widens, running deep and green as it curves graciously around Ashprington Point, narrowing as it passes heavily-wooded banks on each of its sides. Ancient oak and beech trees rise like aged sentinels, sheltering and guarding the timeless course of the river as it weaves its way towards Dartmouth and release to the open sea.

Numerous flocks of piscivorous birds abound in these wooded areas, and it was here that one such bird, perched high up in the branches of a spindly pine tree, sat motionless, scrutinising the underwater movement of the shoal.

The osprey's glowing yellow eyes bored down, penetrating the water and x-raying the fish with pinpoint accuracy. Eyes rivetted in concentration, the bird of prey was oblivious to the sudden blueish green flash of a kingfisher jetting downriver. Calmly, it opened its hooked black bill, and rising effortlessly from the branch of the tree, it hovered over the river, shadowing the shoal as it darted round the Point.

Like a textbook example, the osprey dropped. Diving with feet outstretched and sighting its yellow eyes straight along its talons, it hit the water and smoothly scooped out a member of the shoal. Clutching the trout in its talons, it rose laboriously from the surface of the river, flapping its powerful wings in a kind of slow motion until it gained suitable height.

Above the trees and with the river far below, the osprey turned in flight and with its wings bent and bowed downwards, it arrowed upriver, abruptly changing course to skim the riverside foliage at Ham Point. Flying high over the medieval tower of St David's Church in the village of Ashprington, it arced in a starboard direction setting a new course for its stick nest high up in the riverside trees, where hungry young ones squawked and squealed in anticipation of their mother's return and the impending feast.

Floating on a breeze that rippled through the stillness of the riverside trees, the distant sound of a church congregation singing their Sunday morning praises whispered over the river as the osprey raised its wings, and with legs and talons outstretched, gently glided onto its nest to the welcoming screeches of its young.

Half a mile due west of the osprey's nest, across the fields of Sharpham Estate and three miles south-east of the Deanery of Totnes, lay the village of Ashprington and St David's Church. Early summer was upon the village and neighbouring countryside. Multitudes of buds ripening on the apple trees heralded an oncoming abundance of fruit, while profusions of bright yellow dandelions in the surrounding meadows cheekily projected their fervour to all who passed by.

It was with a feeling of joy and jubilation that the congregation of St David's Church lifted their voices in praise to the words of Isaac Watts' hymn, 'All Glory to Thy Wondrous Name', rising to a crescendo in its final verse until eventually disappearing across the pastures of Sharpham Estate and on towards the river.

Peering over his spectacles that sat precariously balanced at the end of his nose, the Reverend Ebenezer Dunn looked upon his congregation, perusing each with deep regard as they came to the end of the hymn of glory.

The warmth of the summer sunshine radiating through the church windows and the heavy gown he wore as an Anglican minister, had agonisingly brought on a trickle of sweat, which was uncomfortably exuding down his back.

A badly-fitting thick tie-wig beneath his Canterbury cap was causing his scalp to itch furiously, but he dared not give way to the temptation of relieving the irritation with a swift scratch as the risk of the wig and cap falling off was too embarrassing to contemplate. It would wait until after the service when he was alone in the small vestry behind the sanctuary. But before doing that, he had important and secret information to give to a member of his flock, sitting somewhere in front of him, waiting for his sign that they were to meet later in secret.

Ebenezer scanned his congregation, not knowing the identity of his contact but trying to pick up on any facial revelation that might indicate who his

11

accomplice could be. There was nothing that could confirm whom it might be. But he or she was there, that he knew. Gently, he pulled on his left ear.

Captain Philemon Pownoll RN, landowner and gentleman of Sharpham Estate, looked sideways at his wife Jane, trying to hide the grin of amusement that was beginning to crease the corners of his mouth. He could see that Jane was struggling to suppress a fit of giggling as she also found the spectacle of Ebenezer Dunn highly comical. To control herself she turned to their young daughter, Jane, with the pretence of adjusting her daughter's bonnet.

"Jane," she whispered, holding her left hand up to her face while her body started to shake with laughter, "just pretend Mama's loosening your bonnet, please, my darling."

"Mama," whispered young Jane, "the Reverend looks like a silly old clown!"

This was too much for her mother, reddening in the face and starting to sweat she turned towards her husband. Seeing his wife's embarrassment, Philemon thrust a handkerchief towards her as silence reigned throughout the church, making it an even more unbearable spectacle. Biting her tongue and concentrating on a small painting of the crucifixion of Christ on a side wall of the outer aisle, she composed herself as Ebenezer's voice rose in an introduction to his sermon. A sudden loud yawn followed by an expulsion of intestinal gas from someone in the congregation cut short Ebenezer's homily, and with titters of amusement resounding around the church, he irately moved to the side of the altar and began preparations for the distribution of communion.

Jane sat with her hand to her mouth, fearful of erupting into uncontrollable laughter as Ebenezer began waggling his bushy eyebrows up and down to shift the position of his badly-fitting wig. A tug at her mother's sleeve and a look of desperation to relieve herself gave Jane the excuse she needed.

Taking her daughter's hand, she hurried out of the church, closing the door with a bubbling of irrepressible giggles.

Customary in the Anglican Church, a short period of reflection and contemplation after the distribution of communion gave Ebenezer the chance to take a short break, and he gratefully slid into the high-backed altar chair as silence descended around the church. His scalp itched furiously but there was no way he could tear off the thick wig to scratch at the agonising torment. It would have to wait.

Looking away from the congregation and jerking his eyebrows up and down while his ears wiggled to and fro in unison, he focused his gaze on the top corner of a glass window behind the altar, where a fuzzy-like buff-tailed bumblebee was scratching frantically at a corner pane of glass. Mesmerised by the bumblebee's efforts to find a way out, and the warm rays of sunlight streaming through the window, Ebenezer found himself drifting away in his thoughts and memories.

It had been two months since he'd arrived at St David's Church as temporary rector, to stand in for the Reverend Nathaniel Terry who had suddenly been taken ill and had not been heard of since leaving Ashprington to convalesce.

"And nor would he be heard of again," smiled Ebenezer to himself.

Unknown to the Deanery of Totnes, who had approved Ebenezer's temporary position, and to the parishioners of Ashprington, the Reverend Ebenezer Dunn was certainly not what he appeared to them to be.

A cough from someone in the congregation disturbed Ebenezer's thoughts, and squinting through half-open eyes he chuckled inwardly at his deception of making them think he was deep in prayer. Only a few minutes had passed since the distribution of communion, so another five minutes in this pose would do no harm. He smiled at the memory of the years he'd spent as an assistant chaplain at a boarding school for young gentlemen in Plymouth and the free time he had found available for him to seek out the pleasures that the city had had to offer.

It had been one cold wet autumn afternoon as he relaxed in the sweetly-scented parlour of Miss Fanny's house of ill-repute on the Barbican. He had inadvertently struck up a conversation with a gentleman who was waiting, as was Ebenezer, for the services of a particularly favourite employee of the house. As they chatted, Ebenezer was impressed with the fervour of the gentleman's belief in the injustices being swamped on the North American Colonists and their struggle to achieve a fairer representation in the British Parliament. Their conversation was cut short by the arrival of Carolina, a sultry, full-lipped beauty who seemed impatient to escort Ebenezer's newly-found acquaintance away and into the excitingly dark confines of Miss Fanny's rooms of pleasure. As they bid their farewells, the gentleman handed him his card which surprised Ebenezer but interested him all the same.

Well, well, he thought as he digested the name on the card. *A Frenchman, here in Plymouth!*

The name, Luc Skorniere, stared up at him from the card with an address of an inn on Plymouth's Barbican roughly legible at the bottom.

I'll pay him a visit, decided Ebenezer, *won't do any harm, something may come from it.*

A polite cough behind him and the soft sensual voice of Annie brought a lecherous smile to his face.

"Now, you naughty, naughty boy," she cooed, "are you going to spank me for being late? You'd better come with me, you naughty boy!"

Philemon watched a slight smile stretch across the minister's mouth as he studied him in the quiet moments of spiritual reflexion.

There's something about this minister that doesn't seem right, he thought. *I'd doubt he'd smile like that if he were deep in prayer!*

He turned to settle his daughter next to him, who was wriggling and fidgeting in boredom and as he bent to whisper a loving message in her ear. His eyes flicked over the congregation seated stoically in the pews behind him.

Barold Raustin, a carpenter and master builder who had undertaken the renovation work of the Pownolls' mansion house on Sharpham Estate several years before, sat upright next to his wife Hilary, a serious look embedded in his features. Behind him sat Stephen Moore, a boat builder from the adjacent village of Tuckenhay who had built Philemon a sailing skiff for his frequent visits downriver to Dartmouth. Next to Stephen sat the ruddy-faced Mordechai Brunt, Sharpham's long-standing herdsman whom Philemon had kept on after he had purchased the estate with the aim of increasing the beef cattle herd. Elijah Hatch, landlord of The Ashprington Inn, sat erect at the end of the pew, his eyes glued towards Ebenezer. Lucy Hatch, Elijah's wife, sat next to him clutching his arm.

With a sigh Philemon sat back in his pew, gently caressing his daughter's hand.

He would be departing Ashprington in two days, leaving behind the peaceful life he had so long been enjoying with his family. The drums of war had begun to beat in the American colonies, emboldening him to retake his commission in the Royal Navy. He would be leaving Sharpham to join his ship, HMS *Blonde*, and then sail as part of an escort to twenty troop transporters to the British-held harbour of Boston, Massachusetts.

But before that, he and his wife Jane were to be guests of honour at the stately home of Saltram House in Plymouth. Philemon's good friend, John Parker, and his wife, Theresa, were holding a dinner party and ball that very evening with a night's stay over for the Pownolls, while young Jane would stay at home, in the care of Betsy Gribble, Sharpham's housekeeper.

A loud clearing of his throat brought about the congregation's attention, as Ebenezer rose from his chair. Glancing up at the high window behind the altar, he noticed that the buff-tailed bumblebee had finally given up in its efforts to find a way out and sadly, lay rigidly still in the corner of the stone windowsill.

Smiling contemptuously at the bumblebee's misfortune, Ebenezer smoothed down the balloon sleeves of his clerical gown and addressed his congregation.

"Brethren, thank you all for attending Sunday Service this morning." Pausing slightly, he scanned the congregation, noticing the serious looks on Barold Raustin and his wife Hilary, the gaze of expectancy on Stephen Moore and the smiling face of Mordechai Brunt.

"Brethren," continued Ebenezer, "as you're all aware by now, war has come to our North American Colonies. Captain Pownoll will be leaving in two days to join his fleet, God bless you, sir. It is my duty to inform you all that the rebel colonists are being helped and assisted to revolt against our lawfully elected government by none other than the French."

"Bliddy Frenchies," screeched Betsy Gribble, Philemon's housekeeper, "us'll give them hell and a bliddy nose to go with it!"

"You'm be right, Bets," shouted Mordechai, clenching his right hand into a massive rock-like fist. "Us'll be ready for them bliddy garlic eaters and give them a bliddy good slap should any of they try comin' up'r river. Bliddy Frenchies!"

"Ar, a bliddy good seein' to," echoed Rufus Mudd, the village blacksmith, turning his oversized balding head in Mordechai's direction and giving him a rotten toothy grin.

"We must be vigilant at all times and keep a good look out for any strangers. Also, beware the stalking Judas," said Ebenezer, smiling inwardly to himself. "He may lurk on any corner, listening as you converse or even gossip with your neighbour."

Silence filled the church as the congregation sat rigidly still, listening intently to Ebenezer's words of warning.

That, he chuckled, *will certainly put the cat amongst the pigeons!*

After the service, Ebenezer waited outside the church to catch the Pownolls.

"Captain," he grovelled, "my prayers and wishes go with you and I will beseech The Almighty for your safe return. Mistress Pownoll," he crowed, turning to face Jane, "I am always at your service. Should you find yourself in need of any spiritual gratification while your brave husband is away at sea, then I am here to serve. I am at your service, madam."

Without any warning, the top of Ebenezer's head seemed to shuffle unexpectedly and as Jane watched wide-eyed, his thick tie-wig and Canterbury cap slid slowly down his forehead to rest perilously over his bushy eyebrows.

Trying to suppress the fit of giggling that was welling up in her, Jane bowed her head towards the minister and tugged at Philemon's arm with an urgency to depart. Taking young Jane's hand, she turned away and with an uncontrollable screech of laughter, quickly walked away towards the church gate, her body quaking with the giggling she had tried to suppress. Philemon, trying to keep a straight face in front of Ebenezer, politely excused himself and rushed off to catch up with Jane. At the church gate, Jane calmed herself, but turning to look back at the minister and finding the whole scenario one of the funniest things she'd ever witnessed, gave way to the laughter that burst out of her, causing tears to stream down her cheeks. All three Pownolls stood at the gate guffawing with mirth until Philemon untethered the pony and trap tied next to the church gate. As the two Janes settled themselves, he flicked the reins and the little carriage moved off in the direction of Sharpham to the accompaniment of their howls of laughter.

Standing alone at the church porch, Ebenezer watched them go, fuming at Jane's blatant dismissal of him. Cursing at the Pownolls' show of disrespect towards him, he tore off his clerical cap and wig, then with an accursed look in the direction of Sharpham Estate, he turned around and strode back inside the church.

Seated in the small vestry, he hastily filled a large silver chalice with church wine, greedily slurping it in great gulps and vulgarly licking the sides of his mouth as it trickled down his chin to stain the white cloth of his clerical gown.

Reflecting on his past meeting with Luc Skorniere in Plymouth, he smiled at the excitement he had felt as he agreed to provide information of any maritime changes in and around the harbour of Dartmouth. He would collect relevant information that would be advantageous to Britain's enemies, acting as a spy for the French in their mission to promote the North American Colonists' cause. With the information he had managed to gather and pass onto Luc Skorniere, he would become rich with the fat purses promised.

Powerful unknown figures had seen him appointed as temporary Rector of the Parish of Ashprington, a perfect position for him to watch and listen, whilst at the same time giving him ample opportunity to mislead his parishioners with fake news of rebel successes and the fear of conspirators within the village.

Worthwhile information would reward him well, and after the war he would disappear to France for a life of pleasure. Soon, his contact would come to the church to pass on the information he had gleaned for Luc Skorniere.

He was ready. Chuckling, he drained the wine from the chalice and glaring contemptibly around the room, he raised his arm and flung the sacred vessel at the bare stone wall facing him.

* * *

The carriage sent by John Parker to convey Philemon and Jane to Saltram House for the dinner party and ball came to a halt outside the open iron gates of the grand stately home. The coachman blew a shrill blast on his horn, then with a flick of the reins, the carriage glided through the entrance to a magnificent carriageway lined with rows of majestic lanterns illuminating the surrounding lawns and gardens of the august residence.

Although early summer was clearly under way, a well-stacked glowing brazier in front of the grand pillars supporting the entrance portico, warmly greeted the arriving guests. Two liveried servants ushered Philemon and Jane into the gracious reception area where a night's stayover in one of the resplendent bedchambers, had been gratefully accepted.

The atmosphere in the grand reception hall that evening surged with excitement and goodwill. Servants cruised between clusters of chattering guests, offering glasses of grape-scented mulled wine that sat invitingly on glistening silver trays, while a strikingly ample stone fireplace, dynamic and alive with logs blazing cheerily, proffered warmth to those who felt the chill of the early summer evening.

As Philemon and Jane gave up their cloaks and hats, a hearty call of welcome rang out across the hall.

"Welcome, dearest friends, welcome indeed," called John as he hurried towards them.

Turning to acknowledge the greeting, Philemon's face broadened into a beam of friendly affection, as John, with arms open, approached them. Greeting one another with handshakes and genial backslapping, John then turned to Jane, and taking her hand he kissed it respectfully, assuring her of his great joy in once again being in their company.

"Welcome to you, dearest friends," said Theresa, who had been waiting patiently at John's side. "It's been several months since we all last met and while we're happy to see you, there is a touch of sadness, Philemon, that you'll be departing from us in the next two days. But let us not dwell on such matters, the night is yet young, and we are here to enjoy and be happy. Jane, as you can see by my size, it's not long now until the arrival of our new baby. Come with me later and see the new nursery we've created, it's so exciting, is it not, John?"

"Absolutely, my darling, yes indeed," replied John. "But now, my dearest friends, Theresa and I must leave you as it's our duty to welcome our guests into the dining hall now that you are all about to be summoned for dinner, but our conversation shall continue."

As Philemon and Jane watched the guests filtering into the banqueting hall, they became aware of a liveried servant hovering by their side. Turning, he addressed Philemon and Jane, "I'm to escort you both to your table as soon as the last guests have entered. Please be so kind as to wait for a moment."

Philemon smiled, his mind going back to his first encounter with John.

They had met at a livestock market in Totnes during the autumn of 1769, and over several bottles of vintage claret, had discovered their mutual interest in the love of the Devonshire countryside as well as both being born Plymothians and owners of large estates.

John had sadly accounted the loss of his first wife Frances, then with a broad grin had proudly announced his marriage to Theresa Robinson, assuring Philemon of the happiness it had brought him. He talked about his ancestral home of Saltram with great pride and described the collection of highly valued and acclaimed paintings that graced Saltram's walls. He spoke of his friend, Sir Joshua Reynolds, also Devon born and knighted by King George III in that year, depicting him as an outstanding portrait painter. Philemon's introduction to the great man had taken place later that year at Saltram's Grand Christmas Ball. Philemon and Sir Joshua had struck up a convivial friendship, and in the new year of 1770, Sir Joshua had agreed to the commissioning of painting Philemon's and Jane's portraits, now proudly displayed on the walls of Sharpham House. Invitations to the estates of Saltram and Sharpham had followed, with Philemon regularly accompanying John on several of his hunting trips where he'd learned of John's commitment as a Member of Parliament for Devon and of his great honour at having been endorsed as a fellow of the Royal Society, but never once did Philemon feel any hint of imperiousness or snobbery emanate from him.

A gentle applause from everyone seated in the banqueting hall greeted Jane's and Philemon's entry where they were escorted to the top table and their smiling hosts. Standing to the side of John, Sir Joshua Reynolds beamed a friendly greeting to Philemon while bowing courteously to Jane. Seating themselves, Sir Joshua turned to Philemon offering him his hand in a friendly handshake.

"My pleasure, Philemon, it's been a few years since we last met. It seems the gentry of England are competing for my services. I've such little time for myself in between my commissions. I'm honoured to make your acquaintance yet again, my friend."

"Likewise, sir," replied Philemon firmly shaking his hand. "It's a privilege to meet with you again. May I inform you that our portraits hang graciously from the walls of our home at Sharpham, giving us and those who view them much pleasure."

"Splendid, Philemon, splendid," replied Sir Joshua, looking over at Jane. "Jane," he said, getting up and taking her hand with a bow, "a pleasure to see you, you are as lovely as ever."

Jane blushed at the flattery of this well-known bachelor. "Sir Joshua, you are as charming as ever, thank you."

"Now, let us to table, dear friends," interrupted John, "a scrumptious banquet awaits."

Over the various courses, Philemon and Sir Joshua engaged in incessant conversation, Sir Joshua insisting at one point that Philemon relate his experience of capturing a Spanish treasure ship during the Seven Years' War and the bounty it rewarded him, to several parliamentary colleagues of John who sat transfixed with fascination and awe at Philemon's detailed and vivid account. Sir Joshua was thrilled with Philemon's association with the sea, as in his youth, he had experienced his own adventures across the oceans, particularly his exploits through the Mediterranean before ending up in Rome where he'd stayed for two years studying the old masters.

"And, it was there, Philemon," he said loudly pointing to his left ear, "that I got deaf in this ear and therefore rely on this contraption to hear what you're saying."

With that, he pulled a small ear trumpet from his pocket and laughing uncontrollably, stuck it in his ear.

"Now, what do you think of that, eh?"

John, looking over at the laughing figure of Sir Joshua, grabbed Philemon's arm and smiling at his good friend said, "A good invention to keep your brushes in while working, Joshua!"

"Ha, well said, John," chortled Sir Joshua. "Perhaps I'll give it a try, ha. But now I need to speak to Jane."

Clutching his hearing aid in his hand, Sir Joshua rose from his chair to press past Philemon and taking a spare chair from the corner of the room, he squeezed in next to Jane.

"Dear Jane," he began, "for some time I've been wanting to create a portrait that extols the innocent. I have been wondering how I can find a perfect example to portray a true vision of innocence and purity. Nothing I have produced in my work of young children captures this theme entirely. I need a face of a young, true innocent, so I would ask you if you and Philemon would permit me to study the features of your young daughter Jane. She is twelve years old now, I know, but it is the age when the look of true innocence is so utterly apparent and this is what I need to capture, even though the final picture will likely be a girl slightly younger than Jane."

"Sir Joshua," replied Jane, "Philemon and I would be honoured, and we'd feel greatly privileged to be able to assist you in any way you'd deem helpful."

"Thank you most sincerely, Jane," smiled Sir Joshua, "I'll contact you with plans and times when I'd appreciate young Jane to sit. She'll be the subject of a new portrait. I think I'll keep the title simple and call it: 'The Age of Innocence'."

"Good friends, one and all," called out John tapping his wine goblet and beaming at his guests, "the evening is yet young and if you listen carefully, you'll hear music floating around Saltram, the orchestra is warming up in the ballroom."

As the Parkers' guests left the dining room for the ballroom, a flurry of servants descended on the tables while Philemon and Jane waited with Sir Joshua for John to help Theresa from her chair. Several of the liveried male servants were clearing away the remnants of the top table when Sir Joshua grasped Philemon's arm. Holding his ear trumpet up to his ear, his voice rang out across the dining room, "Philemon, when you depart for The Colonies, which port will you and your company arrive in?"

Flushed with the excitement of the evening and a little too much wine, Philemon responded loudly without any thought of who may be listening, "We'll be leaving, all being well, in ten days. I have the command of HMS *Blonde* as part of an escort for a convoy of troop carriers we'll be accompanying to the port of Boston, in Massachusetts."

Unknown to those left in the dining hall, the ears of a liveried servant crossing the room suddenly pricked up, a smile forming as his eyes focused on Philemon.

"Boston, Massachusetts," he repeated silently to himself and hurried from the room.

At the entrance to the ballroom, Philemon gazed with avid appreciation at a room that never failed to impress him. A galaxy of candles enthroned in glittering chandeliers proudly flaunted the Rococo plasterwork of the elaborate ceiling. Admirable paintings and portraits charmed the finely-decorated walls, one of which Philemon recognised as that of Theresa and her young son John, by Sir Joshua. A tap on his shoulder signalled he was needed and turning he looked upon the radiant face of Jane.

"Come, Philemon, we're needed on the dance floor. I'm sure you'll remember the dance to the tune they're going to play, we danced to it when we first met."

Jane took his arm as they glided onto the dance floor where guests, including John and Sir Joshua, had lined up for the first dance. Seated on a chair, Theresa sat fanning herself, tapping her feet to the music as it drifted around the ballroom and then out of an adjacent window to disappear over the grounds of Saltram.

In the early hours, flushed and exhausted from their exertions on the dance floor, Philemon and Jane bade their goodnights to their hosts, and following one of Saltram's servants, retired to the lavish bedroom the Parkers had allocated them. Arms encircling one another in the sumptuous four-poster bed, they drifted off into a contented sleep, Jane reliving the entire evening in her dreams, while Philemon sailed the Mediterranean with John and Sir Joshua at his side.

Chapter 2

The evening chorus of little riverside frogs peeping out their mating calls from the banks of the River Dart, drifted across the pastures of Sharpham Estate to seep through the windows and cracks of St David's Church, where the Reverend Ebenezer Dunn waited in the penetrating twilight for the arrival of his co-conspirator. The sign of a discreet pull on his left ear during the morning service, had signalled to the mysterious informer he had important information to impart and it was at this hour, as evening fell, that their covert rendezvous would take place.

The creaking of the heavy church door slowly opening brought Ebenezer stealthily out of his pew and into the shadows of the side aisle where he watched the broad shape of a cloaked figure slip through the opening and into the duskiness of the church. Concealed within the deep hood of his cloak, the figure stood quietly in front of the baptismal font enveloped by the ever-growing darkness around him.

"Where you'm be?" it whispered.

"Over here, in the side aisle under the painting of The Four Evangelists," replied Ebenezer in a hushed tone.

"Keep your distance," the figure murmured moving in the direction of Ebenezer's reply.

"What have you got for me?" it asked.

"Some navy news," said Ebenezer, trying to make out who this mysterious person could be. "News that Captain Pownoll of Sharpham Estate has retaken his commission in the Royal Navy and will leave for Chatham Docks in two days to join his ship HMS *Blonde*. He will captain the ship which will be part of an escort accompanying a convoy of twenty troop carriers to the American Colonies. They'll be leaving within ten days under the command of General John Burgoyne."

"Which colony?" demanded the figure. "And what harbour?"

"That I don't know," replied Ebenezer staring into the dark shadows where the figure stood.

"How did you come by this news?" asked the figure.

"The woman who cleans the church, Betsy Gribble, she's also housekeeper at Sharpham for the Pownolls. She overheard Captain Pownoll discussing it with his wife, and being a gossipmonger, she jabbered it out to me, the very next day. I have warned her, under the threat of her going to hell, that she is not to mention this news to anyone. The threat of hell will keep her mouth shut. She will now report everything she hears at Sharpham to me. She really believes I have the power to send her to hell, foolish woman!"

"Find out which colony and harbour," the figure instructed.

"My reward will be forthcoming?" stammered Ebenezer.

"In time, Reverend, when you give me your next news," hissed the figure turning towards the exit.

The church door slammed shut as Ebenezer stood completely still in the darkening gloom puzzling over the identity of the contact. Above him, a solitary beam of moonlight shot across the nave of the church lighting up The Four Evangelists, who seemed to be looking forlornly down to where he stood.

Sitting back in the church pew, he scowled at his failure to secure payment for the information he had given. He would have to wait until he provided new facts that would interest his contact and Luc Skorniere, and only then would he be paid for the information he had just passed over. He wanted money, as much money as he could get. Being a traitor to his country was of no concern to him, provided it paid well. And anyway, he had improved the Ashprington smugglers' profits since he had joined them. He grinned at the thought of his merry band of smugglers, all rogues at heart but well thought of amongst the village people. And then there was Squire Maddock of Darton Hall, a villainous promoter of the Devon smuggling barons. He had heartily welcomed Ebenezer and his group into his illicit organisation, seeing Ebenezer as a profligate village parson who was cleverly using his position to pursue hedonistic ambitions of self-indulgency and wealth, objectives the Squire recognised and applauded. As an ardent follower of the ideologies of hedonism himself, he was always pleased to welcome fellow disciples into his circle where he would manipulate them for his own benefit. A sudden realisation of sitting in complete darkness jolted Ebenezer upright. Getting to his feet, he stumbled through the darkened church and into the vestry, then lighting a candle he snatched a bottle of church wine and slumped onto a high-backed chair next to the robing table. Greedily, he gulped down half its contents and with a weary snort of disappointment, stretched out on the chair, shuffling himself into a comfortable position. He grinned at the recollection of a smuggling venture he and his band would undertake for Squire Maddock the following night and the fat purse it would bring.

Spread-eagled on the chair and gripping the half-empty bottle, his eyelids drooped as his mind conjured up pictures of the riches he would amass through his smuggling and acts of treachery. His arms dangled over the sides of the chair as his head lolled back, his lips blubbering to the sound of his snoring.

A little puddle of church wine began to form as the contents of the bottle he still flimsily clutched, slowly dripped onto the cold stone floor beneath him.

* * *

Two days later, to the sound of the first cock crows, Philemon rode out of the grounds that surrounded Sharpham Manor. His heart was heavy after the tearful farewells he had shared with his two Janes, but commitment and a fervent allegiance to his king and country had compelled him to make the decision to re-join the Royal Navy and war against the North American rebel colonists.

He reined his horse to a halt at the top of a hill, wanting to take one last look at his estate. Turning his horse around, he gazed down on his land that sloped down towards the waters of the River Dart. A sudden feeling of regret at his leaving and the twinges of homesickness began to bite at his heart. His eyes travelled along the timeless flow of the river as it gently wound its way past the boundaries of his estate, a river that was integral to the lives of all who worked and lived in its proximity, yet was also a thing unto itself. The Devon countryside that rolled back from the river never failed to take his breath away – a natural patchwork of greens and reddy browns that stretched like a great tartan hemmed together by boundless lines of thick green hedgerows. The variety of deciduous trees that formed the woodland on the banks of the river had grown for hundreds of years to provide majestic arrays of colour each autumn. Fields to his right and left, bathed in the early morning sunshine, radiated their richness in lush emerald greens and soft claret reds.

The distant sound of a five-barred gate slamming shut, accompanied by the lowing of beef cattle being driven to pasture by Mordechai Brunt, broke the spell. Easing his horse back in the direction of Ashprington village and hence the road to Plymouth – where young Watt Huckle, stable lad at Sharpham, would collect his horse later in the day – Philemon pulled his tricorn hat firmly down on his head, clicked his tongue and with a great sigh rode away from his estate and home for the stage coach, that would take him eventually to his ship in Chatham and war in the North American colonies.

Chapter 3

A strong breeze gusting off the water of Plymouth's oldest wharf known as 'The Barbican', whistled along its waterfront, fanning a row of seedy looking inns that overlooked its jetties and quays. Badly-fitting doors rattled on their latches, as a fading picture board of a ginger cat sitting next to a musical instrument resembling a fiddle, swayed back and forth above the door of the old dockside inn it touted.

Settling his horse in the rear of the Cat and Fiddle Inn, the traitor stretched his arms before him, creaking his neck and breathing in the salty brine that wafted off the sea, pleased that his ride from Ashprington across the fields and woodlands to this part of Plymouth was over. He could now enjoy the hospitality of the inn and deliver the news regarding Philemon Pownoll to the French master spy, who waited for him there. Smiling to himself at the thought of the bag of silver he'd collect for the information he'd got from the treacherous Anglican minister of St David's Church, he chuckled with pleasure, promising himself a hearty meal followed by a rumble in one of the inn's bedchambers with Nancy, the inn's busty serving wench and whore.

Pulling down his tricorn against the wind, he made his way towards the inn.

Raucous laughter and boisterous conversation met him as he opened its door and stepped into the smoky and rowdy atmosphere. Nobody paid him any attention as he stood by the door, peering at the ruffians who crowded over the tables, intent on their drinking and gambling. A sudden tap on his arm forced him to turn around sharply.

The flushed chubby cheeks and full ruby red lips of Nancy stared enticingly up at him as his eyes rested lecherously on the pair of enormous fleshy bosoms bursting from her bodice.

"He be over there, lover," she said, indicating a wooden booth in the far corner of the inn. "Would you be wantin' ale and maybe a little bit of fancy after? It'll be a shillin' if you do."

"Bring me ale, Nancy, and I'll 'ave me shillin's worth later," he said tearing his eyes away from her voluptuous breasts.

His contact sat pensively, drawing on his long clay pipe, his eyes darting from table to table studying the faces of the unruly and bawdy rabble wallowing in the inn's sleazy and squalid atmosphere.

"You have news?" he asked, as the traitor from Ashprington took his seat opposite.

"I do," he replied, "or I wouldn't be in this den of filth. Do you have my payment?"

"In good time," replied the Frenchman in perfect English, showing no trace of a foreign accent.

Nancy appeared at their booth with two mugs of ale, slapping them soundly down on the table's solid wooden surface, making sure she gave both men a good eyeful of what bulged beneath the top part of her stained and grubby gown. Holding her hand out for payment, the French spy dropped her a few coins, dismissing her with a flick of his hand thus showing her the contempt she knew he had for her. As she left, she made a rude gesture towards the booth only to be grabbed by a drunken sailor who forced her onto his knee to snuggle his ale-sodden face into her bosoms, much to the mirth and lewd encouragement of the companions seated around him.

"Oi 'ave reliable information," began the traitor, ignoring the distraction and speaking in a hushed tone. "The estate owner of Sharpham Manor, Captain Philemon Pownoll, 'as rejoined the Royal Navy, and with 'ees ship, HMS *Blonde*, will partake in escortin' a convoy of twenty British troop carriers, under the command of General Burgoyne, to the American colonies. They'm be departin' from Chatham Docks probably within ten days. Captain Pownoll left his 'ome early yesterday mornin' and was travellin' to Chatham via the stagecoach links from here in Plymouth, so he should be arrivin' in a few days. Oi expect you'm be wonderin' which harbour they be 'eadin' for. Oi doen know yet but oi assures you oi'll know within a few days."

"We already know," said the Frenchman enjoying the look of surprise on the traitor's face. "Never mind how we know, but it was the port the convoy would be sailing from and when that we didn't know. Also, we needed to know how many troop carriers would be sailing, so what you've told me will be essential to our plans. It's a bonus for us to know that it's General John Burgoyne who'll be commanding the troops, excellent information."

The traitor drained the last of his ale and sat back with a contented look, but curious how the French spy knew of the American port where the convoy would be headed. The need to get back to Ashprington before he was seriously missed began to play on his mind.

"My money, if you'm please, sir," he said.

"Ah, yes, of course," replied the Frenchman smiling, "your thirty pieces of silver!"

He pulled a leather bag from under the table, and making sure nobody was looking their way, opened it and withdrew a small cloth bag fastened at the top by two leather laces.

"Your payment," he said, tossing the bag of silver coins into the traitor's outstretched hand. "You know how to contact me when you have more news for us," he said, rising from the table. "Instruct my man at St David's church to keep his eyes and ears open, we want more regular information that can help our American friends in their struggle against the British. It won't be long before France enters the conflict to defeat Britain once and for all."

The traitor watched as the master spy momentarily paused at the door to glance back at the rabble, now filling the tables and nooks of the inn, then with a nod in his direction, he quietly opened the door and was gone.

"Nancy," bellowed the traitor, "more ale now. Bring me a plate of mutton and potatoes too. Your shillin's in me purse for when oi've supped well."

On the far side of the inn, Nancy looked up, giving the traitor a vulgar but promising gesture, giggling wickedly at the thought of earning another shilling.

Outside the Cat and Fiddle Inn, Luc Skorniere, French spy and devotee to his principal, Charles Gravier, comte de Vergennes, quickly finished writing a coded note then hurried along the Barbican to where a small sloop lay moored at the side of the wharf. The light of a lantern burning below deck showed him someone was on board. Scrambling along a well-used plank wedged between the wharf and the sloop, Skorniere slithered down the slippery ladder of the open trap door to the hold, where the light from the lantern shone dimly through the top of a filthy hold door window. Gently knocking on the hold's door, he called out softly, "Raymond, open up. It is I, Luc Skorniere."

The door squeaked half open and Skorniere squeezed his way into the dingy confines of the sloop's living quarters. Four men sat at a table drinking wine from wooden cups and smoking long stem pipes. The air was thick with pipe smoke and the sour smell of cheap red wine. A small thin man with the features of a weasel looked up, squinting through one good eye, the other hidden beneath a stained leather eye patch. Covering his head was a grubby bandana, while two flintlock pistols jutted out of a thick leather belt buckled to his waist.

"We'll be leaving for the Breton coast on the tide in one hour," he said, not getting up to acknowledge Skorniere. "What do you need?"

"What port will you be heading for?" asked Luc.

"Brest," replied Raymond.

"Perfect," said the spymaster, "I need this note put into the hands of the harbour master, Jean de Claire, it is urgent and most secret. You must insist that he delivers it to Monsieur Gravier, le comte de Vergennes, personally in Versailles within three days. I need not remind you, Raymond, that were you to lose this note or not deliver it, then your life and the lives of your crew here will end extremely quickly. Is that clear?"

"You need not threaten us, monsieur," replied Raymond sourly, "it will be delivered. I take it that my recompense will be awarded on delivery of this note. A full bag of silver?"

Luc looked at Raymond with the disdain he had felt towards the rabble in the inn.

"Of course," he said, "Jean de Claire will pay you your silver. On your return, I will seek you here. Do not try to find me."

With a contemptible look at Raymond and his crew, Luc pressed himself through the hold door and as his footsteps faded over the gangplank and into the night, Raymond hawked up a wad of phlegm, directing it accurately into the spittoon next to the galley.

"It's a fair wind to France, mes amis, up with the sails. The tide is up."

Luc watched the sloop pull away from its mooring, and under the light of the full moon he followed it as it sluiced out of the harbour, disappearing into the darkness of the open sea and on course for the French port of Brest. The information on Philemon Pownoll he'd received that evening from the Ashprington traitor would soon find its way into the hands of France's Foreign Minister and espionage chief, Charles Gravier, advocate of the North American Colonists' cause and admirer of Pennsylvania's recently elected representative to the American Second Congress, Benjamin Franklin.

Chapter 4

Elijah Hatch took down the last barrel of brandy in the cellar room of the Ashprington Inn, muttering to himself of how unfair it was to tax the hard-working country folk on what was for some their greatest pleasure and only source of relaxation, the drinking of alcohol in his inn. It had only been that morning the excise men had ridden through the village, stopping to examine the inn's stock of alcoholic spirits and wines, and to warn Elijah of the punishments served on those caught smuggling.

He was dogged with mixed feelings that all would not go well that night, but the thought of his investment in the contraband and the eagerness that his wife Lucy portrayed, convinced him the risk of dealing in smuggled merchandise was worth the gamble. On the one hand, he would satisfy his customers with cheaper brandy and rum, and he was sure the Excise men would not be returning to Ashprington for a good while. No-one in the village whispered to the Excise and Revenue men, they knew what would happen if they did. But on the other hand, should he be caught out, then he knew he would likely dance to the hangman. A supply of alcohol and lace from France awaited the village band of smugglers that night. Squire Maddock of Darton Hall would purchase most of the supply, providing a good profit for the band of six smugglers taking the risk.

Resting the barrel of brandy on a ledge, Elijah considered the other members of his smuggling band.

Barold Raustin, a carpenter and master builder, forever greedy to make more money by any means, married to Hilary, a distant relation to Squire Maddock.

Stephen Moore, a boat builder in the adjacent village of Tuckenhay and nephew to Obadiah Tucker of Dittisham, a hard man and fisherman but a smuggler first and foremost who with his two sons, operated off the French coast using Stephen as their link to dispense their contraband.

Mordechai Brunt, herdsman at Sharpham Estate, steadfast in his loyalty to the Pownolls but not averse to filling his pockets with illegal cash.

The Reverend Ebenezer Dunn, a hedonist and charlatan, otherwise known to the village community as the respectable temporary rector of the parish of Ashprington.

Watt Huckle, a stable boy at Sharpham, who longed to be completely accepted by the group but who served them in any way he could, looking up to them with the utmost esteem and veneration.

A strong military presence had been building up along the South West Coast, primarily around the ports and fishing harbours since war had been declared with the North American rebel colonists, and with the threat of France joining sides with the rebels, security along Britain's coastline was being tightened.

Dartmouth and relays along the River Dart were being manned with more soldiers with orders to assist officers of the Revenue in their efforts to snare smugglers. Elijah knew he and his cohorts would have to be extra careful that night and be back in the village with the merchandise hidden in the church cellar before the first cock crowed.

They'd row down the river in Stephen's boat to Obadiah Tucker's boathouse on the bank of the River Dart, adjacent to the small harbour of Dittisham, where Obadiah and his two sons would be waiting with the contraband. Lucy and Watt would wait with the wagon at the Pownolls' boathouse for their return. All being well, they would be back at the church with the consignment before Squire Maddock's men came to collect the major share.

Squire Roger Maddock, cousin to the owners of Darton Hall, had moved into the Hall on the recent death of the last occupant, Rawlin Maddock. The Squire's role as caretaker, until the family decided who would eventually take over, had been a perfect opportunity for him to encourage the smuggling rings in and around the towns and villages close to the River Dart. Ashprington was one such village.

"Elijah," Lucy called from the bar, " us'll be needin' another barrel of cider. Rufus here's gettin' thirsty!"

Later that evening as the last customer left the bar, Lucy extinguished the candles and slid the bolts across the inn's heavy oak door. Elijah opened the cellar door that led onto the inn's stable yard, and letting themselves out, they waited in the darkness for their smuggler cohorts to arrive. All was still and quiet. Lucy waited in the shadows while Elijah coupled the horse to the wagon, and it was not long before three figures, shrouded in their cloaks and hoods, silently appeared as Elijah led the horse and cart out into the stable yard.

31

"You'm all be ready, gentlemen?" whispered Lucy stepping out from the shadows.

"Stephen's bringing his boat up to the Pownolls' boathouse now," said a voice pulling back his hood. "We'll take the usual trail that leads from outside the grounds of Sharpham, down through the woods and along the riverbank to the boathouse. There will be no problem to get the wagon down there, it all worked well last time and it has not rained much for some time. Stephen and Mordechai will be waiting for us at the Pownolls' boathouse. I've received notification from Squire Maddock that his two men will be at the church just before dawn to collect his share."

"Will his men have the money for us when us hands over his part of the supply, minister?" asked Barold pulling back his hood and glaring at Ebenezer.

"Yes, yes, yes," answered Ebenezer irritably, "the Squire will see to it that we're paid. Don't worry, Squire Maddock's an honourable man, he won't let us down."

"An honourable man?" laughed Barold. "Bollocks, he be a bliddy rogue, and you'm knows it, Reverend."

"Come on," whispered Lucy, "us had better be goin'."

"Good, wagon's all ready and waitin'," said Elijah. "Watt, you'm drive with Lucy up front with you. Me, Barold and the Reverend will ride in the back."

Towards midnight, the wagon left the rear yard of the inn. A consignment of contraband awaited them in a fisherman's storage shed in an inlet next to the small harbour of Dittisham on the River Dart. A fat purse would be theirs on delivery of the consignment for Squire Maddock of Darton Hall, but the risk of being caught by detachments of the Revenue patrolling the river was a threat they would have to contend with. As a dark cloud passed over a full moon, Watt guided the wagon out of the village and onto the wide country track that led to Sharpham Estate and the boathouse on the bank of the river, where Stephen and Mordechai would be waiting.

* * *

Watt grasped the reins of the wagon as it bumped and rattled its way along the rough track of the wooded riverbank. Barold cursed aloud at every bump, threatening to tear young Huckle's head from his shoulders should they incur yet another violent jolt.

"Can't you drive this bliddy cart any smoother, boey?" he shouted. "My arse baint be smacked so hard since oi be a lad at village school."

"Ssh, keep your voice down, Barold," hissed Ebenezer. "We'll be passing Sharpham Manor, high up above us on this bank. We don't want anyone to hear your moaning."

"Bollocks," mouthed Barold at Ebenezer.

Looking away from Barold, Ebenezer whispered up to Watt, "Watt, look out for a lantern between the trees, it'll be Stephen and Mordechai. We'll be there pretty soon."

The wagon bumped along the rough path passing gaps in the trees where beams of moonlight lit up scattered bunches of wild woodland flowers. A sprinkling of late bluebells strewn across the damp woodland glistened up at them like cashes of discarded sapphires, while the odour of earth loam mingled with decomposing woodland vegetation made the atmosphere around the riverbank close and thick.

Apart from the few shreds of moonlight, the woods on each side of the river were as dark as St David's Church's cellar, the tall silhouettes of the trees rising like ghostly wraiths, guarding the hidden mysteries of the forest at night.

The small lantern carried by Lucy shed only a little light for Watt to guide the horse by, but it didn't allow for the thick knotted tree roots sticking up from the ground to be seen and avoided. More jolts and bumps brought silent curses from the three squatting in the back, Elijah putting a finger to his lips as he noticed Barold about to yell out another expletive.

Ebenezer was just thinking of jumping off the wagon and making his way along the path through the trees when Watt called out that he could see the light of a lantern a few hundred yards ahead between the trees.

"They'm be there, look, between them trees up there, a light."

Stephen and Mordechai walked a few yards down the riverside track to meet the wagon as it trundled towards them; Stephen stretched the lantern he was carrying out in front of him while Mordechai cleared away some branches and rotting tree stumps that blocked their path.

"Come on," said Stephen in a low voice, "the boat is tied up at the end of the jetty. Obadiah'll be waitin with our merchandise."

One by one, the five of them climbed down the wooden ladder strapped to the side of the jetty and climbed into Stephen's sixteen-foot, double-ended river boat. It was a well-made craft, built by his own hands with room for the five of them and the contraband they would bring back. Two sturdy oars rested in their oarlocks, Barold and Mordechai grasping them in their powerful hands, ready to row down river. Elijah settled himself in the bow holding a lantern at arm's length while Ebenezer made himself comfortable in the stern next to Stephen. They were ready.

The lantern did not provide much light but the moon at its fullest, shone far ahead down the river. Lucy and Watt were to stay with the horse and wagon at the Pownolls' boathouse to await their return. Watt had already settled the mare with a bundle of hay to munch, and as Stephen made ready to cast off, Elijah looked up at Lucy.

"Journey down to Dit'sum be under an hour, then about half hour to load and under an hour comin' back."

"I know, Elijah," said Lucy giggling devishly, "unless Revenue comes up river, as you'm be goin' down."

All five in the boat looked up at Lucy, straight-faced and tight-lipped.

"Doen't you go temptin' gremlins, Lucy Hatch, nuthin's gonna happen," retorted Barold, scowling at Elijah's wife.

Stephen cast off and the boat glided out into the centre of the river, the current gently taking it as Barold and Mordechai dipped and pulled their oars in unison. They coasted down the river's moon-speckled waters, Ebenezer making himself more comfortable in the stern while peering warily into the murky shadows of the passing riverbanks.

It was not long before the river widened as they passed a creek leading to the village of Stoke Gabriel. Rowing closer to the river bank, they saw an owl gazing down at them from an overhanging branch of a riverside tree, its wide yellow eyes staring in indignation at their gall in thinking they could cruise past his habitat and disturb him at such a time of night.

The quietness was broken by Elijah, "Down there be Stoke Gabriel, oi've a cousin, Noah Hatch, ee'm be landlord of the four-hundred-year-old Church House Inn there. Must visit 'im and take 'im some brandy, when us gets back."

"What a good idea," said Ebenezer. "Think I will come with you, never know what might come of it. I expect he knows a good many people of importance in the village."

"Oh, that he does, Reverend, that he does, sure enough," replied Elijah.

Quietness descended around them, Stephen whispering to Barold and Mordechai to bring the boat back into the middle stream of the river. Ebenezer felt the change of flow as the boat smoothed its way back into the middle stream. Sitting back in the stern, he gazed up at the night sky, mesmerised by its beauty. Moon beams lighting up the river in front of them shone over the water like pale bands of silver, while an abundance of twinkling stars hanging above them in the night sky looked as if they had been strung together by pieces of invisible string. All he had to do was raise his hand and grab them from their ties. Spellbound by the spectacle, he raised his arm, stretching it far into the night sky, his hand moving to clutch at nothing but thin air.

"Somethin troublin' you, Reverend?" Stephen asked looking at Ebenezer in a puzzled way.

"No, no," replied Ebenezer recovering himself. "Just, erm, a touch of cramp. Where are we now?"

"Passin' Bow Creek on our right. That be Tuckenhay down there, the hamlet where oi lives and works, there's one bootiful beach down by the creek."

Barold and Mordechai had built up a good rhythm and the boat glided through the water with ease, helped on by the ever-strengthening current in the centre flow of the river. The riverbanks on each side were getting further away from them as the river widened. Stephen tapped on Barold's and Mordechai's shoulders, "Bring the boat closer into the right-hand side of the river. Over there, to the left, be Galmpton Creek, you cannot see it in this darkness, but it means that just round this bend in the river us'll be approachin' Dit'sum. Slow down and let the current take us then turn closer into the side when oi tells you."

The boat slowed down as it came nearer to the right-hand side of the river. Elijah knelt in the bow holding the lantern straight out in front of him while Stephen squinted downriver waiting for the bend to appear.

"Careful now," he whispered to Barold and Mordechai, "us's comin' up to the bend. Use your oars to guide us round, then turn sharp right. There be a little inlet at the mouth of the harbour on our right."

The boat glided round the bend and then as Stephen had instructed, Barold rowing on the left side, used all his strength to turn the boat sharp right while Mordechai picked up the turn and in unison with Barold, rowed them into the mouth of the harbour. Far ahead, the lights of Dittisham shone out across its small harbour, lighting up a modest fleet of fishing boats bobbing up and down against their moorings.

"Here," said Stephen raising the tone of his whisper, "turn right now, tiz the inlet oi told you about."

Barold and Mordechai quickly turned the boat into the darkness of the inlet, bumping it up against the side of the bank and tipping Ebenezer headlong towards the bow. Barold roared with laughter at the comical sight of the minister spread-eagled across the deck, desperately clutching onto the boat's side.

"Ha, ha, ha. Stay in your seat, Reverend, when we turn, us doen want you gettin' there before us, do us? Ha, ha, ha."

"Quiet," demanded Stephen. "Look, a light at the end of Obadiah's jetty."

As Stephen's boat coasted up to the end of the jetty, the massive frame of Obadiah Tucker flanked by his two sons came into view. Obadiah, fisherman, smuggler and a man certainly not to cross, watched as Barold and Mordechai directed the boat up to a roughly put together ladder hanging from the jetty's side. One by one they climbed up to face the daunting presence of the most feared smuggler along the River Dart.

"Well, well, it be all you scallywags agin," he said regarding each one of them with a ferocious glare. "Oi hope you'm got me silver, Reverend, or you'm baint be goin back as 'appy as you came. The merchandise be stacked in yonder boathouse at the end of this 'ere jetty. Better you'm get it away before Revenue smell it. Ain't that right, young Stephen?"

"Ar, proper right, uncle," said Stephen.

"'Eem be a good boey," said Obadiah pointing at Stephen and glaring at Ebenezer. "My dearest sister, 'is Ma, bless her departed soul, bringed him up proper good. Jethro, her husbind, good man too. Bliddy good boat builder. Taught Stephen everythin' about boat buildin'. Ain't that right, Stephen?"

"Ar, proper right, uncle," said Stephen, smiling at his two cousins.

"Yes, yes, yes," interrupted Ebenezer impatiently, "we have heard it all before, Master Tucker. Enough of your family history now, our time's very precious. We can't stay here listening to you going on about your sister, time's getting on."

Nobody moved or said anything, all eyes were on Obadiah as his face changed into a ruthless look of resentment, a cold stare fixing on Ebenezer, who began to tremble as he realised the grave mistake he'd just made. Wide eyes followed Obadiah as the smuggler stretched himself to his full height, his left eye twitching furiously above the deep red knife scar that ran down to below his jaw. Absolute terror welled up in Ebenezer, freezing him to where he stood as a manic contortion spread across Obadiah's face, his left eye twitching frenziedly. Ebenezer's sudden fart and the helpless wail that screamed from the pit of his stomach did not stop Obadiah shooting out his right hand to grasp Ebenezer round his neck. Lifting him in a vice-like grip, he swivelled him round and dangling him over the edge of the jetty, he roared a series of profanities into the face of the terrified parson.

Holding the trembling minister at arm's length over the edge of the jetty, he pulled out a long skinning knife with his other hand, thrusting it towards Ebenezer's throat.

"Uncle, no," yelled Stephen, "'ee be a minister. Mama wouldn't want this."

Ebenezer's legs kicked furiously into thin air as Obadiah continued to hold him over the side and then turning at Stephen's plea, he dropped him onto the floor of the jetty, looking down contemptuously at the cringing whimpering figure lying beneath him.

"Doen you'm ever cut me orf agin or even try to, minister, coz next time, and oi promise you, us'll gut you from crotch to gullet. Parson or no parson, oi'm tellin' you. Do you understand, minister? Now you'm gives us the coin, collect the merchandise and fuck orf back to your village where you'm does your parsonin'. Next time oi sees thee, you'm better be careful. Understand me, minister?"

Ebenezer watched Obadiah and his two sons walk away down the jetty while Stephen, carrying the bag of silver coins, followed with Mordechai. Elijah went over to help Ebenezer to his feet while Barold stood alone grinning and trying to suppress the laughter that was brimming up inside of him. As Ebenezer struggled up from the floor of the jetty, Barold burst into raucous laughter, bellyaching and pointing at the helpless minister.

"Ha, ha, twaz when you farted, Reverend, I pissed meself laughin', honestly thought you'd follow through, never seen nuthin' so funny for a long time. The look of terror on your face, when Obadiah had 'ee danglin' over the jetty with your little legs kickin' away like 'at, oi just 'ad to look away, ha, ha, ha. What a sight! Ha, ha, ha."

Shaking with anger, Ebenezer stood glaring at Barold, his fingers caressing the soreness around his neck, then pushing himself away from Elijah, he staggered over to where Barold was still in the throes of convulsing with laughter.

"That damn heathen will burn in hell's fires," he croaked staring in the direction of Obadiah, "and you, Barold, will be there with him for the disrespect you show to me, a minister of the church."

"You'm be no more a minister of the church than one of Mordechai's bullocks," replied Barold. "And doen you threaten me with hell, you'm be goin' there before oi."

"Tiz enough now," yelled Elijah at Barold, "come on, Stephen and Mordechai be loadin' the boat."

Small casks of brandy and rum stacked next to similar containers of wine filled the middle space in Stephen's boat, while rolls of French lace cluttered the bow and stern. Wedged between the contraband, Barold and Mordechai rowed them away from the jetty where Obadiah, giving Ebenezer a grimacing stare, watched them snake their way beyond the lights of Dittisham harbour and out into the dark waters of the River Dart.

They made their way round the bend smoothly and as they passed Galmpton Creek, Stephen indicated to Barold and Mordechai to take the boat further over to the right side of the river as they wouldn't have to fight the current so hard. As before, Ebenezer sat in the stern of the boat next to Stephen, amidst the rolls of French lace, as did Elijah up in the bow.

They all seemed pleased with the full light the moon gave as it lit up their way ahead, even though Elijah persisted in holding the lantern at arm's length over the bow. Blackness Rock and Blackness Point loomed up ahead of them as Barold and Mordechai laboured with the oars. The musket shot fired from behind them echoed over the river like a crack of thunder, erupting the wildlife along the banks into a screeching and squawking flurry. With a jolt, the two rowers dropped their oars.

"What the bliddy hell was 'at?" screamed Mordechai.

"Oh shit, no," yelled Stephen looking behind him, "'tis the Revenue. Doen you stop rowin', carry on as fast as you can."

Looking back over his shoulder, Ebenezer saw the light of a lantern swinging back and forth from the bow of a hastening river boat, the silhouettes of its occupants working hard with their oars to gain on them. It was probably no more than two hundred yards behind, the resounding commands of the officer on board echoing across the river.

"Elijah," shouted Stephen, "ditch that lantern now."

The light from the lantern went out in an instant while the laboured breathing of Barold and Mordechai heightened as they dipped and pulled their oars, straining at every stroke with an urgency of the hunted.

"They're gaining on us," wailed Ebenezer. "Oh my God, we're all going to hang."

Another musket shot cracked into the night sky above them. A tall figure in a red coat and black bicorn stood erect in the bow, a sliver of moonlight illuminating the flintlock pistol held in his hand.

"In the name of His Majesty King George III, I command you to stop and move your craft into the side of the riverbank. We are the Revenue and order you to surrender now."

"Pull harder, lads," shouted Stephen to Barold and Mordechai, "their boat 'tis heavy with Revenue men, they will have to row faster to catch us."

"But they are," screamed Ebenezer, "and they are gaining on us, we'll all hang!"

"Pull in now," came another shout from the Revenue officer, "we'll fire on you unless you stop now."

"Faster, lads," shouted Stephen, "when oi tells you to turn sharp right, you'm do it as if Obadiah himself be after you and breathin' down your necks."

"Git down," hollered Elijah, "flatten you'mselves, muskits."

Barold and Mordechai ducked just in time as a volley of musket fire raked over them, the sound of the musket balls tearing and ripping through the foliage of the overhanging trees. Steadying themselves, the two rowers grasped their oars and with a spurt of super human energy, rowed as fast as they could, disregarding the lashes they received from overhanging branches, their breathing sounding as though their lungs would burst at any moment. The Revenue boat remained behind them but had fallen back a few lengths while the soldiers on board reloaded their muskets.

"Git closer to the side," yelled Stephen, "those over'angin' branches are blottin' out the moonlight, 'tis darker there and us'll be comin' up to the turn soon."

As their boat glided into the darkness of the overhanging riverside trees, Stephen squeezed his way past the casks of alcohol that took up most of the space in the middle of his boat, to the bow where Elijah knelt squinting ahead. Settling himself, he peered out into the darkness, scrutinising the murky outline of the bank while glancing over his shoulder to check the whereabouts of the Revenue boat.

"Reverend," he called, "be they closin' on us?"

"Yes, they're not far behind us," called back Ebenezer. "But they're towards the middle of the river. I don't think they can see us here in the dark."

As if Ebenezer's comment was a cue, the Revenue officer's voice rang out across the river, "We know you are there, come out towards the middle stream of the river. Give yourselves up now. If not, we'll be forced to sink you."

Ebenezer quailed at the threat, sliding himself down further to the floor of Stephen's boat.

"Now, lads, right turn now, be sharp," cried Stephen, "and then, row hell for leather across the mouth of the creek."

As quick as a flash, the boat turned, Barold and Mordechai rowing as fast as their arms would go to cross the mouth of Stoke Gabriel Creek and safely reach the other side.

"Now, slow down, that's it. Now quickly turn left, into this here little inlet."

Stephen's boat glided into the darkness of the small channel. Branches covered the whole area, it was pitch black, and not even a moonbeam broke through the thick foliage. A vast patch of reeds covered the area of water and a mossy smell of fungus on rotting tree stumps filled the area. They sat, not daring to breathe as the darkness pressed in on them from all sides. Barold and Mordechai, still grasping their oars, sat panting after their super-human effort, while Ebenezer squatting in the stern, clutched the sides of the boat trembling in utter terror.

A gentle hush from Stephen brought them all to attention as the sound of oars dipping in water was heard entering the creek. Curious sounds filled their watery hideaway as they peered through the chinks in the foliage for the first sign of the Revenue boat. The dim glow of a lantern gliding slowly towards their sanctuary alerted their senses as they strained to hear what conversation might be taking place amongst their pursuers.

Murmurs could be heard coming from the Revenue boat, growing louder as the vessel crawled through the water at a snail's pace, practically coming to a halt at the entrance to where the men from Ashprington sat shivering in trepidation.

"No sign of them, sergeant," said the officer who had commanded them to surrender.

"I could swear they turned into the creek, sir," replied the sergeant. "It's dark, I know, but the moon's giving enough light for us to have seen if they had carried on upriver. I'm sure they turned in here and my guess is they're rowing like hell down to Stoke Gabriel."

"Mm, you could be right," agreed the officer, "or, they're holding out under the cover of the riverbanks."

"Could give the banks a blasting, sir, might flush them out," suggested the sergeant.

"Yes, sergeant, that is what we will do, and if that does not flush them out, we'll carry on down to Stoke Gabriel and head them off before they've a chance to unload whatever they're smuggling. Carry on."

"Muskets at the ready," hollered the sergeant, "aim into the darkness of the riverbank. Fire."

A crescendo of noise filled the area around the inlet where the five of them were hiding as six musket balls peppered the trees and foliage, scattering splinters of bark and wood everywhere. Silence followed for a short interval while the soldiers aboard the Revenue boat reloaded their muskets, the light from their lantern becoming dimmer as their boat slowly moved away downriver. Ebenezer, shaking in horror, counted six more musket sallies and then there was silence.

"Have they gone?" he stammered, looking desperately through the darkness.

"Not sure," whispered Stephen, "better stay where we are for a while, in case they'm be out there waitin' to see if us comes out."

All five sat rigidly still, biting their tongues with their eyes tightly shut, not daring to cry out as a sudden swarm of little river flies crawled over them, biting into their flesh and sucking their blood. Not being able to bear it any longer, Stephen pushed away part of the overhanging foliage to look out over the creek. By the light of the moon, he was able to see snippets of the river and turning his head in all directions, he could see no sign of the Revenue.

"Right, lads," he whispered, "us's goin' out. Oi think the Revenue's gone on down to Stoke, but they will be back lookin' for us when they find out we are not there. Ready?"

The two rowers slowly dipped their oars and the boat coasted out of the hideaway into the murky waters of Stoke Gabriel Creek.

"Make a right turn," said Stephen softly, "back into the Dart and then upriver and home. Keep over to the left side, it be more sheltered from the moonlight."

Under cover of the overhanging foliage, the five desperate smugglers sat without speaking as Barold and Mordechai summoned up their last fraction of energy to row upriver. Every now and again all five would look back to see if the Revenue had seen them and were hot on their tails. At one point, Ebenezer uttered a startled whimper as he thought he saw the outline of the Revenue boat far behind him, but nothing seemed to be following them.

They began to sense that Sharpham and the boathouse were getting nearer as they passed familiar landmarks along the river, hoping that Watt and Lucy would still be there waiting for them. They knew that they had to get the contraband to St David's Church before Squire Maddock's men arrived at dawn, and time was now getting on. A light mist floated over the boundaries of Sharpham Estate as they rounded a bend in the river.

"Look, up ahead, a light," called Elijah craning his neck over the bow of the boat. Everyone peered ahead to see the light of a lantern swinging to and fro over the river, and as their boat came closer, they all nearly cheered aloud as they recognised the frail figure of Watt, beckoning them towards the jetty where he stood holding the lantern with Lucy waiting anxiously at his side.

Watt threw them the mooring rope as Stephen's boat bumped up against the side of the jetty. Two of them scrambled up the ladder while Barold, Mordechai and Ebenezer began to hand them up the contraband. Lucy stood next to Elijah as he stacked the casks and lace onto the floor of the jetty.

"Us heard the muskits," she said, looking fearfully at her husband.

"Be it the Revenue?"

"Not now, Lucy, us'll tell you later. Here comes Watt with the wagon, you can help us load it. I will tell you everythin' later. Make sure you take our brandy and rum from the supply. Doen' want Squire Maddock to have what's ours after all the trouble us's had."

Watt brought the horse and wagon up to the end of the jetty where they loaded the contraband onto the cart. When it was done, Stephen towed his boat inside the boathouse securing it next to Philemon's skiff. There was no way he'd row it back to Tuckenhay that night, the chance of the Revenue being out somewhere on the river and close to Bow Creek was too probable. He knew that as Philemon was away with the navy, his boat would stay undiscovered as Jane rarely came down to the boathouse. He would stay the night in the Ashprington Inn and collect it the following day, and if everything seemed quieter, he would row it back then. Mordechai and Watt would leave them at the boathouse and head up to the small estate cottage where Mordechai lived and the living quarters above the stable that accommodated Watt.

"Lunch time in the Inn, you two," called out Elijah, as Mordechai and Watt disappeared up the steep slope that led to the mansion house.

"Ar, oi'll be there," came Mordechai's reply, "but Watt'll be busy in stables."

The wagon was ready to go as Stephen made his way out of Philemon's boathouse and as he scrambled up into the rear, Lucy flicked the reins and they trundled off under the first rays of a dawning sky, bumping and rattling along the riverside track in the direction of Ashprington and the secure hideaway of St David's Church's cellar.

Chapter 5

Betsy Gribble looked up from her work of cleaning the church pews as Ebenezer hobbled down the nave, looking much the worse for wear. She noticed he walked with a stoop as if his back was too stiff to bear himself upright, and as he turned to speak to her, she gasped at his bloodshot eyes and the red ring that circled his throat.

"Well," he demanded, "have you got any news for me from Sharpham?"

"No, Reverend," she replied, gaping at the thick red mark around his throat, "but there be something you'm maybe interested to know."

Ebenezer watched her fiddling with the cloth in her hand, her eyes cast down and not looking directly at him.

"What is it then, woman? Out with it!"

"Oi ain't told no-one, Reverend, us'll only tell you. Doen you send me to hell, Reverend, please."

"Foolish woman. What is it then?" shouted Ebenezer.

"Well, 'tis like this, you'm see."

"No, I don't see, tell me now."

"Well, there be a gentleman comin' quite regular like to the manor, he come yesterday and early again this mornin' just after breakfast, before oi left to come here."

"Yes, yes. What's his name and what's he doing there?" demanded Ebenezer.

"Oi doen know what his name is or what he be doin' there, Reverend. But oi heard Mistress Jane callin' him Sir Joshua or somin' like that. And he has always got a big leather bag slung o'er his shoulder."

Mm, perhaps I should pay Mistress Pownoll a visit one morning, he thought.

"Now, get on with your work and don't forget my house needs doing after you finish here. Do not go jabbering around the village what you've just told me, you know what'll happen. You will go to hell, Betsy Gribble, hell fire and damnation for eternity. I have the power to send you there, and don't you forget it."

Ebenezer turned and walked away, wondering who the mysterious Sir Joshua could be. At the church door he stopped, and looking back at Betsy, he noticed the fearful look on her face as she busily dusted the church pews, mumbling the Lord's Prayer and occasionally looking up in supplication at the large silver crucifix that overhung the altar.

"Foolish woman," he muttered to himself and let himself out of the heavy wooden door.

The five smugglers had arranged to meet in the Ashprington Inn that lunch time. At dawn, Squire Maddock's men had given them the message that he wanted to see them all at Darton Hall late that afternoon. They would receive payment for his consignment of the contraband and there was something urgent that he wanted to discuss with them; it would be in all their interests.

Ebenezer let himself into the smoky atmosphere of the inn, recognising the broad back and blonde unkempt hair of Mordechai sitting at a table with his back to the door. Opposite him sat Stephen and Barold, both listening to what Ebenezer supposed was Mordechai's appraisal of the previous night's events. As Ebenezer approached them, Barold looked up,

"Well, well, look what the cat's just brung in!" he said, slurring slightly and nudging Stephen.

Ebenezer ignored the insult, indicating to the inn's serving maid to bring him a mug of cider while he seated himself next to Mordechai.

"Well," he said, staring unintentionally at Barold's ever-purpling nose, "Squire Maddock wants us all up at his Hall later today. He will pay us for what he had from us earlier and inform us of whatever he has got in mind for us."

"Oi reckons he has got another job for us," said Barold taking a gulp of cider from his half-empty mug, "It'd better be a good 'un!"

Elijah suddenly appeared, looking tired and ashen. "Us can all go up in the inn's wagon. Five o'clock here."

"Naw, count me out," said Mordechai. "Got beef herd to see to. But oi'll send young Watt, he can be my eyes and ears at the meetin'."

"Fair doos," said Elijah, "oi will 'ang on to your share of our reward for the consignment. Be here later this week sometime, and us'll give it you."

Mordechai nodded towards Elijah, looking up at him and taking a long draught of cider. "Ar, proper, thank you, Elijah."

"Us be bliddy lucky to get away from them Revenue bastards," said Stephen.

"Ar," agreed Mordechai, "as me stiff arms keep remindin' me."

"Us will have to lie low for a while, Reverend," said Stephen. "Revenue men will be all over the river. Can't take the chance of goin' down to Uncle Obadiah's yet."

Nor ever again for me, thought Ebenezer, caressing his neck and going cold at the thought of meeting up with Obadiah again.

From the corner of his eye, Ebenezer saw Rufus Mudd licking his lips and pawing the inn's serving wench as she delivered a fresh mug of cider, his plate-like hands groping her buttocks as she bent over the table next to him to retrieve some empty mugs.

"Where's my cider, girl?!" shouted Ebenezer, appreciating her rear figure as she stretched over the table to reach the last empty mug.

"Oi ain't forgotten you, Reverend, us'll be comin' pretty quick."

"Arr, and Rufus too by the looks of him," hollered Barold, grinning at his companions and causing those seated next to Rufus' table to roar with laughter and bang their tables approvingly.

"Molly, behave and bring us more cider," shouted Elijah, glaring towards Rufus' table.

Mordechai drained the last of his cider and pushing back his chair, he smiled at his cohorts. "Us'll see you during the week, Elijah. Got a lot of work up at Sharpham with beef herd. Mistress wants top acre cultivated too. Young Watt'll fill me in with news of Squire's meetin'."

They watched as Mordechai made his way through the inn and out through the heavy oak doors.

"Cider for the gentlemen," said Molly hovering next to Ebenezer with a supply of drinks. "One for you, Reverend," she said, moistening her lips as she slowly leaned over him with a mug of cider, revealing what was bursting over the top of her low-cut gown.

"Lovely, Molly, thank you," spluttered Ebenezer, his eyes as wide as saucers, "simply lovely!"

Molly placed the mugs of cider round the table and as she left, she caught Ebenezer's eye, moistening her full red lips with a slow lusty movement of her tongue, causing him to quake and stare lecherously as she flittered past him.

Barold was quick to see the carnal look of desire spreading over Ebenezer. "Now, now, Reverend," he chortled, "you'm looks like you'm come over all funny like. You'm be sweatin' too, Reverend. Ha. Keep your 'ands in your pockets, case they'm go lookin for something Molly got. Ha ha. That there red ring Obadiah give you round your throat's gone all purple. Ha, ha, ha, ha."

"Just like your nose, Barold," said Ebenezer, draining his cider and appreciating the loud guffaws that erupted around the table. Pushing back his chair, he stood up and made for the inn's door, confirming to Elijah that he would be back at five to join them for the journey up to Darton Hall and their meeting with Squire Maddock. At the door, he noticed Molly being pawed again by Rufus Mudd, the blacksmith's mammoth-like hands roughly groping around the rear area of her tight working gown, while he slobbered and grunted in excitement. As she turned, she caught Ebenezer's eye, smiling salaciously at him, her dark eyes boring into his with the promise of something extra yet to come. Trembling, he let himself out and hurried up the road towards the church house, provided by the Deanery for its ministers. Letting himself in, he collapsed onto one of the small lounge sofas located in the front parlour, and as tiredness overwhelmed him, he felt his eyes closing, but vivid pictures of Obadiah Tucker and their escape from the Revenue forced him to keep awake and allow a brief spell of contemplation.

As temporary rector of St David's Church, Ebenezer had dispensed with all evening church services, falsely claiming to the Deanery that temporal work in the parish took up most his time. He had no intention of visiting any of his parishioners, be they sick or in need of any spiritual help. He chuckled at how easy it had been to lie to the fools in Totnes and convince them of his true commitment in striving to do the Lord's Work!

There would be no new information for the local spy to carry down to Plymouth this coming Sunday, so he must remember to refrain from the pulling of his ear, but with luck he'd hear something relevant to report the following week. Perhaps he would have something after paying a visit to Jane Pownoll in a few days. His contact would only meet with him when there was something worthwhile. Who this traitor could be, he had no idea, but he came from the village, that was for sure, and probably well-known to him, but when they met he was always in the shadows and concealed under a dark cloak and hood. Perhaps he should pay Luc Skorniere a visit in Plymouth, maybe he would disclose the identity of this mysterious confederate.

He was suddenly jolted out of his meditation by a loud knocking on his front door. Swearing and scowling at the interruption, he struggled off the sofa, pulling down his tie-wig and impatiently smoothing down the creases of his clerical attire.

"If that's the stupid Gribble woman," he said to himself, "I will threaten her with the fires of hell. That will terrify her for weeks, the foolish woman!"

His deep frown disappeared into an expression of pure delight as the sensuous face of a smiling Molly met him as he opened the door.

"Mmm, Molly, please come in, my dear," he heard himself utter in a shaky tone.

"Why, Reverend, you look like a naughty little boy, drooling over a tasty tart he shouldn't have," she said, pouting her full red lips at him. "Oi be here to give you a little company and to take your mind away from that awful red sore round your neck, oi hopes it not be botherin' you too much."

"No, not at all, Molly, come into my parlour and relax," he quivered.

As he helped her out of her shawl, she brushed his cheek with her lips, sending an overwhelming spasm of excitement shooting up his groin. Grinning at the low-pitched croak of desire that rumbled from his trembling lips and the obvious bulge in the crotch of his breeches, she floated away from him, sighing and pretending to look with interest around the room. He watched her with unequivocal lust as she walked across the parlour, swaying her hips and looking over her shoulder in his direction, moistening her lips with her tongue in the way she had previously done in the inn, and then pretending to look with curiosity at the trinkets that adorned the neat little tables in the four corners of the room. Finally, she stepped back to where he stood, taking his arm and looking enticingly into his eyes,

"Oh, Reverend," she cooed, "may I ask for a little brandy or even a sherry afore us has some company."

"Why yes, Molly, indeed," he said, shaking in anticipation. "French cognac, would a large one be a pleasure for you? And please, Molly, call me Ebenezer, not Reverend."

"Oh, Ebenezer, yes, a very large one would definitely be a pleasure for me!"

Ebenezer swallowed hard, feeling the skin tighten around his sore neck as he poured two large French cognacs, aware of Molly stretching out on the sofa he had previously been relaxing on. With his hand shaking, he offered her the cognac.

"Thank you, Ebenezer," she purred, sitting up and loosening the strings of her gown and bodice. "Help me up, please."

48

Sweat pouring from under his thick tie wig and shaking with apprehension, he took Molly's hand, and helping her up from the sofa, she stepped out of her gown to stand naked in front of his wide-eyed trembling frame.

"Oh, Ebenezer, you are a naughty parson!" she giggled. "You're drooling over a tasty tart, but if you ask me nicely, I'll let you taste it first and then…well then, you know it'll be yours to enjoy!"

* * *

Elijah's wagon bounced and shook as it trundled along the rough track that led across the fields of Totnes towards Dartington and Squire Maddock's Hall. Mordechai was busy with his herd of beef cattle at Sharpham and so, unable to be with them, had sent Watt to be his eyes and ears, and it was Watt, sitting up front next to Elijah, that caused Barold to holler angrily at the boy.

"Shut the fuck up, Watt," he shouted. "You'm been dronin' on and on since us left Ashprington. Us'd appreciate a bit of peace and quiet back here, we'm all be knackered, specially the Reverend, he looks shagged out, red ring and all. Ha, ha, ha!"

Ebenezer squinted at Barold, wondering whether he knew that Molly had called on him earlier. Obviously not, or Barold would have twisted it into a farce that the whole village and surrounding hamlets would be laughing at now. But he had to be careful, that was for sure, although he looked forward to the next exciting and self-indulging encounter with Molly. Nobody would know, and Molly had promised him so, gratefully accepting the golden guinea he had forced into her hand, knowing this was payment for her silence and a future engagement when she'd willingly succumb to his unnatural and freaky sexual demands to which she knew she was not in any way averse.

The track widened into a broad carriageway as they dropped down from the high fields of Totnes onto the level pastureland of Dartington. Their route took them alongside the River Dart, past two stone gatehouses, signifying they had entered Darton Hall property, and up along a narrow winding carriage track that spiralled upwards, leaving the river as a serpentine feature far below.

Elijah pulled back on the reins as the wagon rolled into the cobblestone courtyard that fronted the medieval hall. Heavy double wooden entrance doors glowered down at them from the top of a well-worn flight of stone steps, warning them that this manor was protected, and no-one could freely enter unless

49

authorised to do so. A side door next to the heavy entrance doors suddenly opened and two liveried servants hurried down the steps to attend them, one of them going immediately to the front of the wagon and taking hold of the horse's harness, while the other approached the five men in the wagon.

"Welcome to Darton Hall," he said, looking up at the group with a faint smile. "Kindly follow me, Squire Maddock is awaiting you in the Great Hall. Geoffrey over there will take care of your horse and wagon."

They followed the servant across the courtyard, their eyes taking in every detail of the magnificent medieval complex. Squire Maddock sat at a long oak table, sipping wine from a silver goblet, his eyes following each of them as they shuffled through the entrance to where he held court. Rumour had it around the village and the outlying districts that the Squire occasionally held secret orgies within the hall's complex, where drunkenness and debauchery lasted several days, with various titled gentry around the stately homes of the West Country coming to indulge their hedonistic desires and fetishes. Ebenezer wished eagerly for the Squire to show him favour and perchance invite him to one of these future soirées.

"Come closer," shouted the Squire, "I'm a little hard of hearing and I don't want to conduct this meeting by bellowing across the hall. There are enough chairs around this table."

Young Watt, awestruck at being in such surroundings, stared at the coat of arms that hung behind the throne-like chair of its current caretaker. Squire Maddock noticed Watt's fascinated expression.

"Goes back centuries, boy," he said, "they were carried at Crecy and Agincourt by my family and will be by future generations to come." Peering over his goblet at Barold he grinned contemptuously. "Well, Barold, and how be your good lady, my relative, well I trust?"

"She was when oi left her earlier and oi hopes she will be when oi returns," replied Barold, sneering at the Squire as though he were a nasty smell under his nose. There was no friendship lost between these two, only disdain from Squire Maddock towards his cousin's husband and complete indifference and contemptuous dislike from Barold towards the Squire.

"Well, yes indeed," said the Squire turning towards Ebenezer. "Reverend Dunn, I'm pleased you all made it here this afternoon and I'm more than happy that our special cooperative is proving successful. The consignment you delivered to my men earlier this morning was meritorious, although I hear you had a nasty confrontation with that oaf Tucker from Dittisham. You have to watch your tongue when in company with that madman."

Stephen, looking across the table at the Squire, caught his eye but said nothing.

"Ah yes, Stephen, Obadiah's your uncle, is he not, and the supplier of the French contraband that I pay you for? I think he could be a risk to our cooperative in future. Convince him to keep his temper to himself or he will find himself dangling from one of His Majesty's gallows on Plymouth Hoe. I heard he almost killed the Reverend here. One word from me and he'll dance to the hangman."

Ebenezer watched as Stephen glared at Squire Maddock, refraining from any comment that might upset the meeting but sure to convey the warning to his uncle who, as Ebenezer was certain, would scoff at Squire Maddock's threat, promising to slit his throat the moment he saw him.

"You also had a lucky escape from the Revenue, I hear," continued the Squire. "Be careful, I'll use my contacts to see where they may be when you're next on the river, but should you be caught by them, then I'd deny all knowledge of you and you'd hang. Probably next to that oaf Tucker on Plymouth Hoe."

The five men from Ashprington were silent, each thinking of the narrow escape they had had the previous night and the finality of the hangman's noose they would have faced. Ebenezer shivered at a fleeting vision of himself, standing on an open cart while a rough noose was placed over his neck.

"But that's not going to happen while you work for me," said the Squire looking seriously at all of them. "I will promise each of you that you'll all get rich with what I'm planning. Now, first things first, take this."

Looking over at Ebenezer, he tossed him a leather bag that rattled with coins as it dropped on the table in front of him.

"That's for the consignment. Everything we agreed upon is in that bag."

Barold's face twisted into a stern look as he watched Ebenezer snatch up the bag and thrust it into the inside of his coat pocket.

"Now, what I have to say next is why I've instructed you all up here. But before I continue, I think we're all in need of some refreshment."

Grinning, he clapped his hands loudly. Three long-legged beauties dressed in flimsy see-through gowns strolled in through the doors, carrying trays of wine and cold meats which they placed onto the oak table smiling alluringly at the Squire's guests.

The Squire chuckled devilishly to himself as he watched Barold and the rest of the group leering lustfully at the three women, their eyes following them as they walked away from the table and out through the heavy wooden doors that led into a maze of dark corridors.

"Pray dig in and help yourselves while I continue," said the Squire smirking. "I have an assignment for you which will take place in twelve days from now. This must be kept most secret, and you all know what I mean by that."

"Where it be, Squire?" interrupted Stephen, reaching out for a leg of cold pheasant, his eyes fixed on the wooden doors at the end of the hall.

"Wait, I'll be coming to that shortly," said the Squire.

"I won't be happy if Obadiah has anything to do with it," voiced Ebenezer looking seriously at the Squire.

"That he won't, you can be sure of that," confirmed Squire Maddock.

"But it won't be a river job this time. It will require you to transport the consignment back here to the Hall on horseback. Transporting it back by wagon will be too risky as the Revenue are checking every road crossing from Exeter to Plymouth. Should you be caught at a road crossing, then you would face the hangman. We do not want that to happen so it is horseback across country. With the right planning, it can be done safely, I'm confident of that."

The five smugglers were silent, not taking their eyes off the Squire.

"What's the consignment?" queried Elijah.

"French cognac for me, that's it," replied the Squire. "In half-anker tubs, that's small casks to you, and pigs' bladders."

"How do we carry that back on horseback?" asked Ebenezer looking perplexed.

"I've agreed to purchase twelve half ankers and twelve pigs' bladders from the leader of the tubmen who's organising this on behalf of the local smuggling barons. That will be two half ankers each and two pigs' bladders each. They will sit your mounts well enough and can be secured tightly with straps that I will provide. I will provide the mounts too. You will leave from here an hour before midnight and return here with my supply before dawn."

"And what be in it for us?" asked Barold, frowning at the Squire.

"Double what I've paid you today, and that I'm sure you'd agree will be a veritable purse."

"Wait a minute, Squire," said Stephen, looking around at the others, "you'm baint told us where it'll be."

"No, and I won't till you all swear to me that on pain of death you'll keep it a secret for all time. Should any of you reveal the whereabouts, then you can expect a visit from some very nasty people."

There was silence around the table as each one thought deeply about Squire Maddock's offer. The temptation of a doubling of the purse was too good to refuse and one by one they raised their hands committing their oath to the Squire.

Nodding, he sat back, pouring himself another wine from one of the many jugs now on the table, studying each of them in turn. Slowly, he drained the wine from the goblet and placed it back on the table.

"Churston Manor," he said.

"Bliddy hell, Maddock," cried Barold, "do you know who lives there?"

"Oh yes, I do, Barold," said the Squire seriously. "Sir Francis Buller."

"Yes, and he be a big-noise lawyer up in London," added Barold.

"Exactly, and it's in London where he is most of the time. He is hardly ever in his home at Churston Manor. I have a spy in service there, he will be waiting for you and you can trust him completely. He knows that on the Sunday of the consignment coming in, Sir Francis and his wife, Lady Susanna, will be in London and not returning until the following weekend. He'll take you to the drop where you'll meet my man, who'll organise my supply and then make sure you all get away safely."

"Very well," said Ebenezer, "but where will the consignment be dropped? Surely not on the doorstep of Churston Manor."

"Elberry Cove," said Squire Maddock, helping himself to more wine. "There's an underground tunnel cut through the cliff from behind one of the outhouses to the cove. It was constructed about two hundred and forty years ago for the very purpose of smuggling contraband and people. Unknown to Sir Francis and Lady Susanna, it is regularly maintained by certain members of the household staff, loyal to the local smuggling barons. I know the barons well, as they know me. The tunnel was also used as an escape for Catholic priests in the time of King Henry and later Queen Elizabeth, and I would guess as an entry for the papist spies who later landed at Elberry Cove."

Taking a long draught of wine, he continued, "There's a French ship coming into Elberry on the night I've told you with a heavy consignment for the local barons and me. The ship will not stay long, so unloading will be organised and quick. That has already been arranged and tubmen from Brixham have been recruited together with a few hard batsmen from Paignton. They know you will be coming and they will have my supply ready and waiting. Your contact there will be the foreman in charge of the batsmen, Solomon Metcalf. I have already told him six of my men from Ashprington will be collecting my share, you will recognise him as he has a hook in place of his left hand. He will sort everything for you and knows he will be paid handsomely by me, so do not worry about his loyalty. Load your mounts and then ride back to me here at the Hall without delay. Now, what do you all say?"

The five of them sat quietly, thinking deeply about the risks and dangers that the venture held. Squire Maddock poured himself another wine and grabbing a chicken leg from one of the trays, sat back scrutinising each of them.

"Oi be in, Squire," said Stephen, nodding in his direction.

"Me too," echoed Barold, smiling at Stephen.

"Me and Mordechai will go definitely, Squire, and thank you for includin' me."

Squire Maddock smiled at Watt's enthusiasm.

"Better count me in too then," said Elijah looking at Ebenezer.

"Yes, and me, Squire, although I'm not too happy about the horseback ride. I'll cope as long as you don't give me a bad-tempered beast," said Ebenezer, looking anxiously at the Squire.

"Per'aps you'd be happy on an old donkey, Reverend, ha, ha," laughed Barold.

"Enough," commanded the Squire, looking sternly at Barold.

"Bollocks," replied Barold, asserting himself in front of the Squire and the others.

"Very well," said the Squire ignoring Barold's comment, "I expect you all here in twelve days on the Sunday night, one hour before midnight. I'll send a reminder to Elijah's inn in ten days."

They sat in silence, their eyes studying Squire Maddock as he drained the final mouthful of wine from his goblet.

"Us'll be here, Squire, doen you worry," acknowledged Stephen looking intently at the Squire. "Each and every one of us."

Chapter 6

Young Jane Pownoll sat as still as a statue as Sir Joshua Reynolds' carbon crayon swept over the white paper page of his sketch pad. His eyes travelled up and down from his pad, one moment resting on Jane's features and then dropping down to shade, outline and illustrate the look of innocence he so wanted to capture in Jane's semblance. Disregarded sheets of paper lay strewn around his feet, as he once again tore the sheet of paper he had been working on from its pad and let it fall amongst the growing pile around him.

Jane's mother watched the look of frustration growing on him, but never once did he lose his temper. He continued to steadily build up the likeness of a prominent feature of young Jane's, knowing it would be the ultimate for his theme.

Several weeks had passed since Philemon had left Sharpham for his ship in Chatham Docks and the voyage to the American Colonies. Jane thought his ship was probably under way as part of the escort for the troop carriers bound for Boston Harbour. As each day passed, the yearning for him to return grew, her heart aching with the melancholy of them being apart, but she was insistent that in the presence of her daughter Jane, she would hide her desolate feelings and be as normal as she possibly could.

Sir Joshua had been a regular visitor at Sharpham Manor ever since Jane and Philemon had given their permission for him to study and illustrate certain features of young Jane's, which he believed to be intrinsic for his portrait. Both had been pleased that he had seen in young Jane the depiction he wanted so much to emulate in his forthcoming painting. A sudden wriggle of discomfort from her daughter caught Jane's eye, and she guessed she desperately needed to relieve herself. Sir Joshua was also aware of young Jane's distress, but a moment had struck when the magic of an absolute likeness was forming, and he could not let it pass.

"Dear Jane," he murmured, "I know it's difficult, but please don't move, I think I've got it."

Young Jane forced herself to keep still, counting the seconds as a means of ignoring the discomfort she was feeling.

"That is perfect, Jane. Now be off with you, my dear, quickly, and thank you."

Jane leapt off the stool, tearing out of the room with an urgency that brought a deep chuckle from Sir Joshua.

"Take a break, my dear," he yelled after her. "Be back in half an hour. I'm sure your mother has an apple and a mug of milk waiting for you."

"That she has," said young Jane's mother, coming over from the back of the room and marvelling at the precise likeness of her daughter's eyes staring at her from the page of Sir Joshua's sketch pad.

"Betsy," she called, noticing Betsy Gribble hovering near the door, "take Jane to the kitchen, there's a mug of milk and a rosy red apple waiting for her."

"What d'you think?" said Sir Joshua smiling at Jane's look of approval. "I got it, indeed I did. It is your daughter's eyes and the look of innocence behind them, that is what I wanted. Splendid, eh?"

"Splendid is certainly the word, Joshua," said Jane, admiring the look of purity that exuded from the image of her daughter's eyes, "It's perfect."

"Have you any news of Philemon?" asked Sir Joshua, gently placing the finished sketch into a section of his leather bag and taking out his ear trumpet.

"Only yesterday a letter arrived from Chatham," she replied. "He wrote that all had been well with the journey from here and he was safely aboard his ship. I expect they will have set sail for Liverpool by now where they will meet up with the troop carriers. Then as the carriers' escort, it is the long voyage across the Atlantic to Boston. It will be quite a while before he sets foot back here at Sharpham."

Sir Joshua noticed the faraway worried look in Jane's eyes as she gazed out of a window, picturing her husband at the helm of his ship. The sudden clanging of the front doorbell announcing a visitor, broke Jane's thoughts as Betsy and young Jane reappeared into the room.

"Oi'll answer it, mistress," said Betsy. "Young Jane's had her milk and apple."

"Thank you, Betsy," replied Jane, indicating to her daughter to resume her pose on the wooden stool in front of Sir Joshua.

Betsy hurried out of the room crossing the wide hallway to open the heavy wooden door of the front entrance. She gasped, more in terror than in surprise, at the sight of the Reverend Dunn standing on the front step.

"Ooh, Reverend, 'tis you. What brings you'm up here to Sharpham?"

"That, Betsy Gribble, will be between me and your mistress," he said curtly. "Pray inform Mistress Pownoll, I am here to see her."

With a nod and a curtsy, Betsy closed the door and hurrying back, gently knocked on the door where Jane was watching Sir Joshua crafting an image of her daughter's mouth and lips on a fresh page of his sketch pad.

"Yes, Betsy, who's at the door?" she asked, wondering why Betsy was shaking and looking as if the Devil himself had come calling.

"It, it be the minister, ma'am," said Betsy trembling. "The Reverend Dunn, from the church."

"Bring him into the foyer, Betsy. I'll be there presently."

Reluctantly, Betsy returned to where Ebenezer stood waiting, letting him into the foyer to await Jane.

"You'm to wait here, Reverend, Mistress Pownoll says she will be with you shortly."

"Very well," replied Ebenezer, his eyes examining the splendour of Sharpham Manor's reception area. His attention was focused on the grand staircase where the two portraits of Philemon and Jane adorned the wall of the stairwell when a polite cough and gentle voice sounded behind him.

"Reverend Dunn, how may I be of assistance to you?" asked Jane, looking somewhat puzzled at his presence.

"Mistress Pownoll," crowed Ebenezer, humbling himself. "I'm honoured to visit you. I trust all is well with yourself and your daughter? I am undertaking my duties to my parishioners with visits around the parish, to ensure the well-being of all," he lied.

"With your brave husband away, I want to offer you my service and to re-affirm my commitment to your spiritual well-being. Perhaps your attendance at next Sunday's service would be in your interest? I didn't see you at our Sunday morning service last week."

"No, Reverend, you did not," replied Jane. "I'm afraid that with my husband being away and with the urgency of managing the estate, I haven't much spare time for gatherings that would take me away from Sharpham."

Jane had to pinch herself painfully to stop the giggle that had begun to form deep inside her. She could not forget the previous hilarious encounter with the Reverend and as she looked at his meek obsequious bearing, the picture of his wig sliding down over his eyebrows suddenly caused an uncontrollable screech of laughter to unexpectedly burst from her. Unable to control herself, she fled back to the room where Sir Joshua, crayon in hand and eyes fixed on young Jane, looked up with surprise at her shaking figure.

"Joshua, please, help me out of this predicament," she giggled. "The minister from Ashprington Church is out there in the foyer. I'm sorry but…" Jane gave way to a fit of bellyaching laughter that brought young Jane off her chair to peep around the corner of the open door at Ebenezer, standing alone in the foyer and looking completely perplexed.

"Stay here both of you," said Sir Joshua, putting down the crayon and getting up from his chair.

"Good day, sir," he called approaching Ebenezer in the foyer. "I'm sorry to inform you that Mistress Pownoll has suddenly felt unwell and can't possibly continue her meeting with you. She apologises most profusely, sir."

"And whom might you be, sir?" asked Ebenezer, looking disdainfully at Sir Joshua.

"Well, sir," said Sir Joshua smiling at Ebenezer whilst inserting his ear trumpet into his left ear, "I am Sir Joshua Reynolds, portrait painter to the royalty and the gentry of England sir. And to whom am I addressing?"

"Pardon me most sincerely, Sir Joshua," said Ebenezer, bowing and smoothing the palms of his hands together in an ingratiating manner, "I am the Reverend Ebenezer Dunn, Minister of Ashprington Church. I do now recall who you are, sir, and may I say, it is an honour and a privilege to make your acquaintance."

"Thank you, Reverend," replied Sir Joshua, "but I must ask you to depart as it not a good time for Mistress Pownoll. May I ask why you have come to pay your respects?"

"Only to seek her well-being and to ask her if she has any news of her husband, Captain Pownoll. I would be interested to know how he fares and as to his whereabouts at sea while we are at war against the American rebels. Knowing this I will pray to the Almighty for his protection and safe return."

"That I cannot say, Reverend," said Sir Joshua, feeling uncomfortable with the implication of Ebenezer's reply. "I bid you good day, sir. Betsy will see you out."

At the door, Ebenezer grasped Betsy's arm. "Keep your eyes and ears open, Betsy Gribble, there'll be news I'll want to hear from this household. You know that hell awaits you if you keep anything from me."

Anguished yet again at his threat of sending her to hell, Betsy watched as Ebenezer walked away towards his pony and trap. As the small carriage disappeared up the hill towards Sharpham's iron gates, she shuddered with dread at the prospect of being sent plunging down to eternal damnation and the everlasting fires of hell.

"I'm so sorry, Joshua," said Jane, still giggling at the thought of the ridiculous sight of Ebenezer, "but I just couldn't help myself. I know it is foolish, but the sight of that man just makes me want to laugh. I find him so ludicrous, so absurd."

Jane related the incident of Ebenezer's wig and Canterbury cap sliding down to rest on his bushy eyebrows, and as they all fell about laughing, Betsy stood silently and despondently in the doorway watching them.

"Oh Betsy," cried Jane, seeing Betsy's distressful look. "What is the matter? You look as though you've received the most dreadful news. Can we help?"

"No, mistress, but thank you," answered Betsy. "Oi just come over all queer like, maybe oi be goin' down with somethin'. Oi best gets meself home. Oi'll be here tomorrow. Thank you, ma'am."

Betsy let herself out of the rear door of the mansion and pulling up the hood of her cloak, she hurried away up the steep hill towards the main carriage track that led towards Ashprington village.

"Dear Lord," she mumbled, "please doen let that devil minister send me down to hell. Oi baint be a bad woman and oi be sorry for any wrongdoin's oi done in me life." She trembled at the thought of Ebenezer's dire warning.

Heavy black clouds were collecting in an already darkening sky as she quickened her pace through Sharpham's iron gates, the first drops of rain beginning to fill the holes in the muddy carriage track. A jingling of a horse's harness made her stop and look expectantly over her shoulder. A horse and wagon appeared over the brow of the hill, the driver urgently flipping the reins to urge the horse on faster. Betsy smiled as she recognised Mordechai.

"Climb up, Betsy," he said, pulling the cart to a standstill, "you'm lucky us was passin'."

Bestsy settled herself next to Mordechai as the horse and cart lumbered on towards Ashprington.

"Thank you for pickin' me up, Mordechai, you'm saved me a soakin'," she muttered as more drops of rain began to fall from the ever-darkening sky.

As they approached the village, Mordechai glanced over at Betsy, surprised at her silence throughout the short journey and of the way she had hung her head without even giving him a glance. Outside the Ashprington Inn, Betsy climbed down from the wagon, thanking Mordechai for the ride and as she scuttled off towards her cottage, she turned and gave him a brief wave. He waved back and was quick to see the look of gloom and despondency implanted all over her face.

"Bliddy hell, Bets, what be up with you?" he muttered to himself, a clap of thunder booming over the village, as he guided the horse and cart into the rear stables of the inn. A sudden burst of heavy rain cascaded down, forming a stream that gushed down the centre of the village, disappearing into the marshy areas below. Jumping over puddles that had quickly formed, he opened the door of the inn and hurrying inside, called out for a mug of cider while shaking the rain water from his mop of wet hair.

The inn was quiet with only a few farm labourers absorbed in a card game in the far corner. Rufus Mudd, the only other customer, sat quietly at a table clasping his pewter mug of cider and looking pleased to see the arrival of Mordechai and the chance of some conversation.

Lucy Hatch smiled at Mordechai as she handed him his cider together with a leather bag that rattled with coins.

"That'll be from Elijah, he's gone over to Totnes but he said you would know what it be for."

Mordechai grinned at Lucy. "Arr, that oi do, Luce, thank you."

"Mordechai, come here and sit with me, 'tis dead in here," called Rufus.

Mordechai dropped a few coins onto the bar for his cider and stuffing the leather bag inside the top of his breeches, he wandered over to the table where Rufus sat clasping his mug.

"'Tis one of they early summer storms blown up," he said looking at Mordechai's rain-matted hair. "What brings you in here this time of day?"

"Had to pick up somethin' from Elijah and have a word with Barold. Have you seen him?"

"He be down in Cornworthy startin' a new buildin' job. Suppose he'll be here soon owin' to this bliddy storm."

"Hope so," said Mordechai. "Barn up at Sharpham's got a leak, dread to think what it be like with this here rain now. Needs a new roof."

Rufus indicated to Lucy to bring him more cider as Mordechai looked anxiously out of a small side window at the torrential rain jettisoning down the thick panelled glass window panes.

"Picked up Betsy Gribble on my way in," said Mordechai, taking a long draught from his cider mug. "She didn't look right, Rufus!"

"Oh yeah, why, what's that then?" asked Rufus, putting down his mug and looking curiously at Mordechai.

"Well, she was all quiet like, not her usual gabby self. When oi dropped her outside here, she wandered orf with a real serious look, as if she had all the troubles in the world on her shoulders. She looked dead frightened about somethin' too, terrified oi would say."

"Maybe she seen a ghost on the way, or somethin' that must have scared her afore you came along," beamed Rufus, his rotten black teeth filling his broad smile.

"Doen know," said Mordechai, draining the cider from his mug and peering out of the side window. "Rain's easin' orf, us'd better git back up Sharpham. Tell Barold oi needs him to look at Sharpham's barn. Keep an eye on Betsy, Rufus. Try to find out what's up with her."

From a side window, Rufus watched Mordechai jumping over a series of puddles that had formed opposite the entrance to the inn's stable.

"Ar, Mordechai, that oi will," he murmured deep in thought, "that oi surely will."

Chapter 7

Charles Gravier, le comte de Vergennes, France's Foreign Minister and Spymaster General, stood by the window of his ornately decorated office in the west wing of the Chateau de Versailles, looking out over a series of majestically designed fountains that proudly proclaimed the immaculate gardens accommodating them.

The government of King Louis XVI of France had its seat in this sumptuous palace, and it was here that France's foreign affairs were planned and executed. His window afforded a grandstand view across the palace gardens, a sight that took in the imposing and stately Grand Canal and the masterful Fountain of Apollo that dramatically rose from the Lake of Swans.

News of secret political and military moves from friendly and hostile countries were delivered here to his office in the palace, the nest of spies he had established ensuring that regular reports and updates reached him. France would soon be at war with Britain, using the uprising of the American colonists as an excuse to become involved in their struggle. Plans would now have to be made and an increase in the monitoring of Britain's military stepped up. Until now there had been no sign of anything significant happening across the channel, until the arrival of a coded note from his spy based in the port of Plymouth.

Charles nodded approvingly as his eyes ranged over the palace gardens, quintessentially designed in their symmetry to display their grandeur as indisputable symbols to France's system of absolute monarchy.

His thoughts turned to the roughly coded note delivered to him two days before from the Brest harbourmaster, Jean de Claire. The British Royal Navy were to escort twenty troop transporters under the command of General John Burgoyne to Boston, Massachusetts. Their aim: to reinforce their military campaign and attempt to break a siege of the harbour that had already begun by a force of colonial militiamen. He had acted immediately and ordered a French frigate to proceed post-haste from Brest to Philadelphia, with instructions to deliver news of the approaching British troop carriers to Benjamin Franklin.

With luck and a fair wind across the Atlantic, the frigate should arrive two weeks before the British were sighted. Gravier knew that the New American Navy was little more than a few refurbished cargo ships supported by a collection of whaling and North Atlantic fishing boats and no match against the might of the British Royal Navy. But a surprise attack by the colonists could inflict some serious damage and may even result in the sinking of a troop carrier. France had lost heavily to Britain in the Seven Years' War and there was now a feeling within the French Court that the time was coming when victory over the British could be achieved once and for all. France would wait and see how the American Colonists fared in their rebellion but would continue to support them with arms until the time was right to enter the conflict and declare war on Britain. Gravier believed the opportunity of ending Britain's ever-growing naval dominance was imminent and then with victory over Britain, France would once again begin to rule the waves. The nest of spies he had established in England were bringing to his attention important and often vital developments of naval and military activity in and around its ports and cities. Plymouth was of major importance and he was pleased with the work his spymaster Luc Skorniere was doing there. He knew that Skorniere had recruited some valuable contacts who were supplying him with worthwhile information, such as the information on the troop transporters he had recently received from his messenger in Brest. He also knew that Skorniere had a network of spies placed in the stately homes of the South West, particularly at Saltram House, the residence of the Member of Parliament for Devon, John Parker. Gravier chuckled to himself at the thought that his spymaster had even managed to infiltrate the Church of England, by placing a corrupt and scurrilous Anglican parson to spy on the parishioners of his own village and the adjacent harbour of Dartmouth. He would wait and see how worthwhile this priest would be to their cause; it seemed that Luc was sure of him. Rubbing his hands together, he turned away from the window and with a smile returned to his desk, calling to his secretary that he needed a coded letter despatched immediately to his spymaster in Plymouth.

* * *

Ebenezer sat in the stern of Stephen's river boat as it drifted away from the Pownoll's boathouse jetty and into the mainstream of the River Dart. At the oarlocks, Stephen and Elijah dipped their oars into the gently flowing water, propelling the craft downriver towards Stoke Gabriel Creek. All three were silent, as their thoughts returned to the horrific night they had experienced on their return from Obadiah Tucker's boathouse only a week before. Elijah had suggested to Ebenezer they follow up his idea of visiting his cousin Noah, landlord of the Church House Inn in Stoke Gabriel, and as Ebenezer was secretly desperate for any information he could pass onto his contact, the idea of listening to any possible fresh news of naval build-ups in the area was too good to refuse. Reluctantly, he had agreed to the quickest form of transport to Stoke Gabriel, Stephen's river boat.

Stephen had agreed to ferry them there as he had an eye for one of Noah's serving wenches. He knew she would be overjoyed to see him and would be all too willing to lie with him in a shady corner of the orchard behind St Gabriel's Parish Church after finishing her afternoon shift in the inn.

Travelling down the river to Stoke Gabriel Creek in daylight seemed to Ebenezer to be quicker than it had been on the night of their venture down to Dittisham and Obadiah's boathouse. With the sun on his face, he stretched out in the stern of Stephen's boat, relaxing to the gentle sound of the river and the heady fragrances of the riverside plants and shrubs. Thoughts of the financial rewards that would be soon coming his way and the easy life it would bring, cheered him. Smiling, he reaffirmed to himself his readiness to lie, smuggle and sell as many secrets as he could gather and then escape to a life of total self-indulgance and pleasure.

The Sunday morning service in a few days would allow him to give the sign to the mysterious informant that the fresh information he would hopefully gain from his visit to Elijah's cousin's inn, would reward him well. His smile broadened at the thought of his collecting what was owed to him from their previous meeting. But Sunday was the night the Ashprington smugglers had an appointment with Squire Maddock and an assignment on horseback to Churston Manor. The thought of that quickly brought him back to where he was and pulling himself upright in the stern, he watched the two rowers turn the craft into the mouth of Stoke Gabriel Creek.

Moving slowly through the water, they passed the camouflaged inlet where they had hidden amongst the reeds and foliage the night the Revenue had blasted the riverbanks to flush them out of hiding. Ebenezer scratched at his chest and arms, still feeling the stings and bites from the swarm of riverside flies that had crawled over them that fearful night.

A loud splash suddenly rocked their boat from side to side, forcing the three of them to jolt upright.

"What the bliddy hell was that?" yelled Elijah.

Suddenly struck with terror at the thought of the Revenue coming up behind them, Ebenezer screamed at Stephen, "Quick, turn into the place where we hid last time, Stephen, be quick. It is the Revenue again. Oh God, what are we going to do?"

Stephen and Elijah pulled up their oars and unable to hold back his amusement at Ebenezer's terrified distress, Stephen let out a burst of laughter that was probably heard all over the river.

"Reverend, calm down, 'tis nuthin' but two young otters playin' yonder. Look around, over there."

Nervously clutching onto the sides of the boat, Ebenezer turned his head in the direction of where Stephen was pointing.

"Look, there," said Stephen, still chuckling at Ebenezer's ashen look, "where the water's ripplin', they'm just dived under. Watch carefully now, they'm be back up in a moment."

Ebenezer gazed at the ripples where the two otters had disappeared when without a sound, two flatheads appeared on the surface of the water, their eyes and nostrils set high on their heads and their long stiff whiskers dripping water. For a moment, time stood still as the two young otters stared at the cause of the sudden intrusion to their fun, then as quick as a flash, they dived and were gone.

"Well," said Ebenezer, "I've never seen such fascinating creatures."

"That they be, Reverend," said Stephen, his eyes trailing down river in the direction of the otters' getaway. "Probably there be a holt nearby with an underwater entrance for them. Doubt us'll see them again. Come on, Elijah, Stoke Gabriel harbour's not far away."

The river boat glided smoothly down the Creek with no more sightings of any otters, although Ebenezer noticed several wide ripples on its far side but sadly no flatheads with long stiff whiskers dripping water rose to the surface.

Stephen and Elijah rowed across the wide expanse of river on their approach to the small harbour of Stoke Gabriel, coasting up to a long wooden mooring jetty that stretched out from a short stone wharf. Stephen tied the double-ended river boat up to a free mooring while Elijah and Ebenezer stretched their legs and gazed around at the activity going on around the waterfront. The harbour was bustling with various riverboats arriving and departing, a large contingency of red-coated soldiers busily loading and unloading the river craft, while others lazily lolled around the wharf chatting and liaising with Revenue men. Ebenezer eyed them with interest, wondering if there was anything worth listening to in their idle talk. Without drawing any attention to themselves, the three men from Ashprington casually walked away from the jetty in the direction of a rough carriage track pointing uphill from the wharf. Stephen led the way, the three of them tromping eagerly up the steep incline, past rows of dingy fishermen's cottages until they came to a welcoming sign announcing the Church House Inn.

Mid-afternoon saw the inn unusually busy, but after witnessing the surge of activity down by the quay, they were not surprised to see the inn teeming with red-coated soldiers and Revenue men. Ebenezer spotted a vacant booth in the far corner where they settled themselves, Elijah trying to catch one of the serving wench's attention. Stephen's eyes were flashing everywhere in the hope of seeing his fancy and when at last he spotted her moving between crowded tables with pots of ale, he jumped up calling out her name.

"Nell, Nell, over here!" he shouted, trying to raise his voice above the din of the chatter filling the inn. He had to holler several times, raising his voice ever louder through the raucous laughter that spilled out over the tables.

Nell looked up and spotted Stephen, her face lighting up as she recognised him through the crowd. Excitedly, she placed the mugs of ale she was holding around a group of red-coated soldiers then wiping her hands down the front of a stained pinafore, she pushed her way through the crowd towards where Stephen stood beaming with joy.

Ebenezer's eyes darted around the busy inn taking in the groups of redcoats and Revenue men who sat deep in conversation.

Mmm, there's a wealth of information to be had here, he thought. *Must get closer to a table when their ale kicks in. That's when they'll begin to talk.*

Stephen flung his arms around Nell as she rushed up to where he was standing. Lifting her slightly off the stone floor, he kissed her passionately on her lips, causing her to whimper and moan in delight.

"You'm be away too long, Stephen," she sighed, hugging him closely.

"Ar, that oi have, Nell. But oi be here for you now, my darlin', and you'm lookin' lovely as ever! These be my friends from Ashprington. Elijah from the Ashprington Inn, he has come to see Noah, his cousin."

"He'm be getting fresh barrels from our stock room, should be out soon enough," replied Nell, smiling at Elijah.

"And this be the Reverend Dunn of Ashprington Church," said Stephen, nodding towards Ebenezer.

"Oh!" said Nell, feigning shyness in front of a minister. "Better watch what I say and do. Eh, Stephen!"

"Not at all, Nell," said Ebenezer, lusting secretly over her firm breasts and well-formed figure. "It's my pleasure to be introduced to you, my dear," he gloated, taking her hand and putting it gently to his lips.

"Oh, Reverend, you'm be a right gentlemin," replied Nell, giggling mischiefly as Stephen's hand stroked her rear. "Now, what you'm all be havin?"

"Ale all round, Nell," said Stephen, kissing her hand.

"Us'll be finishin' in an hour, Stephen," she whispered into his ear. "Perhaps us can go for a stroll in the orchard behind the church? Oi knows a nice quiet spot where no-one goes."

Stephen smiled at Nell, pursing his lips in a sensual way. "Absolutely, my booty, can't wait for that."

Nell giggled to herself as she glided away towards the bar, noticing that Noah was now out of the stock room and busily filling up mugs of ale for the waiting serving wenches to carry to the crowded tables.

"Three tankards of ale, Noah," said Nell, "for the gentlemen in the far booth. Your cousin Elijah from Ashprington be there and looking out for you."

Noah Hatch looked up expectantly, following Nell's pointed finger to the wooden booth at the back of the Inn.

"Well, oi never," said Noah, "ain't seen Elijah for some time. Oi'll take the ale over to them, Nell, you'm carry on with other tables. You'm be finishin' in an hour anyways."

"Don't I just know it," uttered Nell, smirking quietly to herself.

Noah ambled over to the booth with the ale, slapping the mugs down on the table in front of them. After much backslapping and hugs with his cousin, Elijah introduced Ebenezer and Stephen to Noah, who immediately recognised Stephen, from Stephen's previous visits to the inn and his liking for Nell.

"Dare says you'm be taking Nell out somewheres later," said Noah looking seriously at Stephen. "You'm just treat her right, boey."

He acknowledged Ebenezer with a hint of suspicion but changed his mind when Ebenezer offered to pay for the next round of ale. Over the next hour, conversation drifted from subjects on the prices of alcohol in each other's inns to how war with the American colonies was beginning to affect them all, when without any warning, Noah turned to Elijah, and with Ebenezer and Stephen well within earshot, said, "And 'ow about your smugglin', you'm old rogue?"

Elijah smiled at Ebenezer and Stephen. "Noah knows about our syndicate," he said. "He benefits from a little brandy oi send to his inn and he keeps his ears open for any news that may affect our trips down to Obadiah."

"Then why didn't you warn Elijah of an increased presence of the Revenue on the river," said Ebenezer, looking at Noah.

"I didn't know they'd be there then," replied Noah earnestly. "Oi only listens out for loose tongues in here and whatever the locals tell me be goin' on down on the quay and parts of the river. As you'm can see, there be a build-up of them redcoats. They'm not only helpin' the Revenue, but there be somethin' goin on here and downriver in Dartmouth. Seems like there be a big build-up of troops and an increase of navy there. Probably got somethin' to do with the war in the colonies." In an instant, Ebenezer became alert.

"Another thing, Elijah," said Noah, beckoning them to come closer as he lowered his voice, "over there at the table just in front of the bar facin' us, be a group of redcoats and Revenue men drinking ale and smokin' their pipes." Noah pushed his face closer towards the others.

"Well, they'm been comin' in here regular like for the past few weeks. Last week they'm were here and after a lot of ale they'm started tellin' me of a chase they'm made up the river at night. They'm said that they had come across a river boat making its way out of Dit'sum and gave chase as it passed Black Rock Point. They'm was sure it be smugglers and after it didn' stop when their officer commanded, they'm fired on it. They'm was impressed at how quickly the boat accelerated away from them as they'm could see, by the light of the full moon, it be fair full of contraband. They'm swore there be five smugglers in that river boat when it disappeared suddenly from sight. There be a sergeant in the group, an 'ard drinkin' man, but that evenin' he told me they'd 'ad the river boat in their sights and was sure they'd get it, but it suddenly vanished into the night. They'm raked the riverbanks with muskit fire but no-one came out from hidin', so they'm carried on down here to Stoke but found nuthin' on the river." Noah lowered his voice even lower, stretching his face further into theirs and whispering, "Now, oi knows it was you in that boat, Elijah, and likely these two here. What have you got to say about that then. Well?"

"What else have you heard, Noah?" asked Elijah, looking at his companions.

"Oi'm comin' to that," said Noah. "Now, you'm bein' family and all that, Elijah, oi would't say nuthin'. But should you be increasin' your illicit brandy supply, then as us be family like, oi thinks that a barrel or two for your hard workin' cousin here wouldn't be missed that much by you, Elijah, would it now?"

Elijah looked at Stephen and Ebenezer, nodding his approval.

"Oi thinks we can arrange that, Noah," said Elijah, staring hard at his cousin, "Now, what else have you heard? Oi knows you'm got more."

"That oi certainly have, cousin, but first let us be having another round of ale, oi thinks it be your round this time, eh?!"

Someone hovering next to their booth brought them to attention and turning, they saw Nell waiting with arms folded. Stephen jumped to his feet and with a smile turned to the group, "Gentlemen, oi has me an appointment with this bootiful young lady. Now if you will excuse me, us'll be makin' our way and will see you, Ebenezer and Elijah, back here when the clock points to ten."

As Noah went to replenish their mugs of ale, Ebenezer turned to Elijah, "Can you trust your cousin, Elijah?"

"Oi have to, Reverend, but he knows our law about splittin' to the Revenue and Excise. He won't say nuthin', and anyway, he is greedy for more brandy that he knows oi've got, it won't hurt us much to let him have a couple of barrels. He has more news about somethin' that may be interestin'. Here he comes, listen to what he says."

Noah hurried back with three full tankards of ale, holding out his hand for payment. Elijah dropped a few coins into his hand, and they sat with their heads close to Noah as he took a gigantic swig of ale, wiping his beery mouth on his sleeve. Studying the two of them, he lowered his voice.

"Two days ago," he began, "on a quiet afternoon when only a few soldiers, locals and Revenue were in the inn, oi had a visit from two gentlemin who settled themselves in the snug next door and asked not to be disturbed. They'm be important gents and oi knew one of them as our Member of Parliament for Devon, John Parker."

Ebenezer listened keenly as Noah continued.

"They'm asked for the best claret oi had in the house, so that's what oi gives them. The other gent be from these parts, oi think a Lord from some grand house just outside of Stoke. I know now he be Lord William Spicer from Armitage House, a mansion not far from here on the old road to Totnes. Folk round here reckons he be an equerry to the King and a member of the House of Lords. Well, oi served them and stood back behind the bar cleanin' mugs and tankards listenin' to what they'm was sayin'. John Parker seemed to be a bit agitated as he spoke to Lord William. This be what oi overheard:

"*'It's really out of the question, William, it's not viable. What does he mean by wanting to come to Plymouth to view the troops and our warships?'*

"*'He's adamant, John. Frederick, Lord North our Prime Minister, has tried to dissuade him but you know our King, once he has got an idea into his head, then it is impossible to make him change it. He has chosen to stay with you at Saltram and that is the end of it, he is coming!'*

"*'Remind me of the date again, William,' said John, holding his head in his hands.*

"*'Lord North has informed his cabinet that the King is intent on announcing a Proclamation of Rebellion, which he plans to give on August 23rd. He will summon his generals to mobilise for complete all-out war with the colonies posthaste. Those troops and naval vessels not already committed to the colonies, will assemble at our ports in a concerted effort to bring this rebellion to a quick end. Plymouth will be a major assembling point and His Majesty will travel there on September 1st to address his troops. He will arrive at Saltram the day before John, so be prepared. This of course is top secret.'*

"*'As it's now mid-May, that only gives us just over three months to prepare,' said John, 'I'll have to discuss this with Theresa as soon as I get back.'"*

Noah looked intently at Ebenezer and Elijah. "That's it, gentlemin, that's what I heard and witnessed only two days ago."

Ebenezer's eyes were wide open. He was stunned with the news and knew that he now had a major hand to play. He kept a straight face in front of Elijah and Noah but inwardly he felt joyous at knowing he now possessed a golden piece of secret information.

What would Luc Skorniere give to know this? he thought.

Draining the last drop of ale from his mug, Noah left them with a parting smile, reminding Elijah of the two barrels of brandy he would expect from him shortly.

Stephen appeared back in the inn on the stroke of ten, looking slightly dishevelled but in good spirits. Neither Elijah nor Ebenezer asked him about his time with Nell; this was a man's private business and was respected.

They walked back to the quay in silence to where Stephen's boat was moored, Stephen occasionally making a grimace and comment about Nell but receiving no remark from the other two. Before embarking, they relieved themselves over the wharf into the dark waters below, Ebenezer still quietly ecstatic over the news he had heard from Noah.

Elijah and Stephen pulled at the oars, taking the river boat out into the wide opening of Stoke Gabriel harbour. They gathered speed through the placid waters, soon entering the Creek under the light of a full moon. It was not long before they glided quietly up to Philemon's boathouse jetty. Elijah and Ebenezer climbed up the ladder strapped to the side while Stephen turned the boat around, with a grin and a wave he pulled at the oars to coast out into the waters of the River Dart and home to Tuckenhay.

Thirty minutes later, after walking back from the Pownolls' boathouse, an exhausted Ebenezer and Elijah staggered into the Ashprington Inn to be welcomed with a brandy from Lucy.

"Well, well, you both look as though you've had more than enough, good day be it?"

"Ar, a proper day, Luce," said Elijah, stifling a yawn.

"Squire's messenger came early evenin'," said Lucy. "He left a message to say Squire awaits your company on Sunday night, eleven o'clock."

Ebenezer looked at Elijah and they both nodded.

"Well, I'm away now," said Ebenezer knocking back his brandy. "See you both at Sunday Morning Service. I expect we'll be going up to Darton Hall in your wagon, Elijah?"

"Ar, that we will, Reverend. Nine o'clock here. I'll inform the others."

Ebenezer smiled with satisfaction as he ambled up the hill to the rectory. Now he had something to tell the mysterious contact who would be sitting in the congregation on Sunday morning, but the cards were now stacked in Ebenezer's favour. He would demand a face-to-face meeting with Luc Skorniere when he'd sell the information he'd heard from Noah for as much as he could get. Grinning

71

broadly, he began to shake with excitement and as he opened the door of his house, he threw back his head and roared with elation, thumping the air as though he had just come into a vast fortune.

Chapter 8

"The King, coming here and staying here! You can't be serious, John?" said Theresa looking earnest and shocked.

"Yes, my dear, I am being serious, and although it is three months away, it is not that long to arrange everything. But what I am most concerned about is the security. We are going to have to allow our home to be searched regularly and to go along with whatever security measures His Majesty's secret service demands. Saltram's in for quite a change to its normal way of life."

"But when he has gone, John, will everything be back to normal? Our baby is due in September, he cannot be here when I am giving birth. What if the baby comes early?"

"Don't think of that my, darling, that won't happen. The doctors have assured you that our precious baby will arrive around the middle of September, weeks after the King has left us and yes, everything will return to normal."

They were suddenly interrupted by a servant hovering at the door.

"Yes, Andrew, what is it?" asked John looking up.

"Sir Joshua Reynolds has arrived, sir, and is waiting in the reception lobby."

"Show him in, please," instructed John.

"Joshua, how good of you to call, come on in and join us. A glass of claret?"

"Good day to you, John, and to you, Theresa," said Joshua, seating himself opposite John and Theresa. "Claret would be fine, John."

"Andrew," said John, indicating to his servant, "and one for me, of course."

"Theresa, you look as though you've heard something stressful. I hope it's not too disturbing for you?" asked Joshua, holding his ear trumpet.

A look from John told Theresa to refrain from spilling out the news of the King's visit to Saltram. John trusted Sir Joshua, but there was a servant in the room, and he knew it best to keep such information from unknown ears.

"I'm as well as I can be, Joshua, and thank you for asking," replied Theresa, smiling. "How is Jane, I haven't heard from her since Philemon sailed to the colonies? I know you've been sketching young Jane's features up at Sharpham House, how's that going?"

"Jane's coping well since Philemon departed," replied Joshua. "But I can see in her eyes that there's a gap in her heart without him by her side. Their daughter Jane's enabled me to sketch such perfect examples of her facial features that truly exemplify the subject of innocence. I shall begin work on it soon. I am still thinking of naming the piece 'The Age of Innocence!'"

"Splendid, Joshua," said John turning to the servant who was hovering near the door. "Andrew, thank you, that'll be all. Close the door on your way out."

The servant nodded once and left the room, closing the door behind him.

"Now, Joshua, you know we've something to tell, and thank you for not pushing us while Andrew was in the room." John took a long draught of claret from his glass. "Yesterday, I stopped off at the Church House Inn in Stoke Gabriel with Sir William Spicer. You know him, equerry to the King and a member of the House of Lords. He lives not far from there and as I was in the area attending a landowners' conference with him, he invited me for some claret and a private chat in the privacy of our own snug in the inn."

"Yes, I know of him, although we've never met," said Joshua looking interested.

"He came straight to the point as we sat alone, informing me that the King will make a Proclamation of Rebellion on August 23rd. The rebellion in our colonies is getting worse and now Parliament and the King want to finish it quickly and surely. By making his Proclamation, he will be calling for all-out war against the rebel colonists and instructing his generals to mobilise those troops not already over there. Now, what d'you think of this, the King has decided he wants to address his troops before they embark for the colonies and he has selected Plymouth for his address, on September 1st. Wait for it, he has chosen to stay here at Saltram, the night before the address."

Sir Joshua looked astounded. "The King, here in Saltram! Phew, John, that's a great feather in your cap and as long as all goes well, a knighthood will be on its way for you pretty soon after."

"Sir William told me that everything is hush-hush and news of his coming must not be let out. Nobody is to know anything about it until he is there at the port addressing the troops. Of course, there is going to be regular security checks here at Saltram before he arrives, we must on no account inform any of our staff of these plans. We will let the staff know that we will be expecting a dignitary from the government to stay here on that date, so they will be prepared. What a surprise they will have when they see who that dignitary is! I ask you again to keep this very secret, Joshua. If news got out, then I can't imagine what could happen."

"The secret's safe with me, John," said Sir Joshua smiling at John and Theresa. "Don't you worry."

* * *

The Sunday morning service at St David's Church was full of worshippers from the village and the surrounding areas. Ebenezer stood alone near the altar, surveying his congregation as they heartily sang the newly published hymn by the reverend Augustus Toplady, 'Rock of Ages'.

His eyes roamed along the church pews, picking out his smuggling cohorts who looked back at him, knowing that midnight would see them saddling up at Darton Hall for the ride across the country to their venue at Churston Manor. Mordechai stood with young Watt Huckle mouthing the words of the hymn. Elijah and Lucy Hatch sat at the back next to Stephen, not taking any part in the singing but looking steadily at their comrades, occasionally whispering to each other, their faces showing the nervous expectancy they were feeling of the forthcoming venture. Ebenezer guessed they were whispering about the night's undertaking and that Elijah was informing Stephen to be at the inn by nine o'clock.

As the congregation settled themselves into their pews, silence reigned around the church. Ebenezer scanned those who were looking directly at him, but he was still unable to get any clue as to whom the mysterious contact could be, but he knew he was somewhere there.

"Brethren," he said, raising his voice to those at the rear of the church, "I'm afraid there'll be no sermon this morning as I'm feeling rather under the weather and can feel my throat getting sorer as I speak," he lied. "I hope you will understand. Thank you and God bless you."

Betsy Gribble sat tight-lipped as he spoke, staring at him through slit eyes. "Oi hopes someone slashes it for you, you'm devil priest," she muttered. Rufus Mudd on the opposite aisle stared at Betsy, remembering what Mordechai had told him that stormy afternoon in the Ashprington Inn. Slowly, Ebenezer raised his left hand to his left ear and with a great show tugged at it, then turned and made ready for the distribution of communion. Betsy had seen the exaggerated pull of the ear and thought it rather strange. *Wonder what he did that for?* she thought. *Be he sendin' someone a signal? Strange that. Oi's gonna find him out, that devil!*

After the service, Ebenezer stood outside the church smiling and nodding at the parishioners as they made their way out. Betsy Gribble ignored him as he made a gesture of recognition, walking past him without even an acknowledgment.

"Foolish woman," he muttered to himself.

The five smugglers, including Watt, crowded round him, confirming that they would all meet up in the inn by nine o'clock that night. As the last of the congregation made their way towards the church gate, Ebenezer returned to the vestry taking a bottle of church wine from a cupboard. Opening it, he sprawled out on the chair next to the robing table and gulped half the bottle down in one greedy swig. He knew the contact had seen the pull of his left ear and would be at the church as dusk settled. Ebenezer would demand an audience with Luc Skorniere, certain of what he would propose to him. He began to tremble as the idea grew in his mind, an idea that would make him rich beyond all his means. The assassination of the King of England at the grand stately home of Saltram House.

With a chuckle he finished off the wine, flinging the empty bottle across the vestry, then throwing off his church vestments, he left the church, slamming the door behind him.

He was about to lift the latch on the gate at the end of the pathway when his thoughts were suddenly distracted by a whooshing sound directly above him.

He gasped in amazement as he looked up at the sight of an osprey flying gracefully over the medieval tower, clutching a fair-sized river fish in its talons. As he watched, enraptured at such an unexpected sighting, the bird turned in flight then gathering speed disappeared over the fields of Sharpham Estate and on towards its stick nest high up in the riverside trees.

Loud laughter burst from the Ashprington Inn as Ebenezer hurried past, anxious to get home where he could have a few hours' sleep and rest before going back to the church for his secret rendezvous. He was surprised to see his front door unlocked as he inserted the key into the lock.

Must have forgotten to lock it on my way out, he thought. *No matter, there is nothing of value for thieves or vagabonds to steal. Ha, as if there are any thieves or vagabonds in the village of Ashprington anyway*, he chuckled.

He let himself in, closing and locking the door behind him, listening for any unusual sounds.

The house seemed peacefully quiet, no cause for any alarm.

A swift brandy, he thought, *and then it's bed and a long sleep.*

He poured a large cognac and was settling down on one of his sofas when he jumped in alarm at a noise coming from his bedroom. He froze, listening intently for it to be repeated. Again, he heard it, a soft murmuring sound followed by what sounded like a deep sigh.

Courage was certainly not one of Ebenezer's qualities; he was in fact a total coward. He had always been quick to stand behind someone in the event of trouble, hiding in fear unless he were the first out of a room when violent situations arose. Standing up from the sofa, he heard it again.

"Oh my God!" he mumbled. "Someone's in the house and in my bedroom. What am I going to do?"

Clutching his glass of cognac, he tiptoed towards the parlour door and standing in the hallway next to his bedroom, he took a deep breath and slowly opened the door. Peeping around the corner so he had a good view of the room, he gasped in surprise as his eyes rested on the naked figure of Molly stretched out on his bed. All fearful thoughts of vagabonds and thieves ransacking his bedroom suddenly disappeared as he stood gaping at the sensual position Molly had adopted. His lower lip started to tremble and the cognac in his glass began to wobble furiously as his hands shook uncontrollably with lustful desire. Molly's legs slowly parted as she opened her eyes, while her tongue licked her full lips enticingly. Seeing him dithering in the doorway, she beckoned him to join her, smiling at the deep groan emitting from him as he watched her begin her foreplay. Not being able to withstand it any longer, he gulped down the cognac and placing the glass on top of a chest of drawers, he flew across the bedroom, leaping on her like a rampant animal, slavering and panting as his hands roughly groped her nakedness. Giggling, Molly let him ravage her, secretly enjoying his primitive love-making. With her head thrown back and her eyes closed, she pulled at his breeches, spurring him on to wriggle out of them swiftly. Grasping his manhood, she groaned in delight, whispering in his ear, "Oh Ebenezer, you are a naughty parson! But do not stop, please."

Ignoring her plea and with his face purpling under the sweat pouring from his brow, he gave a stuttering sigh and with a heavy shudder, was quickly spent.

* * *

The sound of the church bell striking six times woke Ebenezer with a start. With one eye open, he focused on an empty brandy glass perched on top of his chest of drawers, then as sleep left him, he bolted upright looking around the bedroom for Molly. There was no sign of her, although there was a definite sign on the left side of the bed that someone had been lying there.

"Molly, Molly," he called, "are you here, answer me?"

Suddenly, he froze.

"The contact," he cried, "he'll be at the church as dusk falls and then it's up to Darton Hall for eleven o'clock. Where are my breeches?"

When he eventually found them, wrapped around one of the bed sheets under a blanket, he staggered out of bed, struggling to get them on the right way. After toppling over onto the floor several times while trying to get a leg inside them, he managed to pull them up and get himself respectfully dressed.

Where on earth did Molly go? he thought. *She could have woken me!*

He left the bedroom checking the other rooms in the house in case Molly had taken herself into another room to escape his snoring, but all were empty and quiet. Before letting himself out, he stood in his hallway, listening once again for a sound that would signal if Molly might possibly be somewhere in the house. There was nothing.

Dimpsy light heralding the oncoming dusk filtered through the stained-glass windows of the church as Ebenezer let himself in. There had been no sign of the contact waiting outside but Ebenezer knew it would not be long before he appeared.

Lighting a candle, he made his way towards the pew below the painting of The Four Evangelists and seating himself, he waited as the evening shadows began to form.

"Look at those four up there, glaring down at me as if they own the place!" he mumbled looking up at the painting. "Ha, what if I care!"

The evening light was failing rapidly when the sound of a door creaking open echoed eerily around the church. Jumping up out of the pew, Ebenezer stood in the aisle, nervously holding the candle towards the shadows.

"Where are you?" he stuttered peering into the darkness.

"Here, in front of the nave," came the reply. " I can see your candle shining under The Four Evangelists."

A shuffling sound coming towards him caused Ebenezer to take a few steps forward.

"That be far enough," said the hooded figure, "what you'm got for me?"

"First of all, I want my payment for the last information I gave you about Captain Pownoll," said Ebenezer.

"Here," said the figure, tossing a small bag towards him that fell to the ground tinkling with sound of coins. "Now, let me have your latest, and it better be good."

"There's an increase in troop movements and a build-up of troops and ships in and around Dartmouth," said Ebenezer staring at the cloaked figure. "Stoke Gabriel seems to be one of the supply centres for this build-up. I was there and the increase in troops is pointing to reinforcements set for the colonies. There are more frigates and ships of the line coming and going in Dartmouth."

"All very well," replied the contact, "but oi wants dates, numbers and facts about what you saw. Give me these and you'll get your reward."

"Wait," said Ebenezer, as the figure turned to leave, "I have serious information, crucially important to your spymaster. I met him once, a long time ago, and he knows I am working with you here, although I do not know who you are. I will give this information only to Luc Skorniere, no-one else. You tell him to contact me for a face-to-face meeting. This is the most serious information he could receive. Should you not inform him of this, then I would not like to be in your shoes when he finds out. Is that clear?"

"What be this news, if it be so crucial?" said the figure.

"I've just told you that I'll give it to no-one other than to Luc Skorniere," repeated Ebenezer.

"But to wet his appetite, oi will have to tell him somethin'," replied the contact.

"Tell him that it concerns King George III and it could have a great effect on the war in the colonies," said Ebenezer.

Silence filled the church.

"Well?" said Ebenezer, sounding impatient.

"Ar, oi'll tell him of that you can be sure," came the reply.

The church door slammed shut, bringing a sigh of relief from Ebenezer. Lowering the candle, he picked up the bag of coins grinning as he tipped half of the contents into his palm. With the light of the candle, he was able to count the coins sitting in his hand, a rough guess as to how much remained in the bag bringing a satisfied smile to his face.

"Ha, ha," he shouted out, "and there's more to come, plenty more."

Chuckling, he grabbed his cloak from the pew. "Yes, plenty more," he repeated, then with a quick look behind at the darkening corners of the church, he rubbed his hands with glee, nodding arrogantly to The Four Evangelists. Making his way to the front of the church, he blew out the candle and letting himself out through the main door, he hurried off towards the Ashprington Inn.

From the dark shadows behind the church's altar, a figure emerged to stand rigidly still, listening for any sign that the minister might return unexpectedly.

Silence reigned within the darkness as the figure slowly made its way towards the church door, turning to bow respectfully to the silver crucifix hanging over the altar. Betsy Gribble stepped out into the duskiness of the church grounds, a slow smile spreading over her face.

"Well, oi have heard it all now. That devil priest is a traitor. Oi have got him now, and he will not dare send me to hell 'coz what oi knows will surely hang him. And that other one, all cloaked up and hooded, I recognised his voice but can't make out who'm he be, but it'll come, of that oi'm certain."

Betsy opened the gate and closing it quietly behind her, she walked away towards her cottage, feeling happier than she had done for a long time.

Chapter 9

The candle lights at Darton Hall twinkled like a multitude of glow-worms as Elijah clicked his tongue at the horse pulling the wagon up the winding riverside track. Sitting up front next to Elijah, young Watt Huckle wriggled with excitement at the thought of the forthcoming venture. This would be his first active escapade with the smuggling gang, and his eagerness to get into the saddle and thunder across the countryside with Mordechai and the rest of them was obvious to them all. He'd make sure they'd all see his bravery, and when he'd been the first to return with his quota of the Squire's consignment, they'd all hail his courage and acknowledge him a true asset to the group. The other four seated in the rear of the cart, looked steadily ahead as it rumbled up the steep incline. Stephen and Barold sat quietly, absorbed in their own thoughts while Ebenezer with eyes closed, relived again the afternoon of discovering the sensual figure of Molly waiting for him in his bedroom. Mordechai saw the lecherous smile growing across his face but paid no attention. His thoughts were of a deep concern of whether Watt would be able to keep up with them and not be too zealous to display futile acts of daring. He knew that Watt would be over-anxious to prove himself, so he would make sure he would ride next to him and keep a protective watch over him.

Large oil lanterns carefully placed around the perimeter, met them as Elijah guided the horse and wagon into the cobblestoned courtyard. A glowing brazier in the centre lit up the ample figure of the Squire, warming his backside while he slurped from a silver cup. The two liveried servants, who had met them on their last visit, stood to attention next to him. Grinning at the Ashprington six, he beckoned them over to join him at the brazier, and while one of the servants took care of the horse and wagon, the other served them with cups of piping hot brandy.

"Well, the horses are saddled, ready and waiting," said the Squire. "Now listen carefully."

The six of them fixed their eyes on the Squire as he continued.

"From here, drop down and follow the river along the track that leads into Totnes. Cross the old stone bridge and make haste up over Bridgetown till you can get back onto country fields. Cut across country through Berry Pomeroy and continue across fields towards Paignton. By-pass the town keeping to the fields and farmland until you come to the wooded area of Clennon. Carry on uphill till you come to the common ground that leads to the fishing town of Brixham. Half-way across this land, you will come to a rough sign nailed to an old oak pointing to a rough carriage track that runs parallel to farm land. Turn into this track, it'll lead you to Churston Manor. My man will be waiting for you. When you are all loaded up, get back here. Should take you just over an hour to Churston Manor, hour and a half to get the contraband and load up, then just over an hour to get back to me here. All being well, just over three hours. I will have your payment ready when you get back. Do not take any risks; if you see any of the Revenue, hide in the shadows until they have past. It is a full moon for you tonight and clear, so that will be to your advantage. Good luck to you all. Come on, the horses are getting impatient."

They followed the Squire out of the courtyard and up a small hill to where the stables were located. The light of the moon shone down on them and the six sturdy horses that waited patiently for them. Attached to each saddle were leather saddle bags which the squire instructed a groom to open and show the six smugglers. Inside each saddle bag were strong leather straps to secure the ankers and pig bladders to their mounts. As an example, the groom demonstrated how to tie the straps carefully, using two small barrels and two pig bladder water carriers on one of the horses.

Squire Maddock then told them to choose a horse and get mounted. Ebenezer had already spotted a docile-looking mare and before the others could decide, he grabbed her reins and lifted himself up into the saddle. The mare stood patiently while Ebenezer shuffled himself into position. As soon as the others were mounted, the Squire clapped his hands and pointed in the direction they were to take. Stephen was the first away, followed by Mordechai and Watt at his side. Barold dug his heels into his horse's flanks and flew off after them, hollering an expletive which made the Squire roar with laughter. Elijah and Ebenezer trotted after them, urging their horses into a canter, as the other four drew slowly away from them.

They crossed the old stone bridge at Totnes as the town clock began to strike the hour of midnight, and were soon making haste up over Bridgetown where they found a gap in the trees to canter across soft pasture towards the village of Berry Pomeroy. Keeping the front runners in sight by the light of the full moon, Ebenezer and Elijah saw they had stopped by an opening at the end of the field. As they rode up to join them, they heard Barold and Mordechai disagreeing about which route to take. Barold was adamant they should take the left turning into Berry Pomeroy village as he had travelled that way before when inspecting a possible building contract. Mordechai, whilst agreeing with Barold, made it clear it was a longer route and should be overlooked in favour of carrying straight on over to a smaller track that wound past Blagdon Manor Farm. They could then ride on over open country, by-passing Paignton in the direction of the wooded area of Clennon. Unanimously, they agreed with Mordechai, directing their mounts to cross in the direction he had proposed. Stephen held up his hand as they were about to exit the field, whispering to look around for any signs of the Revenue. Barold's horse snorted with impatience as they sat their mounts peering into the darkness and listening for the slightest sound that would warn them of the King's customs men.

A sudden loud gasp from Watt broke the silence as he pointed across to what seemed like a wooden 'T' standing erect in the shadows of a group of trees. A basket-like object hung from the cross beam of the 'T', gently swaying in the night's breeze. They urged their horses forward, stopping in front of a creaking metal cage that hugged the decomposing remains of a corpse hanging from the beam. Birds had obviously had a feast on the unfortunate body, having pecked out the eyes, leaving only dark sockets that were now infested with wriggling maggots. The nose was missing together with the left cheek, and the whole spectacle reeked of an unearthly stench that made each one of the Ashprington six shudder with terror.

"This be Hangman's Cross," said Mordechai staring at the corpse.

"Ar, 'tis that," echoed Barold, and without choosing his words carefully, continued, "He was likely a thief or maybe even a smuggler!"

"Oh my God," cried Ebenezer, "you mean, is that how we could all end up?"

"Enough now," said Elijah, "us have been here too long. Come on," and he tapped his heels into the sides of his horse and trotted away with the others following after him.

They rode down the narrow country track in single file, none of them speaking, as the sight of what they had just witnessed likened them to a similar fate should they be captured. The barking of a dog warned them they were approaching Blagdon Manor Farm, and digging their heels into their horses' flanks, they raced past the farm buildings. Ebenezer hung on to his mare's mane, the noise of the thundering hooves setting off more incessant barking from the farm's dogs. They would be long away before the owners came out to investigate why the dogs had been barking so aggressively.

They galloped on across fields that were bathed in the light of the full moon, always careful to slow down and stop at a crossroads to look out for signs of the Revenue. So far, they had seen nothing to indicate any cause for concern. The ground began to slope away as they spied a densely wooded area lying at the bottom of a steep valley. Ebenezer, riding next to Mordechai and Watt, asked if it was the wooded area of Clennon.

"Ar, 'tis Clennon all right," replied Mordechai, "not far to go now. Just hope the Squire's man will be waitin' for us yonder them woods."

As the ground levelled out, they followed a track that led through the trees where the darkness was only occasionally interrupted by beams of moonlight stabbing through the trees. The sounds of owls and night creatures scurrying out of their way into the dark confines of the undergrowth kept them alert as they followed the narrow woodland track deeper into what seemed the heart of the forest. Staring into the dark shadows of the trees, Ebenezer wondered what creatures were discreetly watching them from their blackened holes, irritated at being disturbed from their nightly routines.

And then they were out and riding under a starlit sky. A grassy hill emerged before them, causing them to urge their horses into an uphill canter. Ebenezer breathed deeply, smelling the salty air of the sea that wafted up from a neighbouring beach below. As they rode over the brow of the hill, they saw that a sea mist had suddenly formed to envelope the area of common ground that Squire Maddock had told them stretched as far as the small fishing town of Brixham. They were not far from their destination. Stephen, spurring on his horse, shouted out he would ride on ahead to look for the sign nailed to the old oak tree and the track that led to Churston Manor. Elijah shouted after him to keep a careful look out for the Revenue; with a wave Stephen galloped away from them, disappearing into the misty darkness covering the common.

* * *

Solomon Metcalf squinted through the sea mist and into the moon-tainted waters of the bay that fronted the three towns of Torquay, Paignton and Brixham. Under the moonlight, shiny pebbles washed clean by the breaking waves covered the cove where he stood, glistening like a hoard of abandoned jewels from a giant's treasure chest. To his right, wooded cliffs stretched far out towards the sea, concealing the fishing harbour of Brixham situated at the southern tip of the bay. A rough muddy track leading up through the wooded cliffs from the cove led to the manor house of Churston Manor, residence of the famous London barrister, Sir Francis Buller, and his wife, Lady Susanna, who being away in London were not expected to return until the following week. A strong mist off the sea half covered the manor house and its outbuildings, veiling a brickbuilt storage shed behind which stood the cliff wall. A heavy wooden door fixed into the cliff wall opened into a secret tunnel that ran steeply down to the pebbly cove.

Solomon tapped the heavy cudgel he was grasping in his right hand against the outside of his right leg, impatient for the arrival of the Marie de France, the French merchant ship carrying the cargo of contraband. The hook on his left hand wavered as he suddenly changed position. Gripping the heavy wooden club between his knees, he reached inside his coat with his right hand, fumbling for the pocket in his waistcoat that held a silver pocket watch he had taken from a sailor in a recent tavern brawl. Pulling it out, he flicked it open,

"Five minutes to one," he mumbled, "where's that bastard Froggy ship, should have been here forty minutes ago. Useless fuckers!"

The squad of batsmen he had recruited from the sleazy inns and haunts in and around Paignton stood around him, careful not to say anything out of place that may cause him to lash out with his cudgel. They all feared him and had cause to, as he had beaten three men to death single-handedly in an argument over monies they'd claimed he owed them from a previous night's unloading job on the quiet beach of Dawlish. During the fight, one of the men had slashed at Solomon's left hand with a filthy skinning knife, cutting into his wrist and nearly severing a vital vein. Days later, the wound, inflamed and badly infected, had begun to turn green. With a carefully sharpened axe, the blade having rested in a glowing furnace for a good hour, Solomon had cut off his left hand with two blows, promptly fainting into the arms of his cohorts surrounding him. An old seafaring fisherman, friendly with Solomon, had cauterised the stub of his wrist, later helping him secure and attach a hook in its place.

Solomon's left arm hung limply at his side, the hook glinting in the moonlight as he put the pocket watch back into his waistcoat pocket. Turning to count that the number of batsmen he had recruited still tallied with those around him, a rush of activity over at the far end of the cove made him look around and glare out to sea. Sure enough, several rowing boats from the French ship were seen coming through the mist towards the cove. The Marie de France had arrived and had silently anchored out in the bay within reach of its pebbly unloading site.

The batsmen were to keep a look out for the Revenue and engage them in a close fight should they be spotted, so keeping them away from the tubmen, who would be unloading the consignment from the rowing boats. Runners would then carry the contraband quickly up to the headland above the cove, where wagons and mounted despatchers waited.

With a crunching sound underfoot, a score of tubmen raced across the pebbles to off-load the cargo from the rowing boats. Solomon watched as they formed a human chain, passing contraband in rapid succession to the runners who carried it up to the wagons on the headland.

"You four," he shouted to a group of his batsmen, "that point on the headland, come on, move it, you bastards. Spread yourselves out up there, three shrill whistles if you see any Revenue fuckers."

The four shot off across the cove, waving their cudgels in the direction Solomon had ordered them.

"You lot," he yelled, pointing to another three, "take the point at the other end of the headland, go now and keep your eyes open." As they scrambled off over the pebbles, he directed the remaining three to stand guard by the wagons on the headland, where runners were unloading the contraband at an exceptional rate. His three men were there in an instant, waving to indicate they were in control, a menacing threat to anyone who intended to pilfer from the wagons.

As the rowing boats returned to the Marie de France to take on more load, Solomon stomped across the cove towards the shoreline, searching the groups of tubmen for their gang leader. When at last he picked him out, deep in conversation with four of the tubmen, he waved trying to catch his attention. The gang leader looked up and recognising Solomon, nodded to him.

Leaving the four tubmen with instructions to wait where they were, he tramped over to where Solomon stood waiting.

"Your lot should be on the next boat," he called, "us'll get those four lads waitin' over there to run it up to you by the track leadin' up to the headland. You'm better be there to take it as there's several light-fingered bastards round here who'd take it without you'm knowin'!"

"Fair doos," said Solomon eyeballing the gang leader, "but you know what the fuckers would get if they tried. Now, it is twelve ankers and pigs' bladders of brandy for the Squire, two ankers for me and a pigskin too. I trust you'm doen have a problem with that. And here," he said taking a small leather bag from his coat pocket, "this be from the Squire, and you'm knows better than to do a runner on me, doen you, you'm fucker?" warned Solomon.

"If them tubmen of yours doen appear, it'll be you oi comes lookin' for. And they'm better have the right number of ankers and pigs' bladders."

The gang leader grabbed the bag from Solomon's outstretched hand, shaking it by his ear and depositing it quickly inside his coat. Then with a toothless grin he said, "No problem with that, friend. Them rowin' boats be on their way back, look over there. Better get you'mself back up there sharpish."

With a quick look towards the returning rowing boats, Solomon turned and crunched back up the cove towards the track that led up to the headland. A dark feeling suddenly overwhelmed him, causing him to stop and survey the scene around him. Although everything seemed to be going well, his instincts were warning him that all was not as it seemed. Something was telling him he should get away swiftly. An inner voice was alerting him and signalling jeopardy. But he needed to wait for the Squire's men from Ashprington to arrive, as he had taken a large payment from the Squire to make sure they got away with his consignment of the contraband. Solomon knew well the Squire depended on him, he was not going to let him down. As soon as the men from Ashprington had left the cove, he planned to round up his men, pay them off, and be well away before the last wagon left the headland. Then, with his own share of the contraband, he would ride away across country to feast and drink in his local tavern. He tapped the flintlock pistol nestled inside the pocket of his grimy greatcoat; it was loaded and ready to use should there be a need.

His thoughts were suddenly interrupted by a series of loud panting behind him as four tubmen, weighed down with contraband, stood sweating and gasping for air. Solomon looked them over with a pitiless grin. "Dump them here, you fuckers, then piss orf quick."

Frowning, he watched them stack the consignment on the pebbles next to him, then looking up anxiously in the direction of the headland he muttered, "Now, where be those fuckers from Ashprington?"

Chapter 10

Stephen suddenly appeared out of the mist, pulling his horse up with a start as the others reined in and came to a halt.

"Oi've found the sign," he told them, "just like the Squire said, nailed to an old oak. Nearly rode past it, but for a gap in the mist. Come on, it baint be far off."

Stephen turned his horse and rode off towards where he had seen the sign, the others cantering after him. They found the track and in single file, they trotted along its uneven surface, peering into the misty darkness ahead for any sign of their contact. Through the moonlight, they made out patches of land eerily poking out from under the hovering mist, the tops of trees peeping up like spindly silhouettes from a horror story. Then without warning, two of the front horses suddenly shied up in terror as a cloaked figure carrying a lantern unexpectedly sprang out onto the track in front of them. Mordechai and Watt riding up front had to control their horses as the sudden shock had spooked their mounts into rearing up and whinnying in fright. The figure, holding up his lantern, stood looking at them, then beckoning with the lantern, indicated for them to follow him further along the track. The mist had lifted slightly, allowing the moonlight to show a fork up ahead. They followed the light of the lantern as it took a left turn at the fork, stopping at the entrance to a spaciously paved courtyard. Thick ivy-covered walls stared out at them at what they guessed had to be the grand Tudor mansion of Churston Manor.

Removing his hood, the figure indicated for them to follow him to a series of metal rings implanted into a stone wall where they could secure their horses. When this was done, they gathered round him, eyeing him dubiously.

"Gentlemen," he said, "I apologise for scaring two of your horses earlier, but I'm pleased you've managed to arrive without any incident. My name is Godfrey and I am the head footman here at Churston Manor. I am also in the employ of Squire Maddock of Darton Hall. I am here to see that you get the Squire's share of the consignment and make sure you leave safely. The ship carrying the consignment anchored in the bay a short time ago. Tubmen and runners stationed down on the cove, are now unloading its cargo where it is being sorted for despatch. The Squire's share of this consignment is waiting for you down there with Solomon Metcalf, gang leader of the batsmen. You will have noticed a fork in the track as we entered the courtyard of the mansion house. The right-hand track leads on to a woodland covering the cliffs above the cove. There's a smaller track there that leads down to the cove from the woods, but we'll go down through a secret tunnel that was cut under the cliffs several centuries ago."

Godfrey noticed the men from Ashprington listening intently.

"Solomon Metcalf and his batsmen are there to fight off the Revenue should they appear while the tubmen and runners are off-loading and carrying the consignment up to the despatchers. There is a Revenue base in Paignton, where a detachment of dragoons assists in seeking out any smuggling activity within this bay. Horse-drawn wagons are now on the headland waiting to be filled by the tubmen and runners who should be loading them right now, the wagons will then disappear into the night. The tunnel will take us down through the cliffs, where we will exit at the mouth of a cave at the far end of Elberry Cove. It will be shrouded in darkness, so no-one will see us coming out. Now, if you would like to follow me, I'll take you down."

"Just one moment," said Barold, looking up at the moonlit walls of the manor house. "What about the other servants, won't they hear all this noise and wonder what the hell's going on down on the cove?"

Godfrey looked at Barold. "There are no other servants here tonight other than Matt, the young bootboy whose tongue was severed in an accident several years ago, so there's nothing to concern you. Matt will water your horses while we are down on the cove, he'll then guard them as we don't know who'll be lurking around while we're down there. Sir Francis and Lady Susanna are not expected to return until next weekend and have laid off their staff until then. As head footman, I was kept on to caretake the manor while they are away in London; they know nothing of my loyalty to Squire Maddock."

They followed Godfrey across the courtyard to the rear of an old stone outbuilding where a thick wooden door clung to the side of the cliff wall. Godfrey produced a key and holding his lantern towards the keyhole, slipped the key in and turned it slowly. The door creaked open showing a black hole descending sharply.

"There's another lantern just behind the door," he whispered. "You sir," he said pointing towards Stephen, "pick it up and take this taper, you can get a light from my lantern."

Stephen lit the lantern successfully and one by one they filtered into the tunnel. A dank stench of wet earth and mould filled their nostrils and as their night vision slowly kicked in, Godfrey slammed the door shut and pushed his way to the front of their single line.

"You with the lantern," he said, his words echoing far away into the dark chamber, "go to the back of the line, so we have a light up front with me and one at the back with you."

They shuffled off, holding one another's shoulders like blind men moving slowly down a line. The light from the lanterns cast long shadows on the dark earthy walls as they felt themselves descending the tunnel's rough stony path.

Ebenezer clasped onto Elijah, fearful of stumbling in the dark. His thoughts were of the past when Catholic priests had used this way to escape the religious persecution of the time. He grimaced in horror at the thought of those who'd fled this way all those years before, forced to flee the religious intolerance that had gripped the country under its kings and queens, and knowing what awaited them should they be caught at the tunnel's end.

A sudden bend showed the light of Godfrey's lantern held high as he pushed at a metal door. A blast of salty sea air accompanied by the sound of waves lapping onto the shoreline flooded up the tunnel. The mist had cleared as they stood at the mouth of the cave watching the scene taking place before them under the light of the full moon.

Watt nudged Mordechai, pointing out to sea where three rowing boats were making haste through the water, their rowers straining at their oars to get back to their ship, a dark shape in the bay. Godfrey locked the brown metal door to the tunnel and led the six of them out of the mouth of the cave and along the bottom side of the cliff wall. They walked across the pebbles, unseen under the shadow of the cliff, until they came to a large rock that stood alone at the top of the cove.

"Wait here," he whispered to Stephen, "I can see Solomon over there checking out a consignment, it has to be the Squire's."

They watched as Godfrey approached a stocky grey-coated man in a shabby tricorn. They saw him take two ankers and a pig's bladder off the pile of contraband and stack them near the track leading to the headland. As Godfrey approached him, he jumped up, thrusting his right hand inside his coat while the hook that had replaced his left hand wavered threateningly in front of Godfrey's face. Godfrey held up his hands in rapprochement, allowing the hook-handed batsman time to realise who it was approaching him. They chatted for a while and as Godfrey turned and pointed towards the six men from Ashprington, Solomon suddenly elbowed him out of the way and stomped across the pebbles towards them, his left arm raised with the hook pointing in the direction of the pile of contraband he'd previously been separating.

"Over there," he hollered, "be the Squire's consignment. This here poppychuke," he continued nodding towards Godfrey, "will take you back to where you'm left your horses. Oi would not hang around here for long, there be the smell of Revenue bastards in the air, of that oi be sure. So, you'm best fuck orf out of 'ere quick with the Squire's brandy."

"Wait one moment," said Ebenezer, looking at the back of Solomon who was about to walk away. He wanted to call Solomon back and demand he delegate some tubmen to carry the supply when Elijah nudged him sharply.

"Shut up, Reverend," he said through clenched teeth. "Doen you'm remember Obadiah Tucker. That there be Solomon Metcalf, he'd rip your throat out with his hook for the slightest negative remark."

Ebenezer swallowed hard, his face turning ashen white as he willed Solomon not to turn around. Unaware, Solomon walked away towards the headland and his gang of batsmen, carrying his supply of the contraband under both arms.

Godfrey led them back across the cove towards the tunnel, stopping to offer to carry one of the pig's bladders for Ebenezer, who seemed to be struggling with his load. He unlocked the metal door and when they had all slipped through into the tunnel, he slammed it tight shut, locking it while Stephen picked up the two lanterns that still burned brightly. Ebenezer clasped the small ankers under each arm, clutching the other pig's bladder tightly between his two hands. The others seemed to be comfortable enough with their load as they slowly made their ascent towards the top of the tunnel.

Watt had to stop half-way up, as one of the pig's bladders he had placed under one arm was slipping out of its hold. Mordechai saw Watt's predicament and stopped to help him wedge it more securely under his arm, then followed him up the gentle incline until they caught up with the others. Panting with their effort, they waited in the tunnel's murkiness for Godfrey to open the door and then summoning up the last of their energy, they staggered back to where they had previously tethered the horses.

Young Matt, the bootboy, was waiting with the horses, having made sure they were watered and well-rested. Barold was first to secure his share of the contraband to his horse, urging the others to hurry so they could make a swift getaway. As the others finished hitching theirs, he looked over to where Ebenezer was fumbling with the straps, not understanding which way to position them and looking totally confused.

"Didn' you listen proper, Reverend?!" he called. "Them straps go the other way. If you'm doen get it right, you'm gonna be here till mornin', on your own too, Reverend. Us'll all be gone, ha ha!"

Stephen came to Ebenezer's aid, turning the straps around the right way and helping him to hoist the ankers of brandy up onto both sides of his horse. Then he strapped the two pig bladders across the horse's lower neck in front of the saddle; Ebenezer was ready to mount up and go.

They all heard the crack of muskets being fired down by the cove. The six of them froze as more shots echoed up from the pebbly beach amidst angry and irate howls. Figures were emerging from the fork in the track outside the courtyard having fled up the cliff path and through the woods in their effort to escape the pursuing Revenue men.

By the light of the moon, a group of tubmen barging into the courtyard saw five of the Ashprington six sitting their horses, the other trying to mount in haste.

"Over there," screamed one, pointing towards them, "quick, git their horses, kill them. The Revenue be comin', us's gotta git away."

"Oh my God," screamed Ebenezer as Barold, Stephen and Elijah spurred their horses out of the courtyard. "The Revenue. Quick, someone help me mount up. Those ruffians will soon be on me."

As quick as a flash, Watt leapt from his horse and placing an upturned hand under Ebenezer's raised boot, he hoisted him up into his saddle. A hard slap from Watt on the mare's rump saw Ebenezer gallop hell for leather out of the courtyard in pursuit of the others. Watt swung back into his saddle as rough hands tried to pull him from his horse and then there was Mordechai kicking and punching the rabble from his mount, urging Watt to get away. Watt's horse shied up in panic as more of the tubmen closed in around them. They all heard the crack and crunch as the hooves of Watt's horse crashed down on the skull of one of the tubmen. The realisation that one of their gang had had his skull crushed scattered the group. With a shout from Mordechai, Watt turned his horse and raced away out of the courtyard with Mordechai thundering after him.

Godfrey had escaped into the safety of the manor house, shutting and bolting the doors. It would not be long before a Revenue officer came banging on the manor's doors, demanding to be let in. Godfrey would claim innocence, telling him he had no idea what had been going on, only that he had been awakened with the noise of the affray. He would mention that this was the residence of the eminent London lawyer, Sir Francis Buller, who was away in London with friends from the House of Lords. He would point out that Sir Francis would be aghast at any insinuation by an officer of the Revenue that his home had anything to do with a smuggling operation. He knew it would cause the Revenue to leave him in peace and not persist in any questioning, and anyway this Revenue officer had smugglers to catch and would not want to waste a moment in his pursuit of them.

Godfrey gazed out of a parlour window as a company of red-coated Revenue men raced into the courtyard, rounding up the group of tubmen and runners who had tried to pull Watt from his horse. He guessed that half of the red-coated detachment were already in hot pursuit of the smugglers, riding across the headland that overlooked the cove and bay in the direction of Clennon, hoping to cut them off before they had managed to get through the woods and over the valley towards Blagdon Manor Farm.

Looking up at the window to where Godfrey stood, a young Revenue officer smiled, and with three of his men following, made his way towards the entrance doors of the manor house. Godfrey shut his eyes, willing the men from Ashprington to flee with all their might. Evading the Revenue would not be easy and to fall into their merciless clutches as smugglers, would certainly guarantee them the hangman. As a resonant thumping on the front doors reverberated around the walls of the empty Tudor mansion, Godfrey slipped into his livery coat and went to open the doors.

Chapter 11

Up on the headland in a small copse of trees that overlooked Elberry Cove, Solomon Metcalf sat, his horse watching the chaotic scene develop on the pebbly beach below. His instincts had told him there would be danger and he had learned to respect the voices that warned him of an approaching threat. From the headland, he had watched the men from Ashprington disappear with the Squire's consignment; it was now up to them to get it safely back to Darton Hall. He could not be blamed if anything went wrong. He had paid his batsmen off and had instructed them to get away from the cove as fast as they could with the promise of beef and ale in his local tavern later in the day. He could smell the Revenue.

He had watched the dark shape of the Marie de France up-anchor and sneak away. As a solitary wagon waited on the headland for the tubmen to load the last of the contraband, he had strapped his two ankers and pig's bladder to his horse and ridden away from the cove in the direction of Clennon where he would take the path through the woods, then instead of continuing up over the valley in the direction of Blagdon Manor Farm, he would take another track into the harbour town of Paignton and his local tavern, 'The Tor Bay Inn'.

He had ridden no more than a few hundred yards across the headland when he heard them. Through the darkness, the jingling sound of horses' harnesses accompanied by an occasional oath was enough for Solomon to turn his horse around and gallop back into the protection of a small copse of trees he had noticed earlier. Calming his horse in the dark shadows, he sat motionless, hardly daring to breathe as the company of red-coated Revenue men pulled up in front of the copse that overlooked the cove.

"Well, well, our lucky night sergeant," he heard a young Revenue officer say.

"This lot will keep the hangman happy. I want you to remain here with half a dozen men. The rest of us will proceed to the cove on foot. You, corporal," he said nodding to a stupid looking fat redcoat, "will stay here with one of the men, guarding our horses."

"Sir," the corporal replied.

"Sergeant," the officer continued, "when you see that we've engaged these smugglers, you and your six men will ride to block their paths of escape. Namely, all tracks out of here towards Paignton, Brixham and Clennon. Is that clear, sergeant?"

"Clear, sir," replied the sergeant.

"Those not detailed to the sergeant or corporal, dismount now and on my order, follow me."

Solomon watched the Revenue men dismount and stand in line behind their officer. The corporal and a private soldier dismounted and gathered the horses together, watching jealously as their comrades loaded their muskets and attached their bayonets.

The Revenue sergeant and the six men the officer had detailed to assist him, sat their mounts looking out over the cove at the remaining group of tubmen and runners who had stayed behind to load the last wagon. Turning to two of his men, he said, "You two will make tracks to Clennon Woods when oi tells you. You two," he said pointing to another couple, "up on the common ground that leads into Brixham, and you," he said pointing to the last couple, "with me at the end of this here headland where it meets the track goin' towards Paignton. Us'll have a good chase on tonight, oi can feel it. Now wait till oi tells you."

The sound of a musket being fired from the headland brought the tubmen to a sudden halt, causing them to panic as they made out military figures charging down through the darkness.

A chilling command rang out across the cove, "Halt in the name of King George III. We are the Revenue. Stop what you're doing and put your hands in the air."

Solomon watched the tubmen and runners scatter towards the cliff path that led up through the woods and the track past Churston Manor. The Revenue were chasing after those who had left it too late to be able to get away from being caught. A volley of musket fire brought down a group of runners clambering to get a foothold at the bottom of the cliff path.

"Follow me, men," shouted the young Revenue officer, as he stormed across the pebbles, giving chase to a group of tubmen who had managed to get themselves up onto the cliff path and were disappearing into the trees.

"Now, you fuckers," yelled the sergeant, "off with you and do not disappoint me. I want at least one of them fucking smugglers brought to me in chains."

Apart from the groans of a couple of wounded tubmen lying on the pebbly beach, silence descended around the area where Solomon sat gently stroking and patting his horse. A few shouts and screams together with an occasional musket shot echoed from the cliff top trees. Peering through the branches that encircled him, he could just about make out the two Revenue men who had been detailed to guard their comrades' horses. They could be no more than twenty feet away from him. He knew he would have to kill them. The flintlock pistol in the pocket of his great coat was loaded and ready to fire; he tapped it reassuringly. Slowly, he touched the heavy cudgel strapped to the side of his saddle, gently withdrawing it from its holding, then he waited.

From his hideout, he heard the rustling of one of the Revenue men moving around in the rough grass directly in front of where he sat. He tried to peer through a gap in the branches, but it was too dark to see much further than the trees that encircled him. He listened, straining to picture the exact position where the soldier could be. An owl hooted from somewhere in the distance, the rustling noise through the surrounding bushes getting louder.

"Where you'm goin', corp?" a voice sounded from outside the hideout.

"Need a shit," came the reply, "'oi'll have one in here, in these trees. Keep your eyes open. Doen want the Captain comin' back here while us's havin a dump!"

The sound of branches being pushed apart and twigs cracking under foot startled Solomon's horse, but the fat corporal was unaware of his encroachment into the hideaway as his desperation to relieve himself was now an urgency. Slowly, without making a sound, Solomon dismounted as the corporal dropped his breeches and squatted within five feet of him. The sound of his squelching fart was the last sound he heard. Solomon brought his cudgel down with such a force that it split the corporal's skull like a mallet opening a coconut.

"You'm alright in there, corp?" called the private sitting with the horses, "Heard a strange noise in there. You'm finished yet?"

Not receiving a reply, the private pulled himself up from where he was sitting, following in the direction the corporal had taken. Gingerly, he poked his head into the darkness of the trees, trying to discern a sign of his comrade. He did not feel the pointed end of Solomon's hook as it shot out from the darkness to rip his Adam's apple from his throat, or the weight of the cudgel that smashed his skull to pulp.

* * *

Ebenezer's horse raced away down the track that led away from the manor house. He could see Stephen, Barold and Elijah ahead, urging their mounts on. He did not dare look around to see if Watt and Mordechai were following, but he thought he heard Mordechai's voice yelling somewhere behind him. The mist had faded, allowing the full moon to shed its light far up the track when he saw his three comrades suddenly pull their horses up and move quickly into the side of the track under the cover of some overhanging branches. Ebenezer caught them up and pulled his horse into the dark shadows where they sat panting with exertion. Watt and Mordechai had seen Ebenezer pull over and followed him to join up with the others.

"What's goin on?" asked Mordechai, gasping for breath.

"Sssshhh," hissed Stephen, "up yonder under the sign on the old oak tree, two Revenue men."

The two Revenue men had already covered the area towards Brixham with no sign of any of the escaping smugglers. With the chance of a break and some brandy they were carrying, they had stopped under the sign nailed to the old oak tree and intent on enjoying several long draughts, they were oblivious to the men from Ashprington watching from the shadows.

"What they'm doin'?" whispered Mordechai sitting behind Ebenezer.

Stephen squinted through a gap in the foliage. "Looks like they'm just chattin' and laughin'," he replied. "Now they'ms swiggin' from a bottle and sharin' it with each other. They'ms takin' their bliddy time over it. Us'll wait here. Keep your fingers crossed they'm doen come down this way."

Ebenezer shook with fright at the mention of the two Revenue soldiers coming after them, his face a picture of terror. A feeling of nausea overwhelmed him as a vision of the hangman and gallows on Plymouth Hoe flashed through his mind. Barold had to suppress his laughter and look away, chortling at the look of intense fear plastered over the minister's face.

"Look, they'ms goin'," whispered Stephen, "ridin' orf in the direction of Brixham. Give it a couple of minutes and us can go. Keep it quiet as they could double back if they'm doen find anythin' that a way."

They left the shadows of their hiding place and slowly approached the end of the track. Pulling up the horses they listened, straining for any sound that would alert them of the two Revenue men returning.

All was quiet as they moved forward onto the common ground, then with an urgency to get away, they kicked their heels into their horses' flanks and took off, speeding away in the direction of the wooded area of Clennon. They had not gone more than a few hundred yards when Watt, riding behind the others, heard a shout from far behind him. Turning, he made out the two Revenue men galloping after them shouting for them to stop. Loosening his rein, he drew up close behind the others.

"'Tis the Revenue, they'm be right behind us," he screamed.

"Oh no, shit no!" yelled Stephen taking a quick look behind.

Barold had heard the warning and spurred his horse on, followed by Elijah who made sure Ebenezer urged his mare into a gallop to keep up with the rest of them. They thundered across the common ground with the two Revenue men close on their tails. The ankers of brandy and pigs' bladders strapped to their horses together with the weight of their riders, were causing the horses to tire quickly. The six fugitives knew this, but the two Revenue men were gaining on them and getting within pistol shot. There was nothing for them to do but to take the chance and urge their horses on faster. Looking over his shoulder, Stephen groaned as he saw the two Revenue men gaining on them.

It must have been a lucky shot, but the ball that flew from the flintlock pistol of one of the Revenue men hit the rear leg of Watt's horse, bringing it down with the sickening sound of legs breaking and a screaming wail of pain. Watt had been thrown clear and was scrambling to his feet when the sight of one of the Revenue men grinning at him victoriously and pointing his flintlock pistol directly at his head made him scream out in fear. Dismounting by Watt's wounded horse, the other redcoat slowly loaded his pistol and placing the barrel next to the horse's head, put it out of its misery.

The others had pulled up their horses at the sound of Watt's scream for help.

They looked on as one of the Revenue men covered Watt with his pistol while the other bound his wrists with rope. Watt looked despairingly around him, stunned and bewildered. Grinning triumphantly at Watt, the two redcoats cut the straps, holding the two ankers and pigs' bladders from his dead horse, securing them tightly to their own horses. Watt looked hopelessly ahead towards his comrades, fear and desperation etched deeply into his face. He began to shiver as one of the redcoats tied a length of rope around his waist, feeding the rest of it out to his partner who sat his horse, grinning at the unfortunate boy.

"No," screamed Mordechai watching from a distance, "he is only a young boey. Hang on, Watt, oi'm comin'."

Stephen and Barold grasped Mordechai's arms, stopping him from galloping to Watt's rescue. There was nothing they could do. The two Revenue men were armed, and it was likely their comrades were not too far away. If they attempted to rescue Watt, they would all likely end up in custody or shot. Grasping Mordechai's horse's bridle, Stephen pulled him away from the scene and with a slap on the horse's rump watched Mordechai ride away with tears of rage streaming from his eyes.

Tied to one of the Revenue men, Watt had to run behind his horse as the length of rope holding him tautened. Looking back over their shoulders as they rode away, the two redcoats drew a finger each across their throats as a grim sign to the onlookers of the fate that now awaited their young captive.

Chapter 12

Ebenezer could feel his horse beginning to weaken as the group descended the hill that led down to the dense woods of Clennon. He knew he had to dismount and give the mare a few minutes' rest, it would not matter if the others wanted to move on, he would only need a short time. At the bottom of the hill, the others had pulled up at the start of the track that would lead them through the woods.

"Can't we rest up a while, my mare needs it," he said dismounting. "I'm worried she may collapse. She is not as strong as the rest of the horses."

"Them two Revenue bastards who got Watt, turned around and went the other way. So's hopefully there baint be no more of them here," said Barold, looking anxiously around.

"Maybe not," said Stephen patting his horse's neck, "but oi doen trust it, best if us moves on and gets right away from this area. Us can rest up a bit when us gets nearer Berry Pomeroy."

Mordechai was quiet, looking as though he were in a daze from the shock of young Watt being captured. He stared towards the top of the hill, hoping Watt would come riding over it. Shaking his head and muttering guiltily under his breath, he blamed himself for the disastrous misfortune. Then unexpectedly, he turned his horse and with a flick of his reins, galloped off through the woods. "Come on, let's get goin'," said Barold, turning his horse and racing off after him.

"I'll wait here for five minutes," said Ebenezer looking at his horse. "I'll catch you up. Better to let her rest a bit and be sure of getting back."

"Us'll wait for you at the fork that leads to Blagdon," said Elijah, looking concerned. "Doen hang about, Reverend, these woods'll be teemin' with redcoats shortly."

Stephen and Elijah turned their horses and disappeared into Clennon Woods, leaving Ebenezer alone with his exhausted mare. Under the light of the moon, he checked that the Squire's two ankers and pigs' bladders were still securely attached to his horse. An urgent need to relieve himself forced him to take a few steps away from the mare and opening the buttons of the crotch area of his breeches, he urinated over the grass at the side of the track. Smiling he looked up at the star-studded sky, remembering how he had tried to snatch one that fateful night they had journeyed downriver to Dittisham and Obadiah Tucker's boat house.

The click of the hammer on a flintlock pistol being pulled back behind him suddenly cut the stillness around him. Shakily, he began buttoning up his breeches, his hands trembling uncontrollably. Fearful of a pistol ball slamming into his back at any moment, he turned around slowly.

Facing Ebenezer with their backs to the entrance to Clennon Woods, two Revenue men sat, their horses grinning at the look of frightful surprise stamped across his face. He supposed they had come through the track in the woods, hoping his cohorts had got away safely and that these were the only two redcoats searching the area at this time of the night. The moonlight showed them swaying slightly in their saddles; he guessed they had been drinking.

"Well, what have us here?" said the one holding the pistol.

"He be one of them smugglers sergeant told us to look for," said the other. "Look at them ankers and pigskins tied to his horse."

"Yeah, he be one of them smugglers alright," sneered the one holding the pistol. "Look at him tremblin'. Do you think he be feelin' cold? Ha. Sergeant will be well pleased with us when us brings him in. Another one for the hang man down on Plymouth Hoe Gallows."

"He doen look much like a smuggler though," said the other redcoat.

"Doen matter to the hangman," said the other. "Theym's all the same when theym's dancin' at the end of his rope!"

Putting on a look of supplication, Ebenezer looked up at the two Revenue men and with his voice shaking, croaked, "I am a minister of the Church of England, you have no right to treat me like this."

"Ha," laughed the one with the pistol. "Will's horse here," he said pointing to his partner's horse, "looks more like a minister of the church than you'm do. Ha. You'm be a smuggler and you'm gonna hang down on Plymouth Hoe like the other fuckers us caught tonight."

Ebenezer watched as one of the redcoats fumbled in his saddle bag, whipping out a near empty bottle of spirits which they greedily finished off in two quick swigs, roaring with laughter at the likeness of Will's horse to a minister of the Church of England.

A dark shadow of a horse and rider coming out of the woods and silently inching up behind the two laughing redcoats suddenly drew Ebenezer's attention. Unaware of what was approaching them, the two Revenue men sat back in their saddles, relishing the moment of fun they were having at Ebenezer's expense. The raucous laughter coming from the one holding the pistol abruptly changed into a stifled gurgle as a stream of blood suddenly jetted out of his throat, narrowly missing Ebenezer. Burbling in a torrent of blood, the redcoat crumpled from his horse, his eyes staring blankly up at his partner who quickly swivelled round to see the cause of this horror. The hook at the end of Solomon's left arm dripped with the blood of the dead Revenue man, while in his right hand he held his flintlock pistol pointed into the face of the redcoat. Smiling, he pulled the trigger. A hissing flash as the hammer sparked the powder in the pistol's mechanism spooked the horses and then in a fraction, the sound of the pistol going off saw flocks of birds rise from the woods, squawking and screeching in alarm. Ebenezer watched in horror as the pistol ball took away half the redcoat's face, the ball pummelling out from the back of his skull, spurting brains and blood everywhere. Looking up at Solomon and then at the two dead Revenue men, who only moments before were alive and laughing at him, Ebenezer felt his stomach urge and turning away, he spewed into the side of the grassy track. Still smiling, Solomon blew on the end of his pistol, replacing it in an inside pocket of his great coat.

"You'm be one of Squire's men from Ashprington?" he said, cleaning off the blood on his hook with a filthy rag.

"I am," replied Ebenezer, trembling.

"Where the others be, and why you'm be here all alone?"

"The Revenue caught one of us, up on the common land as we left the track from Churston Manor. We were running our horses flat out and with the weight of the Squire's consignment, mine soon began to tire. My mare there is not as strong as the rest and she needed to rest up a while or she would give up on me before we got back to Dartington. The others carried on while I waited for her to cool down."

"Which one of you was caught?" asked Solomon.

"Watt Huckle, young stable lad at Sharpham Estate. He's only sixteen," replied Ebenezer.

"Doen give him much hope," said Solomon.

"Why are you here?" asked Ebenezer. "I thought you would be long gone, with the Revenue all over the place."

"'Tis a long story," said Solomon, "but my way back to Paignton on the other side of this here wood was blocked by three Revenue bastards. Oi had to turn back through the wood and when oi heard these two dead fuckers laughin' and threatenin' you, us knew you could do with help. Recognised you from the cove as oi came out of the end of the woods there. You were with that fop Godfrey, good job he got you all back to your horses before those Revenue fuckers arrived."

"Yes, but our escape from the manor was hindered by that rabble who fled up through the clifftop woods. We very nearly didn't make it," said Ebenezer.

"Ha, come on," said Solomon, "your mare seems rested enough to carry on. Us'll ride with you up over the valley until we reach the track that goes past Blagdon Manor Farm, then us'll cut across country and into Paignton by the back route. Best for me not to try the direct route from here."

"What about those two?" said Ebenezer, pointing to the two dead redcoats.

"Leave the bastards for the foxes," said Solomon. "Horses will find their way back and then the Revenue will be out lookin' for them. Come on, time is gettin' on."

Ebenezer mounted his mare, checking that the straps holding the Squire's supply was still secure, then turning his horse, he followed Solomon into the darkness of Clennon Woods.

They rode up over the valley of Clennon, Ebenezer happy that his mare had rested as he could feel her restored energy as they climbed the hill. The full moon shone down, lighting up the pastures they crossed. Whenever they approached a track or carriageway, Solomon would halt, carefully surveying the land around them for possible signs of the Revenue. When he was happy it was safe, they continued.

Familiar landmarks prompted Ebenezer to think of Watt and how he was coping. He wondered if he had been taken to Paignton's gaol and if he were being questioned. He suddenly went as cold as ice, his eyes widening in horror as the realisation struck him.

"Oh my God," he screamed, "what if he talks? What if he tells the Revenue about our smuggling syndicate, the Squire and worst of all, ME?!"

Quailing at the thought that Watt would incriminate him, he slowed the mare down on their approach to the track where Elijah had told him he would wait. He watched Solomon pull up at the fork ahead, acknowledging Stephen and Elijah who were anxiously waiting for Ebenezer to join them. As Solomon chatted to them, Elijah peered out into the distance where Ebenezer was slowly approaching; standing up in his stirrups, he beckoned to Ebenezer to hurry up.

"Very nearly didn't make it," gasped Ebenezer, trotting up and looking into their relieved faces. "If it hadn't been for Solomon here, I'd be in a filthy Revenue gaol now awaiting the hangman. I can't thank you enough, sir."

Grinning at the three of them, Solomon turned his horse towards the opposite fork in the track and looking back over his shoulder, called out, "Should any of you fuckers be passin' through Paignton, or you need help, you'll find me in the Tor Bay Inn. Pass my respects on to Squire Maddock."

They watched him, a fleeting silhouette in the moonlight hunched forward in his saddle, thundering away down the track until he rounded a bend and disappeared into the night.

"You'm can tell us what happened in them woods later, Reverend," said Stephen, turning his horse round. "Us had better make haste."

"What if Watt tells the Revenue everything?" said Ebenezer, looking anxiously at them.

"He won't, Reverend, of that oi am sure," yelled Stephen, urging his horse forward.

Ebenezer gave a fretful look as Elijah hastened his horse after Stephen, and with a shake of his head, followed them into the darkness of the track that would take them past Blagdon Manor Farm and on over the fields to Totnes and Darton Hall.

They crossed over the old stone bridge at Totnes hearing the town hall clock strike the hour of four, then followed the river away from the town until they saw the candle lights of Darton Hall above them. Squire Maddock was waiting with his two servants in front of the glowing brazier as they rode into the courtyard. Leaving their mounts, they followed the Squire into the Great Hall.

Barold and Mordechai sat at the long oak table staring at goblets of wine the Squire had provided. When the other three were seated, the Squire looked at each one solemnly.

"Now, one of you, tell me what happened."

Stephen raised his hand and when the Squire nodded, Stephen began to give him an exact account of the whole escapade, from the moment Godfrey had jumped out in front of them on the track leading to Churston Manor to when finally, Solomon Metcalf had left them to make his way back to Paignton.

Squire Maddock listened, not taking his eyes off Stephen. When Stephen had finished, the Squire sat back, his eyes closed as if trying to picture again in his mind's eye, the events of what he had just heard.

"There's no way we can get young Watt back," he said, opening his eyes.

"But, Squire," interrupted Mordechai, "you'm got powerful friends who would help, surely?"

"Not in a smuggling case as simple as this," replied the Squire. "Watt was caught trying to escape from the Revenue with contraband attached to his horse. It is plainly obvious he had been taking part in the offloading and was trying to get away. He will be considered a smuggler, just like the others they caught. He will be found guilty, of that there is no doubt."

"And will he hang?" asked Barold.

"I'm afraid he surely will," replied the Squire.

"What if he talks and incriminates us all?" asked Ebenezer, looking ashen.

"Well, there's no evidence any of us took part in that smuggling event, only Watt's word. That is, if he does give us away," said the Squire frowning.

Mordechai stared at the Squire, a look of utter despair written all over him. "Watt will never give us up, that oi knows for certain."

"Let us hope you'm be right, Mordechai," suggested Elijah, stroking his neck.

"I doubt that the Revenue will pursue an enquiry," said the Squire. "Although Watt will likely be encouraged to name his confederates at his trial. The Revenue have a handful of smugglers they rounded up, they will be happy for them all to hang, as an example."

"What do you mean, Squire, encouraged to name his confederates at his trial?" asked Ebenezer anxiously.

"Well, the prosecution will have already established his guilt, and it will be in the interest of the court to know the names of his cohorts who got away. But without any evidence that can be directed at us, then there is little the Revenue can do, apart from putting us under surveillance."

"Listen," said Mordechai raising his voice, "oi have told you that Watt will not talk. He won't give our names away at his trial, believe me, oi knows."

"I truly hope you are right, Mordechai," said Ebenezer.

"Now, matters aside," said Squire Maddock tossing a large leather money bag in the direction of Ebenezer, "as I promised, double payment for your efforts, although I lost out on two half ankers and two pigs' bladders, not to mention a horse from my stables. So, if there is nothing more to discuss, I will bid you all a very good night or should I say good morning. I will send word regarding the next consignment. Anything from Obadiah Tucker, I will gladly have. In the meantime, I will find out about Watt's whereabouts and keep you informed. I doubt there will be a trial until the next assizes in Plymouth, probably in two or three weeks."

Squire Maddock watched them leave the hall, deeply concerned over Watt's arrest by the Revenue. The implications of Watt confessing everything could certainly lead back to him and his association with the smuggling barons; he would have to do something and do it quickly.

Waiting in the courtyard for the horse and wagon, Barold looked over at Ebenezer. "Oi will be wantin' my share later today, Reverend."

"Ar, 'tis fair to share out today, Reverend," echoed Stephen.

"Yes, yes," replied Ebenezer with a yawn, "be at the church midday."

They travelled back towards Ashprington without a word being spoken, Barold and Stephen snoring as the wagon rocked its way along the country tracks. Mordechai sat staring out at the shadows around them, thinking of Watt and blaming himself for not riding to his rescue. Elijah sat guiding the horse through the meadows and woodland tracks, deep in thought as to whether he would partake in another smuggling venture. Ebenezer, still anxious about being intimidated by Watt, wondered when he would hear from the French spymaster in Plymouth regarding his proposal of a face-to-face meeting. Hopefully there would be news soon.

Elijah took a shortcut across one of the fields of Sharpham, pulling up within easy reach of where Mordechai could get back to his cottage.

"Midday then," uttered Mordechai as he heaved himself off the cart.

"Us'll stay at the inn, Elijah," said Stephen stretching his arms.

Nodding at Stephen and with a wave of his hand towards Mordechai, Elijah turned the wagon round for the short haul on to Ashprington village.

Early morning activity in the village was well under way as Elijah guided the horse and wagon into the rear yard of the inn. Lucy came hurrying out as she heard them approach, anxious to know what had caused them to return at this hour of the morning. With a grunt and a murmur of being at the church at midday, Barold made off towards his cottage, leaving Ebenezer to make his way up the hill towards the rectory and a few hours' sleep. As he let himself in, he felt the early morning chill throughout the whole house and looking into the parlour room, was pleased to see that Betsy Gribble had laid a fire ready for him to light.

While the kindling wood crackled and hissed in the flames, he warmed his hands, relieved he was now home safe and sound with a purse bulging with coin. He would share out the payment with the others later in the church. With a yawn, he bent and shovelled some coal onto the fire and then pulling off his tie-wig, he made his way into the bedroom.

As he tumbled onto his bed, he heard the church clock strike the half hour of eight.

"Just over three hours," he mumbled as pictures of Elberry Cove, Solomon Metcalf and the two dead Revenue men flashed in front of his eyes. Sleep came quickly, his dreams filled with a never-ending chase across the common land of Churston, while a haunting vision of a petrified Watt Huckle being taken to the gallows on Plymouth Hoe loomed before him again and again.

Chapter 13

Montague Parker, Justice of the Peace for the district of Paignton, looked up from reading a hastily-written report of the arrest of a group of smugglers earlier that morning. Standing in chains opposite him, behind an old oak table in a back room of the Revenue building that served as the Magistrate's Court, six dishevelled and sorry-looking prisoners stood with their heads bowed. Holding a perfumed lace handkerchief to his nose to expunge the foul and offensive odour emanating from the prisoners, he regarded each one with a look of contempt and disdain. As the duty Revenue officer read out the prisoners' names, pausing after each name to emphasise the charge of 'Arrested whilst Smuggling Contraband', Montague's attention was drawn to the frail figure of a young prisoner chained in the middle of the group. Eyeing him with curiosity, he signalled to the Revenue officer to approach his table.

"Captain," he whispered, "the thin small one in the middle of the group. What say you?"

"Caught, your worship, riding away from the scene with two half-ankers and two pigs' skins of French brandy attached to his horse. We know what he was carrying came from the French ship that had just unloaded at Elberry Cove. We now know there was a band of them who got away on horseback; they must have had their horses hidden above the cove, maybe in the grounds of Churston Manor. There is no evidence that anyone from Churston Manor was involved. Two of my men saw the gang exit the track that leads down to the manor house and as they raced away, my men gave chase. A lucky shot felled his horse and we arrested him, but the others got away. We have been trying to find out the names of his accomplices, but he refuses to comply."

Montague stared at the trembling figure of Watt, obviously not a seasoned and practiced villain as those standing with him.

"You, lad," he said, raising his voice to the group of prisoners and pointing in the direction of Watt, "give me your name and where you are from."

Watt looked up into the stern face of Justice Parker. "My name be Watt Huckle, sir," he croaked, "oi be stable lad on the Sharpham Estate outside the village of Ashprington. My employ be with Captain Philemon Pownoll, sir, he be away with the Royal Navy in the colonies."

The mention of Sharpham Estate and Captain Philemon Pownoll struck a chord with Montague. He had heard of Philemon Pownoll from his elder brother John, when he had last visited him at Saltram House in Plymouth. He would have to inform John of a possible smuggling syndicate going on in the village of Ashprington, and an urgency for John to notify Captain Pownoll. But maybe this frightened young lad would give him the names of his cohorts.

"Now, Watt Huckle," said Montague, "there is evidence of you being implicated with these others in the crime of smuggling contraband. The Revenue officer here has informed me that you are likely part of a group of smugglers who were involved earlier this morning on Elberry Cove. You will be found guilty of smuggling, Huckle. You know what the punishment will be, but the court will be lenient with you on condition you supply the names and details of your cohorts. Do you understand me, lad?"

"Oi doen know of any cohorts," stammered Watt, "there baint be no group of smugglers."

"It's a shame you refuse to comply, Huckle," replied Montague. "Very well, I will leave it for the court to decide."

"Stand to attention in front of the magistrate," bawled the Revenue officer.

Montague Parker stared authoritatively at each of the six prisoners chained in front of him. "The six of you will be transported to Plymouth Gaol forthwith, to await trial on the charge of smuggling contraband. Judge Edmund Pickering will hear your cases at the next assizes in two weeks. Take them away."

* * *

Ebenezer was awakened by three sharp knocks on his front door. Rubbing the sleep from his sore eyes, he stumbled from his bed and with a yawn, made his way towards the door. Opening it, he found no-one there; the porch was empty. Looking down the garden pathway, he failed to see any sign that someone had approached his door. Scratching his head, he turned to go back into the house when he saw a note pinned to the left-hand side of the door. Quickly, he snatched it and hurrying back inside, grabbed his spectacles from the table in the parlour. Opening the note, he carefully read:

Our face-to-face meeting, Reverend. Be at the Cat and Fiddle Inn on the Barbican in Plymouth, noon tomorrow.

There was no signature on the roughly-written note, but Ebenezer guessed it was from the French master spy, Luc Skorniere.

Well, well, he thought, *one mention of the King, and things move quickly. It will be a pleasure to meet you again, Monsieur Luc Skorniere.*

He placed the note on top of the mantlepiece in the drawing room and as he was getting ready to leave the house for the church, he suddenly had a chilling thought.

What if someone discovers this note?!

He froze in fear as he pictured the implications the note could lead to and quickly retrieving it from the mantlepiece, he cast it onto the glowing embers of the previous night's fire. The note burst into flames as soon as he placed it on top of the hot embers and with a satisfied grin, he picked up the money bag containg the double payment from Squire Maddock, threw his cloak around his shoulders and let himself out of the front door.

Luc is obviously interested, he thought. *Just wait until I present my plan!*

The church clock struck the hour of midday as he hastened up the hill towards the church. He chuckled smugly as he re-read the note in his mind. Now he would be able to demand a huge purse from the French master spy, knowing that the information he had was not going to be overlooked. It would make his fortune. Clutching the money bag from Squire Maddock, he opened the church door and looking over his shoulder to make sure no-one was following, he hurried inside.

Four anxious faces, seated in the pews below the painting of the Four Evangelists, watched him as he locked the door with the key he always carried.

"Five equal share-outs, Reverend," demanded Barold as Ebenezer opened the money bag.

"Six," interrupted Mordechai, "you'm forgettin', Watt."

"He won't be needin any money where he is goin'," replied Barold, smirking at the others.

Modechai's hand shot out, grabbing Barold by his throat but before Barold could retaliate, Elijah gripped Mordechai's collar with both hands, shaking him

111

violently and yelling, "Be we an undisciplined rabble? Let go of him, Mordechai, I will not have us behavin' like this. And you, Barold, should be more careful of what you'm say and when you'm say it. Mordechai be right, six equal share-outs. Us'll decide what to do with Watt's share when us knows what will happen to him. He may get transportation to some plantation somewhere, who knows?"

"Unlikely, now us's at war with them colonial rebels," said Stephen.

Mordechai took his hand away from Barold's throat, Elijah watching them with a frown.

"Do that again, Mordechai, and oi will seriously damage you," said Barold, glaring sternly at Mordechai. Mordechai ignored him as Ebenezer tipped the bag of silver coins onto the seat of the pew where he was seated.

After sharing out the contents of the bag, all eyes stared at the remaining pile resting alone in the middle of the pew.

"Who is going to look after Watt's share then?" said Ebenezer looking at each of them.

"Not Barold," demanded Mordechai.

"Bollocks," replied Barold, glaring at Mordechai.

"I will," said Elijah. "That be if everyone here agrees."

"Ar, good, Elijah. Oi agree," said Stephen nodding.

They all agreed that Elijah would take care of Watt's share until his trial was over. But then Stephen raised a question that brought anxious looks to them all.

"What happens when Mistress Jane finds out Watt has been taken by the Revenue and will likely hang for smugglin'?"

* * *

Mordechai lay awake that night in the one-bedroomed tiny cottage the Pownolls provided for their head herdsman. Thoughts of Watt and the horrifying conditions he was probably enduring kept flashing through his mind. Stephen had been right when he had raised the question of Jane Pownoll finding out about Watt's involvement and of his incarceration by the Revenue. The two orphaned ploughboys Watt shared living quarters with above the stables, would soon begin to ask questions as to his whereabouts and would eventually inform Jane that Watt had failed to return to Sharpham. Jane would immediately confront Mordechai and a search would ensue. It would not be long before the truth was known, and Watt's confinement identified. An investigation would then take place that could lead to the uncovering of the five remaining Ashprington smugglers.

Mordechai lay in his bed, a cold sweat forming as he stared into the darkness around him. He knew he would have to go to Jane the following morning, but how would he find the words to explain Watt's disappearance without implicating the others. There was no way he would say anything that could possibly suggest the involvement of the other four in the smuggling. He lay staring up at the darkened ceiling, racking his brains for a plausible story, and then it came to him. Time and time again, he rehearsed in his mind what he would tell her, nearly convincing himself of its credibility, until sleep finally overcame him.

Chapter 14

Jane rose early that morning. It was not unusual for her to rise at 5 am as both she and Philemon believed in being on hand for those of their workers who started work on their estate earlier than others. Sir Joshua would be arriving early for a sitting with young Jane, which normally took most of the morning. Betsy usually arrived at 7 am to start the cleaning, and as the cook was down with a bout of flu, Jane would prepare the breakfasts herself. Mordechai always finished with the herd when Betsy arrived and he, Watt and the two ploughboys breakfasted at a table in the barn just after 7 am. Jane would ask Betsy to prepare the table for them, while she readied the pot of oatmeal and warmed the bread. It was going to be a busy morning.

Mordechai sat at the table staring at his plate of piping hot oatmeal without speaking, a serious and distant look spread over his face. Slowly he picked up his spoon. Opposite him, the two ploughboys, Thomas and Samuel, scooped up their remaining grains of oatmeal with thick pieces of bread, wiping their bowls as if they had not eaten for weeks.

"Mordechai?" asked Samuel. "Where be Watt? He ain't been here for a few days now. Be he alright?"

When Mordechai did not answer, the two boys stared questioningly at him across the table.

"Mordechai?" said Thomas raising his voice.

"You'm needn't shout," responded Mordechai, "oi heard you first time."

"What has happened to Watt, have you heard from him?" asked Samuel.

"Naw, doen know nuthin' of his whereabouts. Now, us's got work to do and so have you. So, stop the jabberin' and git on out to pasture, Old Abe will have them ploughs ready. Git you'mselves orf now."

Mordechai watched the two lads scamper out of the barn, both nearly bumping into Jane and Betsy who were coming into the barn to clear away the breakfast bowls and mugs.

"Mordechai, good morning to you," beamed Jane.

"Mistress," replied Mordechai, springing to his feet.

"I trust all is well with the beef herd, and everything in general?"

"Ar, that it be, ma'am, thank you."

"But Mordechai, I can see that something is troubling you. It is spread all over your face. Is there anything I can help you with?" asked Jane, looking concerned.

"Well, er, yes there be, ma'am, but a private word with you would be of great help."

"Of course, Mordechai," said Jane, seeing Betsy hovering by the breakfast table. "Come to the house in an hour."

"Ar, that I will, mistress. Thank you."

Jane collected the last of the breakfast bowls, wondering what was concerning Mordechai, when she realised that Sir Joshua would be arriving that morning for a sitting with young Jane.

He'll have to cope alone with Jane, she thought. *Looks as though Mordechai needs my help.*

* * *

Mordechai knocked gently on the scullery door at the back of the mansion house, silently rehearsing the words he was going to say.

"Mistress be in the drawing room with Sir Joshua, Mordechai," said Betsy opening the door. "Wait you here and us'll go and announce you."

Mordechai repeated the opening line of the half-truth he would deliver to Jane, a story that would protect his four companions but would not fare well for him.

"Thank you for coming, Mordechai," said Jane, entering the scullery with Betsy trailing behind her. "Now, what's the problem and I'll do my utmost to help."

Jane noticed Mordechai's eyes looking over her and turned to see Betsy lingering in the doorway.

"That will be all, Betsy, thank you. The upstairs bedchambers need attending."

"Mistress," replied Betsy with a curtsey and left the scullery.

Jane closed the door and turned to face Mordechai.

"I'm sorry, Mordechai, but I have a guest here who's sketching young Jane, so I can't remain here with you for long. Pray tell me what's troubling you."

"Thank you, mistress," replied Mordechai. "'Tis about Watt, ma'am. There be a lot of trouble."

"Tell me, Mordechai," prompted Jane, looking curious.

"Well, Watt has been arrested by the Revenue down Paignton way, ma'am."

"Watt, arrested?!" said Jane aghast. "What on earth for?"

"Smugglin', ma'am, and oi am to blame."

"Sit you down here at this table and tell me exactly what has happened," said Jane pulling out a chair from under the scullery table.

"Watt had heard from a stable lad he knows down in Churston Manor that there be a French ship comin' into Elberry Cove midnight last Sunday. The ship contained a consignment of contraband for a smuggling baron in one of them mansion houses near Kingskerswell. Well, they'm was recruitin' for tubmen and despatch riders to deliver the contraband to a safe house. Watt only mentioned this to me, but oi thought it a good opportunity to make some coin so oi pushed Watt to find out more about it."

Jane's eyes were fixed on Mordechai as he reeled off his story.

"Well, the next day Watt tells me of a gang leader who was recruitin' for the baron. Oi doen know no names, mistress, only that they was recruitin' in an ale house in Paignton. So's on my afternoon orf from here, about ten days ago, us rides down to Paignton, finds out what ale house they be rercruitin' in and signs me and Watt up as despatch riders for the contraband drop. Oi thought it would go all smooth like, and me and Watt would be back here at Sharpham well in time for work in the mornin'."

"Was Watt with you at the ale house?" asked Jane.

"No, mistress, Watt didn' know nuthin', he didn' even know oi had gone there. When oi told him about bein' despatch riders, he said he didn' want nuthin' to do with it. I made Watt do it, mistress, honest, it be all my doin'."

"How was Watt caught?" queried Jane.

"We had loaded our horses with the supply for the baron and we be ridin' across the common ground at Churston when the Revenue gave chase. It was a lucky pistol shot as they rode up behind us, it brought down Watt's horse and he got taken."

"Did you try to help him?" asked Jane, unable to believe what she was hearing.

"Us tried, mistress," said Mordechai, stifling the tears that were welling up in his eyes. "One of the despatchers ridin' next to me stopped and pulled at my horse's bridle as oi stopped to try to help Watt. It was too late to help him, so we galloped away. Watt would still be here if oi had not encouraged him. Oi should be in that gaol, not Watt. It is not right, mistress, 'twas all my bliddy doin'. What can oi do, ma'am?"

"It is not what you can do, Mordechai, it is what we can all do for Watt. You said he was taken by the Revenue. I expect he was taken to the gaol in Paignton and then later before the magistrate. God knows where the magistrate could have sent him. Probably either to Exeter or Plymouth where they hold the assize courts. I am going to discuss this with Sir Joshua Reynolds who is here in the drawing room with young Jane. Then I hope to see our friend John Parker at Saltram House. He is also the MP for Devon, so he has got investigative powers. One way or other, we will find where Watt is being held, and hopefully a chance of getting him back here to Sharpham. Now, I want you to come with me and relate the account you have just told me to Sir Joshua Reynolds. Come along now."

Mordechai followed Jane out of the scullery and along the wide hallway to where Sir Joshua sat sketching a feature of young Jane's. On entering the drawing room, Jane looked at her young daughter. "Jane, my darling, Mama has some important news to discuss with Sir Joshua. Go to your room now and play or occupy yourself in some way until we call you."

Jane leapt off her stool, happy to be released from the dreariness of sitting still for so long. "Can I go into the garden at the back Mama, please? It's such a lovely day," pleaded young Jane.

"Yes, of course you can. Stay only in the back garden. Promise me?" said Jane, smiling at her daughter.

"Promise, Mama," she called out, already half-way down the hallway.

"Joshua," said Jane, looking seriously at the great man, "this is our head herdsman, Mordechai Brunt. Mordechai has been in our employ ever since Philemon and I took over here at Sharpham. We have always had the greatest regard for him and trusted him in every way. What he has just told me throws a dark light on our trust for him, but it is not for me to condemn him. Not until we get to the bottom of his story and find out what exactly is happening. Now, Mordechai, relate to Sir Joshua what you have just told me."

Mordechai turned to face Sir Joshua and began his lie.

Sir Joshua listened intently to Mordechai's account of Watt's capture by the Revenue. Nodding, he turned to Jane, "This is going to be a difficult one, Jane. If he has already been committed to stand trial at the assizes, then there is not a lot we can do. Wait a minute!" he said, looking up at Jane. "Paignton, yes, well, well. If I am not mistaken, the magistrate for that district is no other than John's brother, Montague. I think we had better take this to John who may then send word to his brother. It will not take long to find out where Watt has been sent and when the assizes will take place. Jane, I think we had better make plans to visit John as soon as possible, say later today after lunch? I know he will be at Saltram, and you, Mordechai, will accompany us."

John was busy in his study when Jane, Sir Joshua and Mordechai were asked to wait in the reception hall by Andrew, Saltram's head footman. On hearing that two of his close friends were at Saltram to see him, it did not take long for John to hurry along the hallway to the reception hall, anxious to know what had brought them to see him.

"Welcome, dear friends," he said looking at them with joy. "What brings you here on the spur of the moment."

"Dear John," replied Jane, taking his hand, "there is a very delicate matter we need to discuss with you. This is Sharpham's head herdsman, Mordechai Brunt, he has a pressing account to tell you that concerns our stable boy, Watt Huckle."

"Why don't you all come into my office?" suggested John. Then turning to his footman, "Andrew, please bring us tea, thank you."

When they were seated, John turned to Mordechai, "Now, Master Brunt, let me hear what has been so urgent for Mistress Pownoll and Sir Joshua Reynolds to have brought you here to Saltram."

Mordechai jumped to his feet and with his voice shaking, related his story of the events of that Sunday night that had led to Watt's arrest.

John sat back, listening attentively, occasionally looking over at Jane and nodding to show he was understanding Mordechai's account while Sir Joshua sat pensively, studying Mordechai as he came to the end of his report.

"It is likely my brother Montague would have been the presiding magistrate," said John. "It is certain that Huckle would have been taken to the gaol in Paignton the night he was arrested. Prisoners normally face the magistrate the following morning. When did you say this took place?"

"Last Sunday, sir," answered Mordechai.

"Then he would have been taken before Montague on the Monday morning. Mmm, today is only Tuesday so it has not been long. My guess is that your stable boy is either still being held in the Paignton gaol, or has mostly likely been committed to stand trial at the assizes in either Exeter or Plymouth. Montague would have committed him to one of those venues. I know that there will not be an assize court hearing for about another two weeks, so that will give us some time to find out where he has been taken. How old is this Watt Huckle?"

"Sixteen, sir," replied Mordechai.

"Dear Jane," John continued, "what I am prepared to do to help, as your MP and close friend, is to journey down to Paignton to see Montague and find out where your stable boy is. Hopefully, should he still be in the gaol in Paignton, then I think we can get him out. But if Montague has committed him to either Exeter or Plymouth, then it will be a difficult matter. Joshua, my trusted friend, will you accompany me please?"

"Absolutely, John," replied Sir Joshua, smiling at his friend.

"And you, Master Brunt, will ride with us. I know Montague has magistrate's business in his small court every Wednesday, so if we plan to arrive after he has luncheoned, he will be in a more favourable temperament. We three can leave from here on the hour of eleven tomorrow. I expect you here in time for our departure, Master Brunt. Jane, we will return directly to Sharpham after speaking to Montague to let you know the outcome. Then I think you should write to Philemon advising him of this news, don't you?"

Jane nodded towards John, showing him her approval of his suggestion of informing Philemon.

"I'll write as soon as we know, John, and thank you," said Jane smiling. "But there is one big problem. If Mordechai goes with you and renders his report to your brother, won't Montague have him arrested for being an accomplice to the smuggling? He's admitted his guilt in his statement to us."

"Exactly," said Sir Joshua, "it will be a dangerous gamble for you, Mordechai."

"No, no," said Mordechai, "oi will take that chance if it means a lighter sentence for Watt. I hold myself responsible anyways, and if they take me, oi will make sure they'm knows it be my idea not Watt's. Oi am goin' with you, gentlemen, and that be it."

"You can take care of the beef herd up until breakfast tomorrow then," said Jane looking up at Mordechai apprehensively, "then prepare to ride here to

Saltram to meet with John and Sir Joshua. You can direct Old Abe to see to your duties while you are away."

Mordechai nodded towards Jane. "Thank you, mistress, oi will do that."

"Ah," said John, getting up from his chair and rubbing his hands with glee, "a gratifying interruption. Here comes Andrew with our tea."

Chapter 15

Ebenezer left the docile old mare he had borrowed from Elijah Hatch in the rear stable of the Cat and Fiddle Inn and made his way towards the front entrance of the seedy-looking public house, where he knew Luc Skorniere would be waiting for him. It had been a long time since he had graced the cobblestones of one of England's oldest wharfs, and pausing at the door of the inn, he breathed in deeply, tasting the salt of the sea and the unique briny aroma of the Barbican.

The inn was thick with the odour of body sweat and stale ale, and looking around at the crowded tables, he tried to make out a figure unlike the rabble of sailors, thieves and cut-throats, who made up the entire clientele of the sleazy den where he stood. A slight tug at his arm made him turn around abruptly. Standing at his side and looking enticingly into his eyes, the flushed chubby face of a serving wench smiled at him, revealing a set of uneven yellow teeth in the wake of heavily painted ruby red lips. Ebenezer's eyes darted down to her heaving chest, where a huge pair of breasts amply filled the front of her grimy gown. Unable to take his eyes away from what was threatening to burst out over the top of her bodice, he managed to stammer out that a customer was expecting him.

"Well, now, lover," Nancy said with a giggle, "he'm be sittin' over there in the far corner, in that booth. Would you be wantin' a little bit of fancy later?"

"Mmm," replied Ebenezer staring at her frontage, "how could I refuse such a wonderful sight!"

"It'll be a shillin if you do," said Nancy, pushing out her chest provocatively.

"Nancy," a ruffian called from one of the tables, "more ale and a look at yer tits. Get over here, we'm getting' thirsty."

Nancy hurried away, and Ebenezer looked over at the booth where Luc was waiting. He would never have recognised him, not that Luc had made a physical impression on Ebenezer's mind when they had first met, but it was something in his voice that seemed exceptional and unforgettable. Ebenezer recognised the tone immediately.

"Ebenezer, we meet again after all these years. I must thank you first for the good work you are doing for our cause. You are much appreciated."

"A little extra in my rewards would give me more appreciation too. But we can discuss that later, Luc. It is my pleasure to meet you again and to see where the information I pass on is received, unlike the hooded contact I deal with in the village. Perhaps you would like to tell me who I am working with there."

"All in good time, Ebenezer," said Luc. "Your contact does not want to be known, especially to you. Anyway, enough of something I will not give you an answer to. I am told you have some special information for us that concerns," Luc lowered his voice, "the King."

Ebenezer jumped as a resounding thump on the table signalled the arrival of two mugs of ale. Looking up, he stared at the tops of two enormous fleshy bosoms being paraded over the table as Nancy bent over Ebenezer to retrieve an empty beer mug. Like the night he had had an impulse to grab a twinkling star from the night sky, so the urge to grasp one of Nancy's bosoms in his hand overwhelmed him. His hand sneaked out, yet again to clutch at thin air as Nancy pulled herself away to stand upright, holding out her hand for payment for the ale. A large grin lit up her face as she looked at Ebenezer and mouthed, "It will cost you a shillin'!"

"Yes, yes, Nancy," said Luc, dropping a few coins into her hand.

Nancy left them with a smile and looking back over her shoulder at Ebenezer, giggled while she walked away caressing her left breast.

"Worthless slut," said Luc, taking a long draught of ale from his mug.

Mmm, couldn't agree more, thought Ebenezer, *but what a pair of tits on her. Must have them in my hands later*, he decided. *Worth a shilling!*

"Now, as I was saying," continued Luc, "the King."

"Before I give you the information, which I guarantee you will never receive the likes of again," said Ebenezer, "I will tell you my price."

Ebenezer licked his lips as Luc eyed him suspiciously.

"Five hundred pounds."

"What!" Luc nearly screamed out loud. "My principal would never agree to such a sum. It is a veritable fortune."

"Exactly," replied Ebenezer, "and so is the information I can sell you. It could mean the end of the war in the colonies and the capitulation of England.

To achieve this would mean the assassination of George III. Five hundred pounds is a small price to pay for such a guaranteed victory."

"*Mon dieu*," said Luc, shaking his head, "I will send word to my chief and should he decide to go ahead, then we can discuss terms."

"There are no terms," said Ebenezer. "Five hundred pounds is the price in cash and a safe-haven for me in France. I am prepared to assist in any operation you may plan to assassinate the King, on condition I'm not the one to pull the trigger or plunge the knife."

"Let me get this right," said Luc. "What you are actually proposing is the assassination of King George III and you have the information of the right time and place of where he will be? Plus, you are willing to help us. Am I right?"

"Right," said Ebenezer, looking directly into Luc's eyes. "And as I said, I will assist in the operation on the condition of the full amount being paid in cash and a safe place of luxury in your country to spend the rest of my days."

Luc considered Ebenezer's proposals, unhappy with his excessive demands.

"Well!" said Luc. "In order to give my chief something to chew on, I'll need a little more. How do you say in English, to dangle a carrot in front of him?"

"Yes, precisely," said Ebenezer. "Tell him the King will make a Proclamation of Rebellion on August 23rd and then summon his generals for all-out war with the American rebels. He plans to review his troops at a certain place on a certain date. There are several prime assembly points where the troops will depart for the colonies, but there is only one where the King will be present. I know that location and the date he will be there to address his troops. What is more, it is not that long away. He will also stay in a pre-arranged location the night before he gives his address. I know that location."

"Bon," said Luc, "I will send word immediately to Versailles. We will have an answer within two weeks, of that I am quite sure. I will send word for you to meet with me again. Until then, keep your eyes and ears open for anything that would be of interest to us. I bid you farewell, Ebenezer."

With a courteous nod, Luc left the booth and made his way towards the door of the inn. Ebenezer sat back staring at what was left in his beer mug, pleased with himself at the way he had handled the meeting with Luc.

"I will be rich," he giggled, "there is no way they will turn down my secret, and they will pay what I have asked. Five hundred pounds and not a penny less."

"Has he left you all alone, lover?" a luring voice sounded next to him. Turning, Ebenezer's eyes widened in complete surprise. Standing as near as she could get to him, Nancy held one enormous breast in her hands, caressing it and brushing her lips over the nipple.

"Only a shillin', lover!" she cooed.

Ebenezer gulped down what was left in his ale mug and springing out of his seat, fumbled for the shilling he had already deposited in the pocket of his breeches. Leering at the whore, he held up the coin between two fingers.

"Lead on, Nancy," he drooled, feeling himself rising to the occasion.

* * *

Mordechai rode into the stable yard of Saltram at exactly eleven o'clock. John and Sir Joshua were already mounted and ready to go, and after a swift salutation towards Mordechai, John raised his arm and waved it in the direction of Saltram's exit. They trotted out of the main gate then urged their mounts into a canter towards the main carriageway to Totnes, and hence across the fields to Paignton.

From Totnes, Mordechai recognised much of the route he had taken with the other five Ashprington smugglers that fateful Sunday night. Passing Hangman's Cross, he noticed there was no sign of the corpse they had encountered that night and wondered when the next poor wretch would be strung up for the theft of a loaf of bread or a smuggled bag of tea.

Approaching Blagdon Manor Farm, John pulled them up, pointing across a turnip field to where the manor house stood.

"We'll cut across this field," he shouted, "and make enquiries at the manor to the whereabouts of my brother."

A liveried servant lugging a wicker basket loaded with firewood, was struggling towards a side entrance as they rode into the manor's courtyard.

"I say, you there, stop a moment," called out John. The man looked around at John's command, dropping the basket in surprise. "I don't know if you know me, but I'm Montague Parker's brother."

The elderly servant looked up at John, ignoring Sir Joshua and Mordechai. "That oi do, sir," he replied. "How may I be of assistance to you?"

"Well, we would like to know if he is here or gone to the magistrate's office in Paignton?"

"Ah, that I know, sir," said the servant. "He left for the Revenue building in Paignton where he has his bureau, at ten o'clock, sir. The good lady, Mistress Parker, be in the house, sir. Shall oi fetch her?"

"No, that won't be necessary," said John turning his horse, "we are in a hurry, just send her my greetings and thank you. I bid you good day."

They rode out of the courtyard, spurring their horses into a canter across the turnip field and back onto the country track that led to a fork, one way going in the direction of Clennon and the other towards the harbour town of Paignton.

Chapter 16

Montague Parker returned to his office after lunching in the parlour room of the London Inn, only a stone's throw from the Revenue building and his office.

He would finish signing the remainder of a pile of documents he had been previously working on and then take a leisurely ride back to the manor house, where he'd change and spend the rest of the afternoon fishing. He smiled at the thought of the peace and quiet he would enjoy that sunny afternoon.

A knock at his door interrupted his thoughts. The clerk to the magistrate's court poked his nose around the half-opened door and coughed politely.

"Sir," he said in a sombre tone, "it's Master John, your brother, with two companions. He needs to see you urgently."

"My brother, well, I never!" exclaimed Montague. "Wonder what brings him here? Send them in, Basset, and bring the port."

"John!" said Montague, opening his arms to his elder brother as the three of them were shown into the magistrate's office. "A pleasure to see you, indeed it is, dear brother, what brings you here?"

"Montague," said John, smiling broadly and clasping his brother in a hug "Something urgent we need to talk to you about."

"Please sit," said Montague, indicating chairs around his desk.

"Thank you," said John. "But first, may I introduce my dear friend, Sir Joshua Reynolds."

"Indeed," replied Montague, shaking Sir Joshua's hand. "I have always had the misfortune to have missed you, sir, when calling on my brother. A pleasure to make your acquaintance."

"And this is Mordechai Brunt, Montague. He is the head herdsman at Sharpham, the estate owned by my dear friend Philemon Pownoll, who is away with the navy fighting the rebels in the colonies."

Looking down his nose at Mordechai, Montague gave him a short nod, curious as to why his brother had brought a peasant farm worker to his office.

126

Mordechai smiled to himself, aware of the obvious class prejudice inherent in this man. Not acknowledging Montague's gesture, Mordechai stared contemptibly at his haughty presence.

"Montague, we need your help," began John. "Two days ago, on Monday morning, you officiated as magistrate to a group of smugglers arrested in the early hours."

"That I did, John," said Montague, a look of distaste spreading over his features.

"In that group, was there a frail young boy of about sixteen, by the name of Huckle, Watt Huckle?"

"There was," replied Montague, "but what has this to do with your visit here?"

"Before I continue, I would like Master Brunt to relate his story to you. As magistrate administering this case, it is important you hear his account."

Montague looked seriously at Mordechai, and then with a wave of his hand, gestured for him to begin.

Mordechai began by reminding Montague of Watt's young age and his status as stable lad at Sharpham Estate. He acknowledged Watt's involvement in the Sunday night's smuggling venture on Elberry Cove but insisted that Watt had been forced to partake in the operation by none other than himself. On many occasions Watt had tried to influence him not to take part, but in the end had followed his lead. He then related his account of the night in question, as he had done so in front of Jane, Sir Joshua and John.

Montague listened to Mordechai's account without interrupting, a stern expression on his face throughout. When Mordechai had finished, Montague sat back, studying him in silence. Then, getting out of his chair, he turned to John and Sir Joshua. "Please excuse me for a brief moment," he said to them, "I have something pressing I need to discuss with Basset. I won't be long."

John smiled at his brother, nodding to him as he left the room. Outside, Montague hurried along the long corridor to Basset's small office.

Entering, he quickly issued an order to his clerk, "Summon the Revenue officer present and tell him to come to my office with two dragoons immediately."

"Yes, sir," replied Basset, jumping to his feet and hurrying out of the room.

Montague returned to his office, putting on a smile as if nothing out of the ordinary was about to happen.

"Montague, dear brother," said John, "I trust you will find it in your power to release young Huckle. As Master Brunt has explained, he was not in favour of this smuggling venture and was only led on by Brunt's insistence he join him. He is a young lad of sound character and some form of minor punishment would be appropriate. Not a committal to the assize courts."

Montague looked at John seriously. "It is too late for that now, John," he said, "I committed him and a batch of other smugglers to stand trial at the Plymouth assizes in two weeks. He has already been taken to Plymouth Gaol, there is nothing I can do now."

Mordechai's face dropped in avid disappointment as he looked desperately at John.

"As MP for the county of Devon, I will take this up with Lord North the Prime Minister," said John, looking at Montague furiously.

"John," said Montague, giving his brother a stiff look, "there is nothing you can do now. Being an MP does not put you above the law. Huckle was found in possession of contraband and arrested escaping from the scene. I am afraid his fate is sealed."

A loud knock on Montague's office door made them look up in surprise as an officer of the Revenue and two armed dragoons rushed into the room.

"Seize that man," ordered Montague, pointing towards Mordechai. "He has just admitted taking part in the smuggling activity at Elberry Cove. By his own testimony, he seems to have been responsible for engaging the prisoner Huckle in the criminal act. As the powers vested in me as Magistrate for the District of Paignton, I commit you, Mordechai Brunt, to be taken forthwith to Plymouth Gaol to await trial at the next assizes on the charge of smuggling contraband. Chain him and take him away."

Too shocked to intervene, John and Sir Joshua watched as the Revenue officer chained Mordechai's wrists and led him away.

"I will be damned if I let this happen, Montague," said John, looking aghast.

"You have no say, John. And another thing, I think you should inform your good friend Captain Pownoll that there is a likelihood of an organised smuggling ring established and operating in the village of Ashprington. I am sure it involves other villagers other than that bumpkin I have just charged."

"Who will be the assize judge when their cases come up for trial?" asked Sir Joshua.

"Judge Edmund Pickering," answered Montague.

"Oh no!" said John, looking seriously at Sir Joshua. "The Hanging Judge!"

"No matter what you say, Montague, I'm certainly taking this matter before Lord North. I realise, as magistrate, you have a job to do, but on occasions a little empathy and compassion in a case such as Watt Huckle's would not be against the principals of justice. Have a thought, dear brother! And now, we must take our leave. I will not thank you for what has just taken place as we came for your help. Now we must explain to Mistress Pownoll the reason for Mordechai not returning, a difficult matter. I hope you manage to sleep easily after administering such justice!"

Looking into the magistrate's rigid face, Sir Joshua nodded politely, shaking his head forlornly as he followed John out of the Revenue building.

* * *

Jane heard the arrival of horses' hooves on the cobblestones of the courtyard fronting the manor house as the sun began to set over the fields of Sharpham. Hurrying out to greet the returning envoys, she stopped abruptly as she made out only two riders. She knew at once that Mordechai would not be returning.

"Jane, my dear," said John, dismounting and handing the reins of his horse to Wilf, a young stable lad who had been brought in to cover Watt's duties, "I'm afraid we have very disappointing news."

"Come into the parlour, both of you," replied Jane, looking seriously at John and Sir Joshua.

Comfortably seated with a glass of claret, John described every detail of the futile visit to his brother Montague, outlining their shock at Montague's cold-handedness in the arrest of Mordechai.

"Well, I suppose it was inevitable Mordechai would be arrested," said Jane, looking anxiously at John and Sir Joshua. "He knew the risk he was taking. He honestly believed he would be helping Watt in claiming that it was all his fault. Do you think the judge will be lenient with Watt, considering Mordechai's testimony?"

"It will all depend on the judge," said John, "but in this case, I am afraid there will not be any sign of compassion or leniency, as the judge in question will be Edmund Pickering. He has a reputation of dispensing swift justice and only considers the facts of the case. When summing up, he will likely direct the jury to find both Mordechai and Watt guilty and then he will administer the penalty of hanging, as he will to the rest of the band of smugglers they caught."

"There is very little that can be done now," said Sir Joshua, looking sympathetically at Jane.

"As MP for Devon," said John, "I aim to bring this matter to the attention of Lord North, the Prime Minister. Maybe he can help in commuting their sentence to transportation or penal service somewhere. It would be better than facing the hangman. But whatever the outcome, the law is the law and Watt and Mordechai broke it and must now pay the price."

"John, I think you should inform Jane of Montague's advice in your contacting Philemon about the smuggling," suggested Sir Joshua.

"Indeed," replied John. "Montague has reason to believe that there is a smuggling ring operating within the village of Ashprington. He has no evidence, but is fairly confident that Watt Huckle was part of that ring, and as it now aspires, Master Brunt is probably connected too."

"If there are others from the village involved, then Mordechai and Watt would never give them away," said Jane earnestly.

"That maybe so," said John, "but Montague thinks Philemon must be informed as both Huckle and Brunt are in your employ."

"I agree," said Jane, "it would be good if both us wrote to Philemon, he would then understand the urgency of the situation. The matter of Watt and Mordechai will probably be over before he gets our news. No matter, he must be informed."

"If there is a smuggling ring operating in Ashprington, then it is very likely Mordechai's story is fabricated," said Sir Joshua. "It is a story to protect not only Watt but whoever is connected to the ring. It would seem that half his story is an honest account but the other half of signing himself and Watt up in the Paignton ale house as despatch riders, is beginning to sound rather fanciful. Mordechai has sacrificed himself, that is plain!"

"How can we find out?" asked Jane.

"I do not know," answered John. "As I am not from the village, I feel I have no say, but as Member of Parliament for Devon, I feel duty bound to investigate, which I will."

"Where have they taken Mordechai?" asked Jane.

"To Plymouth Gaol," answered Sir Joshua.

"Montague has directed him to stand trial at the assize sittings in two weeks," said John. "He will likely stand alongside Huckle and the rest of those who were caught."

"Oh my God," sighed Jane, "I just do not know what we will do with the herd now that Mordechai's gone."

"Jane, you are not to worry," said John taking her hand. "I will instruct one of our herdsmen to come here forthwith. It will be done first thing in the morning."

"I am so grateful, thank you, John," replied Jane smiling.

"And now Jane, Joshua and I must bid you goodnight as we have to ride back to Plymouth before it gets really dark."

"I will be here the day after tomorrow for what will be the penultimate sitting with young Jane," said Sir Joshua. "Until then, a very good night, Jane."

"Just one moment," said Jane. "I think Betsy's still here, upstairs with young Jane. I'll call her, she can instruct the stable lad to bring your horses."

Jane was surprised to find Betsy in the hallway already cloaked for going home.

"Ah, Betsy, there you are. I thought you were upstairs with young Jane."

"No, mistress," replied Betsy, "Young Jane's put herself to bed as her was feelin' tired. Oi was waitin' till they'm gentlemen finished and Wilf brung their horses. Then as you'm promised me, miss, Wilf can drive me back home in the wagon."

"Yes, of course, Betsy. We have finished, so could you go and instruct Wilf to bring their horses and then he can take you back home. Thank you, Betsy, and I will see you tomorrow morning."

"Ma'am," said Betsy with a slight curtsey.

Wilf talked away incessantly as he drove Betsy back to Ashprington in the one-horse wagon that Mordechai had favoured for his visits to the village and the Ashprington Inn. Betsy took no notice of Wilf chattering, she was high on what she'd heard John Parker say while she listened quietly outside the door of the parlour. He would investigate the nest of smugglers within the village, and as MP for the county of Devon, she knew he would be only too interested in hearing information about a traitor within their midst. As Wilf rambled on, Betsy began to think of how she could confront the MP with the news that she knew of something bigger than just a smuggling ring within the village. She smiled to herself knowing that she would have to present evidence to John Parker proving

Ebenezer's guilt of treason, but she would find a way to entrap the traitor and rid herself of him once and for all.

Chapter 17

Mordechai looked through the bars of the prison wagon as it came to a halt outside the gates of Plymouth Gaol. Bright sunlight flooded the inside of the wagon as a guard wrenched open its doors, causing Mordechai to look away until his eyes became accustomed to the strong glare that shimmered over this part of the Barbican. A pungent smell of faeces and urine mixed with the stench of rotting fish and salty brine made his stomach urge as his guard hammered on the thick oak doors of the dilapidated building that towered before them.

"'Nother one for the assizes," he grunted, as a mean-looking brute ushered them through the doors to wait in a dark corridor, while he collected the paperwork from Mordechai's guard.

"You'm be a felon goin' for trial at next assizes," he barked glaring at Mordechai. "Rations be one pound of bread per day and one cup of water. If you'm be wantin' any extras, then you pay me what oi tells you, and oi'll see what oi can provide. Be that clear, felon?"

Mordechai stared into the bestial face of the gaoler, unable to say anything when a searing pain bent him double as the warder's heavy cudgel smashed into his stomach.

"Be that clear, felon?" the brute bellowed.

Gasping for breath and feeling he would vomit at any moment, Mordechai straightened up, his eyes focusing on the gaoler's primeval features and the toothless smirk that stretched across his face.

"Clear," he stammered.

"Move on then," bawled the gaoler, pushing Mordechai down the dark corridor and tapping his heavy cudgel against the outside of his leg.

Mordechai stumbled along the dank stone corridor, conscious of the grunting and snorting of the gaoler following behind. At intervals, dimly-lit oil lanterns secured to the rough stone walls shed a little light, producing long eerie shadows of both prisoner and gaoler descending deeper into the gaol's damp soulless confinement.

"Wait," the brute commanded, as a thick wooden door loomed up in front of Mordechai. Choosing a key from the brass key ring that hung from his belt, he unlocked the door and pulled it open. Mordechai reeled back in horror as an overwhelming stench of excreta engulfed the area. Desperate cries and groans, pleading for water and help, echoed everywhere.

"Git on there, felon," laughed the brute, "the stink you'm kin git used to, but the cries and moans will haunt you all the way to the gallows."

The gaoler pushed Mordechai further through the doorway into another dimly-lit passageway where rows of filthy cells, secured by heavy wooden doors with eye-level observation grilles, glared callously out at them.

"You'm be joinin' them felons what arrived here on Monday," the brute said. "Assize court hearin' be in ten days. You and the rest of them smugglers got Judge Pickering hearin' your cases. It will be the gallows for you all. Ha, ha. Come on, you'm be in that cell up there."

Outside the cell, Mordechai waited while the brute felt for the appropriate key. A heavy shove in his back and he was inside, reeling again at the foul stench that greeted him. The door slammed shut and there was silence. A rasping cough in the far corner of the cell told Mordechai he was not alone and as his eyes grew accustomed to the dimly-lit room, he was able to make out a row of bodies lying on beds of straw. He hoped he would find Watt on one of them.

"Welcome stranger," a voice called out. "There be a bed for you at end of this line, next to the lad. Have you anything to eat or even a little baccy?"

"No, nuthin'," replied Mordechai, squinting towards the far corner of the cell.

A sudden movement below him made him gasp as he felt his ankle held in a vice-like grip. Looking down, he was able to make out the ragged form of a filthy miscreant, grinning while he tightened his grip on Mordechai's ankle.

"All new arrivals have something worth havin'," he hissed. "Gi me yer shoes."

Mordechai was about to grab the lowlife by his hair and pull him up, when to his horror he saw in the dim light of the lantern, a multitude of pus-seeping sores covering the creature's face. Straightening up, he lifted his other foot and kicked out at the wretch with all his force, booting him squarely in the head.

The scream of pain, as Mordechai's left foot slammed into the side of the creep's head, roused the other inmates into an excited babble of laughter and hand clapping.

"Good on you, brother," a voice rang out from the far corner opposite to where Mordechai had been heading. "Fuckin' little creep had it comin'. Better sleep with one eye open, he will cut your throat with the piece of slate he been filin' down."

"Thanks for the warnin'," said Mordechai making his way over to the far corner.

Watt was sitting up on his bed of straw, a broad smile filling his face.

"Oi knew it be you, Mordechai, but why you'm in here, have they arrested any of the others?"

"Naw, they'm safe enough, for present anyway," said Mordechai staring at Watt. "'Tis a long story, we have time enough here for me to tell you, but it seems oi have to keep an eye on that pus-ridden creep who wanted my shoes. Oi gave him a good one, right in the side of his bliddy head oi did."

"He be a nasty one, Mordechai," said Watt peering down the row. "He was one of them who stormed into the courtyard at Churston Manor as we was mountin' up to leave. He was the one who yelled out to kill us and take our horses. Then the Revenue got him and these others. They put me with them in Paignton Gaol till we came before the magistrate later that mornin'. All of these here were at Elberry Cove that night. Oi would not trust any of them, Mordechai, none of them, they's a bad lot. Now tell me what has been happenin' since the Revenue got me. Did all the others manage to get away and what said Squire about me bein' caught?"

Mordechai lay back on his bed of straw, promptly sitting back up with a jolt as a swarm of bugs and insects streamed over him. Watt smiled. "Can't do nuthin' about they, Mordechai. Bliddy bugs everywhere here. You will have to get used to them bitin' and crawlin' all over you. Seems if you kill one, two more appear to take its place."

"Bliddy little fuckers," said Mordechai, swatting an insect crawling up his arm. "Now, you be listenin', Watt? I'll begin on the night after you was taken by the Revenue."

Watt lay back listening to every word, picturing in his mind the series of events that Mordechai recounted. His eyes widened like saucers as Mordechai related the story he had made up to explain Watt's disappearance to Jane Pownoll and the subsequent re-telling of the story to Jane's friends and the pompous Paignton magistrate.

The sudden scurrying sound of rats scuttling along the sides of the cell brought on an abrupt silence amongst the prisoners. Watt's expression stiffened in terror as a piercing howl from the prisoner lying on the opposite bed of straw cut through the silence around them. Swivelling round to see the cause of the terrified scream, Mordechai stared in horror at the sight of a furry creature, the size of a cat with a tail the length of a man's arm, crawling over the prisoner's head. With its front teeth protruding like a set of sharpened knives, it crouched over its victim's neck, then with an arrogant look around the cell, it opened its jaws and plunged down on the prisoner's ear, biting and gnawing it in a diabolical frenzy. Springing to his feet, Mordechai leapt over to where the terrified prisoner lay screaming. Grabbing the giant rat by its tail, he pulled it off the prisoner's ear, slamming it repeatedly against the rough stone wall. With his hand covered in the blood of the rat, Mordechai peered around the cell, then with a yell of disgust, he swung the dead vermin towards the lowlife who had tried to steal his shoes. The rat landed next to where the cretin had been watching and with a leering grin, he snatched it up, licking his lips and sniffing its blood-soaked fur. Clasping it jealously, he scowled at the prisoners next to him and with his middle finger raised towards Mordechai, quickly tucked it under the straw where he lay.

"He'll eat that raw," said the prisoner Mordechai had saved. "Several of these bastards catch the rats and eat them. Even though we be starving, oi could never do that. Dirty fuckers they be. Thank you for what you did, brother. Have to say oi be scared of they vermin, oi just freeze when they starts crawlin' all over me, specially they big uns, and there be a fair few of they in the pack what oi've seen, like the one you got off me. I kin tell you they ain't frightened of us. It is always at this time of day they come scavenging through the cells. Rumour has it, they devoured a young lad in one of the cells down the end of the corridor not long ago. Rather face the hangman than be eaten alive by one of they fuckers. Anyways, you saved my ear even if it be pissing out blood, oi owes you, brother. I be Joe, Josiah Winks."

"And I be Mordechai. Us had better be ready for them vermin when they come agin," said Mordechai, turning back towards Watt.

"The gaoler what brought me here, said us'd get a pound of bread and a cup of water once a day. When does he come with it? Doen suppose oi will be lucky enough to get anythin' today."

"Early mornin's," replied Watt, "no idea of time down here, but us knows it be early mornin' when rations come 'cos us asked one of the gaolers what brings them what time he always comes to us, and he said early mornin'. He be here long time before you came in, Mordechai."

"So, it probably be getting' on for night-time now," said Mordechai.

"Ar, that it be," agreed Watt.

Quietness descended around the cell as sleep came to most of the prisoners. A cacophony of snoring soon broke the silence, while the wretches who could not sleep swatted and slapped at the lice and insects crawling all over them. Curses rang out from the victims as the pests mercilessly bit and sucked the blood and pus seeping from their open sores and boils.

Mordechai lay awake, listening to the sound of Watt's disturbed breathing as the lad slept in a nightmare of dark dreams. He remembered the gaoler telling him there were ten days before the assize trial. If Watt had been correct, then he could gage the passing of days by the delivery of their morning rations. He shivered at the prospect of his trial. A cold awareness of his fate stabbed at his soul, the gallows or transportation. Whatever the sentences, he and Watt would suffer; he hoped to be there with him, to give the lad courage in his final moments, and for Watt to attest to the devoted friendship he had always had for him.

He was suddenly alerted by a strange gulping sound coming from the end of the row of snoring prisoners. Through the gloom of the cell, he made out the shape of the lowlife who had tried to take his shoes; what he saw turned his stomach. Sitting up cross-legged on his bed of straw, the creep's face was buried into the side of the giant rat he had pulverized against the wall. A wet slurping sound echoed around the cell as the wretch gnawed and sucked into the side of the rat, then as he looked up for a gasp of breath, Mordechai's stomach urged as the cretin sneered through a layer of thick blood and drooping entrails that had stuck to the pus-seeping sores on his cheeks and chin.

Mordechai turned away, sickened at the sight. He must try to keep awake, wary of the warning that the rat eater would come to slit his throat. There was no indication of time in the cell, only that it would be early morning when the gaoler arrived with their bread and water. As the snoring of the prisoners echoed around the cell, Mordechai lay awake, listening and ignoring the insects and bugs nipping at his skin. He waited, feigning sleep, waiting for the voracious sound of the rat eater's feast to stop, for then he knew the time would have come for him to have to kill him.

Chapter 18

Mordechai lay on his back in a field of lush green grass, his beef herd grazing peacefully beside him. His eyes ranged across a vast, seemingly endless blue sky where small birds cut across his vision, swooping, diving and spiralling over the richly colourful fields of Sharpham Estate.

The gentle sounds of the countryside floating around him had lulled him into a composed sense of serenity. He was at peace, happy and content within his home and surroundings.

A sudden rush of foul breath, the kind of nauseating smell that exudes from rotting excreta thrown out into the streets on hot sticky days, suddenly disrupted his tranquillity. The putrid smell worsened and turning his head to check the cause of the outrage, he jumped in fright as the hairy, snot-dribbling face of one of his bullocks appeared directly over him, the face seeming to enlarge in repugnancy as its foul breath seethed over him.

Without opening his eyes, Mordechai forced himself awake. He had dropped off while keeping vigil and the foul-smelling breath in his dream meant only one thing; the rat eater was upon him. Not moving a muscle, he felt the hot rancid breath of the creature, knowing it was moving closer in over his face.

Slowly, he opened his eyes. Long filthy hair dangled from the cretin as he leaned over Mordechai, panting and dribbling yellow saliva from his blood-stained mouth. Scores of pus-seeping sores threatened to weep their poison over Mordechai's face, as the stinking rat eater bent low over him, snarling and spitting out his bitterness.

"Oi am goin' to kill you, fucker. Slit your throat with my slate knife. Then oi will take your shoes and cut your toes off one by one and toss them to the rats when they come prowlin' here later."

Frozen in terror, he could only watch as the loathsome felon licked the side of his razor-sharpened weapon. Shutting his eyes tight against the horror before him, he failed see strong hands fasten themselves around the rat eater's throat.

He waited for the cretin's knife to sear across his jugular and then darkness to envelop him. Nothing happened, he could feel the hold the moron had on him slowly weakening. With renewed strength, he raised his head, gasping at the bulging red eyes and the deeply purpling face swaying over him. Rough hands pressed tighter around the creep's neck while thick nail-bitten fingers shook with heightened effort as they squeezed the worthless life out of the noxious rat-eating creature.

"Told you oi owed you, brother," Joe spluttered breathing heavily as he let the corpse crumple to the floor. "Now, what be us goin' to do with him? You best think of somethin' quick." Without a word, Mordechai jumped up and grabbing the rat eater's shoulders, indicated to Joe to take the corpse by his ankles.

They staggered past the sleeping inmates to where the dead lowlife had had his bed of straw and dumping him down on it, Mordechai groped around until he found the remains of the rat. Ripping off its hind leg, he turned to Joe. "Force the creep's mouth wide open," he instructed, "and keep it open." Mordechai pushed the rat's leg into the open mouth, forcing it deeper into the middle of the throat. "Now close the mouth but leave it open a little, pull the tongue out so it looks as though it is lolling against his lips."

Mordechai placed the half-eaten rat into the dead rat eater's palm and closing the fingers around it, he stood up surveying the scene. "Look at the bulge in the bastard's throat," he said, "gaolers will think this lowlife choked on the leg."

"Ar, that they will, brother, good thinkin'. Now let us be back to our beds before they come with mornin' rations."

No sooner had they lain down on their beds of straw than they heard a key grate in the lock of the cell door. Mordechai watched as two gaolers shuffled in, one carrying a sack of stale bread, the other a bucket of water.

"Alright, you bastards," one of them called, "hands off cocks and line up 'ere." One by one, the felons pulled themselves up, coughing and groaning at the early hour.

Watt stood close behind Mordechai as they formed a line in front of the two gaolers. "Looks like one of you doen wanna wake up," said one of the gaolers, looking over at the form of the rat eater lying prostrate on the bed of straw. "Go on, Silas," he said turning to his partner, "put that bucket down and give the bastard a good kickin', might wake the lazy fucker up."

Silas put the bucket down and wiping his grubby hands down the sides of his breeches, approached the dead rat eater. "Git up, you'm lazy piece of shit," he yelled, kicking the corpse in the back.

"He didn' move, Silas," said Jonas, the other gaoler.

"Must be havin one pretty dream. Give him another one." Silas gave an almighty kick into the corpse's back and seeing no reaction, bent down, pulling the dead rat eater up by his collar.

"Fuckin' hell, Jonas!" he hollered. "Looks like the bastard be dead." Jonas dropped the piece of bread he was about to give to a prisoner and scuttled over to where Silas was gawping at the corpse. "Look there, Jonas, he be graspin' summin' in his hand."

Jonas took the rat eater's hand, prising the stiff fingers open. "A half-eaten rat, Silas. The fucker's been gorgin' on rat, the dirty bastard."

"The fucker!" said Silas, looking closely at the corpse. "Look there, Jonas, in his throat, somethin's lodged in there. Oi will open his mouth and you stick yer fingers down his throat and pull whatever be stuck in there out."

Reluctantly, Jonas put two of his fingers deep down into the rat eater's throat, pulling out the hind leg of the giant rat. "He must have choked on the leg. Got it stuck there as he was gorgin' on it."

"Well, us can take him out after givin' out the rations," said Silas. "One less for the hangman in a few days!"

"Ar, we kin throw him in that freshly-dug lime pit where they put those fuckers what died last night," said Jonas grinning. Back on their beds with their bread and mugs of water, the prisoners cast looks of shocked surprise at the sight of their dead cellmate clutching the remains of a rat in the palm of his hand.

"Serve the fucker right," said one, "never did like the bastard anyway!"

"One of the gaolers forgot to give me a mug for my water when oi came in here," said Mordechai looking over at Silas.

"Go over and git the dead bastard's one," said the gaoler smirking. Mordechai found the rat eater's tin mug under the filthy bed of straw. Live and dead black beetles fell out of it as he shook it, wishing he could wash away the disgusting stains and bits of rancid flesh that stuck to its sides. Grimacing, he nodded to Silas to fill it with water from the bucket. He knew it would be the only cup of water he would have that day.

The two gaolers finished handing out the bread and water and while Jonas took what was left of the rations out of the cell, Silas dragged the corpse of the dead rat eater out, slamming the door and locking it behind him. In the quietness of the cell, the prisoners listened to the faint sound of the two gaolers hauling the corpse down the dark corridor and on towards its disposal in the freshly-dug lime pit.

Mordechai looked across at Joe, who grinned back at him, raising his mug of water in a gesture of a toast. Smiling, he put his index finger to his closed lips, signalling their secret would remain untold and stay buried in the lime pit alongside the other unfortunate prisoners who had given up and died during the night. Mordechai nodded and with a sigh, picked up his pound of stale bread, wondering how soon it would be before the scurrying sound of the rats would be heard scuttling up from their dark holes to further terrify and torment the pitiful wretches languishing near him.

Chapter 19

Ebenezer sat in his parlour sipping brandy and thinking of how he would get out of England once the King had been assassinated. Of course, Luc Skorniere would have to help him and provide a safe passage for him to reach his luxury hideaway in France. He giggled as he saw himself a frequent guest at the French Royal Court, honoured and esteemed as a hero of France, rich beyond all means and a popular affiliate of the hedonistic circles that filled the court. A loud knocking on his front door brought him back down to earth.

"Shit," he muttered, "can't they leave me alone. If it is Molly though, I'll give the shameless minx a right seeing to. Wonder where she's been, seems to have disappeared completely from the village."

Rising at the thought of what he was going to do to Molly, he hurried out to open the door. A frown of disappointment creased his features as he beheld a serious-looking Squire Maddock standing in the porch.

"Reverend Dunn, or may I start calling you Ebenezer?" asked the Squire.

"Please, I'd be honoured, Squire," replied Ebenezer. He wondered as to the Squire's friendly approach and what he may be after.

"I've something most urgent to discuss with you, in fact, it's been playing on my mind since last seeing you. It's now most serious, Ebenezer," he said.

"Please come into my parlour," said Ebenezer, allowing Squire Maddock to pass him and enter the house. "A brandy or a sherry, Squire?" Ebenezer asked, indicating for him to sit.

"A brandy, Ebenezer, please, and make it a large one if you don't mind."

Squire Maddock seated himself and knocking back his brandy in one swift gulp, sat back studying Ebenezer intently. "I don't know if you've seen any of your cohorts recently, those of your merry band who assist you in supplying me with, let's say, overseas produce?"

"No, as a matter of fact, I haven't," replied Ebenezer, "I haven't visited the inn for a few days now. I've had temporal work to do outside of the village and a recent diocese meeting in Plymouth," he said, lying. "I've been meaning to catch up with them, perhaps I'll see them at morning service this coming Sunday. Why, is there a problem, Squire?"

"Yes, there certainly is," replied the Squire, smiling at Ebenezer's overt lie and holding out his empty glass for a refill. "The one called Mordechai has admitted to a Paignton magistrate of being a despatcher for the smugglers in the Elberry Cove heist, and is now in Plymouth Gaol along with the lad Huckle. He claimed it was all his doing." Ebenezer nearly dropped the two glasses he was replenishing, his eyes widening in shock and dread. Pulling himself together, he carried the drinks to where the Squire was seated, offering one to the Squire and then seating himself shakily.

"Yes, Ebenezer, I know what you're thinking," said the Squire, taking his glass and smiling at the amount Ebenezer had inadvertently poured. "The magistrate has written a report for the judge stating that he is certain Mordechai is covering something up and that there were others from Ashprington involved in the venture. If both are offered a deal to save themselves from the hangman by naming their confederates, then I am sure they'll name us all. And that, Ebenezer, will mean you being arrested and hanged on Plymouth Hoe."

"Bbb…but what about you?" stammered Ebenezer in terror.

"I have a plan and if it works out, then we'll both be safe. The plan will involve you, Ebenezer; in fact, you'll play a major part in it."

"Will it be dangerous?" said Ebenezer feeling the blood rush from his face.

"If you'll kindly replenish my glass, I'll come to the point and explain the plan. Don't worry, you won't be subject to any physical danger, of sorts."

Worried about the last two words of Squire Maddock's reply, Ebenezer half-filled the Squire's glass and returned to his seat and sat back waiting for him to continue.

"It's plainly obvious, Ebenezer," said the Squire taking a long swig from his glass, "that Mordechai and Huckle will have to be silenced."

"What do you mean, silenced?" said Ebenezer, feeling a tremor of fear run down his spine.

"Not permitted to name their accomplices by being sent to the hangman immediately, their trial and conviction are over," replied the Squire.

"But you can't interfere if the judge compels them to name their cohorts and offers them a penal sentence to do so."

"Precisely," said the Squire, "but what if the judge does not offer them this opportunity and sentences them to hang. Sentence to be carried out, say, within a day."

"Would be better for us," said Ebenezer, "but would he do it?"

"Well, the judge hearing their case would possibly play to plan," said the Squire. "Now, to save us both, this is what I've planned. Huckle and Mordechai must die, and they will, without revealing our names or the names of your cohorts. They'll hang on Plymouth Hoe within a day of being convicted and sentenced."

"I hope you're right, Squire," said Ebenezer. "But what makes you so sure your plan's going to work, you haven't explained it yet."

"The judge hearing their case is Edmund Pickering. He is, let's say, an acquaintance of mine and a devotee to my circle of hedonists. I have planned to hold a soirée at the hall in three days' time when certain members of the gentry and those in high office will attend for a hedonistic two-day programme of pleasure. Edmund Pickering has already accepted my invitation and will be there prior to his officiating the assizes in Plymouth. You, of course, Ebenezer, will attend too."

Ebenezer sat back elated with the Squire's last sentence. It was as though he had at last achieved his life-long ambition, to be amongst those chosen to fulfil their self-satisfying desires in a totally pleasurable and free-for-all atmosphere. The Squire noticed Ebenezer's changed expression and with a rakish smirk, continued with his plan, "Edmund Pickering has some unusual fetish tastes. He enjoys pleasure with both sexes and has an appetite for bondage and masochism. I will arrange for him to partake in these open activities over the two days of revelry. Now, this is where you come in, Ebenezer."

"You mean for me to participate in these games?" said Ebenezer, feeling excited at such a prospect.

"Yes and no," replied the Squire, suppressing his laughter at the comically aroused look on Ebenezer's face. "Three days from now, my guests will arrive at the hall for the start of the two-day orgy. You will be there as a new member of our circle. No-one asks questions as to what we do or where we are from. We are just a circle of bodies intent on enjoying the maximum amount of pleasure we can derive. I will introduce you to Edmund Pickering without giving details of who you are. It will then be up to you to gain his trust. You will shadow him, and at times encourage him to go to the utmost in his depravity. On the second and last day of the orgy, when you can see he has completely satisfied his lust, you will invite him to accompany you into the Great Hall for a gluttonous banquet. I will be waiting there, where you'll escort him into a quiet side room that I'll point out to you. It'll be there that you'll blackmail him by pretending that you're a writer with the well-known 'Gentleman's Magazine' and a colleague of the devout Anglican and moralist, Dr Samuel Johnson, who regularly writes articles of current interest for the magazine. You will trick Pickering into believing that you're working undercover for the magazine, to investigate the secret world of immorality amongst the hierarchy and those in high positions. Sexual deviancy and hedonistic pleasures are what you have uncovered, and you are going to expose Edmund Pickering as a depraved and nefarious partaker in these sinful practices. Pickering will fall for the ruse and it will be then that you blackmail him."

"I see," said Ebenezer, "I'll use the scandal of exposing him as a way of forcing him not to offer Huckle and Mordechai a chance of life by revealing the names of their cohorts."

"Exactly," affirmed the Squire. "You'll insist he sentences them to hang the following day of the trial, so they have little chance of naming us."

"So, the trial will take place in seven days?" said Ebenezer. "Let's just hope Pickering agrees to my demands and silences them once and for all. I have no feelings for them, I only used them as part of my plans to make my fortune. I'm sure you understand that, Squire."

Squire Maddock nodded, glad he'd found an ally in this profligate priest. "Just remember, Ebenezer, that you'll be playing the part of a writer. So, I suggest you find out as much as you can about 'The Gentleman's Magazine', and of course the great literary critic and essayist, Dr Samuel Johnson."

Ebenezer smiled inwardly, grateful for Squire Maddock's scheme that would keep him safe from the hangman and allow him to pursue his ultimate plan of the assassination of King George III and the rich purse it would bring. He would look forward to his part in the scam ahead.

Sitting back, he raised his glass. "Good health to you, Squire, and may the Good Lord bless your plan." Tilting his head back with a grin, he swallowed his large measure of brandy in one gratifying swig.

* * *

Luc Skorniere hastened along the wharf of the Barbican, his eyes searching for a sign of Raymond's sloop. Early evening on the waterfront saw numerous vessels at their moorings. He was sure Raymond had returned the previous night and if so, he would be in possession of a reply from his chief, Charles Gravier, accepting or rejecting Ebenezer's proposal. The sloop was there, moored in its usual place, inconspicuous amongst a variety of other vessels bobbing up and down on a gentle swell. He made his way up the rough gang plank, slipping slightly on some wet seaweed that had somehow found its way up onto the rotting passageway. The sound of silver coins jingling in a leather purse in Luc's greatcoat warned him to be careful of his footing, but on looking around, there was no sign of anyone following or lurking in the shadows. Luc descended the slippery ladder that led to the hold and the dingy quarters where he would find Raymond. A soft light glowed from a top window in the door of the hold. With a gentle knock, he listened for voices inside. Everything was quiet and still.

He knocked again louder this time, gently calling out for Raymond. The soothing sound of water lapping against the sides of the sloop was the only sound echoing around the vessel. He called out again, "Raymond, open up. It is I, Luc Skorniere." He tried the handle on the door, turning it easily until the door opened and he stepped in. A single candle encased in a holder glowed from the top of a rickety table at the side of the hold. "Raymond, where are you? Wake up." Silence enveloped the cabin as Luc cast his eyes around the dirty hold. An old wooden table in the centre of the room showed off a row of empty stained wine jugs standing amongst crusts of stale bread and filthy unwashed plates. An overwhelming stench of stale fish, sweat and mouldy tobacco filled the area, causing Luc to cover his nose with his hand as he called out Raymond's name once more. "Raymond, I'm here. It's me, Luc Skorniere."

No reply in the enveloping silence meant Raymond and his crew had already left the ship. Luc guessed they had gone to a seedy inn somewhere on the Barbican. He could only wait for their return and hope Raymond was carrying the reply he so wanted from Charles Gravier. With the sweep of his arm, he knocked the wine jugs and mucky plates off the table, then pulling up a chair he sat and waited.

Raymond and his three crewmen staggered away from the inn they had been revelling in, pausing to urinate over the side of the wharf while hawking up wads of phlegm which they laughingly levied into the ripples of water below them.

Guffawing drunkenly, they lurched off towards their sloop, halting at the gangplank to leer and gesticulate at two passing whores.

When the two prostitutes retorted with a volley of crude and filthy language, the four Frenchmen cheered and clapped encouragingly as one of the whores raised her skirts and lewdly gyrated her naked womanhood in front of them. With whistles and shouts, Raymond and his crew stumbled up the gangplank, holding on to each other amidst their bellyaching laughter. Luc heard the noise of the returning Frenchmen and prepared himself for the surprise they would get when they found him waiting in their quarters.

Raymond was first to enter, blustering through the door without realising the cabin door was unlocked.

The sight of Luc sitting at the table and staring at him through the dim light of the candle sobered him in an instant.

"*Mon dieu*, is that you, Monsieur Luc, how did you get in here?" he slurred.

"The hold door was unlocked, Raymond, and I just walked straight in. You should be more careful when leaving your boat. I dare say, you may have some valuable items kept here, like a letter for me from Jean de Claire in Brest?"

Raymond smiled, nodding towards Luc.

"That I have, Monsieur. We returned from Brest on the tide early this morning. Jean de Claire presented me with a letter for you when he found us in a quayside tavern before we sailed. He told me it was of the utmost importance, and for your eyes only. I have it here, monsieur, but the sound of my silver tinkling in its purse will remind me of where I have put it."

Luc frowned and taking out the leather purse of silver coins from the inside pocket of his greatcoat, he slammed it on the wooden table.

"The letter first, Raymond."

Raymond sidled over to his berth, and opening a heavy chest, drew out a wax-sealed paper envelope. Turning back to where Luc sat watching him, he slowly handed it to him.

"Thank you, you have done well, Raymond," said Luc getting up from the table and depositing the envelope into his greatcoat pocket.

"*Merci*, monsieur," replied Raymond, shaking the leather purse against his ear. "Until next time, eh?"

"*Absolument*, Raymond," replied Luc. "I shall come to you."

Raymond watched Luc push past his three crewmen and open the hold door. With a glance back at his courier, Luc nodded and with a touch to his forehead, disappeared out of the door and up the ladder to the deck. Raymond pulled the strings of the leather purse, tipping its contents onto the table.

"*Au revoir*, monsieur," he murmured, staring at the silver coins before him.

Luc hurried along the wharf in the direction of the Cat and Fiddle Inn. He would settle in his usual quiet booth at the far end of the inn, and in the glow of a table candle, he'd go through Charles Gravier's reply, hoping it would affirm what he'd been waiting to hear. That the present King of England had only a limited time left to live, and that France would be preparing to finish England's command of the seas once and for all.

Chapter 20

It was not long after Squire Maddock had left Ebenezer's house that a gentle knocking was heard on the front door. With an irritable curse at another interruption, Ebenezer made his way towards the door, expecting to find the Squire back again with some added extras to his plan. Instead, he was surprised to see an extremely well-dressed gentleman standing in his porch with an elegant two-horse-drawn carriage waiting outside the gate at the bottom of the garden. The driver of the carriage, sporting a tricorn hat and black greatcoat, sat erect in his seat, holding the reins of the two placid horses.

"Reverend Dunn?" the gentleman asked.

"Yes, that would be me," replied Ebenezer. "And to whom am I addressing?"

"My name is John Parker of Saltram House in Plymouth. I am the Member of Parliament for Devon and if I am not disturbing you too much, I'd be grateful for you to listen as to why I'm here."

Ebenezer's expression changed immediately and in a grovelling tone, he invited John Parker into his parlour.

"A sherry or a brandy, sir?" said Ebenezer, indicating a seat on one of his two sofas.

"Thank you, Reverend. A sherry would be most welcome," replied John.

"And to what do I owe the honour of your visit, sir?" asked Ebenezer feeling rather puzzled.

"I'll come straight to the point, Reverend," said John sipping at his sherry. "I believe there's a smuggling ring established in this village and as your Member of Parliament, I feel it my duty to investigate. I have been informed that there's a strong possibility smuggling is being organised from this village and certain members of the village are active in its operation. I have written to my good friend Captain Philemon Pownoll, who is away with the navy, informing him. His good lady wife, Mistress Jane, is also very much aware of this. You are probably aware that two men from the village have recently been arrested on a charge of smuggling. One of them was the head herdsman at Sharpham Estate, and the other the stable lad there. The stable lad, by the name of Watt Huckle, was caught with smuggled items attached to his horse as he tried to escape the Revenue near the Churston Manor residence of Sir Francis Buller. The two of them are now in custody in Plymouth Gaol awaiting trial at the forthcoming assizes next week. They both refuse to name their cohorts, but I am certain that there were others involved and likely from here in the village of Ashprington."

Ebenezer could feel the blood rush from his face as he listened in horror. John paused to take another sip of sherry, not taking his eyes off the minister.

"As acting rector of this parish, Reverend, I've come to you first, as you may be able to help in suggesting who may be tied up with this practice and if there are any villagers you would possibly suspect. You know many of the church-goers here who may have given you suspicions of being involved in smuggling. I need not remind you, Reverend, that the authorities treat smuggling as a most serious offence. On many occasions, stiff sentences have led to the smugglers involved being hanged on Plymouth Hoe. As your Member of Parliament, I ask for your cooperation in uncovering this smuggling ring and suggestions of who may be profiting from it."

Ebenezer's mind was working fast. He would have to show willing to this parliamentary gentleman who expected his full support, but how could he deflect his interest away from Ashprington.

"Another sherry, sir?" said Ebenezer, hoping for a little extended time to think.

"You're most kind, Reverend," replied John handing him his glass.

Ebenezer took his time pouring the sherry, racking his brains for a justification to veer John Parker's attention away from this village. As he put the decanter back on the sideboard, his eye caught sight of a full bottle of French cognac. In an instant, he had his answer and with a smile returned to where John Parker was seated.

"I'm most surprised to hear of these terrible accusations against our village, sir," said Ebenezer solemnly. "I appreciate your concern and your dedication in trying to find out who's responsible. I will offer you all my help and be at your command, but I can honestly say that I have no reason to suspect or believe there's any smuggling going on here in the village of Ashprington. Yes, I have heard of the arrest of the two miscreants you mentioned. They are unknown to me, as they have never set foot near the church. But I have heard rumour, in and around the village and those who work the river, that these two felons were connected to a smuggler who uses the River Dart to transport his illegal merchandise. I'm also going to tell you that this sinner and smuggling racketeer helped to organise the smuggling heist on Elberry Cove a few weeks ago. He has nothing to do with our village, and I can swear upon our holy church that there is no smuggling ring here. You are looking in the wrong place, sir. Turn your attention to the village of Dittisham on the River Dart, there you will find your smuggling ring led by this arch villain. Obadiah Tucker is the man you want, sir."

"Well, I thank you most graciously, Reverend," said John smiling at Ebenezer. "My next step will be to catch this scoundrel in the act of bringing back his contraband. I'd be most grateful if you'd assist us in our planning, Reverend."

"I'll assist you readily, sir," said Ebenezer, thinking rapidly, "but on one condition. That my name and the name of our village be left out of all communication you may have in apprehending this sinful man. In helping you, I need your assurance we will remain anonymous. I think I will be able to gather intelligence for you that'll help you make your arrest soon. There are eyes and ears in this village that will confess to me knowledge of his whereabouts and movements."

"Very well, Reverend, anonymous you will be," said John getting up from his seat. "I'll give you two days to try to furnish me with the information that will enable us to catch him and his cohorts. I will send word to you of where we can meet. Maybe it would be best if I don't come here to your house. Perhaps you can come to Saltram, I will send a carriage for you that morning. It won't be a Sunday, so you'll be free from your pastoring."

At the front door, Ebenezer watched him alight his carriage, and a flick of the reins from his coachman saw the Member of Parliament for Devon disappear down the cobblestone hill. Exhausted, Ebenezer returned to his parlour, wondering how he would find information about Obadiah Tucker's movements. Again, the sight of the cognac bottle gave him his answer.

"Of course," he cried out, "Stephen, he'll know."

Pouring himself a large one from the bottle that gave him the inspiration to lie about Obadiah Tucker, he chuckled at the thought of the oaf swinging from the gallows on Plymouth Hoe.

"Revenge is sweet," he said laughing, "and you'll burn in hell, Obadiah Tucker, for what you did to me!"

A serious look suddenly spread over his face as he realised what was ahead of him that week.

Only two days from now, he thought, *before John Parker sends his coach for me. Three days before Squire Maddock's soirée takes place, and after all that, a Sunday morning service when I return from Darton Hall. I'll be drained.*

Staring at the measure of cognac in his glass, he sneered contemptibly, then raising the glass high above his head, he hollered loudly, "To you and your filthy black soul, Obadiah Tucker. You'll see the gates of hell opening before your very eyes as you choke your last breath on the gallows, and I'll be there to watch you dance."

* * *

Barold looked up from staring into his cider mug as the door to the Ashprington Inn opened.

"Well, well, look what's just walked in," he said, nudging Stephen next to him.

Ebenezer sauntered over to their table, pleased to see Stephen smiling up at him.

"Mug of cider for me, Lucy," he called out, "and another for my two friends here."

"'Aint seen you for a while, Reverend," said Barold, draining his cider. "Been holidayin'?"

"Very funny, Barold," said Ebenezer. "No, I've been busy with the church."

"Nice seein' you, Reverend," said Stephen. "Me and Barold just been talkin' about poor Mordechai. Us heard he be down in Plymouth Gaol along with Watt."

"Yes, I have also heard that news," said Ebenezer.

"Problim is," said Barold, "if they tells they bastards down there about us, then us'll be for it. Won't take 'em long to come lookin for us."

"That won't happen," said Ebenezer. "Neither Watt nor Mordechai will name us, of that I'm sure."

"Bliddy hell, Reverend, if that there judge sentences them to hang, then us'll have to go down Plymouth Hoe and see them orf," said Stephen, watching Lucy bringing their cider.

"Ar, that'd be right and fittin'," said Barold, "us'll all go down in Elijah's wagon."

Lucy placed their cider in front of the three of them as Elijah joined them at the table looking tired and worn from worry. With a long face she walked away, glaring at Rufus Mudd who dared tell her to get a move on and bring him more cider. The atmosphere in the inn was gloomy, no laughter and only a slight hint of conversation. Customers sat at their tables sombre and muted, their thoughts centred on the popular characters of Mordechai and the young stable lad whom they'd very likely never see again.

"Stephen," said Ebenezer in a hushed tone, "I had a visit from the Squire's valet the other day and he informed me that the Squire's interested in acquiring some more merchandise from your Uncle Obadiah. Would you know if he's planning another fishing trip with your cousins off the French coast fairly soon?"

Elijah, hearing Ebenezer's question, bent forward across the table.

"If you'm be planning another trip down to Obadiah's, you'm can count me out," he said, staring at Ebenezer and Stephen.

"Oi'll be in," said Barold, "don't you take no notice of him. He has had it up to his neck from Lucy. She just doen want him involved no more. Frightened he will get caught like Watt and Mordechai and end up on gallows. Ah!"

"We're not planning anything yet, Barold. Squire would just like to know if there'll be a prospect of some merchandise coming our way soon."

"Well," said Stephen, lowering his head and dropping the tone of his voice, "oi was only down seein' me cousins yesterday. Had a really good day with them down Dit'sum. Uncle Obadiah was getting his boat ready for a fishin' trip. He told us theym'd be bringing back a load of merchandise, like we had for the Squire when us got away from them Revenue fuckers on the river few weeks back."

"When will they be setting off?" asked Ebenezer, trying not to sound too keen for a quick answer from Stephen.

"Depends on weather," replied Stephen. "Uncle reckons it be fair to sail end of this week. They'll be away a good ten days before us'll see them back. Too late to tell him Squire will have his supply, but us can just row down there like last time and as long as us has silver, then he will let us have whatever what he has got."

"So, Stephen," said Ebenezer, not showing his elation at uncovering what John Parker wanted to know, "are you sure they'll set sail then? If you're sure, then I can inform the Squire."

"Oh yeah, us's sure enough. When Uncle Obadiah starts his twitchin', then us knows he can't wait to git away. They'll definitely be sailing at end of this week, and you'm can tell Squire they'm definitely be returning loaded with merchandise after ten days."

"I certainly will, Stephen," said Ebenezer, picking up his mug of cider with a smile. "You can be sure I will."

Chapter 21

Charles Gravier looked out of a window in his office at the scores of gardeners tending the immaculate symmetrical lawns of the Sun King's Palace of Versailles. Over the past week, he had deliberated day and night on the proposal his top spy, Luc Skorniere, had sent him via his messenger from Brest. He'd been tempted to discuss it with members of the King's cabinet and even King Louis XVI himself, but he knew there'd be such a divided opinion that he'd decided not to consult with any of them and had come to a final decision himself. On the one hand, if all were successful, then he'd be hailed a hero of France but on the other hand, should it be a disaster, then he'd deny all knowledge of the plan, claiming the attempt on the King of England's life was but a rogue attempt by a gang of fanatics. He had burnt the coded letter from his agent, leaving no trace of its top-secret content. Charles' messenger, Jean de Claire, had no knowledge of its details or what the confidential reply consisted of. That reply should reach the master spy in Plymouth within the week.

Charles Gravier was a strong patriot of his country and an ardent defender of France's system of absolute monarchy. Unrest with this system was beginning to raise its head across France and any small uprising or demonstration was ruthlessly put down, its perpetrators dragged out and executed as examples to those with rebellion in their minds.

Revolution was coming, and Charles knew that something had to be done to deflect the growing discontent across the country. King Louis and many of his ministers were blind to this fact, dismissing news of the starving masses and the unrest it was bringing as lies spread by France's greatest enemy, England. If France could bring about a climactic international occurrence, raising its standing in the world above that of England's, then revolution within its borders would be squashed and replaced by zealous feelings of nationalism. This reasoning had prompted him to make his decision and without consulting the King, Charles had coded a top-secret reply, instructing Jean de Claire to make certain it was safely delivered into the hands of Gravier's master spy in Plymouth without fail.

* * *

The light from the candle on the table in front of the booth where Luc sat filling his long-stem pipe, flickered dimly in the shadows of the far corner of the Cat and Fiddle Inn. He had ordered a mug of ale from Nancy as he'd entered the inn and was now waiting for her to bring it to his table. He would act as though he'd nothing better to do than sit and drink ale, letting her know he wanted to be alone and not disturbed. A few extra coins in her flabby palm would guarantee him the privacy he needed to study and digest the reply, and then think carefully of his next movements. He lulled the impatience that was gnawing at him to open the letter in the pocket of his greatcoat; there would be time enough. He had learned through countless secret operations to control his impulses and remain calm and patient, even though his nerves itched with temerity. Nancy slapped his mug of ale onto the table, holding out her hand for payment.

"On yer own, lover?" she asked, casting her tongue provocatively over her ruby red lips.

"Yes, I am, Nancy," said Luc smiling up at her. "And I'd appreciate to be left alone here in the booth. I'm sure you'd be able to see to that, my dear," he added, producing a silver coin with a wink.

"I think that can be guaranteed, lover," she replied, depositing the coin in some deep recess of her grubby gown. "If you'm feel like a little fancy, just call me over, lover. You'm know it'll only be a shillin'!"

"No chance of that, filthy slut," he mumbled, watching her walk away swaying her ample hips.

He lit his pipe with a taper, fired by the flickering flame of the candle in front of him. Sitting back, he drew on the pipe, sucking the smoke deep down then exhaling a richly scented cloud that hovered around him like some eerie spectral vapour. Taking a long draught of ale, he licked his lips contentedly and took the letter out from his greatcoat pocket, gently slicing open the top of the envelope with his pocketknife. Holding the letter in two hands, he leaned forward over the table allowing the full light from the candle to shine over the paper. As he had expected, the letter was in code and calling Nancy over, politely asked her to bring him a quill and ink. When this was done, he deposited a few coins into her

157

hand for her trouble then sliced open the sides of the envelope. Spreading them as an open sheet next to the coded letter, he began to decipher. Luc worked steadily, peering at Charles Gravier's coded words in the dim light of the candle. Several times he would stop and look up to see if he were being watched or if any-one was approaching his table, but the inn was quiet, and Nancy had been paid to assure him of his privacy.

Finally, with both sides of the envelope covered in writing, he folded the original and tucked it into the pocket of his greatcoat, calling out to Nancy to take away the quill and ink and replenish his mug of ale. He gulped at the ale, taking long draughts to satisfy his thirst, then with a quiet belch, opened the sides of the envelope and began to read the decoded instructions thoroughly.

Cher Luc,

After great deliberation, I myself have decided that France can only benefit from the assassination of King George III of England. If successful, Great Britain will be thrown into turmoil, so affecting their plans for a quick end to their war with the American rebels in their colonies. This undoubtedly will be a great opportunity for France to regain its international power by declaring war on Great Britain and rallying to the cause of the American rebels. With the defeat of Great Britain in the American colonies and chaos and confusion on the streets of England, France will then strike at their heart with an invasion of the discorded isle.

Inform your contact that I personally agree and accept his conditions for the assassination of the English King. The amount of five hundred pounds will be paid to him in two instalments. Half immediately after the assassination and the other half when he arrives here in France. I will of course arrange suitable and pleasant accommodation for him within the area of Versailles. The arrangements and planning of this assassination will be entirely down to you and your contact. I have not informed any of King Louis' government or King Louis himself, regarding this operation. Should you fail, then I will deny any knowledge of this. You know what you yourself must do in the event of any failure. I trust you to destroy these coded instructions immediately after reading them. Keep me informed about your planning and when we can expect turmoil to flood the streets of Britain.

Charles Gravier, le comte de Vergennes.

Luc sat back in the booth, thinking seriously. "Well, Ebenezer," he said to himself, "you're going to be a rich man, but you're going to have to work for it and take major risks. Even though you will not hold the dagger that will kill the King, you most certainly will be present wherever it takes place. That I surely promise."

Taking the original coded letter from his greatcoat pocket, he held the top of it into the flame of the candle until it caught fire, and as the flames raced down to its ends, he dropped it onto the stone floor beneath him, crushing the black carbon remains under his booted foot. The same he did with the deciphered words on the opened envelope, watching as the flames licked their way down to its end before being crushed into nothingness on the inn's cold stone floor.

Thinking back to his meeting with Ebenezer, he remembered Ebenezer's claim of King George making a Proclamation of Rebellion to Parliament on August 23rd.

Couldn't be much longer after that when he'll address his troops, he thought. *Ebenezer's sure he knows when and where he'll address them. Could be any port on the south coast. And yes, he will be staying somewhere important the night before his address to the troops. This is where the assassination will take place. I have my spies working in several high-class mansions along the south coast. As soon as Ebenezer names the place of where and when the King will stay, then I will send word to my agent. We have not much time and it's going to take a great deal of planning. Next step is to send word to Ebenezer that I need to see him tomorrow. Once I know the date and place of the King's nightover, we'll make our plans to create the greatest turmoil this country has ever known.*

Draining the last drop of ale from his mug, he stood up from the booth and making his way towards the front door of the inn, he looked back to where Nancy stood watching him. With a grin and a gesture of farewell, he opened the door and was gone.

Somethin' strange about him, thought Nancy. *Oi knows he has a room above this inn. Us'll ask along the wharf if anyone knows more about him. Might even get me shillin' orf him sometime, ha. Us'll see.*

Luc walked a little way along the Barbican, turning into to a narrow side alley that led up between rows of dilapidated slum terraces. Half-way up, he stopped outside an open door where raucous laughter spilled out onto the alley where he stood. A rotting wooden sign hanging above the door humbly advertised the hovel as 'The Hole in the Wall Inn'.

Entering, he looked around the tiny crowded bar. A handful of filthy looking slum-dwellers lolled up against a damp stone wall, laughing and drinking rough cider from stone mugs. A toothless gin-ridden hag with her legs wide open, sat grinning on a three-legged stool, enticing the men around her to stroke her vagina for the payment of half a penny.

Luc's eye caught sight of a puny misfit, deep in conversation with a heavily-bearded-looking villain who looked as though he would be more at home in one of England's lunatic asylums. As Luc caught the misfit's eye, he indicated to him to step outside into the alleyway. He had an urgent message for him to take and darkness would soon be descending over the rough track that led across the fields to Ashprington.

"Take this note to the rector's house in Ashprington, like you did before," said Luc, covering his nose and standing well away from the reeking youth. "Make sure you pin it firmly to his door. Give three loud knocks and then leave quietly. A horse will be waiting for you in ten minutes, behind the Cat and Fiddle Inn. The ten minutes will start when I leave you. Take this shilling and there will be another one waiting for you when you return. Don't look for me, I'll find you here."

Luc hurried away, leaving the youth staring after him. He hastened back to the rear of the Cat and Fiddle Inn and into the stables, directing the stable lad to saddle a horse forthwith with instructions to present it to a ragged-looking youth who'd be turning up for it shortly. Depositing a purse of coins into the stable lad's hand, he left and sprinted across the courtyard, hiding behind a stone wall where he would have a clear view of the entrance to the stable. It was not long before the bedraggled youth appeared, making his way up the alleyway. He was met by the stable lad leading the saddled horse out of the stable. Luc watched the youth spring into the saddle, then turning the horse around, he sped out of the stable courtyard and out onto the cobblestones of the Barbican, where he raced away towards the track that would take him across country fields to the village of Ashprington and Ebenezer's house.

Chapter 22

Ebenezer sat in his parlour, his mind racing around his commitments for the week. His visit to Saltram House was only two days away, followed by the blackmailing of Judge Pickering the day after. He sniggered to himself at the thought of the information he would give to John Parker that would see the end to Obadiah Tucker and his two nasty sons. His mind jumped to the grand soirée at Darton Hall in three days' time and how he was going to make his way up there when three resounding knocks on his front door made him jolt up with alarm. Wondering who it could be, he smoothed down his tie-wig and hurried to open his front door. The porch was empty and looking around in the dimpsy light of the approaching evening, he found no sign of anyone.

Strange, he thought, *there were definitely three knocks on the door, probably those rough urchins from one of the poor houses behind Rufus Mudd's smithy playing, silly beggers.*

Turning to go back inside, he shivered as a cold gust of wind blew back his door, revealing a note pinned to the middle. Tearing the note from the door, he hastened back to his parlour, the note clasped in his hand. Opening it, he read:

Ebenezer,

The time has come. I need to see you most urgently regarding the reply I have received from France. Tomorrow midday, at the same inn as before.

Luc.

Wide-eyed with what was written in the note, he staggered over to his sideboard and trembling, poured himself a large cognac. *"The time has come,"* he read again from the note.

"It's on," he shouted with glee. "I'm going to be rich. They have accepted my demands. Oh yes, I will be there at the Cat and Fiddle tomorrow, and then afterwards a celebration with that brazen whore Nancy and for only a shilling! Ha, ha!"

* * *

In the far corner of the Cat and Fiddle Inn, Luc sat waiting for the hour of midday. Nancy wandered over, curious as to why he was sitting alone and looking a little anxious.

"You'm be waitin for someone, lover?" she asked, protruding her enormous breasts.

"Yes, I am, Nancy," replied Luc. "The gentlemen who was here a few days ago. I believe you took his shilling!"

"Ha, him," she said, "an odd gentlemin, to say the least. Wanted more from me than just a shillin's worth. Bit twisted if not perverted oi'd say, didn't take him long before he was spent !"

"Well," said Luc, "when he arrives, show him round here please. There will be a few coins for you if you keep this area quiet and free from customers. Thank you, Nancy."

Nancy smiled, sensing some extra earnings coming her way; if the strange looking gentleman about to arrive fancied anything extra, then she would oblige, but for more than a shilling.

"He be here, lover," she said looking towards the door of the inn.

Ebenezer strolled up to where Luc was sitting, smiling lecherously at Nancy, who stood thrusting out her huge breasts and pouting lewdly towards him.

"Two mugs of ale, Nancy," demanded Luc, snapping at the inn's whore. "Please sit, Ebenezer, we've a lot to discuss."

Taking his time, Luc lit his pipe, pondering at the look of expectation on Ebenezer.

"I've received a reply from my chief in France," he said dropping his voice. "Before I tell you his answer, I assume you're still willing to assist France in the assassination of the English King?"

Ebenezer looked at Luc steadily. "I most certainly am, Luc, as long as there's agreement on my price of five hundred pounds and a safe haven for me in France."

"Very well," replied Luc, "I'll begin by telling you that my principal has agreed to your proposal."

Ebenezer's eyes lit up with joy. "And my fee?" he asked greedily.

Luc nodded. "Your fee has been agreed."

Ebenezer could not help letting out a whoop of elation, his face a picture of the avarice that lay deep within him.

"But," said Luc, supressing a smile, "your fee will be paid to you in two separate instalments."

Ebenezer's face fell, a concerned look over-riding his look of joyous greed.

"How do you mean, two separate instalments?" he asked.

"The first instalment of two hundred and fifty pounds will be paid to you immediately after the assassination, if it is successful that is. The second instalment will be paid when you have been re-located to France. But there is another condition and that is, you will be present at the time and at the location when King George is assassinated."

"But that wasn't our agreement," said Ebenezer, looking shocked. "My price was to inform you only of the place and of the time where the King would be staying before addressing his troops. I also said that I'd tell you of the place where he'll make his address."

"Yes, Ebenezer," replied Luc, "but you promised explicitly that you would also assist in the assassination and give us all your help. We have now agreed on the amount to be paid to you, but we also hold you to your pledge. You cannot renege on this assurance. It was your promise of giving us your complete assistance that clinched this deal."

Luc pushed his face forward towards Ebenezer's, his eyes boring into the minister's. "Should you not fall in with our demands, Ebenezer, then you can expect a visit one night from our very own assassin. I wouldn't want you to end your life so quickly and miss out on the luxury chateau we're planning for you near Versailles, not to mention the vast amount of money we're going to pay you."

Ebenezer stared at Luc open-mouthed, his lower lip starting to tremble as he realised the cards were now stacked in Luc's hand. The threat of a visit from their assassin should he not comply, was too terrorising to think of. He had no alternative but to go along with Luc's demands and then insist on his help in escaping to France. The offer of luxury accommodation and the fortune that would go with it was too tempting to ignore.

"Very well, Luc," said Ebenezer, "where shall we begin?"

"I want to know where and when the King has arranged to stay on the eve of addressing his troops, and then where his address will take place."

Ebenezer stared at Luc, thinking crucially. "Before I tell you, I want your guarantee of a quick and safe passage for me out of England after the King has been assassinated, the first instalment of my money paid to me there and then."

"Absolutely, Ebenezer," said Luc, "as soon as you tell me what I want to know, then I'll tell you how we'll get you out of England."

Ebenezer nodded. "The King has arranged to stay at Saltram House in Plymouth on the night of 31st August, the eve before he gives his address to his troops after a big parade on Plymouth Hoe. Saltram House is the home of John Parker, the Member of Parliament for Devon. Now, what are your plans for my escape?"

Luc smiled with satisfaction, now they could begin the planning. *Saltram House*, he thought, *it's ideal!*

Ebenezer shuffled on his seat as Luc took a taper to the flickering candle, slowly re-lighting his pipe.

"I will arrange for you to be taken out of England immediately after the assassination," he said, drawing deeply on the pipe. "A sloop moored here on the Barbican will sail directly after you've boarded. The crew are loyal patriots of France and work for me. I have been told the tide will be in our favour, so a quick departure is guaranteed. We will have to move quickly as it won't take the authorities long to seal off all exits into and out of Plymouth. Your first instalment of two hundred and fifty pounds will be waiting for you on board the sloop. We will sail to the port of Brest in Bretagne where one of our agents will escort us to Versailles. There you'll be taken to your new residence and paid the second instalment of your money."

Ebenezer sat back, pleased with what he had heard. Providing he could be one of the first away, he was happy, but there would be an element of danger.

"Who'll escort me from Saltram House to the Barbican where the sloop will be moored, it's a long way on foot?" he asked.

"Don't concern yourself with that now," replied Luc. "If it is not me, then I'll arrange for someone to be with you. I'll definitely be accompanying you on the sloop to Brest."

Two mugs of ale were suddenly slammed down on the wooden table of the booth, a grinning Nancy holding out her hand for payment. Luc dropped a few coins into her hand and as she picked up the two empty mugs, she glanced at Ebenezer, moving her tongue lewdly over her lips.

"Only a shillin', lover," she mouthed.

Ebenezer watched the whore swagger away, looking back over her shoulder and mouthing what was now clearly understood. He shivered with the excitement of what was yet to come with this immodest and shameless harlot. "Only a shilling," he said to himself and grinned.

"We'll meet again, Ebenezer," said Luc. "I'll send word. Look out for a note attached to your door, it will tell you where and when. Of course, should there be any other worthwhile news of troop build-ups, then let my agent in your village know by signalling him. You will always be rewarded for useful information. I've a great deal of planning to do now, so until we meet again, I'll bid you farewell."

Ebenezer watched Luc make his way out of the inn. Tomorrow he would have to be up early as John Parker's coachman would be collecting him for his visit to Saltram House. "But that's tomorrow," he mumbled, "now I'm ready for that dirty slut. Nancy," he yelled, "get your tits out and your fat backside over here now. I've got a shilling in my hand."

* * *

Nancy grinned as she watched Ebenezer leave the inn. He had not taken long with her and she'd managed to force some extra coins from him for taking him in her mouth. She swilled her mouth out from a half-filled mug of ale left on the bar, then with a grubby shawl wrapped around her shoulders, she made her way out onto the cobblestone street. Standing back from the inn's door, she looked up at the cockled glass windows that pouted out over the street. Which one was Luc's? Candlelight flickered dimly from an end window and as all the other windows were veiled in darkness, she guessed the end window had to be Luc's. She would find out.

At the far end of the street outside the Duke of York Inn, an old wooden bench looked over part of the wharf where various fishing vessels were moored. Local whores paraded around this seat selling their favours to the drunken sailors and fishermen leaving the inn. Nancy knew that nothing escaped the whores' attention around this area, and picking up her skirts, she hurried along in its direction.

As she approached, the raucous laughter of two whores struggling to hold up a drunken sailor against an outer wall of the inn filled the area. Nancy watched a bushy-haired whore push her hand down the inside front of the sailor's breeches, while the other whore attempted to loosen his belt. Unable to stand upright, the sailor slid drunkenly down the side of the wall, grabbing onto the whore whose hand was firmly buried deep inside the crotch area of his tight-fitting pants.

Stuck together, they rolled over and over on the damp cobblestones, the sailor screaming in agony as the harlot tried in vain to yank her hand from the inside of his breeches. The shrieks of laughter from the two whores and the agonised screams from the unfortunate sailor had brought a crowd of drinkers from the inn to stand around, guffawing and whooping at the comical scene taking place. The arrival of a brutish-looking giant of a man, the inn's landlord, quickly quelled the boisterous noise outside the inn. He grabbed the whore on the ground by her thick hair, yanking her hand out of the sailor's pants, then as she struggled to her feet, he gave her a backhander which sent her sprawling over the luckless sailor. Helping her partner to her feet, the two whores tumbled onto the wooden seat, bellyaching with laughter as the sailor pulled himself up. With an agonising whimper, he glowered at the two harlots and with his hand between his legs, staggered unsteadily away, looking over his shoulder while slurring insults and threats of retribution.

Grinning at the two whores, Nancy approached them.

"Well, well, it be Nancy from the Cat," said the one who had tried to loosen the sailor's belt. "'Aint seen you for a while. How's business in the inn?"

"Nuthin's changed, Rose, nor ever will."

"You'm still chargin' a shillin', Nance?" asked the one with the thick bushy hair.

"Ar, that oi be, Daisy," answered Nancy. "Bit more regular than bein' out here on the streets. How's you'm doin'?"

"Had us a party of them Frenchies last night, from one of them fishin' boats out over there by the wharf. Me and Rose did four of 'em, two each at the same time. One of them had an eye patch and was rough as hell on Rose. Bliddy sore after. Anyways, what you'm doin' over 'ere, changin' patch?"

"Naw, Cat and Fiddle's like home to me now," replied Nancy. "Gets me shillin's worth quite regular like. What oi wanted to ask you be about the gentlemin who's always in the Cat; he's got a room above the inn too. Sits in a booth at the back of the inn most of the time. Tall and handsome, always carries a leather paper case round with him."

"Oi sees him round this part quite regular," said Daisy. "Propositioned him once, last week in fact."

"Did you have him?" asked Nancy, feeling a twinge of jealousy.

Rose looked at Daisy curiously. "Ah, he just looked at me like I was a piece of shit and told me to bend over for one of they stray dogs that roams round the slaughter house on other side of Barbican."

"Cheeky bugger!" said Rose. "But us saw him couple of nights back. Didn' us, Daise?"

"Ar, we did, sure enough," said Daisy. "Me and Rose was doin' a bit of business down by where they fishin' boats is moored. Little clump of trees right in front of where they Frenchies 'ave their boat tied up. Well, us was given knee tremblers to our clients whom us sees quite regular like. With me back up against the tree, oi had a good view of the Frenchies' boat. Anyways, as me client was given me plenty, oi sees that gentlemin walk up the Frenchies' gang plank, slip on a bit of seaweed and then disappear down an open trap on the deck. Didn' see him come back up. After our clients done their vinegar, me and Rose hung around waitin' for some more business when along comes they four Frenchies drunk as skunks. When they'm started gesticulatin' at us and calling out, Rose lifts her skirt and shows them her muffer. Thought us'd do some business with them there and then but they buggered orf inside the boat. Me and Rose went up the Duke for some gin and much later we meet up again with them outside the inn. Bliddy hell, they shafted us good and proper but paid us well. The one with the eye patch who did Rose was called Raymond. Told her he would look for her again in the Duke."

"So, you never saw the gentlemin with the paper case come orf the boat?" asked Nancy.

"Naw, oi told you. After them Frenchies went inside the boat, me and Rose looked around for some more business but there was nuthin' about, so us went back up to the Duke. Never saw him again after that."

"Look, Nance, us's got to leave you," interrupted Rose, "there be some gentlemen strollin' along the wharf. Come on, Daise, business."

Rose and Daisy hurried away leaving Nancy to wonder why Luc had gone aboard the Frenchies' boat.

Mm, she thought, *interestin'. Wonder who he really is? And that strange lookin' acquaintance of his who can't keep it up for longer than oi can hold me breath, he's an odd one. Didn' taste nice either!*

Pulling her shawl up over her head, Nancy hurried back along the wharf. She thought of the clandestine meetings Luc often had in his regular corner booth. *Everyone what seems to meet him there*, she thought, *looks as though they'm reportin' somethin' important to him. Then they listen to 'im like he is givin' serious instructions to them. Who the bliddy hell is he?*

She thought it strange he had never groped her or lusted over her ample bosoms. She had given him enough opportunities of having her. And that nasty grovelling creep who was with him earlier, looking as though he had just won a fortune. He disgusted her with his weird sexual demands, and all for a shilling! "He be no better than a wild dog," she muttered, "lickin' and spittin' on me when he's aroused. Good job he spills it quick. Us'll charge him more next time, the disgusting little shit!"

As she approached the inn, she stopped to look up at the far window that had previously shown the light of a candle flickering within the room; there was nothing only darkness. The sudden noise of the door to the inn opening forced Nancy back into the shadows. Luc stood in the doorway peering up and down the street. She watched him walk away from the inn and then stop to look back over his shoulder as if to check no-one was following, then pulling his tricorn down firmly over his forehead, he hurried away, his leather paper case held firmly under his arm.

Us'll wait till he returns, she thought, *then follow him upstairs and find out which room has.*

Taking the shawl off her head, she pushed out her chest, and with a carefree smile, walked into the inn. She'd make sure the far corner booth was kept free, as she knew Luc would return there for his usual night cap, then as he left, she'd shadow him and find out if his room was the one where she'd seen a candle flickering behind the window.

Chapter 23

"There's something about him, John, that just doesn't seem right," said Sir Joshua, looking out of the grand parlour window that overlooked the front gardens and the majestic carriageway of Saltram House.

"I'm sorry, Joshua," replied John Parker, "but I'm convinced the Reverend Dunn is right about the smuggling ring in Dittisham, and of that scoundrel Obadiah Tucker. When the Reverend arrives, he will give me the information I've asked him to provide. We'll then know when Tucker and his cargo of smuggled goods will return and where on the river he'll offload them. I will arrange for the Revenue to be waiting down on the river to trap him. We'll force Tucker to give us the names of the smuggling barons he works with in this area of Devon, then after they've all been arrested, tried and hanged, I can report to the House that the illegal act of smuggling in this part of Devon has been firmly quashed."

"Well, I hope you're right, John," said Sir Joshua, sounding uncertain.

"I've asked you to attend this meeting, Joshua, as you're familiar with the smuggling case of Mordechai Brunt and the stable lad of Sharpham, Watt Huckle. Their trial is set to begin next Tuesday. We can inform the judge that we're investigating a new angle on the case, which will prove Obadiah Tucker to be the ringleader and mastermind of the smuggling heist at Elberry Cove; he may delay their trial until we can provide him with actual evidence. This should prove that Mordechai's statement was untrue, and he had been lying to protect Tucker and his gang. With the chief culprit sentenced to hang, Mordechai and Watt may get away with a lighter sentence of, say, transportation to the Indies. It's really all about convincing the judge that there's more to this case than the present facts show."

A gentle knock on the parlour room door saw John's footman Andrew enter the room. "Sir," he said softly looking at John, "a minister from the church in Ashprington has arrived by the name of Ebenezer Dunn."

169

"Thank you, show him in please, Andrew," replied John.

"Gentlemen, I am truly honoured to be here," said Ebenezer, smiling as he was shown into the room.

"It's a pleasure to have you here, Reverend Dunn. I believe you've met my good friend Sir Joshua Reynolds."

"I have indeed," replied Ebenezer, bowing courteously to both John and Sir Joshua. "We met on one of my pastoral visits to Sharpham Manor. I'm anxious about the spiritual care of Mistress Jane Pownoll while her good husband is away with the navy."

"Er hum!" uttered Sir Joshua, pretending to clear his throat.

"Now, please be seated, Reverend. Would tea or something a little stronger be to your taste?"

"Tea would be most gratefully accepted," replied Ebenezer, wringing his hands in a grovelling manner.

John looked up at Andrew, who was hovering near the door. "Bring us tea please, Andrew, thank you. And now, Reverend, I trust you have some important information for us. Sir Joshua is aware of the smuggling that has been going on but does not know of the scoundrel Obadiah Tucker or of his lair in Dittisham. So, I'd appreciate you telling us as much as you've been able to find out about him and his smuggling operations."

"Absolutely, sir," replied Ebenezer, putting on a serious and solemn look. "As I informed you, sir, when you visited me, Obadiah Tucker is the smuggler you are looking for. He operates from his base near the harbour of Dittisham on the River Dart and uses an old boathouse there to keep his smuggled goods."

"Excuse me, Reverend," interrupted Sir Joshua, "but how do you know of this?"

"From certain members of my parish, sir," replied Ebenezer. "After my visit from your good friend here, I made enquiries from certain individuals who work the River Dart and who, let us say, have had the misfortune of dealing with Obadiah Tucker in the past. Apart from the information I have told you, they also told me, in strictest confidence, that it was he who had masterminded the smuggling venture near Churston Manor not long ago. As I am their minister, gentlemen, they trust me explicitly and regularly confide in me. At this point I need to stress that there is absolutely no smuggling going on in our village of Ashprington. If there were, then I should most certainly know about it. The two miscreants from the Sharpham Estate, who are now in custody awaiting trial for assisting in the smuggling heist at Elberry Cove, are unknown to me. I've heard that they were known to Obadiah Tucker's two sons in a friendly manner, so I assume they were with them when the lad Huckle was caught."

A knock on the parlour door indicated tea had arrived.

"Ah, the tea!" said John. "Put the tray on the table over there, Andrew, we can serve ourselves."

The three of them watched as Andrew placed the tray of tea on the table and with a single nod towards John, he left the room gracefully.

"Please continue, Reverend, while I serve the tea," said John.

"Obadiah Tucker is a dangerous man, gentlemen. Two of my parishioners, who have their fishing boats moored next to Tucker's, were reluctant to provide me with the information I am now going to give you for fear of being physically harmed by Tucker, or even killed, should he find out what they've reported to me. It was one of Tucker's sons who told them, after consuming too much alcohol. You must appreciate, gentlemen, that I can't disclose their details."

"Yes of course, Reverend, we understand," said John, handing Ebenezer a cup of tea.

Ebenezer sipped at his tea and then placing the cup on a little side table next to him, continued, "Obadiah Tucker's son told them his father was preparing for a smuggling trip to the north coast of France under the guise of fishing those waters. He and his sons would be leaving at the end of this week and would return after ten days. They would be bringing back supplies of cognac, wine, fine lace and tea. He even offered my two parishioners the chance to purchase some of the merchandise. So, in about twelve days from now, Tucker will be returning with his fishing boat laden with contraband. He will return through the harbour of Dartmouth and then up the River Dart to his base in Dittisham, where he will unload his consignment. It'll be there where you can catch him."

"Where exactly is the old boathouse he uses?" asked Sir Joshua.

"That I'm not completely sure of," lied Ebenezer, wanting to tell them the precise location but careful not to rouse their suspicions. "If I'm not mistaken," he said slowly, putting on a questioning look, "they told me there was a small inlet at the side of Dittisham harbour as you approach it going downriver from Totnes. At the end of this inlet, there's a jetty that leads to his boathouse."

Ebenezer looked at the serious faces of John and Sir Joshua, hoping they had fallen for his lie. He felt quite pleased with his tall story and of the way he'd presented it. He could well start believing it himself!

"And that's all I've managed to find out, gentlemen."

"It's more than enough, Reverend," said John, turning to Sir Joshua and nodding his approval. "Now we have the place and the time of when and where he will be returning, we'll catch him red-handed. Thank you, Reverend. I am sure we'll be successful in catching the rascal. We will leave with a detachment of the Revenue when we can determine the right time of the tide. We will leave with plenty of time to conceal ourselves in our positions before Tucker returns. It'll be best for us to travel in a separate boat, leading the Revenue downriver until we approach the inlet you mentioned."

Ebenezer suddenly froze, nearly choking on the tea he was sipping. Looking at John, he stammered, "We...did you say we, sir?"

"I certainly did, Reverend," answered John, smiling with enthusiasm. "With you with us, we're not likely to miss the entrance to this inlet near Dittisham harbour. Seems like your parishioners have given you a good description of where it is, so I would prefer you to accompany us, Reverend, and assist in the navigation. You'll also be able to witness the taking of this blackguard and his crew."

Ebenezer felt the blood drain from his face; his hand holding the cup and saucer began to shake.

"Reverend, you seem to have come over rather strange," said Sir Joshua, jumping out of his chair and rushing over to rescue Ebenezer's cup of tea before it fell from his hand. "Are you alright, sir?"

"Yes, ye...I'm alright, thank you," he stuttered. "Must be a chill coming on me. Oh dear. I think I should return home immediately."

"Of course, Reverend," said John. "I'll arrange for Andrew to advise the coachman to take you straight back to Ashprington."

"Come, sir, we'll escort you out."

"You're most kind, gentlemen, my prayers and thanks are with you," said Ebenezer, feigning illness.

As they left the grand parlour, Ebenezer's eyes flashed around the area they were passing through. Would the King be cut down here, or in the suite of rooms the Parkers would provide for him? The grand staircase loomed into view as they neared the spacious reception foyer, an ascending line of exquisite paintings following the gleaming marble stairs upwards towards where Ebenezer assumed King George III would be accommodated.

Several liveried servants cruised past them, busy with their household duties. Ebenezer wondered which of them was Luc's spy and assassin. At the main doorway, Andrew stood waiting for the carriage to arrive and without looking over to where they stood, announced in a soft voice that it was approaching.

"I'll send word, Reverend," said John, "of when we'll spring the trap on Obadiah Tucker. We'll travel with a detachment of the Revenue from Totnes, it will be only a matter of days now before we catch the rascal."

Sir Joshua looked at Ebenezer nodding at John's words.

"Forgive me, but when we last met," said Ebenezer turning to John, "you promised me and our village anonymity. Why, may I ask, are you including me in the capturing of this sinful scoundrel?"

"I most certainly did, Reverend," replied John, "but as I said before, we will need you to pinpoint the exact location of Tucker's boathouse when we approach Dittisham. I assume you will need to speak to your two parishioners again to be sure of the precise spot where we can set our ambush. Please do not worry, Reverend, you will be well-hidden from Tucker's sight. The soldiers of the Revenue will make the arrest and as Member of Parliament for Devon, I will serve him and his sons with the arrest warrant. You and your village will not been named in any communication, nor will be in the execution of catching this villain."

"Thank you," said Ebenezer, not entirely convinced he would be an invisible onlooker. Shakily, he mounted the coach with a feeling of utter dread.

As the coachman flicked the reins and the coach rumbled out of the gates, he sat back, a dark frown deeply engraved on his features. The word 'we' kept echoing in his mind.

"Looks like the tables may have turned on me," he muttered. "There's no way I can get out of this one without disclosing it's all a fabrication. If by any chance Obadiah sees me and recognises me, God forbid, he will implicate me and then it will be all over, that is if he doesn't cut my throat first. I will have to make sure I'm completely out of sight when he's caught. Oh my God, what am I going to do should he see me?"

As the coach trundled along through the Devonshire countryside, he suddenly bolted upright. "Tomorrow," he yelled out, "the Squire's orgy, and I haven't practiced or researched anything about 'The Gentleman's Magazine' or Dr Samuel Johnson. Well, I will have to play it by ear and hope Edmund Pickering is stupid enough to believe me. As soon as this damn coach gets me home, I will have the rest of the day to think of something to convince him of whom I'm not."

As the coach lumbered up the hill towards his house, he was surprised to see a fine one-horse carriage parked a little way up from his entrance. After thanking the coachman for his comfortable ride, he made his way up his garden path to where a smiling Squire Maddock, standing next to a large brown box, stood waiting for him.

Chapter 24

"Squire, how delightful. Please come into my parlour," said Ebenezer, fumbling for his front door key with one eye on the mysterious box.

Squire Maddock gently put the box onto the parlour's floor, smiling at the look of curiosity on Ebenezer's face.

"A brandy, Squire?" asked Ebenezer, not bothering to wait for a reply and pouring the Squire a large one.

"Absolutely, Ebenezer," replied the Squire. "Now, I suppose you're wondering what's inside this box, eh?"

"Well, I am, actually," said Ebenezer, handing the Squire his brandy and looking curiously at the box.

"It's a toga, Ebenezer. A Roman toga."

"What on earth!" exclaimed Ebenezer.

"Before you start asking me all manner of questions, let me explain," said the Squire grinning at Ebenezer. "The toga is for you, to borrow, of course. I did not mention when we last met that I always have a historical theme for my soirées. I have come to let you know that the theme for tomorrow is Ancient Rome. Those attending have already been informed of the theme and will therefore arrive appropriately attired in costume. You are to be Cicero, so you will need to wear a toga. There are instructions in the box as to how to fold and wrap it round you. I suggest you start to practice when I've left."

"And you, Squire?" asked Ebenezer looking a little uneasy, "who will you be?"

"Gaius Julius Caesar," replied the Squire. "Although he wore a toga while debating in the senate, I've chosen to wear what he would have worn while on campaigns with the Roman Army, the attire of a Roman General."

"You mean the knee-length tunic, helmet and cuirass?" asked Ebenezer, stifling a giggle.

"Well, yes and no," said the Squire, sounding serious. "Of course I will not be wearing the helmet and cuirass, that won't be practical for the occasion. But a red knee-length tunic, high lace-up sandals, a belt and dagger and a red cloak, yes."

"Well, well," said Ebenezer chuckling, "I can't wait to see it!"

"Let's be serious now, Ebenezer," said the Squire, looking impatient. "Edmund Pickering's coming as Nero. He is rather rotund and decadent, so he'll fit the part. When we are all assembled in the Great Hall and I'm welcoming everyone, I'll introduce you as Cicero. We never use our real names on these occasions, only the names of the characters we are portraying, so remember to address the judge as Nero until you finally spring the trap on him. After you've taken him into the Great Hall for the banquet and you've diverted him into the private room that I'll indicate to you, then you can refer to him by his real name, so dropping the charade. You will use the name Septimus Sniff, and don't forget it. You are a writer specialising in the disclosure of immoral and secret organisations around the country and have already been commissioned by 'The Gentleman's Magazine' to write an article. You are undercover and have managed to slip into this private rendezvous of hedonists by deceiving me as to your real identity and purpose. The rest is up to you."

"Yes, I understand," replied Ebenezer, "but please tell me, Squire, who is Septimus Sniff?"

"Ah ha," said the Squire grinning, "a name of no concern or consequence, Ebenezer. A name engraved on stone, a headstone, in fact. While walking my hounds early this morning, they bolted into a cemetery after a rabbit. On chasing after them, I eventually found them devouring the unfortunate coney over a grave. A headstone planted at the top of the grave with the name Septimus Sniff engraved on it, stared sadly down at the two dogs as they tore the rabbit apart. The name has stuck in my mind ever since. A name that can't be traced to the living."

"Very well, Squire. Septimus Sniff, I shall be," said Ebenezer.

"My guests will be arriving for luncheon tomorrow," said the Squire. "I'll send a carriage for you at the hour of eleven, so you'll be there before they arrive. That will give us a short time to go through any outstanding details we may have forgotten. Now, is there anything you may wish to add, Ebenezer?"

"Yes, there is, Squire, but not about tomorrow. Please sit back and give me your glass. Another brandy, as this may well take more of your time than you expected."

Looking seriously at the Squire, Ebenezer told him everything about the visit from John Parker and of his own trip to Saltram House and what was discussed there. When he had finished, he sat back studying the look on the Squire's face.

"Well, Ebenezer," said the Squire, "a clever bit of deflection, I must say. That rogue Obadiah Tucker has it coming, and he will surely hang once John Parker makes his arrest. But mark my words, it will not be easy. Tucker will fight like a devil to avoid capture, no matter how many dragoons the Revenue have with them. I don't envy you being there, make sure you're not seen by him at any cost."

The Squire sat quietly, looking at his empty glass. "There is one thing that troubles me though," he said, indicating for Ebenezer to refill his glass. "John Parker will try and influence the judge to delay the trial until Tucker can be charged as the instigator of the Elberry Cove heist, which we know you convinced Parker to believe. Ha, a good bit of deception, Ebenezer. But this may prove a problem for us."

"How so, Squire?" asked Ebenezer, handing him another brandy.

"Well, should the judge agree to wait for Tucker to be tried alongside Huckle and Mordechai, it wouldn't be long before it became clear that Tucker was innocent of the Elberry Cove escapade and suspicion fell on us. Tucker will recognise Mordechai, as he was with you the night you collected the contraband for me from his boathouse. Tucker will claim his innocence of the Elberry Cove venture and Huckle and Mordechai will likely say he had nothing to do with it. By recognising Mordechai, Tucker will put two and two together and name you as the organiser out of spite. Under the pressure of rapid questioning from a good prosecuting barrister, it won't take long before Huckle and Mordechai fall into the trap of naming us in connection with Elberry Cove and dealings with Tucker and his sons. The naming of others in your syndicate will follow. Tucker will surely hang for being caught red-handed with a full cargo of contraband, but Huckle and Mordechai could get a lighter sentence for having named us. You would not stand a chance. John Parker would come after you for pulling the wool over his eyes and then you would be for the noose on Plymouth Hoe. Naming Obadiah to John Parker may have caused you more of a problem than you realised."

The Squire took a long draught of his brandy before continuing, "We're lucky, Ebenezer, that the judge is Edmund Pickering. It is now more important than ever for you to threaten him that you're going to expose him, he may then cooperate. Huckle and Mordechai must hang once the sentence is given. Their trial starts on Tuesday, and under Edmund Pickering, it will be over by the end of the day. Pickering must not allow John Parker the delay. There will be a week after the trial before Tucker returns to his lair and is arrested by John Parker and the Revenue. Hopefully by then, Huckle and Mordechai will have danced to the hangman and we will be safe. If not, it'll be the worst for us and a rendezvous on Plymouth Hoe gallows."

"Oh my God!" stammered Ebenezer. "What can we do, Squire?"

"We know that Huckle and Mordechai must be executed before John Parker and the Revenue return with Obadiah Tucker and his two sons. But what if the Revenue did not return with them? What if they were shot trying to escape or trying to kill you and John Parker? Think about it, it would be better for us if they were not brought back, it's always best to plan ahead and so be doubly sure. As you'll be there, you could help to make that happen; in fact, you must make it happen, Ebenezer, or we'll both end up side by side on the gallows on Plymouth Hoe."

* * *

Nancy's pulse quickened as Luc entered the inn on the stroke of midnight. A few of the tables were still occupied at this late hour with a handful of sailors playing cards and drinking steadily, but apart from them, the inn was quiet. She watched him saunter over to his usual corner booth, place his leather case on the side of the table and look around for someone to serve him. When he caught sight of her, he beckoned her over.

"A large brandy if I may, Nancy," he said smiling at her.

"That be good for a nightcap, lover," she said, rolling her tongue over her lips, "and maybe a little fancy before you retire? Only a shillin', lover."

"Just the brandy, Nancy, and hurry it up please."

Nancy returned with his brandy and as he handed her a few coins, she noticed the tiredness in his eyes.

"Been hard at work then?" she asked. "'Tis gettin' late."

"That's my business, Nancy. Now if you would kindly leave me in peace and bring me another one, I'd be most grateful."

Luc downed the brandy in one gulp, watching Nancy walk away, then sitting back he closed his eyes thinking of the plan he was formulating for the night of 31st August and the assassination of George III. Earlier, he had been to see Raymond aboard his sloop and over a few bottles of good wine, had demanded his cooperation in being part of the plot. He had realised he'd have to recruit Raymond completely into his nest of spies, and in order to gain his loyalty, he'd have to tell him of the plan to assassinate the King of England. Raymond had listened without interrupting, nodding and agreeing to Luc's demands. His part in the plot was to be ready with his sloop to take Luc and another conspirator out of England to the port of Brest immediately after the assassination. With a smile, he had satisfied Luc that there would be no problem concerning the tide as it would be in their favour for that time of day.

Jean de Claire would be waiting for them in Brest where he'd transport them to Versailles. Raymond's job would be over when they arrived in Brest, but he would remain there until contacted. Luc had been pleased with the way Raymond had pledged his loyalty and the enthusiasm he had shown towards Luc's proposal. He arranged for Raymond to be available with his boat for future secret meetings when they would discuss plans for the assassination. At no time during their conversation did Luc mention Ebenezer's name in connection with the plot; it was enough for Raymond only to know that there would be two escapees.

Luc opened his eyes to see Nancy hovering before him with another brandy. Thanking her and dropping a few coins into her hand, he knocked it back and picking up his leather paper case, bade her goodnight. No sooner had he closed the door of the inn than Nancy hurried after him, keeping well behind him as he entered an outer side door. Silently, she followed him to a wooden staircase that wound its way up to the bedrooms above. As his heavy footsteps tromped up the stairs, Nancy followed, treading each stair delicately as though they would collapse at any moment. She paused in the shadows at the top, squinting through the dim light of a solitary lantern attached to the far wall of the landing. Luc fumbled his way along in the dusky light, stopping outside a door at the far end. As he peered down the gloomy landing, Nancy watched him take a key from his coat pocket then unlock the door and let himself in. She had been right, the candle light she'd previously seen glowing from an upstairs window, had been his window. She had found his room.

She would wait until he left the inn the following day and see if she could find a way into the room. Her hunch that something not quite right about this mysterious gentleman would soon come to light. The answer, she was sure, lay in his room.

Chapter 25

The Squire's carriage came to collect Ebenezer just before eleven o'clock. He had spent several hours the night before practising the wraps, tugs and holds the toga required to be worn properly, and with a final look at himself in his bedroom mirror, he grunted with a contented air of satisfaction. Letting himself out of the house, he hitched up the toga and hurried down his garden path to where the carriage waited patiently on the cobblestone hill. As he ascended the first carriage step, an unexpected gust of wind buffeted the bottom of the toga, hoisting it up above his waist and revealing him in his loose and baggy underwear. At that very moment, Betsy Gribble turned a corner at the end of the hill. Glancing up towards Ebenezer's residence, she stepped back aghast, her eyes widening in abhorrence at the spectacle of the minister fumbling to get into a carriage, wearing nothing but his underwear and what looked like a large white sheet ballooning around his midriff.

"That devil priest," she muttered, "just look at him, disgustin' man! Wonder where he be goin' lookin' like that? Your time's comin', you traitor, us'll catch you out. All oi need be proof and Mr John Parker to hear you'm traitorin' this country. Next time you'm pulls at that ear, then us'll be waitin' behind the altar in the church to catch you out. Then us'll see who's goin' hell. You'm devil priest!"

Red in the face and panting breathlessly, Ebenezer finally managed to get the toga under control and sitting back in the carriage, tapped on the inside roof to let the driver know he was ready to go. As the carriage descended the hill, he glimpsed Betsy Gribble standing outside the Ashprington Inn watching the carriage trundle past.

"Foolish woman," he mumbled.

Squire Maddock was waiting in the courtyard as the carriage carrying Ebenezer rolled into Darton Hall's medieval square. A grin of amusement spread across his face as he observed Ebenezer hitching up the bottom of the toga while descending the three steps of the carriage. The Squire could not help a gentle clap, chuckling at the obvious awkwardness and discomfort Ebenezer was experiencing.

"Well, Cicero," he chortled, "don't you just look the part!"

"Yes, yes, yes, Squire. It's difficult enough keeping it together in this blustery wind."

"Caesar, Cicero, we must address ourselves by our assumed names."

"Of course, Caesar," said Ebenezer, smirking at the Squire's knobbly knees under the short red tunic he was wearing. "My feet are freezing, as probably are yours in these open sandals," he added.

"Come, Cicero," said the Squire, "let's go inside. My servants are giving final touches to the luncheon tables and a small ensemble I have engaged are tuning up to provide soft Roman-style music of the era. They will be playing throughout the day and up to midnight. They'll really set the scene musically for what we'll be getting up to!"

Inside the Great Hall, Ebenezer's eyes widened with delight at the various scantily dressed servants hurrying to and fro, setting up the tables for what promised to be a truly gluttonous lunch feast.

The tables in the hall were laid out in the shape of a horseshoe, the Squire's throne-like chair positioned in the centre of the top table, where he'd sit alone, but with a clear view of all his guests. The two tables leading off the top table were to accommodate ten persons each, the guests sitting opposite each other on each table. Each guest had been appointed a place, their Roman names delicately quilled on a card. Ebenezer noticed the name Cicero placed at the top of the right-hand table.

"You'll be seated up there at the top of the table opposite Nero," said the Squire pointing to Ebenezer's table place. "He'll drink and gorge himself excessively until he throws up in one of the sick buckets my servants have placed next to each chair. Do not look so disgusted, Ebenezer, this is indulgence, Roman-style. You can be sure all my guests will satiate themselves to the extreme. But you, Reverend, must stay controlled and clear-headed. Do not forget to refer to Pickering as Nero and to me as Caesar, you know you are here to save us both from the gallows. Only indulge in whatever pleasures come your way when you are in the company of the judge. You must convince him you are here for your own personal amusement and gratification. Show him you have no inhibitions when it comes to sexual performance with any one of the beautiful women who will approach you. Follow him around and encourage him in his depravity, he must feel he has your trust. He will wallow freely in his perversions, as will all my other guests. Leave quietly at midnight, my coachman will be waiting for you in the courtyard to drive you home. He will be outside your house at eight tomorrow morning to bring you back when you'll spring the trap on the judge before we all assemble for the final feast in the afternoon. So, are you ready to play Cicero?"

"Absolutely, Caesar," replied Ebenezer with a grin.

The sound of several hunting horns signalling the arrival of the carriages carrying the first of the Squire's guests suddenly resonated across the courtyard.

"Come, Cicero, the games will begin," said the Squire, making his way towards the doorway and the steps that led down from the Great Hall.

Ebenezer stood aside as the Squire welcomed his guests into the hall, each one attired in Roman costume. He scanned the newly-arrived guests closely, hoping he would not recognise any of them. The majority looked older than Ebenezer and were obviously from the aristocratic and upper-class sections of society. It surprised him to see a handful of middle-aged ladies greeting the Squire vigorously, giggling and flattering him on his choice of costume while he pretended to fawn over them in an over-exaggerated and beguiling way.

Another blast of a hunting horn caused Ebenezer to look out over the square as a two-horse carriage trundled across the courtyard to draw up below the steps. He watched as a portly individual stepped unsteadily out of the carriage, smoothing down his toga and adjusting a brightly coloured medallion that hung from his neck. Looking up at the entrance door, he hitched up his toga and climbed the short flight of steps to where the Squire, having just been released from the middle-aged ladies, stood beaming his welcome. Nero had arrived.

Ebenezer followed the two of them into the Great Hall where the ensemble of four musicians were playing tunes from the Wisdom of Minerva, the music gently drifting around the Great Hall. Guests stood around in small groups, chatting and laughing while gladly accepting small goblets of sherry from the scantily clad servants. Squire Maddock took his position at the top table and beaming heartily at his guests, tapped the table for silence.

"Dear friends," he began, "welcome to Darton Hall and our two-day hedonistic programme of pleasure."

A round of cheering and applause greeted the Squire's opening.

"Whilst you are pleasuring in some of the rooms where, let us say, special games will be provided for your preferences, there will be a continuous supply of food and wine available here in the hall throughout the day, until we feast again later tonight. Those of you who may look for a short break between your physical pleasuring, may care to attend some brief discussions on hedonism. The ideas of the great Aristippus, a student of Socrates, who held the belief that pleasure is the highest good, will be debated in the rooms marked with the word 'debate'. You have all been allocated guest rooms for the night's stayover. The two liveried servants standing by the doors to the hall have a list of your accommodations, they will gladly assist you whenever you feel the need to retire."

After taking a long draught from his goblet, the Squire beckoned Ebenezer to join him. Holding up Ebenezer's arm, he addressed his guests, "Dear friends, it is my pleasure to introduce you to a new member of our circle, Cicero."

The Squire's guests stared intently at the smiling figure of Ebenezer and after a short period of silence, greeted him with a fervent round of applause, some of them shouting out their greetings.

"Thank you all," said the Squire. "Now, if you'd search for your table places, then the feasting shall begin."

Ebenezer ambled over to his table place, nodding to those who smiled at him and occasionally shaking the hand of a welcoming member of the group.

Everyone stood in silence behind their chairs, waiting for a signal from the Squire. Semi-naked serving girls floated around the guests pouring wine into their goblets. From the corner of his eye, Ebenezer noticed two effeminate looking male servants in tight-fitting breeches filling the middle-aged ladies' goblets, the ladies pretending to swoon at the sight of them while running their hands over the fops' backsides.

Scanning his guests, the Squire raised his goblet. "The King," he said loudly and took a long draught.

"The King," everyone echoed, taking long draughts from their chalices.

Ebenezer smirked at the toast.

"Before we begin to feast," announced the Squire, "we will toast ourselves thrice over."

The semi-naked serving girls and the two male waiters hovered by, ready to refill the goblets, the middle-aged ladies stretching out to grope at the two male servants, who had orders from the Squire to spoil and pamper them.

"To our circle and to hedonism," hollered the Squire, raising his goblet and draining it in one long draught.

This was echoed around the room, the guests draining the wine in their goblets in one long swig. Two more repetitions of the toast followed. Some of the guests were crudely dribbling wine down the front of their costumes while Judge Pickering, amongst others, licked his red-stained lips, belching openly in satisfaction. The wine was strong, its affects already showing among the middle-aged ladies who were giggling and pawing at the male servants every time they passed by.

"Well, Cicero," said Judge Pickering, looking at Ebenezer across the table, "your first hedonistic soirée. To your health, sir."

Judge Pickering raised his goblet in a toast, downing the wine in the freshly filled vessel in one long swig. Wiping his stained lips on a napkin, he chuckled in pleasure, ogling at three semi-naked girls cruising through the doors of the hall pushing a sumptuously laden food trolley.

"Ah ha," he slurred, rubbing his podgy hands together, "the first course."

Ebenezer turned to see a huge roasted wild boar's head displayed on a bed of oranges being pushed into the space between the two tables where it halted directly in front of the Squire's table. In one rapid movement, the Squire sprung from his chair, plunging his eating knife into the top of the boar's head. Cutting a neat circle, he sliced then speared half of the boar's brain onto his knife. Pulling the dripping knife out of the opening, he stuffed the squashy organ into his mouth and with a swig of red wine, sat back chewing into the soft fleshy mass.

Pointing at Ebenezer to take out the other half of the brain, the Squire and his guests began a series of chants, urging him on to follow the Squire's example. Ebenezer picked up his knife looking at the chanting faces around him and the neat circle at the top of the boar's head.

"Go on, Cicero," slobbered Judge Pickering, "it's an honour. Spear the rest of the brain and eat it with relish. All new intakes to our society are given this honour. Go on."

Ebenezer held his knife over the open circle where the Squire had cut out half of the boar's brain. As the chanting of the guests came to a crescendo, he plunged his knife into the boar's opened skull, piercing the other half of the brain and extracting it in one quick movement. Holding up the dripping knife and with eyes tightly shut, he crammed the soggy grey matter into his mouth to the cheers and clapping of the guests around him. Chewing into the pulpy lump, he looked over at the Squire who grinned back at him, nodding in approval. A long draught of wine helped him swallow the foul-tasting piece.

The Squire's guests heartily tucked into slices of the boar's head, the ears and tongue going to Judge Pickering who had been first to claim them. Throughout the following courses of pheasant, lobster, venison, small songbirds and peacock, copious amounts of wine were drunk, the guests getting drunker by the course. Ebenezer, heeding the Squire's warning, refrained from taking too much wine and tried to engage the judge into various topics of conversation. He watched as the corpulent minister of the court gorged himself through the courses, one moment grabbing numerous small songbirds in one fleshy hand, then snatching up thick pieces of peacock breast in the other. He crammed them alternately into his mouth, grunting with pleasure as he devoured each handful, his beady little eyes roaming the table for ever more delicious delicacies.

A gentle touch on Ebenezer's right arm made him turn to see who wanted his attention. The cold grey eyes of a thinly framed man who looked to be approaching old age stared at him. The name Crassus glared out from the card on the table.

"There's more of those semi-naked girls waiting in the rooms for us later," he drooled, moistening his thin lips. "They're into anything we want them to do. Nero sitting opposite, likes them to whip him on his bare buttocks first and then he will have two of them together. He knocks them about sometimes when he's really worked up."

"Really," said Ebenezer raising an eyebrow. He was just about to ask Crassus where the rooms were located when a loud groan followed by the urging cry of 'Huey' made him look back to where Judge Pickering, with head bent into a bucket, was spewing up the six courses he'd been gorging on. Several of the guests who had been watching the judge, applauded him as he struggled back up in his chair.

Smiling at Ebenezer, he raised his goblet, taking a long draught of wine, "Ah Cicero," he slurred, "that'll make room for more. Would you mind asking Crassus on your right to hand me that dish of raw oysters."

A sudden change in the tempo of the music alerted everyone. The doors of the Great Hall opened as two young women wearing nothing but veils over their faces danced gracefully into the hall. They moved lithely to the music, stretching their bodies and gyrating their lower halves provocatively towards the watching guests. They began to stroke and touch each other erotically, moving in and out

186

of sensual embraces as the music became faster. Ebenezer watched them, fascinated by the lascivious scene. The rapid beating of a drum signalled a crescendo as the two dancers collapsed to the floor, intertwining themselves into a display of lustful fondling. Groans of delight echoed amongst the guests as the two dancers lifted their veils to tongue-lick each other's lips and mouths. Ebenezer sat open-mouthed in disbelief, not a sound emanating from him as he gazed at the face of one of the performers. Paling, he raised a hand to cover his open mouth, and looking again he scrutinised the flushed face of one of the dancers. Astonishment turned into alarm as he watched the two performers standing to rapturous applause from the Squire's guests. He had eyes for only one, the one who had knocked on his door the afternoon after he had returned from the smuggling trip to Obadiah's boathouse. The one who had somehow got into his house and surprised him in his bedroom. The one who had suddenly disappeared from the village but who now stood breathing heavily and staring directly at him. Ebenezer stared back into the dark seductive eyes of Molly.

Chapter 26

Nancy's shift at the Cat and Fiddle wasn't due to begin until mid-morning but wanting to be sure Luc had left his room, she arrived at the inn as Ned Cuttle, the landlord, was opening its doors to a bright sun rising over the Barbican.

"You'm be early, Nance," he said, looking at her in surprise. "What brings you here so early?"

"Morning, Ned," said Nancy, "couldn't sleep. People above me were having their early mornin' barny, and when he started knockin' her about and her started screamin', oi ups and left. Can't walk the streets till us starts work, so oi decides to start early. That bein' alright with you, Ned?"

"Ar, if you wants, Nance. Can't pay thee till your proper shift time starts though."

"Doen you worry about that, Ned. Mistress Cuttle up and about yet?"

"Ar, that she be, cleanin' day for 'er. Them rooms above the inn, 'er's got contract from Digbys, the landlords, to clean 'em once a fortnight. Today be the day."

Nancy's eyes lit up as she saw a way of getting into Luc's room.

"What about they what rents them, have they to be out while Mistress Cuttle cleans them?" asked Nancy crossing her fingers.

"Ar, they'm do. I expect they'm be leavin' shortly. There be only three of them rentin' now. They'm usually comes in for some ale and bread before they'm goes orf somewhere."

"Does Mistress have the keys to them rooms?" asked Nancy earnestly.

"Ar, she do, Nance."

"Got an idea, Ned," said Nancy, sounding excited. "Would Mistress mind if oi used me time before oi starts me shift to help 'er clean one of 'em rooms, us got nuthin' else to do till customers start arrivin'?"

"Oi'd think she'd be delighted, Nance," said Ned, "'er be out back in the scullery, go and ask her."

Dora Cuttle looked up from scrubbing her husband's-stained underwear as Nancy made her way into the scullery.

"Mornin', Nancy," she said, putting the scrubbing brush down onto a soapy washboard, "you'm be here early."

"Ar, that oi be, mistress. Us's got some time before me shift starts and oi be wonderin' if you'm would like me to help 'ee clean one of 'em rooms above the inn. Master Cuttle told me it be room cleanin' today."

"Bless you, Nancy," said Dora. "Us'd be well pleased for the help. Must wait till the gentlemen rentin' leaves them. They'm usually comes into the inn for breakfast. Then us can start. Oi can't pay you for the help, Nancy."

"Naw, that doen matter, mistress. Us's nuthin' better to do till me shift starts. Be a pleasure to help you."

"You'm get back into the bar, Nancy, and when you'm sees the three gentlemen comin' in for breakfast, give us a shout."

Nancy returned to the bar where Ned was slicing some bread and cheese in preparation for the early breakfasts when the door opened and in walked Luc followed by his two neighbours. They nodded to Ned and Nancy, Luc not giving Nancy any indication that he was surprised to see her at that time of the morning. All three wanted ale with a plate of bread and cheese and a few onions thrown in. Nancy wandered over to Luc's usual booth where he sat filling his pipe.

"Mornin', lover, it be a fine day ahead out there."

"Good," replied Luc. "Please bring me some ale, Nancy, thank you."

Nancy returned with a mug of ale, together with a plate of bread and cheese and an onion.

"You'm be goin' far today, lover?" she asked subtly.

"Why yes," replied Luc, "to Exeter, if you want to know. I have business there. Now, I'd appreciate it if you'd kindly leave me to have my breakfast without having to answer any more questions."

Nancy left with a thankful smile, returning to the scullery where Dora was hanging up Ned's underwear on a line stretching across the room.

"They'ms all havin' breakfast, mistress," she said.

"That be good then, Nancy," replied Dora. "Us'll wait till they'ms finished and gone then us can begin. You take the room at the far end of the landin' up there, and then us'll do the other two rooms. Cleanin' rags, soap and buckets in that cupboard over there. Hot water'll be ready soon."

"What about the key to get into the room?" asked Nancy.

"Us's got the spare key, dear. Us'll give it you when us gets up there."

Nancy sat down on a stool next to the cupboard, feeling it was her lucky day. She watched Dora hanging up Ned's underwear, happy she did not have a man to wash and clean for. Luc would be finishing his breakfast shortly and then he would leave for the early stagecoach to Exeter. All she had to do was to wait.

Luc swilled his mouth with the last of the ale in his mug, the juice of the strong onion still searing parts of his tongue. He had lied when he'd told Nancy he was going to Exeter on some business. He was meeting his spy from Saltram House in an inn, adjacent to a small wharf in Totnes where local timber was loaded onto foreign ships. The inn, being out of the way of prying eyes and situated in a quiet spot overlooking the River Dart, was an ideal location for the clandestine meeting Luc had planned. There he would discuss his plans for the assassination and inform his spy of the time of the next meeting which he'd arrange to be held on Raymond's sloop. Checking the time on his pocket watch, he picked up his leather paper case and cramming a remaining piece of cheese into his mouth, left the inn to hurry off towards the stagecoach pick-up point at the end of the Barbican.

Dora had filled two buckets with hot water, and as the last of the upstairs tenants let themselves out of the inn, she and Nancy made their way into the bar, laden with cleaning rags, soap and each carrying a bucket of hot water.

Ned was busy clearing away the empty plates and mugs from the tables.

"They'ms all gone, Ned?" asked Dora.

"Ar, last one left few seconds ago," he replied, not bothering to look up as the two women struggled out of the inn.

Up on the dark landing where Nancy had watched Luc from the shadows the night before, Dora searched through a string of keys until she found the one that would fit Luc's door. "'Ere you'm be, Nancy," she said holding up a bold brass key, "this be the one for that room at the far end. When you'm finished with that room, there be a privvy opposite. Oi'd be grateful if you could give it a clean-up. Doen you worry about emptyin' the container, old Seth from the poorhouse empties that with the help of a young boey from the workhouse. They'm be emptyin' day after tomorrow. Just give it a spruce-up, Nancy, and thank you, dear."

Nancy nodded and taking the key, made her way down to the door of Luc's room; it was the right key and the lock turned easily. Opening the door, she let herself in, standing as still as a statue as her eyes darted to every corner of the room. An old wooden table acting as a writing desk, stared questioningly at her from beneath a bay window where an ink pot and quill peeped up cheekily beneath a mound of scattered papers. A high-backed chair pushed slightly back from the table as though someone had just risen from it, brushed the sides of a neatly made-up bed that stretched along the sides of a flowery papered wall. Stacked up against the wall opposite, a nest of three small tables neighboured a shiny wooden chest of drawers that seemed dwarfed next to a haughty looking dark oak cupboard that rose to an inch of touching the ceiling. The room reeked with the pungent smell of pipe tobacco.

Putting the bucket down on a rug in front of the door, Nancy approached the table. Numerous written papers glared up at her. These meant nothing to her as she was unable to read, but a shiny blue symbol etched onto the top of a document jutting out from under a pile of notes suddenly caught her eye. Delicately extracting the document from under the pile, she held it up towards the light from the window where the bold symbol of a golden crown mounted on a blue shield exhibiting horizontal rows of golden lilies, proudly gazed back at her. The Fleur-de Lis, emblem of France and the French monarchy, gazed out arrogantly from the top of the document she was holding. Further documents and letters with the colourful symbol displayed came into view before her as she rifled through the papers on the table. She knew she had seen such a symbol of golden lilies on a blue background somewhere before, but where, she couldn't quite remember; perhaps it would come to her later. She wondered what may lay hidden in the tall cupboard that seemed to be glaring down at her.

Carefully opening one of the doors, she looked gingerly inside, a musty smell meeting her as she peered into its dark confines. A row of jackets, breeches and shirts hung from one side while more papers and files were stacked on the other side. She was just turning to close the door when the sight of a silver coin caught her eye. Peering closer at the coin and then into the dark recess of the cupboard, she cautiously parted the longer items of the hanging clothes. It was too dark for her to see into the back of the wardrobe but stretching her head further into its niche, she was able to make out a fair-sized wooden chest lying snugly at the back. Extending both arms, she stretched herself full length until her hands touched the top of the chest. Opening it, she felt around inside, her hands feeling the soft texture of leather bags. Clasping one, she withdrew her arm gasping in surprise at what she held.

A medium-sized leather money bag fastened with laces tinkled to the sound of numerous coins. Unfastening the laces, she tipped some of the contents into the open palm of her hand. Silver coins glinted up at her as she peered closely into the bag.

"Bliddy hell," she muttered, "must be hundreds of pounds in that chest."

As she gazed transfixed at the coins in her hand, a shout from Dora outside on the landing brought her back down to earth.

"Nancy, you'm finished in there yet? Us's gonna start on other room now. Don't you forget the privvy."

Quickly, Nancy replied, "Just finishin', mistress, be out soon. 'Aven't forgot the privvy."

Dropping the coins back into the bag, she retied the laces and stretching out towards the rear of the cupboard, placed the bag back into the chest amongst all the others, then closing the top lid, she wriggled out making sure she straightened the row of hanging clothes before closing the cupboard door behind her.

Better do a quick bit of cleanin' so it smells as if someone's been at work in here, she thought.

After giving the room a brief clean-up and making sure the water in her bucket looked dirty, she picked up the rags and soap and as she was about to leave, her eyes rested on the document with the emblem of the Fleur-de-Lis lying on the table.

Us'll take that, she thought, *oi'll find someone who can read it for me, then us'll know what he's up to.*

Picking it up from the table, she folded it and thrust it into a deep pocket in her gown then clutching the bucket she left the room, closing the door and locking it.

Later that night, as Nancy was hurrying along the Barbican after completing her shift at the inn, she stopped as she passed the copse of trees where she remembered Rose telling her how she'd seen Luc slipping on the gangplank on his way onto the Frenchies' boat.

What made Nancy stop so abruptly was the sight of a flag fluttering in the moonlight at the stern of the boat. Reaching inside the deep pocket of her gown, she pulled out the document she had taken from Luc's table. Holding it up to the moonlight and looking at the symbol at the top of the page and then staring at the flag fluttering at the back of the boat, she recognised the resemblance. A blue background with golden lilies. The document in her hand showed the full emblem of France but while the flag had only three lilies, two next to each other and one below them, the design of the lilies was the same as those in the symbol on the document. And all three lilies lay on a background of blue, the same blue as in the symbol on top of the document.

Bliddy hell, thought Nancy, *he must be a Frenchy as the symbol on his documents are similar to that there flag on the Frenchies' boat. That picture must be something to do with France, probably their national emblem. He be up to somethin' with them Frenchies on that boat. Us'll find out soon enough when oi follows him and oi bet he'll lead me all the way here.*

Chapter 27

While the wine flowed amongst the guests in the hall, conversation about the erotic display of the dancers spread around the tables, most lusting over the dancers' performance and hoping they'd get the chance to be paired with one of them at the start of the Squire's special games. Judge Pickering, his eyes wide with fanciful lust, looked over at Ebenezer,

"That dancer with the dark hair," he slobbered, "that's the one I want, Cicero. Looks like she'll be into anything, what d'you think?"

"I'm sure she will be, Nero. As I am the new member of the circle, it'll be me who has first choice of the Squire's lovely playthings, should she be available then I'll choose her and give her to you. What d'you think about that?"

"Well, I'm rightly pleased, Cicero. She'll do me good and proper, I'm sure."

"That she will," said Ebenezer, a plan forming in his mind. "But may I add a condition to that, Nero?"

"You may," replied the Judge licking his lips, as thoughts of what he would do to Molly played on his mind.

"The condition is that you allow me to accompany you and watch you dominate the little vixen."

"Ha," giggled the Judge, "a voyeur if I'm not mistaken."

"Absolutely, Nero," grinned Ebenezer.

"I've no problems with that, whatever turns you on, Cicero. But do not interfere if I slap her around a little after she's beaten me on my…" the Judge lowered his voice, "bare buttocks!"

"Naturally, Nero," said Ebenezer stifling a laugh. "Now, if you'd excuse me for a moment, I'm in need of a breath of fresh air."

"Not at all, Cicero, do not be long, Caesar's going to offer the pairings shortly. I don't want to miss out on that hot little dancing minx!"

Ebenezer slipped out of the hall, hoping that Molly would be waiting somewhere along the dark corridor. He knew she had recognised him by the long stare she had given him, and he was sure she'd want to know what he was doing at such a soirée. Peering into the shadows, he suddenly jumped in shock.

"Ebenezer, you are a naughty, naughty parson!" a sultry voice whispered in his ear.

Turning, he felt Molly's breath on his neck, her face touching just below his ear. "Why, us'd never have believed a reverend such as you, Ebenezer, would have dared attend one of these orgies, but there again, oi ain't that surprised. But how do you come to be here?"

"I could ask you the same, Molly," said Ebenezer, feeling her body pressing against his.

"Oi be one of the Squire's troop of women," she replied. "His valet found me in the inn one quiet evenin' when a rumour of a smugglin' venture be goin' on somewheres down Brixham way. Oi agreed to come here and meet the Squire the next day. He offered me a better standard of livin' 'here at Darton Hall if oi'd come and work for him. Us be a troop of lively girls here who doen mind pleasuring the gentry whenever the Squire tells us to. Us gets good rewards for doin' it and comfortable lodgins too."

I'm sure, thought Ebenezer. *The crafty old devil never told me he had a concubine of pretty harlots holed up here that he rented out to the gentry!*

"Now, why you be here, you'm naughty parson?" asked Molly.

"Never mind that now, Molly, it's a long story and you'll have to trust me. I need you to help me, and I think that a golden guinea tomorrow before the final banquet starts, would help, would it not?"

"That it would, Ebenezer, and an explanation of what all this be about."

"Absolutely, Molly, you'll have that along with the guinea if you do exactly as I ask you. But please do not call me Ebenezer here, I'm Cicero."

"Mmm, name suits you. Us'll whisper Cicero when us's havin' company later."

Perhaps much later, thought Ebenezer, not fancying following on after the Judge had finished with her.

Ebenezer explained what he wished her to do, mentioning that he would be there watching while she was servicing the guest. He omitted telling her that the guest liked to knock women around while sexually turned on and hoped Molly would agree. He made her promise that at no time would she reveal his own identity and always address him as Cicero. What he did not tell her was the plan he and the Squire had made to blackmail the Judge and the effect it would have on a trial taking place in Plymouth within a few days. He went on to lie that her guest for the special games would be an extremely wealthy duke, under the assumed name of Nero. To add to the incentive of the golden guinea, Ebenezer took a chance telling her the Squire would also be providing her with a guinea, as a bonus for keeping Nero more than pleasantly occupied. Molly's eyes widened with ardour.

"Better get started then, Eben… sorry, Cicero," she said with a mischievous giggle.

Ebenezer sidled back into the hall, slipping into his seat opposite Judge Pickering, who by this time was quite drunk.

"Aha, Cicero," he slurred, "Caesar's just about to announce the pairings. Look!"

With a glance at Ebenezer, the Squire rose from his chair as the conversation around the tables quickly dwindled.

"Friends," he said aloud, slurring his voice, "it's time for you to be off with your pairings. Some of you will have to share and I know you willingly will."

The announcement was greeted by loud applause and cheering, accompanied by a resounding banging on the tables. Faces around the tables gazed at the Squire then turned to look at the doors as servants waited for the command.

"Let the fun begin, open the doors," he boomed.

The doors of the hall opened to the entry of a dozen beautiful women, all clothed in see-through gowns. Following, three of the young male waiters minced past the middle-aged ladies, their tight breeches emphasising the hardened muscles in their thighs. Swooning and fanning herself rigorously, one of the middle-aged ladies, much the worse for drink, leapt from her chair to grab one of the young men, stroking his behind and rubbing herself lewdly up against him. After much laughter and table rapping, the obnoxious duchess was escorted back to her chair.

Ebenezer picked out Molly standing in front of the group, her eyes darting from him to where Judge Pickering sat. The Judge's beady little eyes gawked with lechery at the troop of horny-looking women standing before him. With a goblet of wine in one hand and a greasy peacock breast in the other, he drooled and lusted over what he saw, a series of deep groans and grunts rumbling out of him.

"I trust that what you can see meets your approval," the Squire shouted.

"Yes!" bellowed the reply from all his guests.

"It is customary for the new member of our group to choose his pairing before you, and he is the only member who can choose a partner. I have a list of pairings and those of you who will be sharing. After I have read out your names, you can then find a room to your liking, relax and gratify your desires."

All eyes switched to Ebenezer who slowly rose from his chair.

"I will choose," he said, "and then give to the member opposite me, Nero. My pleasure is to watch and enjoy the satisfaction he will experience."

"Very well," bellowed the Squire with a grin towards Ebenezer, "the pairing I have already allocated to Nero must also join you, so Cicero, choose now."

Ebenezer walked across the hall to where Molly stood and taking her hand, returned to his place at the table where Judge Pickering sat gloating and slavering in excitement.

"Joy," the Squire called, "you will join them as you were the one I had chosen for Nero." A tall slender blonde detached herself from the group and swaying her hips to the fascination of those awaiting their pairings, glided over to where a grinning Nero sat utterly elated.

Ebenezer, the Judge, Molly and Joy left the hall quietly as the Squire began calling out the list of pairings.

"There's a comfortable room at the end of this corridor," said Molly, taking Judge Pickering's hand and smiling seductively at him. "Cicero has chosen to watch while the two of us entertain you, Nero. Is there anything that you'd particularly like to start with?"

Flushed with abundant goblets of wine and excessive amounts of rich food, the Judge could only gaze in enthrallment at the two women. As he opened his mouth to try to speak, a thunderous fart exploded beneath his toga.

"You naughty little Nero," said Molly looking at Joy, who suddenly burst into helpless giggling. "Naughty boys will be punished for farting like that!"

"Oh yes, please," slurred the Judge, "you can punish me by taking down my underwear and thrashing my bare buttocks. But you must do it naked."

The soft sound of a cithara playing more tunes to the Wisdom of Minerva drifted along the corridor as Molly guided them into the room she had previously mentioned. Impatient to start, Judge Pickering began to pull off his toga, ogling at the two women slipping lithely out of their see-through gowns.

Several sofas had been placed around the room and as the Judge stood scrutinising them, Molly and Joy guided him to a spacious recliner where he sprawled on his back and began fumbling with his underwear.

Ebenezer watched from the shadows, snickering quietly to himself as the Judge turned himself over to lie face down, while the two women helped him out of the capacious pair of underpants fastened to his midriff. The sight of his massive dough-like buttocks wobbling around like giant-sized marshmallows, caused Ebenezer to thrust a fist into his mouth for fear of bursting out into uncontrollable laughter. This was made even funnier for him when Molly and Joy started to thrash the judge on his buttocks, each wielding a thin bamboo stick.

"Take that you naughty, naughty boy!" yelled Molly, caning his buttocks.

"One of you stand in front of me, quickly," he shrieked, tears of pain forming in his eyes, "I want to see you naked."

The sharp sounds of thwacks on his bare buttocks followed by his whimpering cries seemed to contrast with the soft Roman music that drifted around the room. Ebenezer watched as Molly stood at the Judge's head, a determined look of dominance on her face as she stood naked, her legs slightly parted and stick raised.

"You'm a very naughty little Nero," she screamed at him. "What you'm be?"

A loud thwack sounded as Joy brought her bamboo stick down on the Judge's ever-reddening buttocks.

"I'm a very naughty little Nero," screeched the Judge.

"You'm be a very naughty little Nero because you farted," screamed Molly again. "Why you'm so naughty, Nero?"

"Because I farted when I shouldn't have," screamed the Judge as another thwack landed on his buttocks.

"And you'm won't fart again in front of ladies, will you?" yelled Molly.

"Ahhh," screamed the judge as another thwack landed on his buttocks. "No, I won't fart again in front of ladies. Now help me up, that's enough of the thrashing."

Molly put down the stick she was brandishing at the Judge and looked over into the shadows at Ebenezer who was wiping tears of laughter from his eyes. He nodded towards her.

As the Judge got himself up level with the two women, he lashed out, smacking Joy on her shoulder. He then turned to Molly, slapping her soundly on her cheek. She was just about to slap him back when she saw the excitement in his eyes and the stiffness of his little man.

"Oh dear, he likes to play it rough, Joy. Oi'll pull him back and you straddle him. Let him slip inside you and oi'll sit on his face. See how he likes that!"

With tears of laughter running down his cheeks, Ebenezer listened to Judge Pickering's heavy breathing, deep carnal groans of pleasure rising from his throat as he rocketed up and down while the two women gyrated on top of him, the noise of his flab slapping around like a netful of thrashing fish. Then, with a gasp and a long stuttering sigh, he was spent.

As he lay panting on the sofa, Molly and Joy joined Ebenezer in the shadows.

"Didn' take him very long," said Joy looking at Molly.

"Naw, that type always loses it pretty quick," replied Molly, grinning at Ebenezer.

The room had half-filled with other pairings, the sound of lustful moans and groans drifting up from the remaining sofas. Judge Pickering lay on the recliner like a beached whale, his heavy breathing echoing around the room.

"Cicero, are you still here?" he wheezed.

"That I am, Nero," replied Ebenezer.

"I trust it was all satisfying for you. It certainly was for me, those gals definitely know how to wield a stick, what!"

"Absolutely," replied Ebenezer. "Truly satisfying, Nero."

"Tell those gals to help me into my toga. I am hungry and there's food and wine in the hall. We will have our fill and then continue back here. What say you?"

"Good idea. Yes, Nero, it is all going very well. I am sure Caesar is as pleased as I am. When you're ready, we'll go back to the hall."

Molly and Joy helped the Judge wrap himself in his toga, leaving his imposing pair of underpants lying on the recliner. They left the room making their way along the dark corridor, the two women swaying provocatively in front of the Judge, knowing his piggy-like eyes were rivetted to their sensuous behinds. They sniggered at the Judge's blatant lechery, swaying their hips enticingly beneath their see-through gowns. Ebenezer noticed the lust growing again on the Judge's face.

Another sinful session to witness after he's gorged himself and I'll have snared him, he thought. *I'll get the Squire to order one of those fops who pamper the old crones to ride him while Joy gives him another thrashing. While that is going on, I'll give Molly a good seeing to in one of the other rooms. Ha, yes, it's going to work, I know it.*

Ebenezer found the Squire in the hall, lolling on his imposing chair while two semi-naked girls fawned over him, one stroking his upper thigh under his red tunic while the other massaged the back of his neck.

"Cicero," he called to Ebenezer, "come and join me, a goblet of wine awaits you."

Judge Pickering was already devouring handfuls of freshly-roasted songbirds, his attention focused on the range of savouries and sweets that filled the table. Molly and Joy waited patiently outside the Great Hall.

The Squire dismissed the two girls petting over him as Ebenezer approached.

"I trust all is going well, Cicero," he said in a low voice.

"It is, Caesar," replied Ebenezer. "After he's finished pigging himself, it's back to the room for another session. The two girls are waiting and have already performed well."

"Excellent," said the Squire. "Do you think all will be well for you to spring your trap on him tomorrow?"

"It will, Squire," replied Ebenezer, "but I ask you to instruct one of those effeminate fops who are pampering those rich hags to come with us for the next session. That will surely seal the Judge's fate for us."

"Absolutely, Cicero," smiled the Squire, "I'll see to it straightaway."

Ebenezer watched as the Squire joined a party of middle-aged ladies being indulged by two of the pretty boy waiters. He noticed the Squire speak into the ear of one of the boys and then turning, pointed towards the Judge and then towards Ebenezer. The fop nodded, flapping his hand in an ultra-gay gesture. Returning to Ebenezer, the Squire grinned at him.

"When the Judge is ready, Ebenezer, just let the boy know and he'll follow. Now, this is an excellent wine."

A loud belch from the Judge rang out across the hall as he reached for yet another jug of wine. Rubbing his hands over his flabby pot belly, he looked around for Ebenezer and seeing him standing next to the Squire, beckoned him over. With a nod to the Squire, Ebenezer made his way over to the table where the Judge stood, his watery eyes flitting around the hall.

"If you're ready, Nero, we can resume with the games," said Ebenezer looking over to where the fops were entertaining the middle-aged crones. The one selected by the Squire turned, and seeing Ebenezer looking his way, flicked his hand gaily, detaching himself from the group and mincing over to where Ebenezer and the Judge stood waiting.

"You mutht be, Nero," said the fop, lisping to the judge.

"That I am, you pretty boy," said the Judge. "And what do they call you?"

"Felixth," he lisped, "in Anthient Rome it meant the Lucky One."

"Well, in that case, I'm about to feel lucky, ha," chortled the Judge, putting his flabby arm around Felix's narrow waist. "Lead on, Cicero, and bring those two little lovelies with you."

Ebenezer grinned at the thought of witnessing further acts of depravity the Judge was about to perform. As Septimus Sniff, the writer, he would invoke them all when springing the trap before the grand banquet the following day.

Chapter 28

The Judge's ample underpants lay on the sofa where Molly and Joy had left them. Enchanted by the drivel the fop was whispering to him, the Judge was unaware that he was without his underwear when Joy tugged at his toga letting it fall around his toes.

"Oooh, Nero!" the fop exclaimed, jumping back and flapping a girlie-like hand over his mouth. "You're jutht right for my little game. Now, if you pleath jutht get down on all fourths, I will slip my clothing off and we can thtart. Joy here can be our leader, we won't need you, Molly dear."

Ebenezer and Molly stepped back, curious as to what the fop intended. The Judge slowly bent himself down, dropping onto his knees then bending forward to support himself on the palms of his hands, his flabby breasts and pot belly wobbling back and forth like three crinkly jellies. Ebenezer watched the fop mince naked across the room to a table that stood unnoticed in the shadows. He returned holding a thick black studded dog collar and a short length of rope in one hand, while in the other a small hunting horn. Joy had slipped out of her gown and was standing naked in front of the Judge, who was now sweating and puffing like an exhausted sow. Fastening an end of rope to the dog collar, the fop slipped it around the Judge's neck and throwing the other end to Joy, he sprung onto the Judge's back like a jockey mounting a horse.

"Molly," he called, "give me the bamboo thtick pleath."

Molly handed the fop the stick she'd used to thrash the Judge and with a whoop and a shrill blast from the hunting horn, Felix kicked his heels into the Judge's thighs as Joy began to pull the Judge on all fours around the room. Felix held onto the dog collar around the Judge's neck, whooping and occasionally pulling it back, encouraging the Judge to neigh like a horse while thwacking him sharply on his bare behind with the bamboo stick.

Ebenezer pulled Molly further into the shadows of the room, both bellyaching with laughter at what they were seeing, the sound of the Judge neighing like a horse while Felix blew on the hunting horn as he gave several sharp thwacks onto the Judge's bare buttocks was too much for them. They collapsed against the wall and sliding to the floor, they shook with uncontrollable laughter while more neighs and whoops echoed around the room.

"Fathter Nero," screamed the naked fop thwacking the Judge's bare behind with the stick, "there'th a foxth under that table, fathter, afore it geth away."

Ebenezer struggled to his feet convulsing with laughter as he watched a naked Joy pulling on the tautened rope attached to the dog collar around the Judge's neck, while the Judge, sweating profusely and purpling in the face, refused to move any further, his head drooping like a stubborn worn-out donkey.

"Enough," croaked the Judge, his tongue hanging from his mouth like a frazzled hound. "That was wonderful, but I can't go on. Felix and you, Joy, take me to the sofa and revitalise me. I'm in need of some soft pampering as you can see by the hardness growing on me."

Felix sprang off the Judge's back, unfastening the dog collar around his neck and with the help of Joy, assisted him to his feet where they staggered him over to the four-seater recliner. The Judge collapsed onto the sofa with a sigh, pawing at Felix as he shifted his flabby bulk into a comfortable position. Joy brought the Judge a goblet of wine which he downed in one, holding it out for a refill. As Joy went back to refill the goblet, Felix positioned his head between the Judge's thighs, his tongue expertly going to work on him. Joy handed the Judge his goblet and when he had drained it a second time, she gently straddled his face while his podgy hands groped and fondled her lower half.

As the carnal groans of pleasure rumbled out from the Judge, Ebenezer took Molly's hand and with a grin of excitement, led her from the room, smiling at the scene he'd just witnessed and the imprint it had left on his mind.

* * *

Nancy looked up from collecting a handful of empty ale mugs as Luc walked through the door of the inn. He looked tired as though he had been working hard which made Nancy wonder what he'd been up to and whether he'd been on the boat she'd seen flying the flag with the three golden lilies. As it was now getting late in the evening, he would be wanting a brandy, and after smoking a pipe, she knew he'd order another as a nightcap before retiring to his room.

"Evenin', lover," she said approaching his usual wooden booth. "Have you had a busy day?"

"Good evening, Nancy," replied Luc looking up at her. "Yes, as a matter of fact, it's been a busy day, thank you. Now, a large brandy would end it nicely if you please."

Nancy walked away, looking back over her shoulder at him filling his pipe. *Oi bet you'm have*, she thought, *and oi'll bet you'm goin' to have another one tomorrow. Oi'll be following behind you and it won't surprise me if you'm takes us all the way to that boat what flies that pretty flag.*

Luc sat back drawing on his pipe, waiting for Nancy to bring his brandy. It had been a busy day, he thought. He had delivered a message for his spy to the servants' entrance of Saltram House that afternoon, he was sure it would be handed on. The message contained instructions for his agent to meet him the next day, aboard a sloop moored in the Barbican opposite a copse of trees that fronted the Duke of York Inn. Luc had proposed the time of eleven in the morning, knowing that the busy time for staff in England's aristocratic mansions usually tailed off at around ten.

He'd given detailed instructions of how to get to the meeting place aboard the sloop, and to look out for the flag flying on the boat's stern that portrayed half of the city of Brest's emblem: three golden lilies on a blue background. He trusted his agent to be there.

Nancy returned with Luc's brandy and settling back with his pipe, he went over again in his mind the plan he had formulated for the assassination. Once his agent at Saltram House had been briefed again and Raymond was sure of his responsibility, he would then arrange the final meeting aboard the sloop which he knew would have to include Ebenezer. The 31st August was only four weeks away, which meant that everyone had to be ready and well-prepared.

"Nancy," he called out, "another brandy before I retire."

Nancy brought Luc's nightcap as he was tapping out the last of the glowing embers of his pipe onto the stone floor.

"Busy day tomorrow, lover?" she asked.

"That it may be, Nancy, but I'll breakfast here after nine. Should you be here at that time, I'd be obliged for my usual: bread, cheese, an onion and a pot of ale. Now, if you would excuse me, I think I'll retire."

Knocking back his brandy, he made his way out of the inn and up the dusky stairwell to where his room was situated at the end of the landing. A small table stood outside the privvy next to his room on which a box of candles had been placed. Taking a candle and holding the tapered part into the flame of a lantern fixed to the landing wall, a dark thought suddenly crossed his mind.

Nancy, he thought, *she's beginning to pry. She has asked me again if I'll be busy. I'm getting a feeling she's up to something, maybe she's not the stupid whore everyone thinks she is.*

Deep in thought, he unlocked his door and holding up the lighted candle, he squinted along the length of the landing. Satisfied that no-one was there, he let himself in, quietly closing the door behind him.

Nancy was at the inn early again the following morning, so surprising Ned as this was the second early time she had arrived well before her shift was meant to start. She explained that she had been awakened early yet again, due to problems going on with some tenants in the building where she lived. Early morning arguments and fights amongst those living in the room immediately above her, had caused her to leave her room early. Ned shrugged his shoulders, not particularly interested in Nancy's problems but pleased she was here to give him a hand in preparing the inn for the day's business.

"Oi can't pay 'ee till shift starts, Nance, but I'm glad of the help."

"Doen you worry about that, Master Ned, us be pleased to help you," replied Nancy. "Anyone been in for breakfast yet?"

"Ar," said Ned, "two of them from upstairs but not the one who sits in his usual booth at the far corner. I expect he'll be in soon, so's you can get his plate ready, Nancy."

Nancy remembered Luc telling her the previous night that he would breakfast around nine. That left just under half an hour before he came in. Getting his plate ready with the bread, cheese and onion, she looked over at Ned. "As me shift starts at a quarter before noon, Master Ned, us'll pop out later to do some jobs us's got to do. Oi'll be back before then."

"Ar, so be, Nance," said Ned, not looking up from washing a pile of mugs.

On the chime of nine o'clock, Luc entered the inn, giving Nancy a dark look that suggested she had done something to upset him.

"Mornin', lover," she called out as he made his way to his usual booth.

When he didn't answer, Nancy's imagination started to fire scary fantasies, that he'd found out she'd been in his room and that it was her who'd taken the document with the emblem of the golden crown on a shield lined with golden lilies. She looked at him, a cold anxious feeling beginning to creep over her.

Better take him his breakfast plate and pot of ale, she thought.

As she hovered before him, he looked up from filling his pipe. "Put my breakfast on the table please, Nancy," he said seriously. "You can see my hands are busy."

"There you'm be," she replied, putting the plate and ale on the table before him.

"And before you ask," he said looking up at her, "yes, I do have a busy day and I'd thank you to stop asking me that every time you see me. Now leave me in peace to enjoy my breakfast."

Luc's eyes followed her as she walked away.

Another thing, he thought, *it's early for her to be working now. I'm sure I've never seen her here much before noon.*

The sound of Ned changing some chairs at a nearby table caught Luc's attention.

"Ned," he called out, "good morning to you, can I have a word with you?"

"Mornin', Master Luc, how may oi be of help to you, sir?"

"Just a thought, Ned, has Nancy changed her shift times?"

"Naw, sir, she's been comin' in early only for the past two mornins. She says she can't sleep in mornins due to barnies goin' on in the room above hers. She helps me out so's us ain't complainin'."

"Mmm, I see," said Luc with a serious frown, "well, thank you, Ned."

Luc finished his breakfast and sat smoking a pipe while looking through some notes he had made the night before on the plans for the assassination. As the clock in the inn chimed the hour of ten, he put the notes away and draining his mug of ale, left without a word. Standing behind the bar, Nancy watched him leave. As quick as a flash, she followed him out, just managing to see him disappearing through the door that led to the rooms above the inn. She stood still, thinking. *Right*, she thought, *now we'll see!*

Going back inside the inn, she called out to Ned.

"Us'll be orf now, Master Ned, got some jobs to do. Be back well before me shift starts."

"So be, Nance," called Ned from the scullery.

Nancy grabbed her shawl and hurried out of the inn. There was no sign of Luc, so she crossed the street to where an old fisherman's shed stood and positioned herself behind the corner of the back panel. Peeping around its corner, she had a clear view of the inn. It wasn't not long before Luc appeared and giving a searching look to his left, he then turned in the opposite direction and hurried off towards the Duke of York Inn. Nancy was sure he would head towards the copse of trees that fronted the boat she had seen flying the pretty flag of the three golden lilies. Taking a deep breath, she followed.

From time to time she had to duck into cover, watching as Luc stopped to check he was not being followed. As they approached the copse of trees that looked out onto the Frenchies' boat, Luc halted. Nancy skipped behind one of the many trees that lined the path stretching along the Barbican. Peering around its trunk, she watched him check the time on a pocket watch he took from inside his coat pocket, then with a lengthy look around, he turned and stepped onto the boat's gangplank that jutted out onto the side of the pathway. At the top, he looked around again before disappearing onto the boat. She waited for a while in case he reappeared, but there was no sign of him. She was just about to leave the cover of the tree when she saw a tall man dressed in what looked like the livery of an aristocratic household stop at the gangplank and refer to a note of paper in his hand. He then turned and cautiously made his way along the gangplank and onto the boat.

Well, there be somethin' goin' on in there, she thought, *us's gonna find out.*

Leaving the tree behind her, she walked towards the boat, her eyes fixed on the gangplank. Should anyone suddenly appear, she knew she had a quick escape route along the path, but once aboard, it would be a different story.

With careful steps, she made her way along the plank, jumping delicately onto the deck. Holding her breath, she stood rock still, listening for any sound that would warn her to make a sharp getaway. All was quiet. Cautiously making her way along the port side and past the sloop's single mast, she came across what looked like an open trap door cut into the deck. A wooden ladder led down into a dark hold and as she bent her head to peer further into the black hole, the sound of muffled voices rose from the darkness below.

Slowly, taking step by step and clutching a rusty railing, she descended into the sloop's dusky hold. At the bottom of the ladder, a few paces in front of her, a small dirty window cut into a wooden door was giving off a dim light. Taking a deep breath, she made her way towards it. She could hear voices coming from behind the door speaking in a language she could not understand.

She listened again with her ear close to the door and then it dawned on her that the language she was hearing had to be French. Rose and Daisy had told her the boat they'd seen Luc going onto previously was run by a crew of Frenchies, which meant whoever was in that room, including Luc, were all French. Wide-eyed with curiosity, she stretched herself up on her toes to squint through the dirty window.

Seated around a table listening intently to Luc were five other men. She recognised the one dressed in livery as the one who had boarded the sloop before she had. Seated to the right of Luc, a small thin man wearing an eye patch, whose features reminded her of a weasel, scratched his head under a filthy looking bandana.

He must have been the one who gave Rose a rough seeing to. She said he'd been wearing an eye patch, she remembered.

Nancy's ears pricked up as she suddenly heard the words 'Saltram House' being repeated several times as the conversation became louder. She watched as Luc turned to face the liveried Frenchman, speaking rapidly as if giving instructions, the words 'Saltram House' being said again and again.

Bliddy hell, thought Nancy, *Saltram House be up Plympton way. Wish oi could understand what's bein' said.*

The conversation in French suddenly quietened down as Raymond left the table to return with two bottles of wine. Nancy watched as the group of spies lifted their glasses to each other in a toast.

"*Sante*," said Luc, "or as they say in English, your good health."

Nancy caught her breath as Luc continued in English, "Until our next meeting, my friends. Two weeks from this day aboard this sloop. The next meeting will be in English as we will have our English counterpart with us. Now let us enjoy Raymond's wine!"

English counterpart? asked Nancy to herself. *Who the bliddy hell could that be. Whomever he be, he be a bliddy traitor.*

Tiptoeing back to the ladder, Nancy clambered up its slippery steps. Scurrying across the deck to the gangplank, she wondered who the Englishman Luc had mentioned could be and if he had ever been to the inn. A cold feeling swept over her as she asked herself if she might have ever taken his shilling! With a quick look behind, she leapt off the gangplank and raced away up the pathway.

The distant sound of a clock striking the hour of midday stirred her back to reality.

"Oh shit," she mumbled, "us's quarter of an hour late for me shift. No worries, oi've made up for it with early mornins, sure Ned'll be alright with it."

Stopping to look back in the direction of the Frenchies' sloop, she breathed in heavily thinking aloud, "Two weeks today, that's what ee'm said, and us'll be there listenin' to what they'm plannin'. They'ms all traitors and spies. Us'll find out, just see!"

Chapter 29

Ebenezer sat in the Squire's coach gazing out of the window at the brightly coloured pastures that an early midsummer morning brought to the rich and fertile countryside of Devon. His mind was occupied with a multitude of flashing thoughts, the blackmailing of Judge Pickering later that day, the trial of Mordechai and Watt, the assassination of George III which would only be a month away and the undertaking with John Parker to snare Obadiah Tucker.

He had left Darton Hall after the night's banquet knowing that the Judge, then quite drunk, would not miss him. He had slipped away quietly to where the Squire's two-horse-driven carriage awaited him in the cobblestoned courtyard. The Squire had managed to steal away from his guests, to see Ebenezer off and to ensure that all would go to plan for the following day's entrapment. He'd smiled as Ebenezer confirmed he was more than ready for the sting.

Far below the hall, the early morning sun glinted off the River Dart as the coachman brought the two horses to a stop in the medieval courtyard. Ebenezer gave his thanks for the ride and hoisting his toga, he hurried up the steps that led into the Great Hall. A few early morning risers greeted him as he made his way towards a long table laden with bread, fruit, cold meats and jugs of sweet wine.

"Cicero," a voice boomed as he was helping himself to the delicacies that adorned the table. Judge Pickering waddled over to where Ebenezer stood, his eyes wandering over the breakfast delights.

"Good morning to you, Cicero," he wheezed, his face puffy and flushed. "Sorry I missed you last night, but I was quite drunk, you know. Retired rather late and woke up still dressed in my toga, what! Ha, well, it is another day. I trust you're looking forward to it, eh?"

"Oh, that I am, Nero," replied Ebenezer with a smirk.

"Come, Cicero, sit with me while we feast on this scrumptious breakfast."

Taking two plates that he piled high with a variety of the food on the table, he shuffled over to where they had been seated the night before.

"Before you begin, Cicero, I'd be grateful if you'd fetch me two goblets of wine. Have a raging thirst on me, thank you."

Ebenezer rose from the table, grinning at the Judge's blatant gluttony, watching him grab fistfuls of cold meats which he stuffed vigorously into an already full mouth.

"Cicero, I trust all is well this morning?" a voice asked. Turning, Ebenezer faced a smiling Squire.

"That it is, Caesar," replied Ebenezer. "All is set for an interesting day. I am sure it will go well. Now, if you would excuse me, I'm on my way to fill two goblets of wine for Nero. Can't keep him waiting, can I!"

"Ahh!" said the judge, licking his lips after draining the first goblet of wine. "It looks like a warm sunny day, Cicero. What say you about taking a stroll with those two hot little minxes we dallied with yesterday? We could go skinny dipping in the river, what!"

Anything but bathing in the nude would have been acceptable to Ebenezer, but knowing he had to keep the Judge's confidence in him, he reluctantly agreed.

"Very well, Nero," he said, hoping the sky would blacken and pour with rain for the rest of the day.

"Have some more wine while I look for the girls."

Ebenezer wandered over to where the Squire, chuckling and chewing on a turkey leg, was moving away from a group of his guests. Still laughing, he turned to Ebenezer. "Remind me to tell you that joke later on," he said, "Looks like you've got something to ask me, Cicero?"

"Nero's suggested we go skinny dipping with the two girls we had yesterday," whispered Ebenezer. "It'll keep him happy. Alright with you?"

Squire Maddock nearly choked on his turkey leg. "You and that flabby lump jumping into the river nude! Ha, ha, what a sight that will be! Tell the girls I approve. Be back in plenty of time for the afternoon banquet; it begins at three and you have got to trap him before the feast starts. Meet me here before you bring him in, we will have a final briefing and I'll show the room where you can take him. Remember our necks are on the line, it is all up to you. Skinny dipping, eh? Ha, what a sight that'll be!"

Molly looked up while listening to the group of musicians playing new themes of Ancient Rome as Ebenezer approached. "By the look on your face, something tells me I'm needed again, Cicero."

"Be careful, Molly, the look on my face doesn't always say what I'm intending. You and Joy are to accompany myself and Nero for a stroll down to the river and then for a…" Ebenezer paused, reluctant to mention nude bathing.

"For a what?" asked Molly with an eyebrow raised.

"For, for a skinny dip!" said Ebenezer hesitantly. "The Squire's approved it."

Molly looked at Ebenezer open-mouthed, then looking around to see that no-one was listening, lowered her voice and with a soft giggle said, "You'm want me and Joy to take all our clothes off and jump into the river with you and that lardy, pig-like mutation of something that would be a star attraction in the circus?"

"Well, I can assure you, it wasn't my idea. It was Nero's," moaned Ebenezer.

"It was N- e- r- o's," whined Molly sarcastically, copying Ebenezer's disgruntled tone. "Us's only jokin," she giggled. "Meet us back here in 'alf the hour, us'll go and fetch Joy. Skinny dippin, ha, ha!"

The Judge, still gorging on a freshly stacked plate of cold meats, wiped his greasy mouth on the sleeve of his toga as Ebenezer re-joined him at the table.

"Well, Cicero?" he said, his eyes widening in expectation. "Are the minxes ready for a bit of aqua play, what?"

"Ready and willing, Nero," replied Ebenezer with a smirk. "We'll meet them in half an hour."

"Phaw, what ho!" said the judge. "Hot little bitches naked in the river, eh! You can watch again, Cicero, while I have them both, what!"

Ebenezer and the Judge followed Molly and Joy into a field and down a grassy track that dropped steeply to where the river gently flowed. At the bottom, the two women slipped out of their gowns to lie naked on the lush grass, soaking up the warm sun. Grunting and breathing heavily, the Judge pulled off his toga, his white spacious underpants fluttering like a flag of surrender in the warm breeze. Not being able to suppress the laughter that was welling up inside of him, Ebenezer walked away towards the edge of the river, chuckling as the vision of the Judge in his cavernous underpants drooling at the two women, stuck in his mind.

"Come on, Cicero, off with that toga," urged Molly coming up behind him. Ebenezer felt a warm hand slip inside his toga to find its way towards where he was already springing to life. Gasping at the surprise of Molly's soft hand on his growing stiffness, he murmured in pleasure, willing her to continue. Grinning at him seductively, she suddenly pulled her hand away and laughing propelled herself headfirst into a deep pool of the river. Gazing after her, Ebenezer watched her stroking out gracefully under the water. And then, as if in slow motion, she kicked her legs and surfaced, rivulets of streaming water funnelling from her silky hair.

"Come on, Reverend," she mouthed silently, "come and get me!"

For a moment Ebenezer was sure he heard her say, "It'll only cost you a shillin'!" but he knew he was wrong as she duck-dived to swim back under the water to where he stood.

Looking back over his shoulder, he chuckled as he saw the Judge fumbling to get out of his underpants while Joy lay stretched out in the warmth of the sun.

Without a thought he pulled off his toga and stepping out of his underwear, took a flying leap into the water below. Holding his breath, he felt the chill of the water enveloping him, and as he surfaced, soft arms encircled him as Molly's full wet lips met his in an ardent sensual kiss.

Towards the middle of the river, a lonely rock loomed up from the water and detaching herself from Ebenezer, she breast-stroked up to it, beckoning him to follow. Not being much of a swimmer, he was reluctant to follow, but the sweet taste of her lips on his and the sight of her glistening breasts protruding from the water was too alluring to turn down. Kicking out, he doggy-paddled over to where she stood on some sleek flat rocks under the water. With her back to a smooth part of the rock, she pulled him close, feeling for his hardness.

Grasping him, she groaned, her tongue licking and caressing her own lips in her wild passion. Ebenezer looked upon her as she writhed sensually against him, his hardness at its limit. With a slight hoist and her breath accelerating into rapid pants, she wrapped her long legs around him, guiding him into her warm moist womanhood. Silence reigned over the Dart and the surrounding countryside, broken only by the moans and gasps that rose from the rock in the middle of the river as Molly gave way to the heightening well of pleasure coursing through her. With a piercing wail, she orgasmed, throwing her head back with gratifying delight as her body shook with spasms of pleasure. Ebenezer grasped her tightly as he felt himself explode into her warmness, panting with elation at the astounding intimacy he'd just experienced.

The sound of high-pitched giggling from the riverbank followed by an almighty splash then a gentler one, told Ebenezer the Judge and Joy were in the river. Slipping away from Molly, he stepped onto the flat stones under the water, and peeping around the large rock, watched the lily-white body of the Judge splashing around in front of Joy while she teased him, floating on her back with legs wide open, then backstroking away as he slipped and blundered after her. Then to Ebenezer's surprise, he suddenly submerged, wading under the water like a great hippopotamus to where she lay floating on her back. Joy's shocked scream of surprise as he sprung up out of the water to grab her in his arms aroused flocks of birds in the riverside trees that suddenly took to flight, squawking and cawing in dismay. Bellowing with laughter, the Judge turned her around in the water and lifting her slightly, pressed her dripping rear into his flabby lower front half.

A slight touch on Ebenezer's shoulder told him Molly was at his side. Smiling wickedly at the sight of the Judge performing with Joy, she clasped Ebenezer's arm, gently guiding him back over the underwater stones to the riverbank and the warmth of the sun in the lush long grass.

Ebenezer chuckled as he watched the Judge trying to clamber up the bank while Joy pushed and shoved him from behind. The Judge, red in the face and sweating all over, reminded Ebenezer of a picture he had once seen of a pioneer trying to push a stubborn mule up a steep mountain slope. Grunting and snorting river water from his nostrils, the Judge flopped down on the grass next to Ebenezer, a swarm of riverside flies and flying insects buzzing around him like bees on a honey pot.

"Damn little pests," he puffed, swatting at several that had settled on his flaccid breasts, "they always seem drawn to me!"

Mmm, thought Ebenezer, *probably the only species that are.*

"My stomach's telling me it must be past the hour of noon," the Judge exclaimed sitting up straight. "A little luncheon in preparation for the sumptuous feast we'll be having later would be a good idea. WOULD it not, Cicero?"

"Absolutely, Nero, it's time we should go anyway," said Ebenezer, thinking of his role as Septimus Sniff.

Molly and Joy led the way up the steep track, stopping halfway up for Ebenezer and the Judge to catch their breath. Looking down at the River Dart that snaked its way through the flat pastures of Dartington and on towards Totnes, and hence past Sharpham Point and Dittisham, Ebenezer pondered on how he'd accuse Judge Pickering of the carnality he'd recently witnessed him performing.

"I'll think of a way," he mumbled, "I'll just have to. Couldn't care a fig about the Squire's neck, but it's mine I've got to save."

With a deep sigh, he fell into step behind the Judge as Molly and Joy pushed on up the hilly path towards Darton Hall and the finale that awaited them there.

* * *

"Don't forget to mention Samuel Johnson," said the Squire as Ebenezer turned to leave the hall after their final briefing.

"I have it all prepared, Squire, trust me," replied Ebenezer. "The Judge will be outside the hall presently."

They had returned to the hall as a light luncheon was being served to those guests who were too hungry to wait for the banquet at three o'clock. The Judge had gorged himself on what was on offer, retiring after several jugs of wine for a siesta, to prepare himself, as he said, for the final grand banquet at three. Ebenezer had proposed they meet an hour before, tempting him with a lie that Felix would be waiting for him in the room where he had performed the horse and jockey charade the previous day. Unable to resist the prospect of an hour with the little lisping fop, the Judge had readily agreed. Squire Maddock had shown Ebenezer the room where he was to spring the trap and as the hour approached two o'clock, he had nodded to the Squire and hurried from the hall. There was no going back now, everything was ready.

Ebenezer waited patiently outside the doors of the Great Hall as servants breezed in and out with various dishes of mouth-watering delicacies.

"A feast fit for kings and queens," muttered the Judge as he shuffled up to where Ebenezer was waiting. "Lead on, Cicero, I shan't dally long with the pretty boy, not with what awaits in the hall at three. Be sure to make him understand that there'll be no horse and jockey games today."

With a smile, Ebenezer turned to walk through the Great Hall when the Judge took his arm. "The other way, Cicero," he said pointing down the corridor, "that's the way to the room we were in yesterday."

"Ah, not exactly, Nero," replied Ebenezer, "that room is presently occupied, Felix has suggested you meet him in a quiet room just off the hall, this way."

The Judge followed Ebenezer through the Great Hall, passing the Squire who nodded and smiled at the two of them. Ebenezer felt the eyes of the Squire following them across the hall to where they stopped in front of the door to the room that would witness their evasion of the hangman or their doom on the gallows. With a glance over his shoulder at the Squire, Ebenezer opened the door and ushered the Judge inside.

A small table with two chairs stood in front of a glass-panelled window where beams of sunlight highlighted the confused look spreading over the Judge's features.

"Are we early, Cicero, or is this the wrong room?"

"No, this is not the wrong room, Judge Pickering," said Ebenezer, putting on a stern voice.

"What, how do you know my name?" said the Judge, his tone changing.

"I know your name and everything about you," replied Ebenezer. "You are an immoral, disgusting abuser of women and boys."

"What?" shouted the Judge, his double chins wavering as his face reddened. "How dare you! I demand to see the Squire, right now."

"If you leave this room now, then your life as you know it, will be over forever," said Ebenezer, looking sternly at the judge.

"Who, who are you?" asked the Judge sounding anxious.

"My name is Septimus Sniff," said Ebenezer, putting on an air of importance. "I am a writer of considerable influence and have been commissioned by The Gentleman's Magazine, of which I am sure you are aware, to write an article exposing the corrupt and immoral practices of the upper classes and those in high positions. I know that you, Judge Edmund Pickering, are a hedonist and a practicing sexual deviant who uses and abuses both sexes for your own self-gratification. My close colleague and friend, Samuel Johnson, also a writer and a moral Christian, is awaiting my report, which he will then submit for publication in the magazine. We are going to ruin you, sir. Publicly expose you through our magazine as a sinful, gluttonous, alcoholic sexual pervert who has no right to pontificate to those unfortunates who come before you in a court of law. My report will find its way to the House of Lords and to those law lords who strongly speak out against such sinful practices that you wallow in."

"This is preposterous," yelled the Judge, "you have no proof. I'll have you arrested before the day is out."

"On the contrary, sir," said Ebenezer. "I have witnesses in this great building who are willing to testify that you, sir, are everything I have accused you of."

"What? Whores and queers," shouted the judge.

"No, sir, genuine employees of the Squire. Coachmen, cooks and servants. All moral Christian folk who are only here as they need to earn a living."

"What about the Squire and the other guests who are here?" asked the Judge, his voice shaking.

"Yes, they will be mentioned in my report as sinful pleasure seekers. But they are not high officers of the law as you are, sir. You are a Judge and should be morally higher than them. But what I have seen is sadly not the case. I have witnessed your depravity, sir, and will describe your depraved actions in detail. Every sinful act you have committed will be printed, together with testimony from those with whom you fornicated and abused."

"But, but surely there is a way you can be persuaded not to print all this," pleaded the Judge, knowing he was trapped.

"Ah, ah," said Ebenezer, "are you attempting a bribe, sir?"

"Well, no, not exactly as you put it, Master Sniff," said the Judge, looking faint and about to collapse. "Perhaps something beneficial to you, or something I could do to benefit you in any way that would help you personally?"

"Wait here, sir," said Ebenezer, "I need some refreshment. I am a Christian, sir, and would not deter from offering you drink. Would a cup of wine be of help to you?"

"That it would, Master Sniff," said the Judge, "and thank you."

Seeing Ebenezer come out of the room, the Squire rushed over, quietly taking him by his arm. "Well," he said earnestly, "how's it going?"

"I think I've got him," said Ebenezer. "I'm letting him stew now while I fetch some wine, then I'll go in for the kill."

"Ah, the coup de grâce," said the Squire. "Excellent. When you have finished, give me a nod then leave him to me and leave. I will have my coachman waiting to take you back in the next twenty minutes. Forget the banquet. I'll call on you tomorrow after your Sunday service."

Ebenezer returned to the room carrying a jug of wine and two goblets. Judge Pickering looked in a worse state than when Ebenezer had left the room; he sat with his hands over his eyes, his flabby frame trembling in apprehension.

"Take this," said Ebenezer, offering a goblet of wine to the Judge.

"If there's anything I can do to stop you printing this about me, then I'd be only too willing," said the Judge, taking the goblet from Ebenezer.

"I feel it my Christian duty to inform the innocent of what goes on in the higher circles of society," said Ebenezer, getting ready to make the offer. "But Christian duty is also to forgive and not to be the punisher. Let him who is without sin cast the first stone. So, Judge Pickering, there may be something that could deter me from using your name in my report."

"Yes, yes, you only have to ask, Master Sniff."

"You are the Judge at the assize court in Plymouth next Tuesday, are you not?" asked Ebenezer.

"That I am," replied the Judge.

"There will be a trial of a gang of smugglers accused of despatching smuggled goods from a French ship that unloaded its supply of contraband on Elberry Cove some weeks ago."

"That will be so," said the Judge.

"Amongst that rabble," said Ebenezer, taking his time, "will be two miscreants by the names of Watt Huckle and Mordechai Brunt. Concerning their guilt, there is no doubt. I expect you to pass the sentence of hanging on the group, but concerning the two smugglers I have just mentioned, they are to hang immediately and without any delay. The following day would be appropriate. I'm not concerned with the other members of the gang, only Huckle and Brunt."

Judge Pickering nodded. "I have your guarantee, Master Sniff, that my name will be erased from your report and the article that will be published?"

"You have, sir," replied Ebenezer.

"And may I ask your reason for this?" asked the Judge.

"You may not, sir," said Ebenezer indignantly. "It is enough for you to comply, and then forget the whole incident as I will, regarding your name and your association with this depraved group of sinners. It was by my deceiving them, particularly the Squire, that I managed to infiltrate this den of depravity."

"Consider your request granted, Master Sniff. Watt Huckle and Mordechai Brunt will hang within twenty-four hours of being found guilty, you have my word."

"Very well," said Ebenezer, "go and feast on the sumptuous banquet that awaits and not a word of this to anyone here, especially Squire Maddock. My sources will report to me on the trial next Tuesday. Good day, sir."

Judge Pickering left the room, not acknowledging the Squire who was busying himself outside the door. Ebenezer filled a goblet with wine, draining it in one quick draught, then looking towards the Squire who had entered the room, nodded to him with a satisfied grin. As Ebenezer walked towards the door, he stopped and turned. "Give this to Molly," he said holding out a guinea, "tell her it's as I promised for a job well-done and by the way, I told her you'd give her one too. It's done, they'll hang within twenty-four hours of being found guilty, and then we'll be off the hook. Best to keep away from the Judge at the banquet. Leave our next meeting until the Monday. I'll expect you in the afternoon."

Squire Maddock nodded.

"Now, Caesar," said Ebenezer still grinning, "if your coachman's ready, Septimus Sniff, or is it Cicero, needs to go home!"

The Squire's coach pulled up outside Ebenezer's Ashprington residence as the church clock struck the hour of four. Weary and in need to shed the ridiculous toga that now hung like a bed sheet around him, Ebenezer nodded his thanks towards the coachman. A sudden thunderous sound of hoofbeats pulling a speeding carriage caused Ebenezer to jump back in alarm, the vibrating noise spooking the two horses attached to the Squire's coach. Looking over his shoulder at the advancing carriage, the Squire's coachman tried to steady his horses as a shrill blast from a hunting horn blared out from the rear of the approaching coach, warning anyone attempting to cross the village hill to get out of the way. As the speeding carriage advanced towards Ebenezer's residence, it slowed down to manoeuvre past the Squire's carriage. Squinting at its window, Ebenezer made out the shape of a single passenger cloaked and wearing what looked to be a naval officer's bicorn hat. As he peered closer, the figure turned to look out of the window, his face looking directly at Ebenezer. With a startled cry, Ebenezer stepped back as the carriage moved by. He watched as it gathered speed to take the route past the fields of Sharpham Estate and on towards the manor house that overlooked the River Dart. Captain Philemon Pownoll was back in Ashprington and on his way to his home at Sharpham Manor.

Chapter 30

Jane looked out of the parlour window at the sound of a carriage pulling up in the drive outside the main doors of the manor house. The afternoon sunshine glinted off the coach as a cloaked figure descended the carriage steps and with his back to the parlour window, stretched up to pay the coachman for the ride. Tossing a coin up to the guard at the back of the carriage, he turned and picking up his bag made his way to the front door. Wide-eyed and with her hand up to her mouth in shocked surprise, Jane let out a shriek of ecstasy as she recognised the smiling figure making his way to the front door.

"Jane," she screamed to her daughter upstairs, "come down quickly, Papa is here."

Throwing open the door, she screeched in delight, tears welling up in her eyes as Philemon stood with his arms open. Not waiting for her daughter to appear, she flung herself into his arms, hugging him close while the tears cascaded down her cheeks.

"Am I dreaming?" she sobbed looking into his face.

"No, Jane, I'm home," he said softly, tears also welling up in his eyes.

"Papa!" young Jane shrieked, appearing at the door and throwing herself at her father. "Oh, Papa, you're home, you're home!"

With his left arm wrapped around Jane, he heaved his daughter up with his right arm gazing into her face and relishing the loving look of adoration that radiated back at him. Out of the corner of his eye, he noticed Betsy hovering by the open front door.

"Hello, Betsy," he said, "would you be so kind as to bring my bag in. Thank you."

"Welcome home, sir," said Betsy picking up his bag.

Holding his two Janes, Philemon made his way into the house, stopping in the grand hallway to breathe deeply the scent and atmosphere of his home. With his eyes closed in a prayer of thanksgiving, he held his wife and daughter close to him as if not wishing this profound moment to pass.

"Come, my darlings," he said opening his eyes, "let us to the parlour. I'm hungry and tired."

"I'll bring tea and muffins, ma'am," said Betsy.

"Thank you, Betsy," said Jane smiling, "and please inform the cook there'll be an extra place at dinner. The Master's home!"

Philemon sat in his usual comfortable chair listening to young Jane's account of her sittings for Sir Joshua Reynolds and the exact likeness of her features he had finalised in his sketches of her. Philemon could see that her mother was itching to talk, but his daughter now held the floor and was not going to be hushed into silence. Philemon let her continue, smiling at her confidence and persistence in being heard. When at last she had run out of words, she ran to her father, snuggling down in his lap while her mother poured the tea that Betsy had brought in.

"Now, Philemon," she said, "this wonderful surprise, what brings you home unannounced?"

Putting the cup of tea his wife had handed him onto a side table next to his chair, Philemon looked over at Jane.

"We left Chatham for Liverpool earlier than expected on May 10. Once in Liverpool, we rested for a day and then set sail to escort the troop carriers across the Atlantic to Boston. All was going well until we came in sight of Boston Harbour six weeks later. I remember standing on the quarterdeck viewing the distant harbour when a warning cry from the lookout in the crow's nest alerted us to a flotilla of enemy vessels approaching us on our port side. I gave instructions for a beat to action stations and to ready our twenty-eight guns. My ship and the other escorts were shielding the troop carriers when the enemy attacked. They were well-prepared for action and must have been waiting for us in the inlets and coves that stretch along the coastal approach to Boston Harbour."

Philemon paused to take several sips of tea, noticing the wide-eyed looks of apprehension on Jane's and young Jane's faces.

"They came at us with such a speed that we only had minutes to ready ourselves. Looking through my glass, I made out a force of several sloops-of-war, some old French frigates and a collection of whaling ships that had been equipped with nine-pounder cannons. Shielding the troop carriers, we turned to meet them broadside, knowing we had superior firepower but expecting casualties in their first attack. As they came into range, they turned, opening fire at the same time as we did. Twelve guns on our port side opened-up, as did the other escorts. Nine-pounders flew over us, whistling as they cut through the air and then there was a deafening crash as one of the balls sliced our mizzen. When the smoke cleared, I saw we had crippled two of their old frigates and blown many of their whaling ships to smithereens. The remainder of their flotilla, much depleted, had turned and were racing away towards safe havens. But they had achieved their purpose, to harry us and inflict damage. The troop carriers were untouched as were the other escorts, but my ship had lost its mizzen and half a dozen of my crew dead. They had known we were coming. Somehow, they had had information of when and where we would be approaching Boston Harbour. They had known about us coming well before we arrived and likely how many troop carriers we were escorting. I believe they were tipped off by a spy before we left England. How that could've been, I'd love to know!"

"When did you get back, dearest?" asked Jane, still wide-eyed at Philemon's account.

"After the rebels had retreated, we took stock of our injuries," said Philemon. "The remaining escorts were intact and able to continue on to Boston Harbour escorting the troop carriers. My ship, however, needed a new mizzen which was not possible to replace in Boston due to a lack of materials and expertise. There is an ever-increasing blockade on the town and harbour there, but our frigates escorting the troop carriers managed to break through without any great difficulty. My ship was ordered to return to Plymouth for the fitting of a new mizzen and with clement weather and favourable winds across the Atlantic, we were able to limp back using only the sails on our fore and main masts. We arrived early this morning. While the ship's in dock undergoing the refitting, I'm on leave to remain here until word reaches me that the ship's ready to sail again."

"There's been some dreadful news, dearest, since you've been away," said Jane. "I wrote to you about a month after you'd left England for Boston. John has also written to you, both our letters concerning two very crucial issues that are affecting us and the village."

"Your correspondence is probably awaiting me in Boston," said Philemon, "but as I've been at sea for the better part of three months, I've no idea of what's been happening. Please tell me, Jane."

"My letter was written to advise you that young Watt Huckle was arrested for smuggling contraband. He was chased on horseback by the Revenue across Churston Common several weeks ago. A lucky shot brought down his horse and he was caught with smuggled containers of French cognac strapped to his horse. He has been sent to Plymouth Gaol to await trial at the assizes which begin next Tuesday. But what is more, is that Mordechai came forward and owned up in front of the Paignton magistrate, John's brother Montague, in being the instigator of Watt's involvement, and to being part of the smuggling heist. Montague had him arrested on the spot and taken to Plymouth Gaol where he too will stand trial along with Watt. It's expected that they'll both be hanged."

"Good Lord!" exclaimed Philemon, unable to believe what he was hearing. "Is there any way we can stop this? This is dreadful, Jane!"

"John's petitioning Lord North our Prime Minister, but there's been no news from him so far. I feel there is not much hope now as it's only three more days until the trial. There's another matter also."

"Not more arrests, I hope," said Philemon.

"No, dearest," replied Jane. "Montague advised John that he strongly believes there's a smuggling ring operating here in Ashprington. John's taken it very seriously as he is the Member of Parliament for Devon and is determined to find out who may be behind it. I believe he has already started his investigations, but I haven't heard from him for some time, so I haven't any more news about it. This was the second issue in our letters to you."

"Well, well," said Philemon, lifting his daughter off his lap and getting up from his chair. "Everything was so peaceful while I was here. War comes, and I leave with the navy and then serious trouble breaks out here at home. I suppose it is lucky in a way that I've been brought back here. I will add my weight behind yours and John's to see what we can do to try to save Watt and Mordechai from the hangman. If their trial is set for Tuesday, it does not give us much time. Jane, tomorrow is Sunday and I know John will be at home. I think we should go down to Saltram House first thing in the morning. Can you see to it that Betsy is here to take care of young Jane while we are away? I know it's Sunday, but this is now vitally important."

"Yes, dearest," replied Jane nodding, "I quite agree. I'll go and have a word with Betsy now. Come, Jane, let us see if the cook's preparing dinner."

* * *

John and Theresa Parker were breakfasting with their young son John when John's footman, Andrew, interrupted them.

"Excuse the interruption, sir," said Andrew, "Captain Pownoll and Mistress Jane have arrived and are waiting in the reception hall."

"What, Philemon here with Jane?" exclaimed John jumping out of his chair in surprise.

John called out to his two friends waiting patiently by the main front doors as he hurried down the long corridor that led to the reception area, his breakfast napkin still tucked under his chin.

"Dearest friends, what brings you to Saltram on this pleasant morning? It is wonderful to see you both. Come, join us for breakfast, we have only just started. Philemon, what brings you back from the navy?"

Smiling at the warm welcome from John, they followed him into the parlour where Theresa, now heavily pregnant, sat beaming with surprised pleasure at their unexpected visit.

"Dear friends, come and join us please," she said looking up at them.

"Andrew," said John turning to his footman, "breakfast for our two guests please."

"Sir," replied Andrew with a nod as he left the room.

"Now, Philemon, please tell us what the cause of this wonderful surprise could be, and what brings you back from the navy?"

Over breakfast, Philemon recounted the attack on his convoy at the approach to Boston Harbour and of his suspicions concerning a spy. He sat back listening intently as John gave an account of the meeting with his brother Montague and of Mordechai's confession. John looked disappointed when he told Philemon and Jane that Lord North had declined to help by interceding on Watt's and Mordechai's behalf. But he himself as the Member of Parliament for Devon, would plead for them in a private meeting with Judge Pickering before the trial opened. He went on to tell them of his brother's concern of a smuggling ring operating in the village of Ashprington.

"This is news to me, John," said Philemon, looking at Jane in a serious manner. "Jane mentioned it to me after relating the account of Watt and Mordechai. I would never have believed it in our village. Who on earth could be behind this?"

"Well," said John, looking seriously at Philemon and Jane, "I went to see the temporary rector of Ashprington Church, the Reverend Ebenezer Dunn, hoping he may be able to suggest any suspicions he may have of anyone in the village who may be involved in any smuggling activity."

"He's a strange one," said Philemon. "I only met him once, outside the church after a Sunday service before I left for the navy. His ridiculous presence in front of the congregation and when he addressed us outside, caused Jane to hurriedly retreat from him in raptures of laughter. I saw him yesterday as I was passing through the village in the carriage that brought me home from Plymouth. He was standing outside his residence wrapped in a kind of white sheet and wearing Roman type sandals laced halfway up his calves. He looked the epitome of ridiculousness. How he could help in your investigations, I have no idea. The man's a joke!"

From the corner of his eye, John saw Jane with her hand to her mouth, trying to supress the giggles that had started in her at the mention of the Reverend's name.

"On the contrary, my friends," said John. "He was most helpful. In fact, he gave me the name of the ringleader of the smugglers and where they operate from. He later made some enquiries, managing to find out that the smugglers would be returning with a supply of contraband about a week from now. The Revenue will be waiting for them. I hope to convince Judge Pickering to postpone the trial until we have this villainous smuggler in custody, together with his admission of organising the smuggling heist that Watt and Mordechai foolishly took part in. This may sway the judge to give them a lighter sentence. Reverend Dunn is certain that this blackguard is the mastermind of all the smuggling activity going on in this part of Devon. When he is hanged, the smuggling will cease, mark my words."

"Who is this scoundrel?" asked Philemon.

"The reverend is certain the rascal's name is Obadiah Tucker. He lies low in his lair off the River Dart, near the harbour of Dittisham. We'll lay a trap and catch him and his crew as they return with their hoard."

"The trial of Mordechai and Watt," said Philemon, "I assume it will be held at the assize court near Plymouth Hoe?"

"Yes," replied John, "on Tuesday at ten o'clock. The judge presiding, Judge Edmund Pickering, has a reputation for speedy trials so I am sure he'll direct the jury to come to a verdict before the day is out. Those on trial, including your stable boy Huckle, were all caught red-handed so there is nothing to disprove their guilt. Mordechai's admitted to being part of the heist, so he will be found guilty. It will then depend on the judge's summing up and the sentences he'll pass down. But if I can convince him, when we meet in private before the trial opens, that I will have evidence that could prove Mordechai and Watt were only taking orders from the ringleader, he may be swayed to postpone the trial until Tucker can be brought before him."

"Yes, I see," said Philemon. "I'd be pleased to accompany you to the trial, John."

"Absolutely, Philemon. Sir Joshua, I am sure, will join us too. May I suggest we meet here at eight in the morning? My meeting with the judge is scheduled for nine o'clock. Now, the ladies look as though they'd enjoy a stroll in the gardens."

"Ha, as a matter of fact, so would I," said Philemon, rising from his chair with a smile.

"Just one moment, before we all go out," said Theresa, looking over at John. "Philemon and Jane are our good friends, John, I'm sure we can trust them to keep the secret."

Intrigued, Philemon sat down again, looking at Theresa and then at John.

"One moment," said John, rising from his chair and opening the parlour door. When he was satisfied no-one was lingering outside, he closed the door, re-taking his seat at the table.

"We trust you both not to say a word to anyone about what I'm about to tell you."

"You both have our silence, on our honour," said Philemon.

"A month from now, a very important person will be coming to Saltram for a night's stay," continued John, looking at them seriously. "The King."

"Phew," said Philemon aloud. "The King? Why so, John?"

"The King will be making a Proclamation of Rebellion to Parliament on the 23rd of August. This means that the colonists in our American colonies taking part in the rebellion, will be formally declared as traitors and rebels to the crown. It is a justification for all-out war and an increase of troops to the fighting. The King will give an address to troops about to embark from Plymouth on September 1. This means he must stay somewhere before the address the following morning and he has chosen here, Saltram House."

"What an honour for you," said Jane smiling at Theresa.

"Theresa and I were going to discuss this with Jane as the time of his visit grew nearer, as you have now unexpectedly returned from the navy, Philemon, we naturally include you."

"My ship will be in dock for at least six weeks," said Philemon.

"In that case," said John smiling at Philemon and Jane, "we'd like you both to be guests at a special dinner we'll be holding for the King on the night of his stay. Sir Joshua will also be present. You will, of course, stay the night yourselves."

"It will be an honour, John," said Philemon looking at Jane.

"Wonderful!" said Theresa grinning at them. "Now, we can talk more about it out in the gardens. I need some fresh air. Come, Jane, we have to talk about what we're going to wear!"

Philemon followed them out to the neatly cut lawns that covered the outside west wing of Saltram. As he watched Jane and his friends stroll happily across the lawn, he couldn't help but think that he'd never have believed it if anyone had told him that a certain nine-pounder cannon ball about to be fired from a rebel's vessel outside Boston Harbour, would later present him with the occasion where he and his wife would meet and dine with the King of England. With a smile and a fateful shrug of his shoulders, he hastened across the lawn, eager to catch up with the others.

Chapter 31

Ebenezer woke to the sound of three resounding knocks echoing around his house. Flashes of the Squire's soirée at Darton Hall had played on his mind throughout the night, his dreams exploding into highly colourful spectacles. Scenes of him speaking in a gay lisp while condemning Judge Pickering quickly changed as he found himself in a river full of naked women, Squire Maddock roasting animal brains over a fire on the riverbank. Molly's face loomed again and again while Judge Pickering stared down at him from his high seat in the assize court, his gavel resounding with three reverberating knocks as he boomed, "You are guilty, Ebenezer Dunn, you shall hang by the neck until you are dead." Ebenezer lay on his back, his eyes flickering around the bedroom as the dream cleared.

"Someone's at the door," he muttered, forcing himself out of bed. "At this hour, on a Sunday morning?"

Opening the door, the early morning sunshine played on his eyes, causing him to shield them with a raised hand; there was no-one there. A note pinned to his door and flapping in the light breeze suddenly caught his eye. Pulling it down, he rushed back into his bedroom looking for his spectacles. Putting them on, he opened the note, noticing at once the date written at the top:

August 14

Ebenezer,

There will be a final meeting two weeks from this date at eleven o'clock in the morning when I'll go over the plans for organising the party that'll take place on August 31 at the big house. The meeting will be aboard a small sloop moored opposite a copse of trees that lie in front of the Duke of York Inn on the Barbican. Look out for a blue flag with three golden lilies flying at its stern. I expect you there without fail.

Luc.

"Ah, ah!" exclaimed Ebenezer reading it through once more. "The party will be the assassination, and the big house Saltram. A meeting on the twenty eighth, eh! It will be easy to find that sloop and good to meet anyone else involved. Yes, I will be there. But Luc'll need to know that John Parker's good friend Captain Pownoll's back from the navy. I wonder if his being back has anything to do with the information of his escorting those troop carriers that I informed Luc's messenger about several months ago. Well, Luc can find that out. But before he does, I'll need to give this information to the messenger. I'll signal him during the morning service."

Holding the note over the flame of a dying candle, he watched as the paper quickly wrinkled up, obliterating everything written on it then finally flittering down to lie as nothing but smidgens of black carbon. Grinning devilishly, he made ready his clerical attire and began to dress for the Sunday service.

The congregation stared impassively at their minister as Ebenezer came to the end of his sermon. Betsy Gribble sat stone-faced, her lips pinched tightly together, her eyes cold slits of loathing. Next to her, the Pownolls's young daughter fidgeted incessantly, while the three remaining members of his smuggling band sat with faraway looks in their eyes. The atmosphere in the church was thick with gloom and doom, the congregation waiting for Ebenezer to speak about the oncoming trial of Mordechai and Watt.

Searching the faces that looked fixedly towards him, he tried again to put a face to Luc's mysterious messenger, but to no avail. Slowly, he tugged his left ear, knowing that someone in the congregation had been alerted. Betsy had seen the signal and knew immediately that there would be a secret meeting in the church between the two traitors later that evening. If the Pownolls had returned home by then, she would make sure she was there, hiding as she had done before in the shadows behind the altar.

"Brethren," began Ebenezer, "Tuesday will witness the day when two of our parishioners will be tried at the assize court in Plymouth for the crime of smuggling. Mordechai Brunt and Watt Huckle will be tried and then sentenced on that day. We pray as a congregation that the Lord will grant the presiding judge to administer a sentence other than capital for our two Christian brothers. Let us stand and recite the Lord's Prayer."

As the congregation prayed for the lives of Mordechai and Watt to be spared, Ebenezer chuckled at the lie he had just directed his congregation to pray for. He would make a point of meeting up with Barold, Stephen and Elijah outside the church after the service. He noticed Betsy Gribble staring at him with her usual look of contempt, occasionally looking sideways at young Jane Pownoll, who looked as though she could not wait for the service to end and be released from its boredom. He supposed that her parents were busy, or even away for the day, as Betsy was obviously looking after her. Little did it matter to him.

After the service, Ebenezer made a short work of the usual greetings and good wishes that certain members of his congregation expected from their minister after a Sunday morning service. Dismissing them quickly, he joined his three smuggling compatriots who stood apart from the rest of the well-wishers.

"Us's all goin down to Plymouth for the trial," said Barold looking at Ebenezer.

"Ar, that we be, Reverend," said Elijah. "Us'll go down with horse and wagon. You'm welcome to join us, Reverend. We'm be leavin early about eight o'clock from the inn."

"Ah well," said Ebenezer, thinking rapidly for an excuse, "I may have to forego it as I've been summoned to the Deanery in Totnes for a parochial meeting," he lied.

Barold and Stephen shook their heads, looking offended at Ebenezer's excuse.

"Well, if you change your mind, Reverend, come down with us, eight o'clock."

"I'm sure you'll let me know the outcome," said Ebenezer, making out he had to hurry away. "I'll meet you all in the inn at lunch time later today."

Although he wanted to go, he could not take the chance of Judge Pickering recognising him as Septimus Sniff. Not that the Judge would pick him out amongst a large crowd. If he were to conceal himself well behind the others, with his clerical hat pulled well down over his face, he would get away without being recognised. And he would be able to know immediately if the Judge was keeping to his side of their bargain by sentencing Mordechai and Watt to hang immediately. Yes, he would take the chance and go with the others. He would tell them later in the inn.

Elijah smiled to himself while filling several mugs of cider and ale behind his bar. The inn was busy, albeit that a cloud of gloom hung over the village at the prospect of the impending trial of Mordechai and Watt. He noticed Ebenezer squeezing past a throng of farm labourers standing around chatting and slurping from their pewter mugs. Catching his eye, he nodded over in the direction of a corner table where Barold and Stephen sat, with a wave of recognition Ebenezer made his way over.

"One for the, Reverend, and the same again for us, Elijah," Barold called out to Elijah as Ebenezer pulled back a chair at their table. "Have you had second thoughts about comin' down to the trial with us then?" asked Barold.

"Yes, I have, they won't miss me at the meeting," he lied.

"So, you'm comin down with us then?" asked Stephen.

"That I will be, Stephen," replied Ebenezer.

"Ar, that be proper, Reverend," said Stephen, looking up at Elijah who had just arrived with their drinks.

"Reverend be comin down with us, Elijah," said Stephen, taking his mug of cider from Elijah.

"Ar, I heard him tell you, Stephen," said Elijah sitting next to Barold.

"Us better stand at the back of the courtroom, in case Mordechai or Watt names us," said Barold. "Then us can make a quick run for it before Revenue grabs us."

"That," said Ebenezer, looking at the three of them with a serious face, "is not going to happen. Mordechai and Watt will not name us, of that I'm certain."

"Oi hope," said Stephen, looking deeply into his mug.

"Changing the subject for a moment, Stephen, is there any news on Obadiah coming back from his venture? The Squire sent word two days ago."

"Ar, there be," said Stephen. "As it's Sunday today, they'll be comin' back next Saturday. He'll have a good supply with him, so tell Squire to get his silver ready. If he wants, he can have it all for whatever Uncle Obadiah prices it at. It will be mostly French cognac, wine and fine lace. Oh, and tea! Yeah, quite a lot of tea, as the tax on it here is gettin' higher day by day. There be a good market now for smuggled tea."

"Mmmm, thank you, Stephen, I'll certainly tell him," said Ebenezer smiling.

"Now, if you are ready for another one, I think it's my round. Refills all round please, Elijah."

* * *

Betsy arrived at the church late in the evening as dusk was beginning to fall. Letting herself in, she stood and listened, concentrating on the slightest sound that would warn her of anyone approaching. Silence reigned throughout as she made her way over to where she had hidden in the shadows before. The sight of the silver crucifix hanging from above gave her a sense of being protected and bowing before it, she offered up a prayer, then slipped stealthily in behind the altar.

Philemon and Jane had returned from their visit to Saltram House late that afternoon, and a lift home from Wilf in the manor's horse and wagon had given Betsy enough time to prepare for her secret vigil.

The noise of the church door creaking open alerted her. She listened to a series of grunts and sighs, guessing it was the Reverend, his footsteps echoing across the nave as he passed the altar and disappeared into the vestry. She pursed her lips tightly, clenching her fists in indignation as she heard the cork being pulled from a bottle of church wine followed by a sloshing sound as it sluiced out of the bottle.

The devil! she thought, *he's probably pourin' it into a sacred chalice.*

The sound of Ebenezer smacking his lips together followed by a loud belch, brought a frown and a sigh of disapproval from Betsy as she strained to listen for the slightest utterance that could incriminate him. She heard him slurp more wine into the chalice and then the sound of a series of wicked chuckles culminating into lusty guffaws as she imagined him behaving irreverently from behind the doors of the vestry.

"Ha, Septimus Sniff, indeed!" she heard him cry out. "He did it, yes he did and they're going to hang. Ha, I am brilliant. Oh yes, that oaf and his two sons will be dancing on the Hoe too, ha."

What on earth? thought Betsy. *And who's Septimus Sniff? Is he part of this devil priest's treacherous cell?*

The opening and slamming of the church door signalled the arrival of Ebenezer's mysterious contact. Betsy listened as the cloaked figure stood by the door breathing heavily.

"Where you'm be?" it called.

"I'm right here," said Ebenezer coming out of the vestry.

"That be far enough," said the figure. "What you'm got for me?"

"Tell Luc that Philemon Pownoll, the master of Sharpham Manor and Estate has returned from the navy. I do not know why he's here or for how long. He must be on leave. But he is a close friend of John Parker at Saltram House and

I've a strong feeling he may be present at the big house at the time of the party. Luc will understand what that will mean."

"Anything else?" said the contact. "Troop movements or anything that may concern the King?"

"No, nothing new there. But give the information I have just told you. It's of the utmost importance to Luc."

"Ar, that I will," said the cloaked figure.

Betsy listened to him leave, the church door slamming behind him.

Oi knows that voice, she said to herself. *He's from the village. It'll come to me soon enough. Now, who could Luc be and what did that devil mean by a party? Us's gonna inform Master Pownoll and Master Parker of this and what oi've heard about someone called Septimus Sniff. But will they believe me? Us'll approach them about this when oi knows the time will be right for them to listen. Till then, us'll keep watchin' that devil priest.*

Ebenezer filled the chalice with the last of the bottle of church wine. Gulping it down, he stopped to take a breath, puzzling over the identity of the contact.

"I'm going to find out who he is and why Luc needs to use him here when he's got a more important person in me. When I see Luc at the meeting, I will insist he tells me who this mystery person is and why he doesn't reveal himself. I cannot understand why he needs a courier when I'm quite capable of delivering the information I get myself. It would save Luc money and maybe he'd increase my reward. Ha, we'll see."

Throwing back his head, he drained the last of the wine and with a loud belch threw the empty chalice across the room, grinning as it clattered against the opposite wall.

"Ha, that stupid Gribble woman can clean that up tomorrow," he slurred.

Betsy heard the belch, jumping in alarm at the sound of the chalice smashing against the vestry's stone wall.

"You sacrilegious devil," she hissed. "Your time's comin', sooner than you'm thinks."

Muttering to himself, Ebenezer left the vestry and lighting a candle made his way towards the church door. Betsy stood motionless in her hiding place, hardly daring to breathe, listening as she imagined him fumbling for a key to lock the church door on his way out. Darkness was beginning to engulf the church as Ebenezer slammed the church door behind him, the sound of the lock turning in the door.

Betsy listened to him lurching down the pathway until silence reigned again. With a deep breath, she left her hiding place, taking the key she was permitted to have as church cleaner from the pocket in her gown. With a respectful bow to the large sliver crucifix, she offered a prayer of thanks for its protection, then letting herself out, she locked the church door behind her and hurried away down the cobblestone hill towards her cottage in the village.

Chapter 32

Squire Maddock sat up from his seat on one of the sofas that graced Ebenezer's parlour, smiling as Ebenezer offered him a generous measure of French cognac.

"He never said a word," said the Squire. "Just sat in his place at the table and gorged himself. I tried some friendly conversation with him after the banquet, but he was reluctant to communicate in any way. As the guests began to depart, he was one of the first away. A quick farewell from him and then he was gone. Now, you fill me in with everything that took place in that room and I hope you're confident he'll keep his side of the bargain."

"Oh yes, I'm sure we'll get what I demanded from him," said Ebenezer.

Squire Maddock leant back as Ebenezer related every detail that had taken place in the room that afternoon at Darton Hall, reassuring the Squire of Judge Pickering's agreement to sentence Mordechai and Watt to hang within twenty-four hours of pronouncing sentence. Ebenezer grinned as he described how the Judge's attitude had changed when told there'd be witnesses to his debauchery, and how his face had fallen on hearing that a copy of Septimus Sniff's report for The Gentleman's Magazine would be sent to the House of Lords for the attention of the law lords.

"It was then that he capitulated and conceded to sentence Mordechai and Watt to hang as I'd instructed. I accepted his plea of not naming him in my report, ha ha!"

"Splendid, Master Sniff!" laughed the Squire. "So let us see if he keeps his promise at the trial tomorrow. By the way, will you be present yourself?"

"Oh yes," replied Ebenezer, "I'll go with my three remaining cohorts. I will make sure I'm up in the gallery behind several large bodies with my clerical hat pulled well down over my forehead. Judge Pickering won't see me there, I'll make sure of that."

"I won't be there," said the Squire, "but I'll have a first-hand report of it, you can let me know more about it when we next meet, Ebenezer, together with details of the hanging of course!"

"I have some further news, Squire, concerning the oaf Obadiah Tucker."

"Ah yes, and your entrapment of him I'm sure," said the Squire.

"I've had confirmation that he and his two sons will be returning in the next five days with a full complement of contraband on board his fishing vessel, so when we trap him, there'll be no escape for him."

"Good," said the Squire, "he's not to be taken alive, Ebenezer. Make sure he isn't, it'll be up to you to find a way."

Yes, up to me again! thought Ebenezer.

"And now I must leave you. A luncheon date with one of the barons in Kingswear. I will await your news of the trial and the news concerning Tucker and his sons. I'll send word."

Outside the minister's residence, Ebenezer watched the Squire mount his carriage, and as the coachman guided it away in the direction of his lunch appointment, another carriage turning into the village caught Ebenezer's eye as it trundled up the cobblestone hill to stop directly in front of him.

"Good day, sir," the coachman called down to Ebenezer. "Master John Parker from Saltram requests your company for lunch. If you would like to step up, we'll be there in under an hour."

"Where?" asked Ebenezer recognising the coachman.

"Why, to Saltram, sir," he replied.

"Just give me a minute to fetch my cloak and lock the house," replied Ebenezer.

Settling himself in the carriage, he knocked on the inside roof to let the coachman know he was ready, and as the horses turned to descend the hill, and hence the road to Plymouth, he wondered what arrangements John Parker had made for the apprehension and seizure of Obadiah Tucker and his two sons.

Ebenezer was not surprised to see Sir Joshua Reynolds present as Andrew showed him into the spacious parlour at Saltram where John Parker and Sir Joshua were already enjoying a pre-luncheon glass of sherry.

"Ah, Reverend Dunn," said John looking up as Ebenezer entered the room, "thank you for coming. A glass of sherry before luncheon is served?"

"You're most kind, sir," grovelled Ebenezer, bowing to John and Sir Joshua.

"Andrew," said John turning to his footman, "if you please, a glass for the minister, thank you."

"I expect you've gathered why we've asked you to lunch with us today, Reverend," said Sir Joshua putting on a smile.

"I've no reason to doubt that it's to do with the plan to apprehend Obadiah Tucker and his two sons, sir," replied Ebenezer sipping at his sherry.

"Precisely, Reverend," said John. "I hope you've managed to find out if Tucker will definitely be returning with a consignment of contraband in five days."

"The information I gave you previously, sir, concerning Tucker's smuggling venture off the French coast is most reliable. What was told to me by my two parishioners cannot be treated lightly. I sincerely believe that Tucker and his two sons will be returning with a full consignment of contraband to his lair in Dittisham next Saturday, sir. I gather the time of the tide on the River Dart will be in his favour for a return at dawn."

"Splendid!" said John nodding towards Sir Joshua.

The parlour door opening brought their conversation to a lull as Andrew announced that lunch was about to be served.

"Come, Reverend, we shall continue over lunch," beamed John, guiding Ebenezer out of the room.

Lunch had been prepared for the three of them in John's ample study, where a well-laid table welcomed them to a first course of game soup followed by a generous sized salmon-trout. A cheese board with fresh fruit would complete the meal while two bottles of good wine from Saltram's wine cellar would be served throughout. Ebenezer's eyes widened with delight.

While two younger footmen served the courses, Andrew poured the wine, not letting their glasses stand idle while they drank with relish.

"As you were saying, Reverend," said John, wiping the sides of his mouth with his napkin, "you're confident that Tucker will be returning with his contraband on the tide at dawn next Saturday morning. Joshua, what say you?"

"Reverend Dunn sounds perfectly sure, John," said Sir Joshua, taking the ear trumpet from his ear. "I think you can go ahead with the plan. We have the trial tomorrow and then there's further planning and preparation for you know what!"

Sir Joshua's last sentence silently alerted Ebenezer. "Further planning and preparation for you-know-what," obviously referred to the King's visit to

Saltram on 31 August. Without giving away any sign of recognition to Sir Joshua's reference, Ebenezer turned to John.

"The plan, sir?"

John looked over at Sir Joshua who nodded.

"Yes, Reverend. The Revenue are standing by with a detachment of dragoons to follow us down the river to where you shall indicate the best place for us to lay our ambush. Now that you have said that Tucker will be returning at dawn next Saturday, we'll have to leave Totnes with the escort in the early hours to be well-positioned by dawn. I will send a carriage to Ashprington to collect you at one o'clock in the morning. The carriage will take you to the wharf in Totnes where we will depart. I have already checked the status of the moon for that week and we're lucky that it'll be almost full, so providing us with necessary moonlight for our journey downriver. Dawn will break at about five, but by then we will be well-hidden and waiting in the place you will show us. The dragoons will be under the command of a Revenue officer and there will be a sergeant there too. We'll catch that scoundrel once and for all."

"What about the rest of the plan, John? I think you should tell the Reverend."

"Yes," said John nodding, "I am sure that you're aware of the trial of Mordechai Brunt and Watt Huckle, together with others accused of involvement in the smuggling heist on Elberry Cove. In fact, we discussed this before, when you informed me that Obadiah Tucker was the organiser of this criminal act. Well, the trial will take place tomorrow as you know and it is my intention to plead with the judge for a postponement, until we can bring Tucker before the court as the mastermind and organiser. I will also plead for a lighter sentence to be given to Brunt and Huckle as they were not in any way guilty of organising this heist, only guilty of stupidly taking part in it. Tucker will surely hang but Brunt and Huckle may only get a lighter sentence of penal service somewhere. As Member of Parliament for Devon, the judge must listen to my plea. Then with Tucker out of the way for good, smuggling in this part of Devon will cease."

Ebenezer suddenly felt sick. Trying not to show any alarm at what he had just heard, his mind was working fast. John would obviously prevent any harm coming to Tucker when he was arrested, so killing him was going to be difficult. The Squire's words kept echoing in Ebenezer's mind. "He's not to be taken alive Ebenezer. Make sure he isn't."

"The trial is scheduled to begin at eleven o'clock tomorrow," continued John. "I've made a special appointment to speak to the judge before the trial starts and so present this new evidence to him. It'll be then that I suggest a postponement in the trial until we've brought Tucker before him in chains."

"The judge may not grant your plea," said Ebenezer, feeling weak at the knees.

"That is also possible," said John, "but in the interests of justice, he must at least consider it."

"Will you be attending the trial, Reverend?" asked Sir Joshua.

"Oh yes, I'll be there, gentlemen," replied Ebenezer, thinking of a way he could divert Judge Pickerings's possible change of direction should he acknowledge and grant John's plea.

"Well, come what may tomorrow, the entrapment of Tucker will go ahead next Saturday," said John. "I'll inform the Revenue to be ready and waiting at the wharf in Totnes. It's an early start, Reverend, but the capture of this arch villain is now a priority, I know you agree."

"That I do, sir," agreed Ebenezer. "And now, gentlemen, it's time for me to depart. Church business is also a priority for me," he lied. "I thank you for a most excellent luncheon, sir, and should I miss you at the trial tomorrow, then I'll await your carriage at one o'clock next Saturday morning."

"You're more than welcome, Reverend, and thank you for being so helpful. We'll apprehend this villain Tucker, and that'll be an end to it."

"That's what you think!" thought Ebenezer as John and Sir Joshua saw him to the front door of the mansion house where the horse and carriage waited.

"Until Saturday, Reverend," said John smiling.

With a wave of his hand from the carriage window, Ebenezer sat watching the grounds of Saltram House pass by, a deep frown creasing his forehead at the prospect of Judge Pickering granting John Parker's special plea. As the carriage trundled through the mansion's gates and onto the carriageway towards Ashprington, he suddenly sat up with a jolt.

"That's it!" he exclaimed. "Septimus Sniff must be at the trial, in full view of the judge. No-one will know him, but the judge will. And Sniff will be staring at him throughout the trial, looks that'll warn him not to renege on their bargain, should he want his name excluded from the damning report that Sniff is composing, ha, ha. I will have a short note emphasising this fact delivered to Pickering's chamber before the trial begins. Ha, this will surely clinch it. Mordechai and Watt will hang within twenty-four hours of being sentenced and Master Sniff will be there to watch them dance!"

Chapter 33

The courtroom in Plymouth hummed with exchanges of conversation as Ebenezer exited a side door to the rear of the judge's bench. Up in the gallery, Stephen, Barold and Elijah looked down on the crowd assembling. A street urchin brought in for a few pennies, walked back and forth swinging a thurible of burning incense to override the stench of body odour that clung to the close and sweaty atmosphere of the courtroom. Wigged and gowned officers of the court scribbled incessantly, their quills scratching away at rough sheaths of paper while the twelve men of the jury sat upright in their box pew, sipping the cheap wine the court provided for its jurors. Theirs would be a busy day.

Ebenezer had found the office of the clerk to the court and handed over the sealed note for Judge Pickering's attention, instilling on the clerk the importance of the note being delivered to the judge before the commencement of the trial. The note warned of public disgrace should the judge renege on their agreement, ending with a line alerting him of the presence and watchful eye of Septimus Sniff in the courtroom. While waiting in the clerk's office, a sudden exchange of overheated and angry voices coming from the room next door had caused the clerk to look up with concern. Through the thin walls, Ebenezer had made out the voice of John Parker raised in frustration as Judge Pickering bellowed his obvious annoyance at him. Ebenezer had guessed that John had been making his plea for a postponement to the trial, and by straining hard he had managed to overhear some of what was being hollered.

"I am the Member of Parliament for Devon and I demand you hear me out."
"This is a court of law, sir, not the House of Commons."
"This is all in the interest of justice."
"You haven't even arrested the blackguard yet! I won't allow it and that's an end to it."

Ebenezer had handed over his note to the clerk, and with a feeling of heart-warming relief, had quickly left the clerk's office and made his way back to the courtroom to face an already packed chamber.

Seeing an unoccupied place in the front row of the spectators' area, he squeezed himself in, turning to give a brief wave to his three cohorts up in the gallery. Out of the corner of his eye, he noticed an angry-looking John Parker exit the same door he'd come out of and make his way to the other side of the courtroom, where Sir Joshua Reynolds, Philemon and Jane Pownoll were seated. People around Ebenezer were busily chatting, some making bets on the outcome of the trial while others eagerly forecast how many would be sentenced to hang. A sudden quietness slowly descended over the room, smidgens of conversation gradually disappearing out of the windows leaving the courtroom bathed in silence. Some stared at the bare walls in silent apprehension, wondering what was going to happen next, others looked anxiously around them. A gasp from someone up in the gallery broke the silence as the distant sound of chains being dragged slowly along a stone floor rose from the dark depths of the courthouse, the sound becoming louder as the ominious rattling approached a side door to the courtroom and then stopped.

All eyes focused on the door, not a sound being heard. A sudden cry of shock from Jane Pownoll broke the silence as the door creaked open. With an anguished groan, she covered her mouth with her hand at the sight of two of the dishevelled prisoners being led through the door towards the prisoners' dock. Mordechai and Watt shackled in chains, shuffled into the dock alongside another pisoner, squinting in the light as they turned to face the court.

"All rise for Judge Edmund Pickering," shouted the voice of the clerk to the court. Everyone stood as a red-faced and perspiring Judge Pickering entered the courtroom. With a stern look towards the three prisoners in the dock, he strode over to take his seat of judgement, indicating to the clerk of the court to get ready to read out the charges against them.

"Before the clerk to the court reads out the charges against the prisoners," said the judge surveying the faces in front of him, "the procedure of the court directs prisoners to be brought up to the courtroom in threes, when the charges against them will be read out. They will be asked to plead either guilty or not guilty to these charges. Should any one of them plead not guilty, then it is for them to convince the jury of their innocence. The jury will listen and then give their verdict. Sitting directly in front of me is the prosecuting council for these cases, Jarvis Grumpweed. None of the prisoners have requested council for their defense." Judge Pickering paused, instructing a court official to pour him a goblet of wine which he hastily drank, indicating for an immediate refill.

"After the jury have given their verdict on each prisoner," he continued, "that prisoner will be taken out of the courtroom until all verdicts on the nine prisoners here today have been given. They will then be brought back to the courtroom for sentencing. I hope I have made the procedure clear. Very well, we can continue. Clerk to the court, please read out the charges against each prisoner and ask how they plea."

"Josiah Winks," began the clerk to the court, "you are charged with being involved in the criminal act of smuggling an illegal consignment of French cognac on the shore of Elberry Cove on the night of the first day of July 1775. How do you plead?"

Joe looked around the court at the faces staring at him. There was not any sign of wanting to understand why he'd done it from those who stared back at him from the public area. Just blank expressionless faces. He turned and looked at Mordechai and with a shrug of his shoulders and a grin towards the jury, called out, "Not guilty."

A murmur of surprise rippled around the courtroom, Judge Pickering raising his eyebrows questioningly.

"Mordechai Brunt," continued the clerk, "you have admitted your involvement in the crime of smuggling an illegal consignment of French cognac on the shore of Elberry Cove on the night of the first day of July 1775 and of being the instigator in encouraging another of the accused to take part. Sentence will be passed on you for your admittance to the involvement of taking part in the illegal heist mentioned. A further charge of being an organiser to the crime of smuggling a consignment of French cognac on the night mentioned and the charge of recruiting the accused to take part in its illegal operation has been brought against you. How do you plead?"

Mordechai stared in the direction of Philemon and Jane, their faces creased with anxiety.

"Guilty to the first charge, on my admission to the Paignton Magistrate. Not guilty to the second charge of bein' the organiser and recruiter."

A rattle of chains and the sound of a crash against the side of the prisoners' dock interrupted the court's procedure as all eyes turned towards Watt who had collapsed next to Mordechai. Bending to help him to his feet, Mordechai noticed the futile look of hopelessness and despair on the boy's ashen face.

Jane Pownoll had seen it too. Unable to bear it anymore, she stood up and shaking with emotion, screamed at the officials seated in the court, "Help him, give him some water, can't you see he's sick. He's only a boy."

"Sit down, madam," bellowed Judge Pickering. "Another outburst like that and I'll have you removed from the court."

Philemon was about to stand up in protest to the judge's remark when John grabbed his arm, shaking his head in discouragement.

"You, boy," said Judge Pickering glaring at Watt, "are you fit to continue?"

"Yes, sir, oi be sorry, sir," murmured Watt, dabbing at a cut to his eye as a result of his stumble.

"Continue," said the judge nodding to the clerk to the court.

"Watt Huckle, you are charged with despatching an illegal consignment of smuggled French cognac and assisting in the operation of smuggling the aforesaid consignment from the shore of Elberry Cove on the night of the first day of July 1775. You are also charged with failing to stop when ordered by officers of His Majesty's Revenue on a chase across Churston Common on the aforesaid night. How do you plead?"

Gripping the sides of the dock and beginning to shake with distress, Watt looked up into the gallery at the faces of Stephen, Barold and Elijah. Barold stood looking down at him tight-lipped and expressionless while Stephen tried to form a smile of encouragement. Watt stared intently into Elijah's eyes, promising he would never give them away. He smiled up at them, trying to tell them they were the only friends he had ever known and wishing they could all be back together in the safety of the village. Then, suddenly overcome with an unexplainable sense of doom, he lowered his head and gave way to the multitude of tears that had been welling up inside of him for days, his body shaking with emotional despair.

"Huckle, how do you plead?" the clerk asked again, ignoring Watt's desperate state.

"Guilty, sir," he stammered.

The courtroom looked on in silence as Judge Pickering directed the gaolers to take Watt away to the lower cells of the courthouse, where he would wait until they brought him up again for sentencing. Watching him limp out of the courtroom, bent and frail in the confines of the chains binding him, Jane buried her face in her hands, sobbing at the poignant helplessness of their young stableboy.

"Master Grumpweed," said the judge loudly, "you may begin your case against Mordechai Brunt who has pleaded not guilty to the charge of organising and recruiting the smuggling heist."

Jarvis Grumpweed stood upright, staring at the jury while gripping the sides of the collar of his gown.

"I put it to you, members of the jury, that this man, Mordechai Brunt, organised the smuggling heist that took place on Elberry Cove on the night of the first day of July, by recruiting those miscreants who are appearing before the court today, and others who are yet to be caught."

"No, that is not true!" yelled John Parker, jumping out of his seat.

"Silence!" bellowed Judge Pickering. "I will not permit your interruption, sir. Another outburst from you and I'll hold you for contempt. Continue please, Master Grumpweed."

All eyes had turned towards John as he stood glaring at Judge Pickering. Most of those in the courtroom that day were landowners and merchants who recognised John as their Member of Parliament, as did those of the jury who now stared in John's direction. All believed John to be a fair and honest representative of their interests. Several of the jury smiled in John's direction and with a polite nod towards them, he retook his seat, knowing he had achieved his purpose.

Jarvis Grumpweed waffled away pompously to the jury without giving any evidence as to why Mordechai had been accused of organising and recruiting for the smuggling heist. To those paying any attention to the pretentious-sounding lawyer, it was obvious that he alone was enjoying the sound of his own voice. Several loud yawns from the gallery and an explosion of someone's pent-up intestinal gases ended his soliloquy and with a lengthy glare at the grinning faces above him, he retook his seat.

"Mordechai Brunt, you may now address the jury," said Judge Pickering.

"Gentlemen," began Mordechai, turning to look at the members of the jury, "Master Grumpweed has presented no evidence to you as to why oi've been charged with this second indictment. Oi have no witnesses or anythin' oi can show you to prove that oi be not the organiser or recruiter of this smugglin' heist," he paused and looking up into the gallery, caught the eyes of Stephen, Barold and Elijah. "My only crime was to partake in its operation and influence young Watt Huckle to join me in its undertakin'. We were recruited by a gang of tubmen and batsmen in an inn in Paignton. I doen know their names or if they still be there, but you'm will probably hear the same from the other prisoners caught by the Revenue when they appear up here for trial. That be all I have to say." With a nod and a smile towards his three cohorts up in the gallery, Mordechai turned back to face Judge Pickering.

"Members of the jury," said the judge, "you have heard the case from the prosecutor and from the prisoner. I ask you now to consider your verdict."

The twelve members of the jury huddled together, nodding and shaking their heads as they whispered their perceptions and views of what they had just heard. Not a sound was heard amongst the spectators, all eyes were fixed on the twelve men in the box pew. Then, with a series of nods, they sat back in their seats as their foreman rose.

"Members of the jury, have you all reached a verdict?" asked the clerk to the court.

"We have," answered the foreman.

"How do you find the prisoner on the second charge of organising and recruiting for the aforesaid smuggling heist?"

Anyone could have heard a pin drop in the courtroom. The silence was absolute as spectators craned their heads forward to hear the verdict.

"Not guilty," said the foreman.

"Yes!" said John, thumping the air and turning to smile at his three friends.

A round of applause echoed around the courtroom, spectators beaming their satisfaction and nodding in agreement with the jury. Ebenezer sat with his head bowed, a frown of deep concern creasing his forehead.

Will this verdict affect the judge's ruling in sentencing Mordechai to hang? he thought. *Mordechai must hang if I'm to be safe.*

Looking up at the bench to where Judge Pickering sat straight-faced, their two eyes met. Ebenezer lifted a copy of the note he had given to the clerk of the court for the judge's attention. A flicker of nervousness crossed the judge's features as he looked down at Ebenezer brandishing the note.

"Silence in court," barked the clerk to the court, his call echoing around the courtroom.

"Mordechai Brunt," said the judge in a serious tone, "whilst being found innocent of the second charge, you are to be held for sentencing of the first charge, to which you have already admitted your guilt. You will be brought back to the courtroom for sentencing after all cases have been heard. Take him away."

Mordechai was led out of the dock, his chains rattling as he shuffled across the courtroom floor. Noticing Philemon and Jane staring at him with looks of compassion, he smiled back at them, willing them to believe in his faithfulness and love for them. As the tears filled Jane's eyes, he nodded to her, letting her know his understanding of what they were trying to tell him. That they believed in him and wanted him back home in the safety of Sharpham.

"Master Grumpweed," called out the judge, "you may proceed with your case against Josiah Winks."

"Thank you, your honour," said the prosecutor smiling at the jury. "Gentlemen of the jury, this will take only a little time. The accused, Joshia Winks, has pleaded not guilty to the aforesaid charge. I call Captain Phileas Crisp of His Majesty's Revenue to take the witness stand."

The young captain, who had chased the group of smugglers up through the woods and into the courtyard of Churston Manor, stood stiffly to attention in the witness box.

"Captain, that man," he said turning to face the jury and pointing at Josiah, "was he one of the men arrested trying to escape from you on the night of the first day of July? And was he in the group who ran from the scene of the smuggling heist, up through the path in the woods overlooking Elberry Cove and into the courtyard of the manor house known as Churston Manor?"

"He most certainly was, sir," replied Captain Crisp. "He's a known criminal, sir, and has escaped justice on several occasions on charges of smuggling and highway robbery. We were pleased to have caught him."

"Thank you, Captain," said Grumpweed. "There'll be no more questions. The jury have heard enough."

"Josiah Winks," said Judge Pickering glaring at him, "you can address the jury now."

"No, us's nuthin to say to them," said Josiah. "Looks like they'ms already made up their minds!"

"Very well," said the judge. "Gentlemen of the jury, please consider your verdict"

The jury huddled together, and in the blink of an eye, they sat back as their foreman rose.

"Have you reached a verdict?" the clerk to the court asked.

"We have," said the foreman. "We find the prisoner Josiah Winks, guilty."

"Josiah Winks," commanded Judge Pickering, "you'll be taken from the courtroom and then brought back for sentencing after all other cases have been heard. Take him away."

As Josiah was taken out to join Watt and Mordechai in a cell under the courtroom, three more prisoners accused of being involved in the smuggling heist were led in to face the court.

"How be it you'm pleaded not guilty?" asked Mordechai peering at Josiah back in the courtroom cell. "You'm was one of them what tried to pull Watt from his horse that night."

"Ha, that oi knows," replied Josiah, "but when you've been arrested as many times as oi have, you'm learns to always plead not guilty. The court has hell of a job most times to prove your guilt. Us be unlucky this time that the fuckers had that Captain as a witness. He recognised me good enough."

"So, all them others what shared a cell with us in Plymouth Gaol be likely to plead not guilty?" asked Mordechai.

"Ar, that be right, brother. But they won't know that that prosecutin' fucker has the Captain as a witness. They will all get one hell of a surprise when he walks into the courtroom."

"How you'm be, Watt?" asked Mordechai looking down at Watt slumped up against the damp wall of the cell.

"There be no hope for us, Mordechai," said Watt looking up. "Might just as well accept it. Us's goin' to hang."

"Naw, doen you give up now, Watt," pleaded Mordechai. "Didn you see Captain Pownoll in the courtroom with John Parker, our Member of Parliament? Us's sure them's doin' somethin'. I expect theym'll talk to the judge and get us a light sentence."

"Ar, oi hopes you'm be right, Mordechai. All oi wants be to get back to Sharpham and ride the horses across them fields again. Be good to see Thomas and Samuel too. Do you think us'll be able to get back there soon?"

Mordechai looked at the faraway look of yearning in Watt's eyes. "Ar, course us will, Watt. You'm just wait and see."

Watt did not hear the cell door open as the three prisoners who'd proceeded them into the courtroom were pushed into the cell, their chains rattling as they stumbled against the rough stone walls. He had let his mind take him back home, to Sharpham Estate and the lush green field overlooking the River Dart where he exercised the horses. For Watt, everyday was a summer's day there, happy to be alone with his horses in the only home he had ever known. Now he was home, laughing and splashing with Thomas and Samuel as they fooled around in the river on their free days. He smiled as he gazed out over the fields of claret reds and emerald greens that sloped gently down towards the river. He felt the joy of being at one with this land, a land he had known from birth. There was nowhere else he would rather be. The countryside of Devon, Ashprington and his home at Sharpham were crying out to him, calling him back like a long-lost son.

It was not long before the final three prisoners were brought down from the courtroom to wait in the cell. Each of the nine who waited in the gloomy silence knew that sentence would soon be passed upon them.

"Prisoners Winks, Brunt and Huckle up now for sentencing," a rough voice called out from behind the bars of the cell gate.

The three of them shuffled out of the cell, their guards pushing them along the dark stone corridor to the flight of steps that would take them up to the courtroom.

The rows of spectators in the public area and up in the gallery stared in silence as Mordechai, Watt and Josiah were led into the courtroom and into the prisoners' dock. Mordechai recognised Ebenezer sitting in the front row, up in the gallery Stephen, Barold and Elijah looked pittyingly down on them. John Parker, Philemon and Sir Joshua sat stony-faced while Jane stared across the courtroom at them with her hand held over her mouth.

"Stand straight and face the judge," called the clerk to the court.

A gasp echoed around the courtroom as the spectators watched a court official place a square of black cloth on top of the judge's long wig.

"Oh no!" cried Jane.

"Josiah Winks," said Judge Pickering sternly, "you have been found guilty of the crime of smuggling contraband into the county of Devonshire. You will be taken to a place of execution on the Hoe in Plymouth tomorrow and hanged by the neck until you are dead. May God have mercy on your soul. Watt Huckle, You are guilty of the crime of smuggling and despatching contraband in the county of Devonshire. You will be taken to a place of execution on the Hoe in Plymouth tomorrow and hanged by the neck until you are dead. May God have mercy on your soul."

"Yes!" said Ebenezer quietly. "And now for Mordechai."

A murmur of surprise suddenly whipped around the courtroom as the spectators noticed the court official extract the square black cloth from the top of the judge's wig. Ebenezer looked up wide-eyed.

"Mordechai Brunt," said Judge Pickering, "you have been found not guilty of the second charge against you, but you have pleaded guilty to being involved in the smuggling and despatching of contraband. You made this confession voluntarily by approaching a magistrate in the district of Paignton. By the surrendering of yourself and by your admission to the magistrate, the law looks favourably upon you. I therefore sentence you to ten years naval service aboard one of His Majesty's ships of war. Sentence to begin immediately."

Watt turned to Mordechai, tears welling up in his eyes.

"God keep you, Mordechai, I love you as my brother."

Mordechai choked back his tears as his hand went out to grasp Watt's arm. He wanted to speak, to tell Watt he would be with him at the end and that he loved him too as brothers do, but he couldn't. The words would not come. He stood trembling with emotion as rough hands pulled him out of the dock.

"Farewell, Watt," he called. "Even though you won't see me tomorrow, oi'll be standing next to you. Believe in that, Watt. Farewell."

As Mordechai was taken out of the courtroom, Ebenezer stared up at Judge Pickering, his lips pulled tightly together while his eyes squinted in rage.

Ignoring the look on Ebenezer's face, the judge turned to the prison guards, "Take these two away, then bring in the next three for sentencing."

John, Sir Joshua and the two Pownolls left the courtroom with looks of utter disheartenment, Philemon supporting Jane who had given way to her intense feeling of grief. At the door of the courtroom, John turned and catching Judge Pickering's eye held it in a lengthy stare, letting him know of his anger at being so abruptly dismissed. He would return before the assizes broke up with the real perpetrator of the smuggling heists, a far more dangerous criminal than the ones the judge had sentenced that day. And then as the maximum sentence was passed upon Obadiah Tucker, he would watch with satisfaction as the foreboding square of black cloth was slowly donned onto the top of the judge's long judicial wig.

Chapter 34

Seagulls squawked and screeched at the brilliant collage of gold and orange hues peppering the sky, as dawn rose over the waters of Plymouth Sound.

As though the breaking dawn was a signal to commence work, the clattering sound of equipment being assembled on the clifftops of the Hoe was a sign that preparations for a day of merrymaking had begun. Colourful marquees began to spring up, barrels of cider and ale were rolled into hastily erected tents, while ditches were dug and filled with firewood to roast the wild boars that would be turned slowly on spits. The sweet smell of toffee boiling and bubbling over campfires wafted around the fair ground atmosphere as more traders and hawkers arrived to unpack their displays of souvenirs and knick-knacks.

Huge crowds were expected that day to enjoy performances from acrobats, jugglers and fire eaters, all designed to wet appetites before witnessing the ultimate climax. At midday, two horse-drawn open carts carrying Watt and the seven condemned smugglers of the Elberry Cove heist, would make their way onto the Hoe, stopping at two long-beamed gallows that rose chillingly at its southern end. Today was the day of the hanging.

Mordechai lay on a bed of straw alone in a cell in the depths of Plymouth Gaol.

After being sentenced to ten years aboard a ship of war, he had been taken back to the gaol until the authorities found a ship's captain prepared to take a convicted criminal as part of his crew. It was quite common for ships of war to take on convicts, allocating them the dirtiest of chores and working them twice as hard as ordinary seamen. When battles broke out at sea, it was these men who were first to board an enemy ship, fighting their way through the decks to commandeer the enemy's vessel. Broadside action relied on the sentenced seamen keeping the supply of cannon balls topped up by repeated runs to the armoury and back. A dangerous job, as the armoury of any ship was a prime target.

Plymouth harbour was filling up with convoys of troop carriers, bringing troops into Plymouth for King George III's address, after which they would sail for the American colonies and war against the rebels. Fleets of frigates and ships of the line were also arriving and anchoring in the Sound, the frigates to act as escorts to the troop carriers. For those arriving for the hanging, it was quite a spectacle.

Mordechai stared up at the damp ceiling in his cell, knowing it was the day of Watt's execution. He was helpless to do anything, only to think of how Watt was coping. He was numb, nothing stirred him. The foul-smelling gruel they'd given him as a breakfast lay untouched by the door of the cell, maggots already settling within the wet mushy pulp. He lay on the stinking bed of straw picturing Watt waiting for the guards to come and take him for the short ride to the gallows on the Hoe. He knew he should be with him, standing next to him as their end came. He closed his eyes praying that it would be a quick end for Watt, praying he would not convulse in agony for too long. Just at that moment, a strange but calming feeling came over him as if someone was there, standing near him. He heard Watt speak, telling him that he would be brave and wanting Mordechai to be proud of the way he'd die. The feeling strengthened as he heard Watt plead with him to survive his sentence at sea, to come through it and return to his life at Sharpham. And then it faded, evaporating through the walls of his cell, leaving nothing but an empty sense of finality.

"I'll survive, Watt, I promise you," yelled Mordechai. "Whatever I face, I'll come through it. And yes, I will return to Sharpham, this I pledge to you, Watt, with every breath in my body."

Elijah guided the horse pulling the wagon with Ebenezer, Stephen and Barold through the crowded streets leading to the Hoe. They had left Ashprington early that morning to guarantee getting front places in front of the gallows. They knew what they had to do for Watt's final moments. Approaching the rough promenade that ran along the length of the Hoe, Elijah spied a stable where they could leave the horse and wagon. Grudgingly, they paid the hostler with what they believed to be more than double the price of what it should normally cost, but today was a carnival day and stables such as this could charge what they liked. With everything finally settled and the wagon parked safely away, they set out on the path across the Hoe.

Philemon and Jane arrived with John and Sir Joshua as the crowds were getting thicker. Jane hid her face beneath the hood of her cloak, her eyes red with the tears she had been shedding. They walked across the Hoe by-passing the food and drink stalls, looking away disdainfully from the merrymaking crowds that thronged the entertainment squares. Jane tightened her grip on Philemon's arm as they reached the two long-beamed gallows where four nooses dangled dauntingly from each beam. Two masked executioners stood next to each of the gallows while two brutish-looking guards glared at the crowd, keeping them well back from the bleak area. Later, a troop of dragoons escorting the two open carts bringing the condemned, would place themselves in front of the crowd.

The men from Ashprington had managed to push their way towards the front of an already packed area in front of the two gallows. At the far end of the front line, they watched as the two brutish-looking guards escorted the Pownolls, John and Sir Joshua, to a front position, John dropping a few coins into their outstretched hands. As the crowd behind them chatted away, Ebenezer's mind was on Judge Pickering and the way he had allowed Mordechai to escape the noose. His sentencing had been done by the book, regardless of the threat that Septimus Sniff would reveal his name. Ebenezer guessed that Judge Pickering had called his bluff but had acceded to half of Sniff's demands as a matter of precaution. He would have to accept it and keep well away from him, the risk of being unmasked being far too great. At least half of the plan had worked, but he wondered what the Squire would think of it.

The noise of the guards assembling outside the cell where Watt and the other seven condemned waited in desolate silence, aroused the dread in them that their time had come. They watched the cell door open, their nerves stretched with the fearful tension that gripped each of them.

"Time's come," barked one of the guards entering and looking around the cell.

"Piss on you!" shouted one of the seven.

"Out, you fuckers, now, or we'll drag you out," shouted the guard.

The prisoners shuffled down the dark stone corridor, their heads bowed forlornly, the rattling of their chains resonating in the grim silence. A door at the end suddenly opened, the bright sunlight causing them to blink rapidly as they were pushed out into the prison yard. Squinting through the bright light, Watt looked up and with a gasp stared in horror at two one-horse open carts, each holding four wooden coffins.

"Move up to the blacksmith and then onto the guards holding the rope," a voice commanded.

The prisoners shuffled up in line to where a stony-faced blacksmith waited to cut away their fetters and chains. He did not take long to extract their chains, waving them on to where several guards stood to bind their hands to their front with strong rope.

Watt found himself standing next to Josiah as a command rang out across the yard, "First four prisoners in line, to the first cart. Mount, then sit on a coffin. Now, move yourselves or we will carry you, you bastards."

Unable to speak and beginning to shake with fear, Watt felt Josiah take his arm and lead him to the first cart. They were the front two and as Watt tried to mount the cart, he stumbled, falling back against Josiah.

"Get that little fucker up and onto that cart or he'll run all the way behind it," yelled one of the guards seeing Watt fall.

"Come on, brother," said Josiah gently, "I'm with you, lean on me."

With help from Josiah, Watt steadied himself and heaved himself up onto the cart, moving hesitantly towards a coffin facing the front. Josiah was up and next to him in an instant. Watt could hear the other prisoners mounting the carts, some groaning and cursing, others breaking down into helpless sobs.

Two clergymen reading from bibles were the last to mount the carts and as each of the prisoners sat on their coffins, the double doors of the prison yard creaked open. The driver of the cart where Watt sat shaking, clicked his tongue and the horse and cart ambled out of the yard to be followed by the other. A small troop of dragoons appeared at the gates, marching alongside the two carts as they trundled along the route that would take them to Plymouth's already bustling Hoe and the gallows that awaited them there.

The crowds on the Hoe were pushing forward to get a good glimpse of the hanging as a city clock chimed the hour of midday. People standing behind Ebenezer were shoved forward as more bodies joined the already surging crowd that were pressing to see the arrival of the two carts. Children sat on their father's shoulders sucking at toffee-coated apples while hawkers pestered anyone they could attract to buy their cheap souvenirs and trinkets.

The ominous tolling of a bell ringing out across the Hoe brought on an eerie silence as the crowd turned to see the two one-horse open carts slowly approaching. Dragoons marched ahead of the carts clearing a way through the crowd as people craned their heads forward to catch a glimpse of the condemned men. A few rotten vegetables were thrown at the prisoners as the carts trundled past, a customary act but frowned upon by the majority in the crowd. As the carts neared the gallows, more dragoons rushed forward to clear a path through the mass of spectators.

Jane gripped Philemon's arm, crying out as she recognised Watt trembling on a coffin in the front of the leading cart. The Ashprington four grimaced at the terrified look on Watt's face, the cart he was in pulling up in front of one of the gallows. As the second cart drew to a halt next to the one carrying Watt, a universal silence fell over the crowd. The driver of the first cart clicked his tongue and the horse moved forward, stopping a few feet from the crowd. Then with a gentle downward pull on the reins, the horse began to walk backwards, so backing the cart up until it stood directly under the dangling nooses. The driver of the second cart followed suit, backing his cart directly under the second gallows while the dragoons parted the crowd to make a runway for the horse and carts.

The two clergymen on the carts asked the condemned men to pray with them, only to be rebuffed by several curses and cries of scepticism. Watt and Josiah nodded to the minister who encouraged them to listen to his words of salvation and then bow their heads in silent confession, asking for God's forgiveness. This they did until the well-intentioned ministers were ordered off the carts by the two masked hangmen.

Watt scoured the crowd, recognising his friends from Ashprington looking up at him in the front row. He smiled down at them holding his head high as his body shook with fear. Before he had left the cell earlier, he'd willed Mordechai to promise he would make every effort to survive the ten-year sentence at sea and return safely to Sharpham. He closed his eyes picturing Mordechai, Thomas and Samuel running through the fields of Sharpham with him, laughing and yelling in the ecstasy of running across the land he loved. With a jolt, he realised he would never see them again. Tears of despair filled his eyes, but he would keep that picture in his mind until the very end. Through his tears he found Philemon and Jane looking up at him, Jane breaking her heart at his torment. He nodded to them, mouthing a farewell and then his thanks for giving him a home.

The carts suddenly rocked as the two hangmen clambered up, each holding up four white hoods. Some of the prisoners stood in silence, accepting the finality of the hooding, others wriggled and cursed as the hoods were pulled down over their heads. Watt swallowed hard, fighting back the urge to breakdown and scream his fear as the vile-smelling covering descended over him.

Feeling the moment was right, Elijah approached the hangman on Watt's cart, whispering up a request to pull on Watt's legs a minute after the noose had tightened around his neck. The hangman nodded, holding out his hand for Elijah to drop the customary payment into his palm.

Watt panted heavily under the closeness of the hood, his body stiffening as he felt rough hands pull the noose over his head, the knotted part resting over his Adam's apple. He jumped, sensing a slight pull on the rope as the noose gently tautened around his neck. It would not be long. A final hush fell over the crowd as all eyes focused on the eight hooded prisoners standing erect on the carts. Unable to control the trembling that was overtaking him, Watt's body began to shake in panic at what was about to happen. Behind him, a prisoner groaned, his bowels opening uncontrollably over his desperate ordeal. At the back of the cart, a prisoner collapsed, sobbing beneath his hood, the hangman jumping back onto the cart to wrench him back up with a slap to his head.

With a final look that the nooses were all set over the prisoners' necks, the two hangmen walked towards the front of the carts, looking up at the drivers who sat ready to cast their whips across the horses' backs. Someone in the crowd called out, beseeching God to forgive the eight about to die and to accept their souls into heaven. A cloak of apprehension fell across the Hoe.

The silence around the gallows suddenly broke into a widespred intake of breath, rising to a voluminous groan as the crowd beheld the moment of death that was about to take place before them.

"Now," screamed the two hangmen standing back as the drivers thrashed the whips across the horses. The eight hooded prisoners were swept from the carts as the horses bolted. As the nooses tightened, they kicked out paddling their legs over thin air, wriggling and jerking as they swung from the gallow's beams. The crowd watched in stunned stillness, some looking away but most unable to take their eyes from the eight struggling bodies that quivered and writhed in their death throes.

Elijah, Stephen and Barold rushed forward to clasp Watt's legs as he kicked aimlessly out into thin air. As they grasped him, sounds of a frantic high-pitched gurgling came from beneath his hood. Holding his legs tightly, they yanked them down swiftly, twisting them so his body quickly jerked to the right and his neck snapped. Staring sadly up at his thin limp body swinging from the beam, they returned to their place in the crowd, Stephen giving way to tears of pity while Elijah shook with saddened emotion. Barold stood gazing at Watt's body dangling before him when, completely out of character, he dropped to his knees as a wave of apologetic grief for having scorned and scathed him on so many occasions overwhelmed him. Ebenezer remained straight-faced, secretly happy that a potential risk to his safety had been removed.

A nod in their direction from the hangman told them they could take Watt's body down from the gallows. Hoisting Stephen up in front of Watt, Stephen cut through the rope above Watt's head, the others holding Watt's body as it released. Barold and Elijah walked over to the open cart that had brought Watt to the gallows, pulling out one of the coffins. As they laid Watt's body in the cold wooden box, Stephen turned to Ebenezer.

"Can't you'm say a few words for him, Reverend, please?"

"Why of course," replied Ebenezer.

With his eyes closed and the others standing with their heads bowed, Ebenezer began to superficially pray over Watt's body, when a polite clearing of someone's throat behind them suddenly interrupted their sombre vigil.

Philemon and Jane stood looking at Watt's body lying in the coffin, Jane trembling uncontrollably with the shock and horror she had experienced at the sight of their hooded stable boy being swept from the cart.

John Parker and Sir Joshua stood a way back, nodding in the direction of Ebenezer. Ebenezer gave a slight wave of acknowledgement towards the two, putting on a look of priestly demeanour and hoping they would not think he had any connection with the body lying in the coffin.

"Reverend Dunn," said Philemon with his arm around a weeping Jane, "we'd like to take the body back to Sharpham for burial. Jane and I feel that Watt would be at peace, buried in the field where he spent his time exercising the horses. It has a beautiful view over the river."

Ebenezer looked at Stephen, Elijah and Barold who nodded their appreciation.

"Very well," said Ebenezer, raising his voice for John's and Sir Joshua's benefit. "As he was from my parish, I'll conduct the burial service for him."

"That will be welcomed, Reverend," replied Philemon. "Now, we have a wagon hired to take the body back to Sharpham, it will be here presently."

As Barold secured the top of the coffin, a horse and covered wagon arrived to take it back to Sharpham. Elijah and Stephen took one end of the coffin while Barold and Philemon took the other. With gentle respect, they placed it onto the wagon then paused with heads bowed.

"Wait for us at Sharpham," Philemon told the driver of the wagon. "We'll be there not long after you."

They watched the wagon lumber slowly across the Hoe, disappearing through the dispersing crowds as Barold, Elijah and Stephen made ready to leave.

"Our horse and wagon are in a stable at the entrance to the Hoe," said Ebenezer.

"Our carriage will be waiting around that area too," said Philemon. "We'll walk there with you."

Ebenezer's three companions walked on ahead while John and Sir Joshua joined Philemon and Jane in quiet contemplation with Ebenezer in front of the two gallows. With a shudder, Jane pulled at Philemon's arm as a sign to depart. Philemon walked away supporting Jane, who silently wept beneath the hood of her cloak. Ebenezer was glad of the chance to convince John and Sir Joshua he was only there to perform his priestly duty while desperately hoping they had not recognised him in the courtroom the previous day.

"Those three ahead of us," he said pointing to the backs of Barold, Elijah and Stephen, "asked me to accompany them on this sad day. They knew of the young lad who was hanged, being of the same village. Although I never knew him, I agreed to be here as he was of my parish. A sad, sad day, gentlemen."

"That it be, Reverend," replied John, "but the real villain will be swinging from that gibbet very soon. Do not forget my coachman will be collecting you in the early hours of Saturday, one o'clock to be precise. Then we will have him, Obadiah Tucker doesn't know yet what he'll be facing."

"Mmm, that he doesn't," said Ebenezer, watching Stephen leading the way back to the stables.

Chapter 35

Ebenezer watched Squire Maddock drain the last of his brandy from his glass, promptly holding it out for a refill.

"Can't do much about it now," he said, gratefully accepting the freshly filled glass. "I agree, Ebenezer, that rogue of a judge must have called your bluff, unless he was playing a very dangerous game in that had you really been a writer about to uncover him, he would've had to find some way to escape the denigration that would very soon be pointing at him. Your report would now be in the hands of Doctor Samuel Johnson and being made ready for publication, ha!"

"Our only problem now is Mordechai," said Ebenezer, looking at the Squire seriously.

"We can only hope he keeps his mouth shut," replied the Squire. "I'm sure he will, because to name us would mean naming his other three accomplices and I'm certain he wouldn't want to do that. Now that Watt is out of the way and Mordechai himself will be out of the way for the next ten years, there's nothing for us to lose sleep over."

"With all due respect to you, Squire," said Ebenezer, "you're forgetting the one other person who can name us, Obadiah Tucker."

"Ah, of course, Tucker," said the Squire.

"Mordechai's being held in Plymouth Gaol until a ship can be found for him," continued Ebenezer. "I don't suppose that'll happen until after the King's address to his troops. Should Tucker, by some unfortunate circumstance, find himself in a cell in Plymouth Gaol near Mordechai and recognises him, then it won't take him long to find out why Mordechai's there. Tucker and his sons are devious and good at intimidating people for their own ends; they will bribe or threaten someone inside the gaol to tell them about Mordechai and then they'll find out about Watt and the hanging. They'll blow John Parker's case right out of the water by naming us as the organisers of the Ashprington smuggling ring."

"Precisely, Ebenezer," said the Squire, "and that is why you must make sure that he isn't put into Plymouth Gaol, or any jail at all. You'll just have to make sure he and his two sons aren't taken alive."

"But how am I going to do it, with a boat full of dragoons and the Member of Parliament for Devon sitting alongside me? It's not going to be that simple."

"Well, you must think of a way, Ebenezer. I am sure you'll be able to think of something, eh? Now, how did the hanging go and when is the burial of Watt going to take place? You were going to tell me."

"The hanging was a gruesome affair as all hangings are, this one in particular," said Ebenezer, looking seriously at the Squire and picking up his glass of brandy. "It wasn't just Watt up there on the cart, there were seven others. Some cursed until the end, one defacated in terror and another sobbed until he was swept off the cart. Watt held himself well, although his body shook constantly with the fear of what was going to happen. They all danced in thin air after the horses had bolted. Elijah, Barold and Stephen rushed over to Watt and yanked his legs until his neck snapped. Then it was over. Elijah paid the hangman for them to do this, also to cut his body down at the end. The money came from Watt's share of the Elberry Cove heist you gave us; Elijah was looking after his share. Those who had no-one to cut them down were left swinging there as an example. I expect their bodies have been enclosed in some type of cage, still swinging from the beams until the birds devour them. After we had cut Watt down, the Pownolls said they wanted to take him back to Sharpham for burial. They will prepare a grave in the field looking out onto the river where he exercised the horses. I have offered to perform the burial service which will take place tomorrow. The following day, I am to meet John Parker well before dawn in Totnes, when we'll journey downriver to lay the trap for Tucker and his boys."

"Mmm, I see," said the Squire. "We can talk about your trip downriver with John Parker later, but first let us go back to the trial. How did Pickering look when he pronounced the sentences?"

"There was one other in the dock with Watt and Mordechai when he sentenced them," said Ebenezer. "I was sitting close to the front of the court with a perfect view of Pickering, and of course him of me. Before the trial began, I had delivered a note warning him of the consequences should he renege on the deal he'd made with Sniff at your hall. I even made a copy of the note which I held up on several occasions throughout the trial. When he sentenced Watt to hang within twenty-four hours, I thought all was going to plan, but when I heard him sentence Mordechai to ten years naval service on one of His Majesty's ships of war, I just couldn't believe it. I stared up at him with looks that would have frightened Satan himself, but he looked steadily away from me, refusing to meet my eye. He had either sentenced him by the letter of the law, or he had called my bluff. I think it were both. I expect he's wondering now whether his name will be defamed or if anything will come of it. I will keep well away from him, not that I'll be in a situation where I'll come across him again. I doubt very much that you'll invite him to another one of your soirées, Squire?"

"Quite!" said the Squire nodding. "Now listen carefully, Ebenezer, if Tucker is taken alive on the Saturday, you lay your trap, and he later goes to the assize court where Pickering will be in attendance. It's quite probable that John Parker will insist you are called as a witness."

"No, no, that's not possible, I have anonymity guaranteed by John Parker."

"Ha, think, Ebenezer," said the Squire, "John Parker wants a conviction for Tucker and his boys to hang. You were the one who gave Parker his name as the ringleader of the smuggling ring, and that he was the organiser of the Elberry Cove smuggling heist. You also made it clear to Parker that he would be returning to Dittisham with a consignment of smuggled goods this weekend and where Parker could trap him. You will be a key witness, Ebenezer, right under the nose of Edmund Pickering. Forget Parker's promise of anonymity, he wants the conviction so he can glory in the fact that he ended the smuggling activities in this part of Devon. We know that is not possible, but he doesn't. He believes Tucker is the sole ringleader and villain. You made him believe so! He'll call you as a witness, it's as certain as day follows night!"

"Oh my God!" cried Ebenezer wide-eyed.

"So, now it's vital," asserted the Squire, "that Tucker and his boys are not to be taken alive, for both our sakes."

* * *

The field where they were to lay Watt that morning, was bathed in summer sunshine. Watt's grave had been dug in a sunny corner at the top of the field overlooking the River Dart, where the gentle flow of the water bestowed a serene and soothing sense of peace over the rich green countryside he was once so happy to have been part of.

Having prayed over the coffin and read appropriate extracts from scripture, Ebenezer asked the mourners assembled around the grave to bow their heads for a moment's reflection of Watt. Betsy Gribble stood with her arm around the two grieving ploughboys, Thomas and Samuel. Jane clasped Philemon's arm while holding young Jane's hand, sobbing gently as she gazed at the lonesome wooden box holding the body of their young stable boy. Elijah and Lucy Hatch squinted somberly through the bright sunlight while Barold and Stephen looked disconsolately upon Watt's coffin. A handful of mourners from the village stood with those who had worked with Watt on the estate, all remembering the innocent young orphan who had loved life at Sharpham. Wilf, the new stable lad who'd taken over Watt's duties, stood at the back holding onto the two plough horses that Watt had tended with dedication and love, their bridles jingling in the silence as they shuffled and then stamped the ground. The woods on each side of the river resonated with the sound of birdsong, the sweet aria of a blackbird singing out its eulogy to the boy it knew who had cared.

With a nod to Philemon, Barold, Elijah and Stephen, Ebenezer recited Psalm 23 aloud as they gently lowered the coffin into the grave.

A table of food and drink in the barn had been laid on for all the mourners after the service. Groups stood around chatting and remembering the times they had spent in Watt's company, but for the four Ashprington smugglers, it was a difficult topic as they'd only been in Watt's company during their smuggling ventures. Philemon wandered over to join the group who stood with Lucy as they listened to Ebenezer grimly acknowledging Watt's courage before he was swept off the cart.

"He was a brave lad," said Philemon. "He died not revealing the names of any of his cohorts."

"But he claimed he didn't have any. It was only him and Mordechai," said Ebenezer looking at the others.

"Well, that's to be seen," said Philemon. "My good friend John Parker and I believe there were others from hereabouts involved. The Revenue will catch them sooner or later. They are probably guiltier of smuggling than Watt was. He paid the price, poor lad. But that's the law!"

Ebenezer swallowed hard, praying that Philemon would not say anything about John Parker's plans of catching Obadiah, especially as Stephen was there in the group. He was sure Philemon knew, but maybe John had not told him who'd be accompanying him. Perhaps John was keeping to his promise of anonymity for him after all.

Not wanting to go any further in the conversation, Lucy tugged at Elijah's arm, signalling for them to depart. Barold joined them and they made their polite farewells to both Jane and Philemon. Stephen had moored his boat down at Philemon's jetty and was in no hurry to leave. Enjoying the spread of cold meats and ale Jane and Philemon had provided, he replenished his plate and refilling his mug of ale, joined Ebenezer at a table in the corner of the barn.

"That be a fine service you'm did for poor Watt, Reverend," he said.

"Yes, thank you, Stephen. It's good he's been given a beautiful resting place."

"Ar, so be, Reverend," replied Stephen. "Remember what us be discussin' not long ago about Uncle Obadiah comin' back with a consignment?"

"Yes, I do, Stephen," replied Ebenezer, hoping nothing had changed.

"Well, if you hear from Squire, tell him that Obadiah be returnin' tomorrow. He will have plenty for the Squire and us knows Uncle'll have to sell it off quick as there's a lot of Revenue activity goin' on."

"Oh yes, I'll certainly tell him, Stephen," said Ebenezer, trying not to sound too interested. "If he's returning tomorrow, what time do you think he'll be back?"

"Well, tide'll be right for 'im early mornin', probably about dawn as oi told you before, Reverend."

"Mmm, so you did," said Ebenezer, just wanting Stephen to confirm again the time Obadiah would fall into their trap. "Good, I'll certainly let the Squire know, and thank you, Stephen, for the information. Now, if you would excuse me, I need to get back to the church. Some important duties."

"Ar, let us know when Squire wants the goods reverend. Doen leave it too long. Catch you soon, maybe Sunday at mornin' service."

Jane and Philemon thanked Ebenezer for conducting Watt's burial service and with a courteous farewell, he left Sharpham for his house in the village. The remainder of the day he would spend quietly at home resting, then an early night as he'd be up at midnight waiting for the coach to take him to his rendezvous with John Parker and the troop of dragoons. He needed the rest of the day to think of a way to prevent Obadiah Tucker and his sons from being taken alive. With a shudder, he knew he would have to find a way of killing them.

Chapter 36

Obadiah stood with his back to the bow of his fishing vessel, peering through the half light of the approaching dawn as the sleepy harbour of Dartmouth disappeared in the wake of his stern. The mouth of the River Dart opened welcomingly before his bow and with a chuckle at having avoided being pulled in by the Revenue on their entry to the harbour, he guided his boat into the channel of the Dart that would take him and his sons back to their hideaway in the inlet next to Dittisham harbour.

Plenty of fish caught off the Breton coast, lay in their icy surroundings down in the hold where his two sons dozed after the night's crossing. A fair wind would have afforded them a speedy trip across the channel but for the extra weight of contraband stacked high in the hold next to the fish. Obadiah had been ready with a large bribe should they have been stopped by corrupt men of the Revenue, but luckily this had been spared and they'd sailed straight through the harbour with no sign of any impending interruption to their homeward course.

"Nearly home, Da," his eldest son announced climbing up from the hold.

"Ar, that us be," said Obadiah squinting through a river mist that had sprung up on their entry into the Dart.

"Better wake your brother, Nate, tell him us'll be approachin home pretty soon."

"'Eem be awake, Da, he's just layin' in his bunk."

"Get him up here now," growled Obadiah. "Us needs all eyes in this here river mist."

Dawn was breaking, allowing a little light to peep through the cloud of mist that hung over the river and the trees that lined the riverbanks. Obadiah grasped the helm, peering through the mist for familiar landmarks that would indicate a turning to his port side and the channel into Dittisham harbour.

"Reef the sail, you two," he bellowed to his sons, feeling the approach to the turning on the port side. Everything ahead was blanketed by the river mist. "Nate, take the helm and keep her steady while oi looks out over the bow," he yelled towards his son. "When oi tells you, you'm turn the fucker 'ard to port."

Nate took the helm, watching his father squinting into the half-light before him.

Leaning over the bow and peering into the mist, Obadiah yelled into the cloud surrounding them, "Ha, you'm can't play games with me, you'm bugger. Us knows this river better than any fucker alive. Oi could sail it blindfolded with no problem and oi knows our turnin' be comin' up any moment."

Nate watched his father pull himself upright, his head bent to one side, his ear listening to the swell of the river as their boat coasted up nearer to the turning.

"Now, Nate, hard to port!" he yelled, his left eye twitching furiously. Nate swung the helm to port, feeling the vessel glide smoothly into the channel that led to the harbour of Dittisham and the inlet to their jetty.

Dawn had risen and was spreading its light across the riverbanks ahead of them. The mist was lifting, and everything was very still. Reaching inside the pocket of his greatcoat, Obadiah pulled out an already opened bottle of brandy and pulling the cork with his teeth, guzzled a good mouthful, wiping his lips on the back of his hand. Taking over the helm from his son, he turned the vessel into the mouth of the inlet, shouting to his sons to furl the sail.

All was quiet as the fishing boat glided along the inlet towards the jetty. Obadiah stood with one hand on the helm, the other holding the now half empty bottle of brandy. A slight breeze rippled the water as they coasted up to the wooden ladder strapped to their pier. Putting his ear to the breeze, an uncomfortable feeling began to creep over him. The silence was unsettling, no birdsong that usually welcomed the dawn, no screeching of the gulls that welcomed the fishing boats back with their hauls, just an overwhelming silence. As the boat bumped up against the jetty, he froze. He had seen a sudden flash of light at the far end next to his boathouse, like a flicker of sunlight reflecting off a polished blade of steel. Something was not right.

* * *

Ebenezer was ready. The parlour clock on the wall over the fireplace told him there were ten minutes to go before John Parker's coach would arrive.

Better wait outside and take a lantern with me, he thought nervously, the butterflies beginning to dance around in his stomach. Wrapping himself in his cloak, he locked the front door of the vicarage and squinting through the pitch-blackness of the night, held up the lantern as he picked his way down the garden path to wait at the side of the cobblestoned hill.

The clip-clopping sound of a horse's hooves entering the village, along with the light of a lantern swinging to and fro in the darkness, announced the arrival of the one-horse carriage that would take Ebenezer to the wharf in Totnes where John Parker would be waiting with the troop of dragoons. He watched as the swinging lantern took a left turn towards the cobblestoned hill where he was waiting, then holding up his lantern, he stepped out onto the hill as the carriage loomed up out of the darkness, the coachman bringing it to an abrupt halt.

John Parker pulled up the collar of his thick greatcoat. August had brought spells of warm sunshine to the summer days that year, but the nights were chilly, especially around open areas near the river. A troop of ten dragoons stood to attention next to a slope on the wharf that dropped down to a wooden platform running along its lower length. Two small naval river boats positioned up against the platform, bobbed up and down at their moorings.

John walked over to the officer commanding the dragoons. "Shouldn't be long now, captain. The Reverend Dunn who's accompanying us should be here soon."

"No problem, sir," replied the young officer. "I'll instruct my sergeant to get the men aboard the boats. Two of my men will row your boat downriver, I will accompany you and the Reverend. The rest of my troop will be in the other boat along with my sergeant, they will be following us down the river so we must keep them in our sight. There's a river mist slowly rising so I hope there won't be a problem once we get going."

"Indeed, I hope not," said John nodding. "We'll have to find a suitable place to lay ambush and keep our heads down when Tucker arrives at dawn."

"Yes, sir," said the captain, "please leave that to us. We'll prepare the ambush."

"Very well," replied John, "but Tucker and his boys must be taken alive. Please make that clear to your men."

"That I will, sir, but I can't insist my men do nothing if Tucker threatens their lives."

"Minimal force then, unless your men are threatened," said John.

"Very good, sir," said the captain. "Sergeant, instruct the men to commence boarding and then wait for orders."

John watched the troop march down the slope to the wooden platform, the light from the moon showing them scrambling aboard their boat while the sergeant directed two dragoons to board the other boat and wait at the oarlocks. The sound of carriage wheels trundling towards the wharf caused John to look up expectantly. Ebenezer had arrived.

With a smile, John saw that his coachman had seen the lights of their lanterns and with a wave of acknowledgment, he watched his one-horse carriage draw up to where he stood waiting.

"Come, Reverend," he said, shaking Ebenezer's hand in a greeting, "the boats are ready and waiting."

John stretched his legs out as he pulled the collar of his greatcoat further up round his neck. Sitting in the stern of the boat, they watched the two dragoons pulling at their oars while the Revenue captain stood at the bow peering into the darkness over the river. Every now and then he would turn around to make sure Ebenezer was alert and following the course they were taking. The moon was three-quarters full but shed enough light over the river for Ebenezer to look out for the familiar signs that Stephen had pointed out when they had rowed down to Obadiah's boathouse only two months before. The lantern in the boat behind them swung steadily in its bow as the river turned them gracefully round Ashprington Point and on past the darkened fields of Sharpham Estate. To his right, he made out the Pownolls' boathouse, the moon shining over the jetty where they'd finally unloaded the consignment of contraband they'd managed to bring back from Obadiah's boathouse that fraughful night. Ebenezer shuddered at the thought of that dire night and the panic he'd felt when the Revenue had straffed the riverbank where they'd been hiding.

A shout from the Revenue captain caused him to look to his left as the boat slowed down at the entrance to Stoke Gabriel Creek.

"Carry on, captain, not this one. I'll tell you when," he called out.

"How long now, Reverend?" asked John, peering out into the darkness at a thin mist slowly rising over the river.

"Just past the next turning on the left," said Ebenezer squinting ahead, "but we'll want the opposite turning which is quite sharp."

"Better let the officer know," said John looking in the direction of the bow.

"Captain," Ebenezer called, indicating for the Revenue officer to join them in the stern, "it's best if you tell your men to manoeuvre the boat further to the right side. We will want the turning opposite the turning into Galmpton Creek.

It is quite a sharp turning. As we take the next bend in the river, tell your men to get ready to turn sharp right when I tell you. I'll come up to the bow with you now."

"I'll come too," said John getting up to follow.

The two dragoons at the oarlocks nodded to their officer as he instructed them to wait for the command to turn sharply starboard after rounding the oncoming bend, then taking the lantern to the stern of the boat, he waved it to and fro several times for the boat behind to prepare to make a sharp turn. As the river gradually gave way to the bend, Ebenezer saw the entry to Galmpton Creek over to his left.

"Now, turn right now, into that channel on the right."

The two rowers turned the boat effortlessly, guiding it into the channel that led to Dittisham harbour, the boat behind them following sleekly in their swell.

"There's an inlet turning just to the right, over there," shouted Ebenezer. "You can just about see it in the light of the moon. That is where Tucker will be heading, his boathouse is at the end."

"You heard the Reverend," shouted the captain, "make for that inlet and pull up alongside the riverbank. I'll signal our other boat to follow."

The two river boats glided into the mouth of the inlet pulling up at the side of the bank.

"Right, everyone out of the boats," ordered the Revenue officer. "Lift them up out of the water and hide them away in the bushes over there. When that is done, check your weapons and line up here in front of me. Sergeant, you take two men and scout up ahead, the rest of us'll wait for you to return. I insist on a blanket of silence, we don't know who may be skulking around near here."

While the two boats were being concealed, Ebenezer and John sat on a fallen tree overlooking the inlet, listening to the sound of the distant river coursing its way towards Dartmouth and the open sea.

"May I remind you, sir," whispered Ebenezer looking at John, "that you've promised me anonymity after this episode is finished. And that I keep out of the action that will take place when apprehending the blackguard and his sons. I trust you as a gentleman, sir, that your word is your bond."

"Why of course, Reverend, and yes, my word is my bond, sir, have no doubts," replied John, looking seriously at Ebenezer.

Ebenezer nodded towards John, pleased with his sincerity but still aware of the Squire's words of warning of John's purpose in bringing Tucker to trial.

267

The sound of the sergeant returning with his two men brought the troop of dragoons to attention, hurrying to form a line behind their captain.

The captain nodded as he listened carefully to his sergeant, his eyes roaming up the dark inlet.

"Good. Take the troop up there now and make sure you are well-hidden. We will be right behind you. The dawn will be up very soon."

He watched his men disappear into the darkness before walking over to where Ebenezer and John sat waiting.

"Gentlemen," he said, "there's a field of thick high grass growing in front of the boathouse and alongside the jetty. It's an ideal place for us to lay our ambush. Come with me and keep your heads well down. Once we have apprehended the smugglers, then you, sir," he said turning to John, "as the Member of Parliament for Devon, will issue them with your warrant of arrest."

John nodded as he watched the young officer take a pocket watch from under his cloak. "It's half the hour of three," he said. "Dawn will be breaking in an hour, I suggest we hurry and join the troop."

Hidden in the long grass at the side of Obadiah's boathouse, Ebenezer wondered how the young Revenue captain would deploy his troop in the forthcoming engagement. A gap in the grass in front of him gave him a clear view along the jetty to the inlet. Everything was still and quiet as the dawn slowly rose around them.

"It's vital that Tucker and his boys are not taken alive, for both our sakes."

The Squire's words rang out again and again in Ebenezer's mind as he gazed through the gap at the empty scene before him.

He would have to keep out of sight when the action started, he couldn't risk Tucker seeing him. He quailed at the thought of Obadiah recognising him and the fate that would befall him should the villain get his hands on him. It was too terrifying for him to contemplate. The butterflies in his stomach were already aflutter, dancing a merry jig to the nervousness that was welling up inside him. Unable to control himself, he gave way to a series of rumbling farts that broke the silence around them.

"Ssssh, can't you hold yourself, Reverend," said John, looking angrily into Ebenezer's reddening face.

A shout coming from the mouth of the inlet of someone ordering a sail to be pulled up, suddenly brought the troop to high alert. Nothing moved in the long grass, all was still. Through his gap in the grass, Ebenezer shivered as he recognised the towering figure of Obadiah at the helm of his fishing boat, the frightening images of reptiles tattooed over his bald head glistening in the early morning sun. The sudden movement of the Revenue captain slowly getting to his feet and drawing his sword, caused Ebenezer to turn his attention towards the young officer making a quick dash out of the long grass towards a large wooden barrel next to the boathouse.

The sound of the dragoons shuffling up on to their knees and aiming their muskets through the long grass at the jetty suggested that action was imminent. Squinting through his spy hole, he watched Obadiah glaring thoughtfully towards the boathouse while occasionally swigging from a bottle of brandy, the twitching of his left eye reminding Ebenezer of the brutish madness in the man. A shout from the fishing vessel broke the silence.

Not taking his eyes away, Ebenezer made out the figure of Obadiah's younger son waving and shouting from the stern as a double-ended river boat being rowed up the inlet suddenly came into view. Ebenezer's jaw dropped in calamitous shock, a wave of nausea sweeping over him. He shook his head in disbelief, trying to clear the vision of the familiar figure pulling in the oars as the boat coasted up next to Obadiah's fishing boat. Peering again through the long grass, he gave a soft groan as he watched Stephen throw a mooring rope up onto the jetty and then clamber up the ladder, beaming and shouting his greetings to his uncle and his two cousins.

Chapter 37

Obadiah stood as still as a statue, his eyes sweeping the jetty and the long grass that wavered in the early morning breeze. He bit his lip in anger as he saw, from the corner of his eye, his younger son Ben scrambling up the ladder to greet his cousin.

"Damn!" he muttered. "What the fuck's Stephen doin' here?"

Standing next to his father, Nate could feel the tension gripping Obadiah. "Somethin' wrong, Da?"

"Down in the hold, Nate," said his father without turning to look at him, "be two muskets. They'm both be loaded, bring them up here now, my pistol be also there, tuck it into your belt and bring that too. Go slowly and quietly as if nothin' unusual be happenin'. Doen you alarm your brother or Stephen."

"But what be happenin', Da?" asked Nate staring at his father.

"Doen you question me, boy," growled Obadiah. "Do as oi tells you. Now go!"

Nate turned and disappeared down into the hold. Not taking his eyes from the front of his boathouse, Obadiah pulled the cork from the bottle of brandy he was still holding and took a long swig. He had seen it again. The sudden flash of sunlight reflecting off steel. His eyes scanned the area around the boathouse searching for the cause. The flash had been swift and rapid coming from behind the wooden water barrell next to his boathouse. The flash could mean only one thing: someone was there, armed with a weapon of steel and waiting for him and his two sons.

The young Revenue captain watched the double-ended river boat coast up the inlet, pulling up next to Obadiah's fishing boat. A young man, not much older than himself, tossed a mooring rope up onto the jetty and then clambered up the wooden ladder, waving and shouting his greetings to those aboard the fishing vessel. Whom he could be, the Revenue officer had no idea, but he knew he had to be connected to the smugglers and the haul of contraband that lay hidden somewhere in the vessel's hold. He smiled at the thought of arresting another smuggler and the praise he would get for it. He knew his men were getting itchy for action but for them to stay hidden and quiet would hopefully encourage the Tuckers to begin unloading their haul. It was then he would give the order to strike. Clutching his sword in his left hand, he raised the hand slightly, shielding his eyes from the glare of the sun, while in his other hand he grasped a flintlock pistol. He watched as Obadiah took a long swig from a bottle, the eyes of the smuggler glued to the front of the boathouse and the wooden barrel next to it. He noted Obadiah's elder son quickly disappear down into the hold, obviously to arrange the unloading. When they were all up on the jetty, then he would give the order.

Thinking rapidly, Obadiah walked across the deck to the trap that led down to the hold. He could feel he was being watched as his left eye twitched furiously.

"Nate," he hissed down into the dark hold, "wrap them two muskets in two blankets and pass them up slowly."

Nate did as his father bid, passing up the two muskets wrapped in two old blankets. "Give us the pistol when oi puts me hand down through the trap," he whispered.

Grasping the flintlock pistol, he withdrew his hand, tucking the pistol under his thick leather belt. Bending, he tapped the outside of his left boot, feeling the shape of the long leather scabbard strapped to his lower leg that held his razor-sharp skinning knife, then looking down into the hold at Nate, he put a finger to his lips. "There be an ambush waiting for us, boy, up in the long grass. Doen know who or how many but us'd take a guess and say it be the Revenue. Now, us ain't gonna hang on Plymouth Gallows, so there be nuthin' for it but to fight our way out and escape through the cave behind the boathouse where us stores the contraband."

"There be another pistol here, Da, and us's got me skinnin' knife under me belt," whispered up Nate.

"Proper, Nate," said Obadiah. "Ben and Stephen doen know about this yet but us'll tell them. Now listen, Nate, what I want you to do is to start bringin' up some of they ankers. Us'll then carry them up to the jetty with the two muskets wrapped in the blankets. When oi tells you, you'm all disappear into the long grass. Give Stephen the spare pistol and us'll make sure Ben has a skinnin' knife which he ain't frightened to use. Them Revenue bastards will have shown theyselves by then so make sure you avoid them, kill them if they try to stop you.

Us'll make our way to the cave and then out through the passage at the back. Oi hid the entrance to it with branches and foilage from the riverbank, do you remember?"

"Ar, Da, that oi do," replied Nate.

"Good," said Obadiah. "Now start bringin' up them ankers and us'll call the others."

Obadiah made his way back to the bow and looking up at the jetty, smiled nonchalantly at Stephen as though he were pleased to see him. From the corner of his eye, he saw another sudden flash of sunlight reflecting from behind the wooden barrel.

"You two lads," he called up, "come on down and help me and Nate unload the consignment. Stephen, what brings you here so early?"

"Come to tell you Uncle that Reverend Dunn said Squire Maddock will have most of your supply."

"Sssh, ok, but keep your voice down, Stephen, and git on down here."

Stephen's face fell, a worried look springing up over his features as Obadiah whispered to him and Ben what was about to happen.

"Us can get away in me river boat," said Stephen, looking at his craft bobbing up and down at its mooring.

"As soon as they Revenue fuckers see us getting onto your boat, they'd shoot us down like us was mad dogs," said Obadiah. "Anyways, us'd have to turn her round and set the oars, take too long, Stephen. Up there in that long grass be our only 'ope. You'm be family, Stephen, us be all together in this. Nate, give Stephen the spare pistol, it be primed, boy. Now as I said, us'll start takin' some of them ankers up onto the jetty. Me and Nate have the muskets wrapped in them blankets. As soon as the Revenue shows themselves, us'll give the word and you'm all dive into the grass. Any fucker tries to stop you, kill them. Make for the cave behind the boathouse where us stores the contraband. Us'll see you at the end of the passageway that leads out t'other side of Ditt'sum harbour. Come on now, start bringin' up they ankers."

Ebenezer lay in the long grass shaking with fear as he watched the Tuckers and Stephen carrying ankers of brandy up from the fishing boat's hold and depositing them onto the jetty. He watched as the four of them stood solidly together, Obadiah and his elder son holding onto what looked like long sticks wrapped in blankets. He could see Stephen looking nervously towards the boathouse, his hand resting on a pistol tucked under his belt. He jumped as a commanding shout rang out across the jetty.

"In the name of his Majesty King George III, put up your hands, we are the Revenue."

Turning his head, Ebenezer saw the young Revenue officer come out from behind the wooden barrel next to the boathouse and approach the jetty. Sunlight glinted off a sword he carried in his left hand, his right hand gripping a flintlock pistol aimed at the four smugglers. In an instant, the ten dragoons spread out in the long grass, raised themselves, muskets ready and aiming.

Obadiah stood watching the Revenue captain walking towards them. Slowly, he and Nate let the blankets wrapped around their muskets drop to the floor of the jetty.

"Now," yelled Obadiah, "into the grass." As quick as a flash, Stephen and his two cousins leapt into the long grass as Obadiah raised his musket towards the young Revenue captain. He did not see the hole the musket ball left in the captain's forehead or hear the thumping sound as the young officer's body hit the wooden floor of the jetty. He had sprung after the other three the moment he'd pulled the trigger, letting the musket fall to the floor. Too late, a volley of musket fire from the dragoons peppered the area of long grass where the four smugglers had fled.

"Good lord!" said John, wide-eyed at the action that had just taken place. "I'm going to tell the sergeant to take command. I think it best if you stay here with your head down, Reverend. It looks like the blackguards escaped to the other side. The dragoons have followed them into the long grass over there, won't be long before we have them. I am going to find the sergeant. Here, take this, you never know if you might need it, it's part of a pair of duelling pistols I brought from Saltram. I have the other, they're both primed and loaded." John handed Ebenezer the pistol then took off out of the long grass in search of the sergeant.

Ebenezer lay where he was, not moving and hardly daring to breathe. His head wobbled with the fear that was coursing through his body. He hadn't been this terrified since Obadiah had lifted him over the jetty and nearly cut his throat. He quailed at the thought that the brute might find him lying hidden in the grass. He knew Obadiah had to die and he hoped that the dragoons would find him and kill him together with his two sons. But what of Stephen. He could not let Stephen find him there. Clutching the duelling pistol firmly in his right hand, he shut his eyes tightly, praying he would not be discovered and identified by any of the four. He beseeched the Lord that the dragoons would find them and kill them before John had a chance to insist that they be taken alive and put into irons.

Stephen ran through the long grass following his cousin Ben; he could hear Nate somewhere over to his left beating a track towards the left side of the field that overlooked Dittisham harbour. He had no idea where his uncle was but the sound of his musket going off still rang in his ears. The shouts of the dragoons resounded over the field and his guess was that some of them were not far behind him. He could still hear the heavy breathing of Nate, close on his left side. Ben suddenly made a quick right turn and tore through the grass, leaving a track for Stephen to follow. He guessed Ben was making for the small path that ran behind the boathouse stopping at the mouth of the cave. The crack of a musket being fired close to him made him dive away to his right side, forcing him to roll through the long grass. He lay on his back looking up at a bright blue sky expecting a bayonet to skewer him at any moment. A shout followed by several cheers from where he had been following Ben made him roll back over and kneeling up, he peered up over at a group of dragoons lifting the lifeless body of Ben. He watched a dragoon sergeant and a civilian rush to where they were carrying Ben's body towards the boathouse. Stephen's mind was racing. He would double back towards the jetty and try to steal his way onto his riverboat while the troop of dragoons were busy searching the field. He was sure he would be able to float away unseen and row to where the cave's tunnel exited at Dittisham harbour, so rescuing his uncle and Nate. Gingerly, he got to his feet and keeping bent, he began to creep back along the way he had come.

Ebenezer lay motionless, shaking from head to foot as the action around him heightened. He had heard the first crack of a musket and the sound of a body hitting the floor of the jetty and hoped it'd been Obadiah's.

He'd been too frightened to look up over the long grass and when the sound of the second musket being fired and the cheers that followed echoed around the field, he was sure that two of the four were now out of it. He lay where he was, gripping the duelling pistol and not daring to move.

Stephen inched his way through the long grass, sure that he was heading in the right direction towards the jetty. Behind him he could hear the shouts of the dragoons, trying to flush out his uncle and his cousin Nate. He could feel he was nearly there, only a few more yards to go. He suddenly froze. A soft whimpering cry followed by the sound of heavy breathing wafted through the grass in front of him. The sound reminded him of a wild forest animal caught in a hunter's trap. He could not go back, the jetty was so near, he'd have to go on through the grass past whatever creature was making the pitiful noise. He dropped onto all fours and began to crawl in the direction of the agonised sound.

Ebenezer suddenly became alert. A slight shuffling noise in the grass ahead of him brought on a spasm of nauseous fear. He stopped breathing heavily, and the pathetic whine that had followed his deep breaths abruptly faded. He had no idea what to do; the shuffling through the grass was getting louder and it was coming directly towards him.

"Oh my God!" he stuttered clamping his eyes shut. "It's the brute. It's Obadiah, I know it is."

"Reverend?" a voice whispered in shocked surprise.

Ebenezer opened his eyes to see Stephen gawking at him on all fours through the grass.

"What the bliddy hell you'm doin' here, Reverend? Why you'm skulking here alone? And why you'm holdin' that there duellin' pistol?"

Terror had overtaken Ebenezer. He stared at Stephen, his body shaking and his teeth chattering in trepidation.

"I…I…I can't say, St…St…St…Stephen," he stuttered.

"Bliddy hell, oi thinks you'm be with them Revenue bastards, Reverend. You'm led them here to take my uncle and my cousins. Reverend, you'm be a fuckin' traitor to us and you'm be damned for doin' this."

Stephen got to his feet, his face distorted in anger at Ebenezer's betrayal.

"Be it revenge for what Uncle Obadiah did to you when us was last down here," he shouted. "You'm didn' know oi'd be 'ere, now did 'ee?"

Ebenezer quaked in fright as he watched Stephen take the pistol from under his belt.

"St…St…St…Stephen, no wait, it wasn't me."

"You'm lyin', Reverend, 'twas you and you'm a coward, you'm always was a coward. And now you'm deserve killin'."

Ebenezer clamped his eyes shut, his legs automatically coming up to shield his body from the impact of the pistol ball that was about to end his life.

He heard the shot ring out but did not feel the smack of the pistol ball tearing into his body. A thudding sound next to him, as something crashed down onto the ground made him open his eyes. He looked in horror at the staring eyes of Stephen lying next to him. A musket ball had taken away the back part of his head. He lay in a pool of blood, his eyes gazing questioningly at Ebenezer like a little boy who had just had his toy taken from him. Ebenezer shuddered, but thankful that another threat to him had been removed. Two dragoons came running through the long grass, their red tunics covered in patches of sweat.

"Be you'm alright, Reverend?" said one. "Us saw the bastard standin' up with a pistol levered at you. Ned here is a bliddy good shot at fifty paces. He saved you, Reverend. Us's still lookin' for two more of the scum. Us'll find them."

"Have you got the main man yet?" croaked Ebenezer. "The big brute with tattooes of reptiles over his bald head?"

"Naw, we ain't got him yet, Reverend, but he be the one us's lookin' for. Doen you'm worry, us'll get the fucker. Won't us, Ned?"

"When you do, let me know please. I'll still be here," said Ebenezer shaking.

The two dragoons disappeared into the long grass, leaving Ebenezer alone with Stephen's body lying next to him. The glazed eyes of Stephen stared out at him, hypnotising him to follow their stare as they trailed his every movement, gaping at him whenever he turned, accusing him of betrayal and sellout. Ebenezer trembled, fearful of Obadiah finding his way to his hideaway and stumbling on him before the dragoons had managed to find him. Turning his face away from the staring eyes, he clasped the duelling pistol tightly, the sound of the dragoons searching the long grass reminding him that the fiend who terrorised the life out of him was still out there, dangerous and highly lethal when cornered.

John heard the crack of a musket being fired from the corner of the boathouse. Looking back over his shoulder, he saw a young lad in his late teens throw the musket down and disappear behind the walls of the boathouse.

"Sergeant," a call came from a dragoon standing in the centre of the long grass, "man down!"

Forgetting the young lad behind the boathouse, John and the sergeant ran through the grass to where a dragoon lay on his back, a deep hole in the centre of his chest.

"Did anyone see where the shot came from?" yelled the sergeant.

"Yes," said John, "a young lad from the corner of the boathouse. He must have found his way through the long grass. Looked like Tucker's elder son. He took off as soon as he had made his shot. I'll go back there and scout around."

"You two," said the sergeant pointing to two dragoons, "take the body over to the boathouse. The rest of you follow me."

As they took off after John, a call rang out from the back of the boathouse.

"Sergeant, looks like there's a cave here, behind the boathouse."

Obadiah turned over the young dragoon he had just slit the throat of, wiping the blood from his skinning knife on the soldier's tunic. He had waited, hidden on the far side of the field for Nate to make it to the boathouse. He grinned at the precision of Nate's shot, proud of his son in the way he was taking after his father. He knew Nate would be halfway through the cave's passageway by now, then it was up to him. A rustling of grass near him had warned of the dragoon's approach. Sliding the skinning knife from the scabbard strapped to his lower leg, he had ducked down and waited – this one would be for Ben. For a split second, the young dragoon wondered why his legs had been pulled away from him as he pitched violently forward. He'd felt the burning sensation of the razor-sharp edge of Obadiah's skinning knife serrate his throat from ear to ear, then a warm expulsion of blood shooting out from the wide incision it'd made, then nothing. Obadiah peered over the top of the long grass, his eyes picking out a civilian rushing towards the side of the boathouse and disappearing around the back. He heard him call out that he had found the cave. Now was his chance; if he could get over to the other side of the field and up near the side of the boathouse where the wooden water barrel stood, he'd stand a better chance of slipping into the cave unnoticed when the dragoons resumed their search. He knew Nate would have covered his tracks and reset the foliage that camouflaged the enrance to the cave's passageway – he had taught his sons well.

Ducking back down, he bent forward and with a stoop, crept away through the grass towards the wooden water barrel at the side of the boathouse and the protection of the long grass that wavered in front of it.

John looked up at the stacks of smuggled contraband occupying most of the area inside the mouth of the cave. One of the dragoons had found a lantern and on lighting it, deep shadows formed around the cavern, but there was no sign of Tucker's son. In a far corner, bushes sprouted green leaves and thick brambles, but there was no sign of him hiding behind them. The cache of contraband would be gladly accepted by the Revenue, together with what lay in the hold of Obadiah's fishing vessel, but this was no compensation for John, who needed the arch villain and smuggler clamped in irons.

"Sergeant," he called, "we've seen Tucker's son run from the scene and regretfully he's escaped us, but there's been no sign of Tucker himself since he dived into the long grass after killing your officer. He must still be here, out there somewhere. We must find him. I want him taken alive and chained, is that clear?"

"Clear, sir," replied the sergeant. "Back out to the long grass, men. Pick up your search where you left off. Two of you take the area on the far side of the field that overlooks the harbour. You'm all heard Master Parker, he wants him taken alive. That's an order, now let's be havin' you outside. We ain't leavin' here till we find him."

Panting, Obadiah stopped to rest, peering up at the side of the boathouse and the wooden water barrel where he had seen the flashes of sunlight rebounding off the Revenue officer's sword. He could hear the dragoons beating through the grass on the opposite side of the field. It would not be long before they found the dead soldier with his throat cut, then while they were lingering over the dead body, he'd make a dash for the cave and follow Nate's escape route through the passageway. He waited, controlling his breathing and listening for the shout that would signal his time to escape.

Ebenezer had heard someone crashing into the grass just in front of him. He guessed the dragoons were searching for Tucker's two sons on the other side of the field so it would have to be John, back from briefing the sergeant. He would tell him the dragoons had shot Stephen, who was about to kill him in his effort to escape and hoped John wouldn't remember him from being on Plymouth Hoe at the time of Watt's execution. He was sure they would not, but then a thought occurred to him. *Best to be sure though*, he thought struggling out of his cloak.

He slung the cloak over Stephen's head, watching a dark stain of blood from the back of the head spread across part of the cloak, then turning back to the gap in the long grass, he squatted down waiting for John to appear. He listened, straining to hear John's voice letting him know he was approaching. Nothing came, everything was quiet.

"Master Parker, is that you sir?" he called out. Nothing moved, there was no reply. "Sir, show yourself please."

A rustling in the grass in front of Ebenezer told him he had been heard. He pulled himself up into a sitting position as he sensed a body shuffling through the grass towards him. "Sir, over here. I'm here."

Ebenezer's face suddenly dropped in horror. A shockwave of terror spasmed through him. He opened his mouth to scream but nothing came out. He started to shake uncontrollably as he gazed transfixed at the sight of a glistening bald head encompassed in reptilian tattoos, snaking through the grass towards him. Panic took over as the bestial face of Obadiah glared through the gap in the long grass, his left eye twitching furiously while the long red knife scar running down from his eye to under his chin glowed through the sweat running from his forehead.

"YOU!" he thundered. "YOU!"

"Ahhhh," wailed Ebenezer, the farts exploding from him like a row of Chinese crackers. "Ahhhhh, oh God, help me!"

"Be that Stephen?" rasped Obadiah in shock, standing and lifting the cloak over Stephen's head. "You'm killed my nephew, you'm fucker."

"M…M…Master Tucker, no, it wasn't me," cried Ebenezer, his head wobbling frantically from side to side in his panic.

"Doen you Master Tucker me, you'm filthy treacherous priest. Us told you what oi'd do to you if oi came across you again, didn' oi, you'm little piece of cowardly shit."

"No, I didn't kill Stephen," wailed Ebenezer. "It was one of the dragoons who shot him."

"Shut the fuck up, priest," hissed Obadiah, taking his skinning knife from his scabbard. "Us's gonna slice your throat open from ear to ear like oi should have done them past two months ago."

Holding the knife in his right hand, he shot out his left hand, grabbing Ebenezer around his collar, then lifting him from his sitting position, he pulled him up close, their faces nearly touching. Ebenezer smelt the sour odour of brandy on Obadiah's breath as he stared in horror at the demonic contortions spreading over the brute's face. Whimperings of terror flittered out of him as he felt Obadiah raise his right hand to slice the skinning knife across his throat.

Shutting his eyes tightly, he waited for the searing pain of the cut that would end his life. A sudden vision of John flashed across his mind as he remembered his words, *"You never know if you might need it."*

Of course, the pistol, he thought, still feeling it grasped in his right hand. *The brute didn't see it and I'd forgotten it in my terror!*

In a flash, Ebenezer raised his right hand, pushing the barrel of the pistol into Obadiah's side just under his raised arm. Before Obadiah could feel it there, Ebenezer found the trigger and pulled. He remembered John saying it was primed, loaded and ready to fire; he prayed John had been right. For a moment, nothing happened and then as Ebenezer saw Obadiah's knife glinting towards his throat, a thunderous explosion rocked the two of them. Eyes staring wildly in surprise, Obadiah staggered, letting Ebenezer fall to the ground and then with a gurgle and a heavy intake of breath, he fell face down into the long grass.

Hearing the pistol shot from where Ebenezer was hiding, John and the sergeant tore back through the grass to find Ebenezer standing over the body of Obadiah, the pistol in his hand wobbling around precariously, his body shaking with the shock of what had just happened.

"Reverend, are you hurt?" shouted John, taking the pistol from Ebenezer's hand.

"No, no, I'm not hurt," said Ebenezer. "Just in shock for the moment."

"Here," said the sergeant, offering Ebenezer a flagon of brandy, "drink this."

Taking a long swig, Ebenezer shivered and looking at John smiled, "I thought it was you coming through the long grass, but when I saw that bald head covered in those vile reptilian tattoos, I thought my life was over. He tried to slit my throat but thank the Lord I remembered the pistol you'd left me. I had no alternative but to shoot him."

"Indeed, Reverend," said John, "but it's a pity that we'll have no conviction of the mastermind behind the smuggling activities in this area. His younger son was shot trying to escape us but there is no sign of his elder son, we think he's got away. And who was he?" he asked, pointing towards the dead body of Stephen, the head still covered with Ebenezer's cloak.

"Tucker's nephew," said Ebenezer. "I don't know his name, but I know through my parishioners that he was part of Tucker's smuggling group. He had come for a large supply of the contraband. He tried to kill me but was shot by one of your dragoons by the name of Ned, I think. He'll verify it."

"Very well," said John. "Sergeant, take the dead bodies to the double-ended river boat that we're now requisitioning. Allocate two of your men to row them back up to Totnes and then organise their burials. We will leave now in the boats we travelled down in. Leave two of your men to guard the fishing vessel, then arrange with your superior to return post-haste to remove the vessel and the contraband in the cave. Reverend, come, it's about time we went home."

Ebenezer sat in the stern of the Revenue's river boat, feeling drained but quite elated it was now all over. Obadiah and Stephen were dead and so there would be no implications towards him as being part of the Ashprington smuggling ring. Mordechai would soon be gone, and John Parker seemed content enough to close his enquiry into the smuggling activities his brother Montague had warned him of. Now he could look forward to the meeting with Luc and the fortune he was going to make with the assassination of the King. With a smile, he sat back and closed his eyes.

Chapter 38

Ebenezer hurried along the pathway on the Barbican, scanning the numerous fishing vessels bobbing up and down at their moorings. In the distance, he spotted the Duke of York Inn, his eyes quickly moving away from it in a line towards the wharf and the copse of trees that fronted it. A clock on the Barbican struck the hour of eleven; he was on time. He stopped in front of the copse scanning the fishing boats until his eyes rested on a blue flag displaying three golden lilies. A gangplank stretched from the side of the boat to the pathway where he stood and taking a deep breath, he gingerly made his way up, stepping onto the vessel's empty deck. An open trapdoor towards the boat's stern suggested the way to where the meeting with Luc was probably going to take place and not seeing anyone around on the deck, he made his way over to the open hole where narrow wooden steps led down to the darkness below. Placing his foot on the first step, he grasped the rusty rail next to it and cautiously began his descent. A murmur of voices coming from behind a door in the dimly-lit hold told him where to go and laying his hand on the brass handle, he gently opened the door.

Five men sat around a table in the centre of what looked like the crew's quarters, a candle burning slowly in the middle of the table lighting up a large-scale architectural drawing of a building. Two empty chairs placed at the top of the table looked as though they were waiting to be occupied. The room stank of body odour and stale fish.

"Ebenezer!" said Luc getting up from his seat. "You're here at last, come over and join us. Raymond, a mug of wine for the Reverend please."

Ebenezer made his way towards one of the empty chairs, nodding towards Luc, his eyes following a thin weasel-looking individual wearing an eyepatch, who had started filling a small mug with a dark reddish wine.

"Please be seated, Ebenezer," said Luc smiling. "Before we start, I'll introduce everyone here to you. Pouring the wine is Raymond, captain and owner

282

of this fishing vessel and a member of my team. Sitting opposite you are two of Raymond's crew, Philippe and Robert, also members of my team. To your left is Andre, whom I think you've already met."

Ebenezer had already noticed an individual attired in the livery of some stately home, turning to greet him his eyes widened in surprise as he found himself looking into the face of John Parker's first footman and trusted valet, Andrew.

"My God, this is a surprise!" exclaimed Ebenezer. "I had no idea. I would never have guessed, Andrew."

"I can't say the same, Reverend," said Andrew grinning. "I've known about you for some time, ever since Luc informed me about you. I already knew about you when you visited John Parker at Saltram to discuss your plans concerning the capture of the smuggler Obadiah Tucker. Nothing of importance misses my attention at Saltram. I'm Luc's spy in the household where all the comings and goings are noted by me and then reported back to him."

"But you don't look or sound at all French!" said Ebenezer looking puzzled.

"But I am French," replied Andrew. "Years of living here in England and speaking your language daily, has caused me to lose my accent. But what is a Frenchman meant to look like, I ask you?"

"Yes, yes, we can debate that all day, Andre," interrupted Luc. "There's another one of Raymond's crew who's gone to buy fresh bread and cheese for us all. He will be back later, Ebenezer. But now we are waiting for one more member of my team yet to arrive. You will soon get to meet your mysterious contact from the village. Ah! I can hear him descending the ladder into the hold now."

All eyes looked towards the door as Ebenezer noticed the brass handle slowly turn. The door opened and a figure in a familiar black cloak and hood stepped into the room. It was difficult to make out who the new arrival was, as dark shadows enveloped the entrance. Closing the door behind him, he walked slowly towards the table where they were all sat. As he came within the light of the candle, Ebenezer gasped in shock at the sight of the individual removing his hood. With mouth agape and eyes as wide as saucers, Ebenezer found himself staring into the grave and sombre face of Barold.

* * *

Nancy looked up at the clock in the Cat and Fiddle Inn as it gave a single chime to indicate the time of ten thirty. She had already cleared it with Ned Cuttle to have an hour off that morning, telling him she needed to shop for a few necessities and that she'd be back in time for the lunch time trade. She would leave in thirty minutes, not for the shops but for the French fishing vessel moored opposite the copse of trees where she knew Luc Skorniere would be holding another meeting. She would make herself busy over the next thirty minutes, wiping the tables down yet again and making sure there were full barrels of cider and ale ready for Ned to serve.

She had been unable to sleep much the night before, thinking about the meeting that was going to take place aboard the French fishing vessel the following morning. She was adamant that she was going to find out what Luc was up to, and she knew she would get her answer by eavesdropping on the secret gathering.

She would do as she'd done before, sneak aboard the vessel and listen at the door in the hold after the meeting had begun. She remembered Luc saying that this meeting would be in English, as an English member of his treacherous circle would be present. She wondered who it could be and if he had ever been into the inn to see Luc, and if he had, had he ever paid her a shilling. She would be there to find out. The clock suddenly struck the hour of eleven and feeling the butterflies jumping around in her stomach, she grabbed her shawl and left the inn.

She hurried along the pathway that snaked its way along the wharf towards where she knew the French fishing boat would be moored. The sight of the blue flag with the three golden lilies flapping gently in the breeze brought her to a stop. The boat's short gangplank stretched before her and looking over her shoulder, and then into the shadows of the copse of trees that overlooked the vessel, she hastened up the plank and stepped cautiously onto the boat's deck. She stood perfectly still, her eyes scanning everything in front of her. There was nothing to give her any alarm and the open trap door towards the stern of the vessel beckoned her invitingly. Tiptoeing across the deck, she made her way towards the steps that led down to the vessel's hold and the meeting that she knew had already started. Once down, she stood listening to the murmur of voices coming from behind the door where she was sure the treacherous assembly were plotting and planning.

Warily, she made her way towards the door, the murmur of voices becoming clearer and more distinguishable. Placing herself at the corner of the door where the hinges allowed a minute gap, she listened to the conversation taking place. Glancing upwards, she noticed the window on the door that she had just managed to look through when she had last been there. Concentrating on controlling her breathing, she placed her ear against the gap, listening to the distinct voice of Luc seeping through.

"I received your information from our mutual contact now sitting next to you, Ebenezer, concerning the return of Captain Pownoll and his likelihood of being at Saltram on the night when we assassinate the King. It's good to know who'll be present there that night, but it won't interfere with our operation."

Barold turned to Ebenezer. "Now you'm knows who the contact in the church be, Reverend. Oi was waitin' for the time when you would cotton on, but you'm never did. Oi was waitin' for you to get suspicious too. Disguised me voice, gurt good it be too, ha ha!"

Ebenezer was too stunned to speak. The surprise of finding out that the cloaked and hooded contact was Barold had shocked the life out of him. Picking up his mug of wine, he took a long draught.

"But you're only Luc's messenger, Barold," croaked Ebenezer, "why are you here at this covert meeting?"

"That, Reverend, you'm'll find out later," replied Barold, taking the mug of wine from Raymond's outstretched hand.

"Us heard about Stephen, poor bugger. Doen suppose it had anythin' to do with you now, Reverend, had it? And Obadiah, I expect you'm pleased he be dead now, ain't you, Reverend?"

"Andre has brought an architectural drawing of Saltram House," said Luc. All eyes in the room focused on the drawing. "He's informed me that the King will be accommodated here."

Luc put his finger on the upper west wing of the mansion. "You can see that there are six bedrooms and two bathrooms. The King will occupy one of these bedrooms while his entourage will take the rest. Andre will know on the day which one, isn't that correct, Andre?"

Andrew nodded towards Luke. "The plan is to assassinate the King at night when the house is quiet, and everyone is off guard. I know there will be armed guards patrolling the house and grounds, as to how many, we don't yet know. Our assassin will be inside the house well before the royal party arrives, hidden in a secret hideaway of the bedroom Andre is confident he will be allocated. We know the arrival is set for six o'clock, late afternoon. As valet to John Parker, Andre has free movement around the house and will make sure he is with the King's personal valet when the King retires. The King is known to favour early nights, so he will be to bed straight after dinner. Andre will slip a sleeping draught into the King's nightcap, then two knocks on the panelled hideaway will inform the assassin that the drugged nightcap has taken effect and the King is asleep."

"How will the assassin make his getaway?" asked Ebenezer.

"There's a passageway leading away from inside the hideaway," said Andrew. "Behind the panelling in most of the rooms, are fairly wide cavities. Many of the original walls to the house date back to Tudor times and when John Parker's father took the building over and had it redesigned and subsequently restructured, some of these outer walls were kept. To bring the rooms in the house up to a more fashionable state of appearance, all the inner wall panelling was renewed in thick oak. It was the late John Parker who had the idea that a secret hideaway should be fashioned in the cavity of the master bedroom on the west wing. I am sure the Parkers will allocate this one to the King. As to why he wanted a hideaway there, there is no answer, so your guess is as good as mine. He did not stop there. Running along the cavity is a passageway that leads to a narrow spiral staircase that drops down to the wine cellar on the basement floor. There is a door from this wine cellar that opens out onto the rear courtyard, this will be the assassin's escape route. I will make my way to the wine cellar immediately after I've knocked twice on the bedroom panelling to indicate the King is asleep. I will be waiting for you at the bottom of the spiral staircase. We'll escape out through the grounds to where the horses will be ready and waiting."

"You said horses," said Ebenezer looking up at Andrew.

"Yes, Ebenezer, four horses. One for our assassin, one for me, one for Andrew and one for you."

"I've agreed for Andrew to sail to France too," interrupted Luc.

"What?" cried Ebenezer. "You mean for the two of us to be with the assassin in that hideaway?"

"Precisely," replied Luc. "It's the only way I can be sure our operation will be successful. If anything happens to our assassin, then we will be there to finish it. You yourself will have to play the part with me and assassinate the King."

"But, but, but…" stammered Ebenezer.

"No buts, Ebenezer. Let us hope we'll only observe and not have to do the deed ourselves. Don't forget our last conversation when I warned you of what will happen should you renege on our agreement."

"Oh my God!" croaked Ebenezer beginning to shake. "But how will we get into Saltram?"

Luc looked at Andrew. "Andre will be waiting for us at the rear tradesmen's delivery door. We will be disguised as bakers bringing freshly-baked bread and cakes for the King's stay. We'll arrive in a horse-drawn wagon and Andre will take care of the rest."

Ebenezer looked around the table at the others who all looked calm and resigned to the fact that it was up to all of them to make this undertaking successful.

"But what about the assassin?" said Ebenezer. "Who is he?"

Luc smiled. "Good question, Ebenezer. If you look to your left, he's sitting next to you."

Slowly Ebenezer turned, and for the first time ever, Barold's face broke into a beaming smile as he looked upon the ashen face of his minister and co-smuggler.

Nancy had heard every word clearly and was agog with what she had listened to. Now she knew what the reference to Saltram House had been about when she had heard it mentioned the last time she'd crept aboard the vessel and listened to the conversation in French. She suddenly felt very scared; there were French spies in the room along with two very nasty English traitors. She wondered who the traitors could be, she would have to look through the window. She remembered seeing an old three-legged stool at the bottom of the steps that led from the deck to the hold. Turning, she tiptoed towards the steps and bending slightly, picked up the stool. Wobbling a little, she managed to get both of her feet onto the seat and very slowly stretched herself up to peep through the dusty glass of the window.

The first person she saw was Luc, standing to the side of two men seated at the top of the table. The angle of the window only allowed Nancy to see the back of Luc, who was blotting out the faces of the two men he was talking to. When he moved away, Nancy gasped. She recognised them immediately.

"Bliddy hell," she muttered, "that's the strange lookin' one who likes to spit and lick me when I get him aroused. And that other one only likes it in me hand;

287

he never paid me the shillin' he had promised. Theym's both traitors and workin' for that Frenchie Luc. Oi knew he be up to summin', he be a French spy. That skinny one with the eye patch that had Rose, must be the one who's gonna take them to France in this fishin' boat after they'ms killed the King. Us'll have to stop them somehow."

The sudden shock of rough hands grasping her legs caused Nancy to scream out in terror as she felt herself being picked up and slung over the shoulder of someone reeking of sour sweat and fetid fish. She glimpsed him open the door and then carry her to the table where he let her drop to the wooden floor.

"Found her looking through the window out there," said the third member of Luc's crew, putting the bread and cheese he had been out to buy on the table.

"Well, well, well, Nancy," said Luc pulling her to her feet, "now what brings you to spy on us, eh?"

Ebenezer watched Nancy smoothing down her gown, feeling himself rising, as he admired the sensuous sight of her enormous breasts falling out over her gown. Nancy saw the lecherous look on his face and feeling sickened, quickly rearranged her clothing.

"Raymond, get some rope and tie her to my chair," ordered Luc, "but first search her."

One of Raymond's crew held her while Raymond rubbed his grubby hands over her, feeling for what may act as a weapon. He thrust his hand into the deep pockets of her gown, pulling out a sheet of paper from one.

"Only this, Luc," he said handing it to his spymaster.

Luc opened the folded sheet, noticing the bold symbol of the Fleur-de-Lis.

"You've been into my room, you filthy slut," he screamed at her. "And you stole this. How much of it did you understand?"

"Nuthin', Luc, honest," cried Nancy, "oi can't read or speak French."

"Ha, if you can't read, you liar, why did you take it? To show it to someone?"

"Oi dunno, Luc, oi just did. Please let me go," pleaded Nancy.

"Tie her to the chair, Raymond," said Luc staring at Nancy.

Raymond pushed her onto the chair, pulling her arms back and tying them tightly. He then used a length of the rope to secure her legs. When he had finished, he stood behind her, his eyes fixed on Luc.

"I'll ask you one more time, slut, why did you take this paper from my room?"

"Oi'm sorry, Luc, oi dunno why, oi just did. Oi can't read French or even English honest, so oi doen know what's in that paper. Just please let me go, oi won't say nuthin', honest."

Luc looked at the tears running down Nancy's cheeks, her sobs echoing around the sides of the hold. Barold and Ebenezer stared at the vicious look on Luc's face while Andrew looked at Nancy with pity in his eyes.

Turning away from Nancy, Luc looked at Raymond and nodded. As quick as a flash, Raymond drew the long skinning knife he had been holding across Nancy's throat. Ebenezer watched in horror as a spurt of crimson blood jetted out of the deep incision, followed by a thick flow that seeped down over her breasts and gown. She tried to scream but only managed a gurgling as her lifeblood ebbed out of her. The room in front of her began to slowly fade, a misty film forming over her eyes. In the distance, she saw the shape of the vile stranger who had spat and licked her while ravishing her in a back room of the Cat and Fiddle Inn, and all for the princely sum of a shilling. The room was waning as she felt herself being propelled away from it. She could vaguely make out the people in it, all looking at her as they became smaller and smaller. They seemed to be calling her, but she heard no sound. Her eyes closed and then there was nothing.

"Get rid of the body now, Raymond," said Luc.

Raymond and his three crew members picked up Nancy's body and left the room.

"She heard too much," said Luc looking at the others sitting around the table.

"Ar, that she did," agreed Barold nodding towards Luc.

Ebenezer and Andrew said nothing, Ebenezer still shocked at what he had just witnessed.

"Now, back to business, gentlemen," said Luc calmly. "Andre, what time would you say it best for us to arrive at Saltram?"

"Well, if the royal party are arriving around six, I'd suggest four thirty, while things are buzzing in the household. Extra deliveries will be arriving throughout the day, so a late delivery of bread and cakes with three of the bakers I will have contracted, won't be looked on as unusual. John Parker will leave a lot of the preparation to me and I will instruct the staff that there'll be an extra order of bread arriving at about four o'clock. The staff don't know that it is the King who'll be arriving. They've previously been told to expect an important member of the government, but John is going to tell them exactly who to expect when he assembles them all after the lunches are over."

"Ebenezer and Barold, I want you here aboard Raymond's sloop the evening before the assassination," said Luc. "Bring one bag only, Ebenezer, that you'll travel to France with, nothing else. You will both be spending the night aboard the sloop. Raymond's three crew members will take rooms at the Duke of York for the night, so both you and I can take over their berths here."

"But I have more to bring than just one bag!" exclaimed Ebenezer.

"One bag with whatever you choose to bring is enough. You won't be coming back, Ebenezer."

Ebenezer stared uneasily at Luc, realising the moment had finally arrived.

"Your staying the night here will give us the chance of going over the plans again. Allain will have the horse and wagon ready for us on the day at about four o'clock. I will have the bakers' clothes here for us to change into. The bread, cakes and tarts, Raymond will see to. Philippe and Robert will be hiding with the horses in a small lane off the main carriage track outside the grounds of Saltram. Barold has elected to return to Ashprington to carry on life as normal. The three of us with Philippe and Robert will ride hell for leather back here when Raymond will cast off as soon as we are on board. A fat purse will await you, Barold, as will yours, Ebenezer. Now, are there any questions?"

Barold grinned at the thought of his pot of gold.

"Just one," said Ebenezer, "Barold, how will you kill the King?"

"I'll slit his throat," said Barold nonchalantly, raising his mug of wine in a toast.

"To the death of the King," said Andrew raising his mug with a smile.

"Yes, to the death of King George III of Britain and Ireland, Vive la France," yelled Luc, standing up and raising his mug.

"Well, here's to my fortune," muttered Ebenezer raising his mug, "and a fair wind to France."

Chapter 39

Philemon handed back the folders containing the sketches of his daughter Jane to Sir Joshua Reynolds, a look of wonderment spread across his face.

"Truly remarkable, Joshua," said Philemon, "you've captured her look in every angle."

"I'm pleased myself," said Sir Joshua. "But what I'm most pleased about is the look of innocence. That's what I was really after."

"Well, you've achieved it, Joshua," added Jane smiling at him.

"When will you begin the work?" asked John, draining the last drop of claret from his glass.

"Not till the autumn, John," replied Joshua. "I have a portrait to finish off, one of the ladies in waiting to Queen Charlotte, it needs just a few more delicate touches."

"Will you still title young Jane's portrait as 'The Age of Innocence'?" asked Jane.

"Yes, that I will, Jane dear," he replied, "that I will."

"Splendid," said John, standing up and looking out of the parlour window that afforded a striking view of the sweeping fields and pastures across Philemon's estate of Sharpham.

"Now, the dinner tomorrow," he said turning to look at the three of them.

"The King's party will be arriving at around six in the afternoon, so we've been informed. It would be best for you, Jane and Philemon, to arrive an hour later when the King will be eager for company and to dine. Joshua will be at Saltram earlier, with myself and Theresa to welcome His Majesty."

Sir Joshua bowed his head courteously.

"It's only the King coming, Queen Charlotte has elected to stay behind. She rarely accompanies him on military matters."

"Dinner will be served at seven thirty after a small reception in the drawing room. His Majesty will retire directly after dinner, I expect. Andrew, my valet, will assist His Majesty's valet in preparing the King for the night. The King has a great interest in the sea, Philemon, and I'm sure he'd be most pleased to hear your account of your capturing the Spanish ship *The Hermione*, and the fortune it held."

Philemon nodded. "Of course, it'd be a pleasure," he replied.

"I'll send a carriage for you both, say just after six?" suggested John. "And of course our guest bedroom on the east wing will be yours, my dears."

"Thank you, John," said Jane.

Philemon poured his two close friends another claret, clearing his throat loudly to gain their attention. "I have some news for you both which I'm sure you'll be interested in," he said, offering John and Sir Joshua another glass of the fine wine.

"I have secured the indenture of Mordechai Brunt to serve his sentence on my ship HMS *Blonde*. He will be in my custody legally, and should I be commanded to another ship in the future, then Mordechai will be attached to it under my authority. He'll be sailing at the lowest rating, a convicted seaman, but at least I'll have my eye on him."

"And a kinder eye than any another captain, Philemon. Good news, sir," said John, beaming with pleasure.

"I'll arrange for him to be taken to my ship after the King's address. We're then sailing straight back to Boston as an escort to the troop carriers."

A gentle knock on the parlour door interrupted their conversation.

"Come," announced Jane.

The door opened slowly to show a gloomy-looking Betsy standing there as though she had the greatest of worries on her shoulders.

"Why Betsy, what is it? You look most worried, my dear," said Jane looking concerned.

"If it pleases you, ma'am," Betsy replied, "oi needs to talk to you all, most seriously. Oi have some very important news to tell 'ee."

"Come in, Betsy, and sit yourself down here," said Philemon, indicating for John and Sir Joshua to stay where they were seated.

"Now Betsy, what seems to be troubling you?" asked Jane looking at her anxiously.

"Oi hope you'm doen think oi be interferin' or anythin', sirs," she said looking directly at Philemon and John, "but it concerns the Reverend. Oi'm certain he be a traitor."

"Would you be referring to the Reverend Ebenezer Dunn, Betsy?" asked John.

"Yes, sir, oi be," she replied.

"Tell us all what you know, Betsy, take your time," said John, looking seriously at Philemon and Sir Joshua.

"Well, sirs, oi've had me suspicions about him for some time now. One evenin' several weeks past, oi'd stayed late cleanin' the church when oi heard him comin' in. 'Twas gettin' dimpsy then and shadows formin' all round the church, so's not wantin' him to be angry with me for bein' late in my cleanin' work and what with him threatenin' to send me to hell, oi hid behind the altar in the shadows. Well, not long after he had come in, oi heard the church door openin' again, and someone else come in. Oi didn' see who'm it could be, but oi heard him plain enough."

"Yes, Betsy, what did they say to each other?" asked Philemon.

"Well, the stranger asked the Reverend if he had any information for him, and the Reverend asked for payment for the last information he had given him. Oi heard the sound of a bag of money bein' passed over and coins tinklin' in it. Then the Reverend tells him there be a big build-up of ships and troop carriers in Dartmouth harbour. He also tells him that Stoke Gabriel be busy with troops loadin' and unloadin' supplies. Then the stranger, obviously some spy or whatever, tells him he wants numbers and dates and unless the Reverend can give him this then he won't get paid. But then, oi hears the Reverend demand the stranger to stop and listen to some very important news he had concerin' the King."

"Good lord!" exclaimed John. "Please continue, Betsy."

"Well, the Reverend tells him that he wants a face-to-face meetin' with someone called Luc Skorniere in Plymouth. He won't say nuthin' to the stranger about the King, only to Luc Skorniere. Well, the stranger tells him he will pass on the Reverend's message and then he leaves. Oi heard the Reverend laugh all devilish like while he be counting some of his coins from the bag and then he hurries out of the church and slams the door shut. Oi waited for a while behind the altar in case he came back but he didn', so oi lets meself out of the church and goes home."

"Have you heard anything more, Betsy?" asked Philemon.

"Oh yes, sir, oi have. It be only a short time past. Us was in church one Sunday mornin' with young Jane, the mornin' you'm both was down in Saltram

House visitin' Master Parker here. Well, the Reverend came to the end of his sermon and stood lookin' at the congregation without sayin' a word. Then, as blatant as ever, he pulls his left ear and with his bushy eyebrows raised, he glares at us all. Oi thought it strange he did that but oi knows him be a strange one, then it struck me that the devil's sendin' someone in the church a message. Didn' take me long to work out that he was tellin' whoever the message was for, to be in the church that evenin' for a meetin' again. So's oi lets meself into the church early evenin' as it was gettin' dimpsy and 'id behind the altar once more. Oi stayed there listenin' and waitin' as it slowly got darker. Well, sure enough, oi heard that devil priest comin' in and he goes straight into the vestry and starts drinkin' the church wine, belchin' too he was and mentionin' someone called Septimus Sniff. Well, oi never heard that name before and he certainly baint be from this here village. Then oi heard the door open and the spy comes in askin' where he be. The Reverend comes out of the vestry and tells the mystery man to give Luc a message. He tells him that you sir, Philemon Pownoll, be back in Sharpham from the navy and would very likely be at the big house for the party. He said it be most urgent for him to tell Luc this news. Oi thought the way they'm was talkin about the party at the big house that it must be somethin' important. The Reverend was most adamant that the news of you, sir, goin' to the party at the big house got to Luc straightaway. It sounded like the reverend thought you'm was goin' to spoil the party sir. The spy then left. Oi been waitin' to tell you this for a while now, sirs, but you'm been too busy, so's oi left it till now. That devil priest tells me he can send me to hell if oi tells anyone about what ever oi heard. Doen let him do that, sirs. Oh, oi nearly forgot, but oi thinks oi knows who the mystery man what collects the information from the Reverend could be."

Betsy paused looking at the four who sat looking at her earnestly.

"Who is, it Betsy?" said Jane gently.

"Oi knows by his voice, it be Barold Raustin, the builder in the village."

"What, Barold?" said Philemon, shocked. "He's done many a job for us here at Sharpham, I can't believe it. Are you sure, Betsy?"

"Yes, sir, oi be, it definitely be his voice oi heard and he be a traitor."

"Philemon," said John, "the big house must refer to Saltram and the party must be the King's stay with us. Oh my God, we have got a nest of spies here and they've somehow got information that the King's going to stay at Saltram tomorrow. That means only one thing, a possible assassination attempt. It is too late to get news to His Majesty to stop the visit; we would never get there before he left the palace. We have got to get hold of Reverend Dunn and Barold. Philemon, you go to Barold's cottage now with Joshua, I will go to the minister's house. Take a pistol with you. We will arrest them, then take them to the Revenue building in Totnes for questioning. Jane, it would best for you to stay here with Betsy. Come, gentlemen, time's passing."

John hammered on Ebenezer's front door, the sound echoing around the porch where he was standing. He waited then hammered again, shouting out for Ebenezer to open the door there and then. There was no sound of anyone in the house. Evening was setting in and the time when Ebenezer should be at home. There was no sign of any candles alight in the house, it looked empty. John knocked again, standing back to look up at the top windows; there wasn't a trace of anyone at home.

He's gone, he thought, *Betsy's warnings came too late. He is a damned spy and I didn't even see it. He must be with whoever's planning the attack on the King.*

John turned around and walked back down the path towards the gate, deep in thought about the danger that would strike his home the following day. At the gate, he saw Philemon and Joshua coming up the cobblestone hill on their horses. When they saw John, they dismounted.

"Barold's not at home," said Philemon. "His wife Hilary told us he'll be away for two days on a building job he's starting near Exeter."

"Mmm, I doubt it," said John shaking his head. "There's no sign of Ebenezer either. His house is all empty and shut up. Something has been planned for tomorrow and they're part of it. We have uncovered two traitors in this village of Ashprington and I believe they're going to try to assassinate the King. We cannot interrupt the King's address to his troops, it's in the national interest. His address could result in bringing the war to a quick close so we must keep the King ignorant of this threat and do our utmost to find the traitors who'll be lurking in or near Saltram tomorrow. It's imperative we keep the King safe and discover whoever may be hiding within my walls."

Chapter 40

Ebenezer stretched his legs, the lumps in the uncomfortable mattress he had spent the night on aboard Raymond's fishing vessel digging into his back. The putrid smell of fish hung heavily around him and on opening his eyes, he saw Luc and Barold in conversation at the table. He listened to Luc, explaining the necessity of having to wait a good five to six hours concealed in the bedroom's secret hideaway before the King fell asleep. It then dawned on him that he too would be cooped up with the two of them, in what would probably turn out to be the narrowest of hiding places. With a disgruntled yawn, he got out of the berth and scratching his backside made his way towards the table. Taking a mug, he poured himself some ale and picking up a slice of bread and cheese, sat listening to their conversation.

"We'll wait there until Andre's sure the King's fallen into a deep sleep," said Luc. "The sleeping-draught that he'll slip into his nightcap will act quite quickly. You, Barold, will slip out of the concealed opening as soon as we hear Andre knock twice on the panel, then when the deed's done, the three of us will make our way along the secret passageway to the spiral staircase that leads down to the wine cellar where Andre will be waiting. If everything goes in our favour, we should be out and back here ready for Raymond to cast off in the early hours, and you'll be well on your way home to Ashprington."

"Sounds perfect," said Barold. "Let's just hope them two Frenchies will be waitin' with the horses."

"What about our disguises?" asked Ebenezer.

"I have a friend who runs a large bakery on the other side of the Barbican," said Luc. "He's French and sympathises with our cause. He employs half a dozen bakers who begin their day baking well before dawn. They are finished by the hour of eleven when they leave the bakery and head off home. He has promised to put by three bakers' smocks and caps that Raymond and Allain will collect when they pick up the bread and cakes after two o'clock this afternoon. Allain

296

will be driving the wagon and he will wait with it while Raymond brings us the disguises. Once we have changed and run through the plans one more time, we'll be ready. Allain will drive us to Saltram where he will leave us once we've unloaded the wagon. Andre will show us where to deposit the bread and cakes, then he'll take us to the King's bedroom where we'll prepare for our long vigil."

"May I remind you of our agreement," said Ebenezer looking earnestly at Luc, "that my first instalment must be waiting on board here when we return."

"Yes, yes, Ebenezer, it'll be here when you return, don't worry."

Ebenezer licked his lips, the avaricious looks of greed contorting his face into diabolical leers of self-satisfaction.

"Raymond will collect it from a loyal compatriot of ours who practices law here in Plymouth. This contact is to be trusted, have no doubts your money will be here."

"I truly hope so," said Ebenezer, his face aglow with the thought of holding the first part of his fortune.

"Barold, I'll be holding your purse until the deed is done. When we reach the horses, you will receive it then. Don't worry, everything will be there as we agreed."

Barold nodded, a slow smile spreading across his face as he mentally calculated his growing wealth.

"And now, gentlemen, I need to run through a few details with Raymond, who's up on deck. Relax here for the moment, I'll return shortly."

As Luc closed the door to the crew's living quarters, Ebenezer turned to Barold.

"The shock of finding out that the mystery contact in the church was you, Barold, has now lessened a bit, so perhaps you'd tell me why you've turned traitor."

"Same as you, Reverend, for the money. Me and Hilary want everything we can possibly get. Oh yes, before you'm asks, Reverend, she knows what oi do, it be her what encouraged me into all this. It was when oi was doin' repair work in the stable behind the Cat and Fiddle, about a year past when oi met Luc. He would often chat and then he started buyin' the ale after oi'd finished workin'. Well, he asked me one evenin', right out of the blue, if oi'd be interested in doin' some work for him. Before he told me what it would be, he offered me a massive purse, it be somethin' oi just couldn' turn down. He just wanted me to wander round Dartmouth countin' the number of frigates and supply ships that was comin' and goin'. Well, us did well on that one and then he asks me to kill someone he said had been watchin' him for some time outside the Cat. Oi spent a few evenin's watchin' outside the inn and sure enough oi sees this fucker leanin' up against the wall who then followed Luc when he came out. One evenin' oi followed them both and when Luc slowed down by the trees near the Duke of York, the bastard stopped behind a tree. He didn' hear me comin up behind him. Oi slit his throat there and then and left him. Luc gave me a purse twice as much as Squire Maddock gives you to share amongst us for his smugglin' jobs. Then Luc asks me to act as his contact with you. Oi was sure you'd recognise me, but oi couldn' turn down his request as the reward oi got from him was well worth it. Ha, that's why oi always said to you not to come near me when oi met you in your church. Oi think oi did a good job of coverin' me steps. No-one in the village, especially in our smugglin' group, had any idea of what oi was doin', ha, ha."

"So, you don't mind killing the King of England then?" asked Ebenezer.

"Nah, oi'd do it twice over if the purse was good," replied Barold with a grin. "What he is payin' me for this 'un is more than what oi got from you for our last two smugglin' runs. Anyways, Hilary's goin' up to Darton Hall to see her relative Squire Maddock, to see if we can take over from you and help him organise the smugglin' business. Her will tell him that you'm buggered orf to France after gettin' involved with these here spies down in Plymouth and that you'm won't be comin' back. I expect I'll have to do some recruitin' now Stephen's dead and Elijah doen wanna know anymore."

"Mmm, well good luck, Barold!" said Ebenezer, feeling doubtful about Barold's aspirations and wondering what the Squire would make of it all.

* * *

Andrew stood at the back of Saltram's impressive dining room, watching as John cleared his throat to address his staff.

"I've gathered you all here to give you important news of who'll actually be arriving at Saltram later this afternoon." John paused briefly. "You know that we have an important guest arriving at Saltram and I'm very pleased to see the house looking in such a wonderful condition. Thank you all. Now, you were told to expect the arrival of a high-ranking official from the government. I can tell you that he'll certainly be a high-ranking official but not from the government."

298

Several curious faces looked closer towards John.

"You were all informed that it would be a government official visiting, but that was only for security reasons. We had to hide his identity as a cover, but I can now tell you that it will be His Majesty King George who will be visiting us here at Saltram. He'll be staying here for one night only, before he gives his address to the troops assembling on the Barbican."

An excited flurry of whispers descended over the staff, some of the young servant girls holding their hands to their mouths to quell the excited squeals that were threatening to burst from them.

"The royal party will be arriving at six o'clock all being well. The pre-planned programme will continue as normal, a reception for His Majesty in the drawing room just after his arrival and then dinner at seven thirty. His Majesty will retire early, and breakfast will be served tomorrow morning at eight. Sir Joshua Reynolds, along with Master and Mistress Pownoll, will also be my guests. At this point, I must instruct you to be on the look-out for any strangers who may be wandering around in the house. I do not want to alarm you, but we must be diligent. Thank you all for your good work. Now back to your stations and be ready for six o'clock."

John left the dining room to see Andrew hovering outside the door.

"Sir Joshua Reynolds has arrived, sir, I've suggested he wait for you in your sitting-room."

"Thank you, Andrew," said John, hurrying off to welcome Joshua.

The grandfather clock in the hallway chimed the hour of three as John opened the door of his sitting-room to see Sir Joshua inspecting a sketch he'd previously made of a farm labourer and donated to the Parker family, hanging from the wall over the fireplace.

"Joshua, you look perfectly ready for His Majesty," said John beaming at his friend who was smartly attired in evening dress.

"Well, yes, John, but you know my feelings towards our present King. It is plain, he doesn't really like me, and I must admit the feeling is mutual. But I shall go out of my way to be charming and supportive of his visit here to Saltram."

"Yes, I do realise that, Joshua," said John, "but it's important for Theresa and me to have the nation's most famous portrait painter here with us at Saltram to welcome the King. I am sure he'll appreciate that. And I thank you, dear friend."

299

"Have you made a search of the rooms, John?" asked Sir Joshua seriously.

"Time and time again, but nothing's turned up out of the ordinary. I've confided our knowledge of a suspected attack on the King with Andrew, he seemed most concerned and will increase the searches as the clock ticks by."

A gentle knock sounded on the sitting-room door and Andrew entered quietly.

"Ah, Andrew, I was just saying to Sir Joshua that you'll increase the inspections around the house as we get further into the afternoon."

"Of course, sir," said Andrew, "but now I need to know which bedroom you've allocated the King?"

"Ah yes, the master bedroom on the west wing on the first landing, it's the largest bedroom on the wing. The door next to it is a bathroom for the King's sole use. His entourage will take the other rooms on that floor. They are all ready and made up. Constant checks please, Andrew, on the bedrooms, the drawing-room where we'll hold the reception and then the dining-room."

"We have a late delivery of bread and cakes arriving at about four-thirty, sir," said Andrew, looking at John seriously. "I'll make sure I'm at the tradesmen's entrance to oversee it."

"Yes, thank you, Andrew. Mmm, fresh cakes, eh! That will please the King, he's got a sweet tooth you know, by all accounts."

Andrew nodded towards John, a smile forming across his serious features.

"I'll want you and two other footmen in the reception hall when the King and his party arrive, Andrew. The two footmen will show His Majesty to his room first, then the rest of his party. You will accompany him and his personal valet. Make sure his valet settles in his room next to His Majesty's and is given everything he asks for. The two footmen will wait in attendance on that landing until the King is ready to be escorted to the reception in the drawing room. Shadow the King's valet from the time they arrive, I hope that is clear? And, Andrew, checks on every room must be made on the half hour."

"Absolutely, sir," said Andrew. "If that is all, sir?"

"Yes, Andrew, that'll be all," replied John.

Andrew hastened along the hallway to the grand staircase that led up to the first-floor landing and the master bedroom on the west wing. He could not help but think that of all the stately rooms in England, this one would be the room to witness the last night of the English King.

Outside the door of the bedroom, he listened to see if any of the chamber maids were inside giving final touches to the room. There was no sound of any movement. With a quick look behind him, he opened the door and stepped in. The room had been beautifully prepared. A fine four-poster bed, made up and ready, stood majestically in the centre of the large square room. A suit of two luxurious armchairs and a sofa stood a little way back from the bed while a gleaming silver dish, brimming with juicy mouth-watering fruit, stood haughtily poised on a highly polished mahogany table. Red velvet curtains draped elegantly from a bow window, while a heap of kindling wood and coal lay in a generous-looking grate, ready to light should His Majesty feel the need for the comfort of a warm fire during the night. The walls of the bedroom were panelled in a rich oak and it was to the far-left side, four panels back from the window that Andrew approached. A wooden grill had been inserted into this panel at about head height, and to anyone who happened to notice it, it would appear as an ordinary air vent. That it was, but it was also a spy hole for the secret hideaway at the back of the panel.

Andrew wondered why John had not thought of checking this secret of the house; he could only think that he may have forgotten all about it or thought that no-one knew of it, apart from his personal footman. Satisfied there was no-one approaching from outside the room, he grasped the thick wooden side of the panel and pushed. The wooden structure slowly moved inwards, revealing a dark square-shaped space. He stepped in, closing the panel behind him by pushing a brass handle attached to its inside. He had been in this hideaway before, furtively spying on important government officials John had invited for a weekend's hunting. What he had observed and heard he had reported directly to Luc. Groping around in the darkness, he felt a small table up against the side of a damp wall, three chairs stood tightly hugging it. He shuffled over to where the grill on the panel shed enough light and a good flow of air to satisfy whoever was hiding there. He must remember to have several candles lit in the bedroom to give off enough light to seep through the grill. This would suffice for the three assassins to see by, although the hideaway would still be shrouded in shadow. As soon as the King or his personal valet entered the room, then whomever was keeping watch from behind the grill had to insist on complete silence within the secret chamber. Leading away to the left, a narrow passageway disappeared into the darkness. This would be their escape route to the staircase that led down to the wine cellar where he would wait for them to appear and then lead them out to where the horses would be ready and waiting.

Pleased that everything looked in order, he pushed the handle on the panel and stepped back into the bedroom, making sure the fitting was securely closed behind him. Quietly, he let himself out and hurrying away towards the staircase, he heard the grandfather clock below, chime the hour of four.

"That's it," he said to himself, "they're on their way. Better get down to the kitchen and the tradesmen's entrance. They can bring the bread and cakes through the kitchen into the large walk-in pantry, then it will be easier for us to slide away to the wine cellar without being noticed. If they are looking the part, then the kitchen staff won't get suspicious. Ha, don't suppose any of them down there know that the King's got a sweet tooth!"

Chapter 41

Andrew watched the horse and wagon lumber slowly up the long driveway, skirting the main entrance to drop down a gentle slope to the rear basement courtyard where he was waiting at the door of the tradesmen's entrance. Hiding a smile at the ridiculous sight of Ebenezer dressed in a blue and white pin-striped smock and a tight-fitting white baker's cap, he sidled over to the wagon.

"Start to unload the bread and cakes, and follow me," he said looking up at Luc sitting next to Allain.

Luc jumped down from the wagon, shouting for Ebenezer to follow him and instructing Barold to stay on the wagon with Allain to pass down the items ordered for Saltram's kitchen. No-one uttered a word as Ebenezer and Luc, cradling loaves of fresh bread and cakes, followed Andrew through the kitchen and into a wide pantry at the far end. Several of the kitchen staff looked up from their work, not taking any notice of the late delivery men but covetously eyeing the sight of the number of delicious cakes and tarts passing them by. After two loads were stacked away in the pantry, Andrew told Luc and Ebenezer to stay where they were while he went to fetch Barold from the wagon and to instruct Allain to leave.

None of the kitchen staff paid any attention to Barold as he followed Andrew through the kitchen to where Luc and Ebenezer waited. Inside the pantry, Andrew held his finger to his lips indicating they keep silent, then moving outside, he made sure the kitchen staff were busily engaged in their work and obviously not bothered with the whereabouts of the three bakers. Satisfied, he indicated for the three of them to follow him out of the kitchen. They hurried along a dimly-lit corridor, stopping outside a thick wooden door while Andrew fumbled around in his livery coat pocket for a key. As he nudged the door open and ushered them in, their eyes lit up at the rows of bottles lying on tiers of dusty shelves. A solitary lantern glowed from its wall holding, shedding a dull light across Saltram's spacious wine cellar.

"Over there, behind the shelves in that corner," he said pointing in the direction of a dark corner of the cellar, "is a spiral staircase. You cannot see it from here, in fact, you cannot see it from any angle in this room. You need to squeeze past that last shelf to reach it, it is in behind there. At the top of the staircase is the passageway I was telling you about that leads to the hideaway in the bedroom they have allocated the King. Come on, that's where we're heading, but first I need to light this taper from the lantern on that wall."

They followed the light from Andrew's taper across the wine cellar to where the last set of shelves gave way to a narrow gap.

Through the gloom, they watched Andrew squeeze past the shelf rack, his glowing taper lighting up the spiral staircase that vanished into the darkness above them. One by one they followed, Ebenezer having to pull his stomach in tightly to inch his way past the narrow gap.

Andrew had previously left a box of candles at the bottom of the staircase, and lighting one from his taper, he led the three assassins up the spiralling stairs, the light from the candle casting ominous looking shadows around them. At the top they shuffled after him in single file, Ebenezer bringing up the rear behind Barold and feeling the hairs on the back of his neck tingling with apprehension. The passage suddenly gave way to a wider square-shaped area that seemed brighter than the narrow confines they had just come through. Andrew stopped by the side of the small table and chairs, moving closer against the wall so they could gather around him.

"Over there on the panel, you'll see a brass handle. Push on it and the panel will open onto the bedroom. Above the handle you will see a grill. Its purpose is to provide an air supply through this wall cavity; it also allows a little light from the bedroom, but for our benefit it will act as a spy hole. If you look through it, you'll have a good view of a four-poster bed and a suit of furniture next to it."

Luc stepped over to it, appreciating its convenient height. Looking through it, he saw clearly what Andrew had described, nodding with approval at the extra wide angles it afforded. Barold and then Ebenezer took turns to familiarise themselves with the view from it after Luc had moved away.

"You must take it in turns to keep watch on the bedroom," continued Andrew. "As soon as anyone enters, then complete silence must be observed, even the controlling of your breathing. From time to time you will see me coming and going. It will be when the King's personal valet and I are preparing the King for bed that I'll drop the sleeping draught into his nightcap. We have been assured that the King never retires without a nightcap, usually a small glass of wine laced with brandy. So, what with that and the sleeping draught, he should be well-away in no time. Barold, two knocks from me will indicate the King is asleep, then when you see his valet and me leave the room, your job begins. I'll make my way down to the wine cellar where I'll wait for the three of you. There will be no burning of candles in here after I've gone, your eyes will soon become used to the dim light in here. When the deed is done, Barold, make sure the panel is firmly closed when you come back in. It's not far down the passageway to the spiral staircase."

Andrew shook each of their hands, and with a man's hug, clasped Luc around his shoulders.

"*Bonne chance, mon ami,*" he said looking into Luc's eyes.

"*Merci, Andre, bonne chance aussi, mon ami,*" replied Luc.

They watched the shadows from the light of Andrew's candle dance across the sides of the passageway as he hurried back along their escape route, the glow on the side of the wall at the top of the staircase disappearing as the flame on the candle was finally extinguished in the darkness below.

"I'll take the first watch," said Luc, stepping over to where the grill on the panel was letting in some of the day light from the King's bedroom. "There's just under an hour before the King's party arrive, so I suggest you two sit yourselves down and grab some rest. Tonight's going to be a busy one, of that you can be sure!"

* * *

The sound of three blasts from a hunting horn outside Saltram's gates signalled the arrival of the royal party. John, Theresa and Sir Joshua stood nervously in the grand reception hall waiting for an equerry of the King to ride up to the main entrance and then, as custom had it, announce the imminent arrival of the King of England.

"Andrew, open the main doors," John instructed. "I can hear hoofbeats coming up the carriageway. It'll be the King's herald riding ahead to announce his arrival."

Controlling his nerves, Andrew opened the doors. The sight of a cavalry officer dismounting and striding towards the main entrance prompted the three of them to step out and stand under the main entrance portico. Plucking the tricorn hat from his head, he bowed affably towards them.

"Sir," he boomed, eyes fixed rigidly on John, "His Majesty King George III requests your hospitality and company. How shall he be received, sir?"

"With a warm and joyous welcome, sir," replied John.

With a nod, the equerry remounted and rode off back down the carriageway to where the royal carriage stood waiting. Smoothing down her gown, Theresa stood next to John, her pregnancy looking obvious in its last few weeks. Behind them, Sir Joshua Reynolds, wondering how he would be received by the King, looked towards the royal carriage and the carriage behind it carrying the King's entourage. Andrew stood with two of the footmen, his face not showing the anxiety running through him as he watched the royal carriage roll up to stop in front of where John and Theresa were standing.

A liveried coachman rushed up to place a wooden block of steps in front of the door, stepping back with a bow. A figure wrapped in a dark cloak and clutching a leather case under his arm, stepped gracefully from the carriage and down the wooden block of steps to stand respectfully beside the door. At the same time, a thin, pale and liveried figure rushed over from the carriage behind to take his place beside the door opposite the cloaked individual. All eyes were focused on the royal carriage as the King disembarked. John and Theresa stood watching, the spectacle of the King of England rolling up to their front door, not quite sinking in. Smiling, the King whispered in the cloaked figure's ear, who then turned and beckoned John and Theresa to come forward to them.

"Your Majesty," he said, "may I present Master and Mistress Parker of Saltram House. Your hosts, sire."

King George offered his hand to John, who took it and bowed courteously while Theresa curtsied with difficulty.

"My dear," said the King, eyeing Theresa's condition, "I do not expect you, in your condition to bend to your King. Please remain upright and take my arm, madam."

With a look of astonished delight, Theresa placed her hand on the King's outstretched arm, smiling with pleasure at John.

"Master Parker, it is indeed a pleasure to meet with you, sir. I trust our night over with you has not presented you with any inconvenience?"

"Not at all, Your Majesty," replied John. "It is an honour to welcome you to our home, sire."

"Splendid," said the King. "Ah, Sir Joshua Reynolds. I have heard you spend a great deal of your time here at Saltram when not engaged on a portrait, eh?"

"Your Majesty," said Sir Joshua bowing to the King. "It is a privilege to meet with you again, sire."

"Indeed it is, Sir Joshua," said the King. "Indeed it is."

While the King chatted to Sir Joshua, the cloaked figure approached John.

"Master Parker, sir, thank you for your welcome. I can assure you the King is most pleased."

John looked at the King's secretary smiling with relief.

"Thank you, Lord Chilworth, that is good to hear. When we last met in London to discuss the evening's programme for the King, you mentioned that His Majesty retires early. We have the reception for him as soon as you feel ready and then dinner at seven thirty. The two extra guests I spoke of when we met, Master and Mistress Pownoll, will be arriving in an hour."

"That will be fine, I am sure," said Lord Chilworth. "As for your two extra guests, the King is delighted to be dining with a sea captain and his wife."

The King's secretary turned to look at the thin pale figure hovering behind him.

"Master Parker, may I present the King's personal valet, Henry Tonks."

Henry gave a short bow in John's direction. "A pleasure, sir," he said.

"Indeed, sir," said John, smiling at Henry. "If you look over to your right, you will see my personal valet standing by the main entrance door. His name is Andrew and he has instructions from me to be at your side when you are assisting the King. This has been cleared by Lord Chilworth."

"Very good, sir," said Henry smiling, "I'll introduce myself when we go in."

"Thank you, Henry," replied John. "And now, Lord Chilworth, I think we should all go in and prepare for the evening. My footmen will show you to the King's bedchamber and then return for the rest of your party."

Luc looked away from the grill in the panel and quickly turning towards Barold and Ebenezer, clicked his fingers.

"Sssssh, not a word, they're coming," he hissed.

Barold and Ebenezer immediately sat upright, their senses sharpening to Luc's warning. Controlling his breathing, Luc peered through the grill, his ears alert for the sound of the opening of the bedroom door. Barold and Ebenezer sat rigidly, still not moving a muscle. The sound of a key in the lock and the door opening instantly sharpened Luc's attention to the limited view in front of him.

Not being able to see towards the door from the angle the grill afforded, he strained his ears towards the babble of voices entering the room.

Two footmen came into view carrying the King's luggage, which they placed in front of the mahogany table. Luc watched Andrew cross the room to light several candles from a lighted taper he was carrying, his eyes following him towards the window where he drew the velvet curtains to shut out the early evening light. Darkness enveloped the hideaway for a moment until the light from the candles grew stronger, allowing a fraction of their light to seep through the grill.

Barold and Ebenezer hardly dared to breathe, their eyes stuck fast on Luc.

"You needn't fuss so much, Henry," Luc heard the King say to his personal valet as they came into view. "I feel quite energetic, even after that long journey, and I don't want to rest now. The Parkers have organised a reception for us before dinner and I think we should go down now."

Luc watched Andrew dismiss the two footmen and then assist Henry in putting the King's bags onto the table.

"Andrew here can escort me down to the reception while you unpack a few of my things, Henry. Then, when you are ready, come and join me. Lord Chilworth, I am sure, will be down there already. But first I should change into something more appropriate for dinner, eh?"

"Sire," said Henry quietly, opening one of the bags.

Luc turned towards Barold who sat rigidly still in the semi darkness. Ebenezer starting to tremble, watched Luc wide-eyed, not taking his eyes from the square grill on the panel.

Silently, Luc beckoned Barold to come to the spy hole.

"Take a good look at your victim, Barold," he whispered. "The King of England."

Barold peered through the grill. His eyes focusing on a tall slim man, probably in his late thirties who stood with his arms extended while a servant helped him into an expensive-looking shiny evening jacket. He noticed that the young man's powdered white wig, pulled tight into his head, enhanced a high forehead, while his large watery eyes, staring out towards the oak panelling, revealed a hint of insecurity and a longing for something that he could never have.

"Ar, that be the one whom's gonna make me a fortune," he mumbled quietly.

John looked up from inspecting the trays of hors d'oeuvres as the King, escorted by Andrew, entered the drawing room.

"Your Majesty," he said smiling, "I trust all is favourable?"

"Absolutely, sir," replied the King, "everything is excellent."

Andrew nodded respectfully and left the room.

The King's secretary, Lord Chilworth, and a group of his entourage noticed the King's arrival and moved over to join the King and John. Sir Joshua and Theresa, entering the drawing room, saw John in the King's group and eagerly joined them, the King immediately moving to Theresa's side to engage her in conversation. Several liveried servants stood by the group, offering glasses of sparkling wine that sat bubbling away invitingly on glistening silver trays.

John stood back with a feeling of joy and relief, happy that the atmosphere was already one of conviviality and warmth. The evening ahead looked set to be a great success and one which he hoped the King would never forget.

A slight cough behind him let him know Andrew needed his attention.

"Yes, Andrew?" he asked.

"Sir, Master and Mistress Pownoll are in the reception hall."

"Excellent," said John. "Tell them I'm on my way."

Informing the King that his two guests had arrived, John excused himself from the group and with a smile of encouragement towards Theresa, left the room.

Philemon and Jane waited a little nervously in the reception hall for John to come and fetch them. It was not every day that one met the King of England.

"Dear friends," called John as he hurried towards them, "I must say you both look most fine. Jane, you look outstanding, my dear. One would say you look as though you are dressed to meet a king, ha! Now come with me and really meet your King."

Philemon gave Jane his arm and with a deep breath they followed John into the drawing room and an introduction to King George III of Great Britain and Ireland.

Luc watched Henry place the King's night clothes onto the bed and then turn it down, so it was ready for the King to get straight into it when he returned to the bedroom after the dinner. He heard the bedroom door open and then saw Andrew come into view carrying a silver tray on which stood two medium-sized decanters and a crystal wine glass. Luc could see that one of the decanters had been filled with red wine while the other one contained the brandy.

"Ah, Andrew, splendid," said Henry looking up, "the King's nightcap, I assume?"

"Absolutely," replied Andrew with a smile, "I'll put it here on the table."

"Well, everything's ready now for when he retires," said Henry. "Master Parker has informed me that you'll be assisting me later in case there's anything I'll need. That is good of you, Andrew, thank you."

"You're most welcome, indeed you are," said Andrew, looking over at the grill and wondering which one of his accomplices was watching.

"I'll wander down to the reception now and wait to see if His Majesty has need of me," said Henry looking at Andrew. "They'll be going into dinner shortly. Will you be serving at dinner?"

"On this occasion, no, Henry," replied Andrew. "We're to dine together in the staff dining room next to the kitchen, orders from Master Parker. I have placed one of Saltram's good clarets on our table. It's breathing now."

"What are we waiting for then, let's go," said Henry smiling with pleasure.

Luc heard the bedroom door close after them, the vision of mouth-watering delicacies filling the tables below, reminding him of how hungry he was. He knew it wouldn't be long before Ebenezer started to complain of his hunger, but to eat satisfyingly now would weaken their senses and that he couldn't afford to let happen. Turning away from the grill, he whispered over to Ebenezer to come and take his turn at the grill.

Just a few more hours, he thought, sitting himself down in the chair, *and providence will again smile on France. What we will achieve tonight will turn the tables in our favour and France will once again be great. Ha, Great Britain will languish under our heel as they should have always done. The time has now come. Vive la France!*

Chapter 42

The conversation around the table in Saltram's dining room flowed as steadily as the wine, the King enjoying the service he was receiving as much as his appreciation for the tasteful and exquisite décor of the stately home. Sitting at the top of the table to the King's right, John looked around at the handful of diners who were all, apart from Theresa, Sir Joshua and the Pownolls, trusted officials of the King's court. Lord Chilworth, deep in conversation with Sir Thomas Gage, who'd been appointed Commander-in-Chief in North America and was to sail to the colonies immediately after the King's address, was obviously discussing important aspects of the King's speech to be given to the troops the following day. The King's physician chatted earnestly away to Sir Joshua Reynolds, relishing the refills of superior claret that Saltram's footmen kept providing. Philemon had the King absorbed in his account of how he, as commander of the sloop-of-war HMS *Favourite*, together with the captain of an accompanying frigate HMS *Active*, had chased down a Spanish merchant ship on its way to Cadiz harbour from the South American port of Lima in Peru. The King sat enthralled at Philemon's detailed description of the action that had taken place at sea on that day in May 1762. He was so taken by the event that when Philemon recounted the vast fortune of gold and precious stones that had been discovered when the ship had finally been boarded, the King whooped in amazement and wonder.

"Well, I never," said the King sitting back utterly spellbound. "What a story, Captain Pownoll. I remember hearing about that during the Seven Years' War, but I never dreamed I would meet the officer responsible for such an amazing capture. Well done, sir, I'm most impressed."

The King then turned his attention to Theresa and Jane, chatting to them with the ease of the skilled conversationalist that he was, the two friends listening in awe to his entertaining repertoire of anecdotes.

John sat taking it all in, pleased with how the dinner party was progressing but aware of the dark cloud that hovered over the whole scene. He had personally made a thorough search of most of the rooms, content that there was nothing there to indicate an attack on the King. He was sure that Andrew had searched the rooms he had not, including the bedroom allocated to the King. He trusted Andrew to make a complete search and was sure he had.

So, he thought, *if Betsy's story is true then where is the threat and where are the spies?*

His thoughts were interrupted by Andrew and Henry entering the dining room. The conversation around the dining table was beginning to peter out as the King's party, having enjoyed a scrumptious four-course dinner with copious glasses of fine claret were now starting to feel a need for their beds.

On seeing Henry and Andrew waiting patiently, the King nodded and rose from the table.

"Ladies and gentlemen," he said looking around the table, "a fine, fine dinner. I thank you, Master and Mistress Parker, for the wonderful hospitality, but after our long journey and the urgency to rise early tomorrow, I must bid you all a very goodnight."

"Ladies and gentlemen," said Lord Chilworth raising his glass, "a toast to our King and may his address to the troops tomorrow inspire them to a victorious conclusion to the rebellion in our colonies. To the King!"

Everyone raised their glasses, their voices echoing around the walls of the stately home as they toasted their sovereign. Grinning, King George gave a wave as he made his way out of the dining room, those around the table bowing and curtsying graciously. At the door, he smiled at Henry and Andrew who bowed courteously towards him. With a nod in John's direction, Andrew turned and followed the King and Henry out of the door and up the grand staircase to the bedroom that only he knew concealed the traitors John had been desperate but unable to find.

Ebenezer jumped with fright as he heard the bedroom door open and voices enter the room. He pushed his ear close to the grill listening intently.

"Pssst," he hissed towards Luc and Barold who were dozing at the small table.

Luc immediately became alert, springing out of his chair and moving silently over to where Ebenezer was peering through the grill.

"They're getting him ready for bed," whispered Ebenezer, moving away and letting Luc take over.

Luc nodded as he watched Henry expertly change the King into his night attire and then take a candle over to the fireplace to light the kindling lying in the grate. It was not long before the crackling of firewood could be heard as the King settled himself in one of the armchairs near the fire. The lumps of coal that Henry had placed over the kindling wood had started to glow and it did not take long before the flames started to lick their way upwards from the grate.

"Andrew, can you prepare the King's nightcap while I get his morning clothes ready?" asked Henry. "A full glass of wine with a large dash of brandy."

Andrew made his way over to the table where the tray with the two decanters were placed. Looking over at the grill, he smiled, knowing that it was probably Luc who was watching from behind the panel. He took off the stoppers from the two decanters and holding the glass in his left hand, filled three quarters of it with red wine finally topping it up with the brandy from the other decanter.

Placing the glass on the table, he turned his body, his back facing the King and Henry, so blotting out their view of the table. Quickly, he put his hand into the pocket of his livery coat and pulling out the small bag that contained the sleeping draught; he opened it and poured the powder into the King's nightcap. Taking a spoon from the cutlery dish next to the fruit, he gave the contents in the glass a swift stir.

"He's done it, he's drugged the King's nightcap," whispered Luc turning to Barold and Ebenezer. "All he has to do now is give it to him and make sure he drinks it. Barold, get yourself ready."

Andrew turned towards Henry and the King, certain they hadn't noticed anything unusual. Picking up the glass, he moved over to where the King sat gazing into the fire.

"I'll take that," said Henry staring at him.

Andrew felt a surge of panic as Henry stood facing him with his hand held out.

Controlling himself, he handed over the glass, fearful that Henry may take a sip to check its purity. With a nod, he turned to the King.

"Sire, your nightcap," he said handing him the glass.

The King took the glass and sitting up, took a long draught, licking his lips with the pleasure of its taste.

"Mmmm, that's good, Henry," he said, taking another long draught.

From behind the panel, Luc watched the King take a second large mouthful.

"Come on, one more long swig and you're done," he whispered, looking round at Ebenezer and Barold standing next to him.

Gazing into the fire that was now blazing away warmly, the King's eyes began to droop. Henry recognised this and taking the King's arm, he gently took the glass away from his hand.

"Andrew," he said, "help me put His Majesty to bed, he's nearly gone."

Andrew took the King's other arm and they tenderly lifted him out of the armchair.

"Let me finish my nightcap, Henry," muttered the King as they sat him on the side of the bed.

Henry put the glass into his hand and the King downed it in one big mouthful.

"A good nightcap, it's done me well," slurred the King, his eyes drooping even more.

"He must be exhausted," said Henry, tucking the King into bed. "I knew he should have rested before going down to dinner. He'll sleep well now, in fact I think we all will."

"Yes, I hope you do!" said Andrew with his eyes on the grill.

A gentle knock on the door saw the cavalry officer put his head round the door. "Just to let you know, Master Tonks, I've set two guards outside His Majesty's door, they'll be here all night."

"Thank you, captain," said Henry.

"Well, I think it's time to retire, Henry," said Andrew. "I have some rounds to make before going to bed, so if you'd like to follow me, I'll show you to your room next door."

"Thank you, Andrew," said Henry, smoothing down the quilt on the slumbering King.

They left the bedroom quietly, Andrew noticing the two guards outside the King's bedroom standing rigidly to attention. Henry bade his goodnights and disappeared into his room, thanking Andrew for his help.

Downstairs, Andrew heard John wishing the Pownolls a good night's rest and as Sir Joshua finished off the last of his brandy, John came out of the drawing room to see Andrew descending the stairs.

"The King's asleep, sir," said Andrew, "and there are two guards outside his room."

"Very good, Andrew," said John, his eyes darting up the staircase and around the hallways. "Let us just hope we're in for a peaceful night. Madam Parker has gone to bed, as have my guests. Sir Joshua will be going up presently. I trust you'll make your rounds now with an extra special check on everything."

"That I will, sir," said Andrew, anxious to get back up to the King's bedroom.

"Well, I'll bid you goodnight then, Andrew. Breakfast is to be served at eight."

"Very well, goodnight, sir," said Andrew with a smile.

Andrew watched John walk away with Sir Joshua to their bedrooms on the east wing of the house. Everything was now quiet. Turning around sharply, he hurried back up the stairs, slowing down to a gentle walk as he approached the guards and the King's bedroom.

"I forgot to take away the tray with the King's nightcap," he said to one of the guards.

The guard nodded and opening the door, Andrew quietly slipped into the bedroom. The candles he had lit earlier had burned down considerably but still gave off a dim light. He stood perfectly still in the quietness of the room, listening to the sound of the King snoring. What was about to happen was for the glory of France, of this he was certain, it was what he had been working and waiting for all these years. The time had finally come. With a glance up at the grill, he smiled and knocked twice on the panel, then picking up the silver tray with the empty crystal glass and the two decanters, he quietly left the room.

Chapter 43

Holding the dagger in one hand, Barold pushed on the handle attached to the inside of the panel. The fitting slowly moved outwards and with a quick look towards Luc and Ebenezer, he slipped into the King's bedroom. All was quiet and still as he stood listening to the gentle snores coming from the four-poster bed. An orange glimmer from the fire and the waning light of the candles radiated a warm amber glow around the room. His shadow danced on the panel behind him, a frightening wraith-like form bending and swaying to the flickering of the candles. He jumped slightly at the noise of the secret panel suddenly being pulled back into place.

No matter, he thought, *it'll be easy to push it open again.*

Lifting the dagger in his hand, he moved towards the bed, his heart beginning to race with the tension of the moment. Looking down on his King, he felt empty of any emotion at what he was about to do, his only concern being the bulging purse he would collect later from Luc. Raising the knife, he turned it round so the razor-sharp blade was in the right position to slice across the King's throat. As he pressed the knife forward, the King suddenly blubbered in his sleep and smacking his lips together, turned over on his pillow, his head facing away from where Barold stood.

"Fuck!" muttered Barold. "Now oi'll have to grab him by his hair and pull him back so's oi can see his throat."

Easing his hand forward to grab the King's hair, a sudden creaking sound of the bedroom door slowly being opened jolted him back. For a split second, Henry froze at the door, his eyes focusing on a demonic figure hunched over the King with a raised dagger. Enraged at the interruption and spitting his fury, Barold turned to see the cause of the intrusion. As he glared towards the open door, a reddish glow from the dwindling fire lit up the maddening expression on his face, giving him a hideous contorted look of a devil from the depths of hell. Henry was suddenly reminded of a scary painting he had once seen as a child, of a demon about to kill and take the soul of an innocent as he slept. The horrific memory quickly faded and shaking his head, he propelled himself towards the bed, yelling for the guards.

Unable to sleep with the worrying thought of an attack on the King, John quietly rolled out of bed and dressed silently, so as not to wake Theresa. He gently opened his bedroom door and slipped out into the silent corridor. A strong feeling of imminent danger followed him as he hurried towards the west wing of the house and the King's bedroom. With a sickening feeling, he raced along the landing, hearing frantic cries of help resonating from the King's bedroom.

Without a care for his own safety, Henry flew across the bedroom intent on saving his King. Barold saw the threat to himself and pulled back from the bed, his first instinct to look for a weapon that his attacker maybe brandishing. There was nothing in the hands of his assailant. Only seconds had passed since Henry had rushed forward to save his King, but his careless charge towards the assassin had prompted Barold to step back. With a careful aim, Barold hurled his dagger at Henry, seeing it bury itself deep in the valet's chest, piercing his heart and killing him before he hit the floor. With a sleep-filled grunt, the King turned over, oblivious to the ongoing drama.

Barold raced towards the secret panel, his mind solely intent on escape. Placing both hands onto its side, he suddenly felt himself thrown forward and powerless to push, nothing worked as he tried harder to heave it open. He felt himself falling, a strange feeling of helplessness pushing him down. He thought it strange that visions of rowing Stephen's boat down the river Dart flashed in front of him, his horseback race out of Churston Manor with the Squire's ankers strapped to his mount, Solomon Metcalf stomping off over the pebbles at Elberry Cove, Mordechai being led away to the cells and the figure of young Watt swinging from the gallows on Plymouth Hoe. The face of Ebenezer flashed before him, taunting him and laughing at his failure to kill the king. He felt himself tumbling downwards, unable to stop, and then there was Hilary beckoning him with open arms, smiling as he buried himself into her loving caress. As the darkness began to envelop him, he made one last effort to raise himself up and speak the loving words he'd always wanted her to hear, but nothing came except a sad sigh as he gave in and let himself go.

John burst into the King's bedroom, aghast to see Henry's body lying in a pool of blood next to the King's bed. He stood bewildered as everything in the room suddenly seemed to mollify into a kind of slow motion. He watched the two guards aim their flintlock pistols at a desperate figure clawing at the side of a wall panel, the flash from their pistols as the powder ignited sending sparks spitting across the bedroom. A deafening crack as the guns fired saw the figure thrown forward as the pistol balls ripped into his back, two bleeding holes appearing below his shoulder blades. John watched open-mouthed as the figure slid slowly down the oak panelling, his fingers scraping the sides as if he were desperately clutching onto the last remnants of his life. As he crumpled to the floor, John heard him try to utter something, but nothing came, then with a sorrowful sigh, he gave up as his life, withered and died.

Luc watched from the grill, stupefied and decimated as his plans shrivelled to nothing before his eyes. Ebenezer stood next to him, trembling with the fear of being discovered and ending up with a noose around his neck on Plymouth Hoe gallows.

"Barold's been shot," muttered Luc. "It's over, we've got to get out of here, now."

Ebenezer looked at Luc, his eyes wide with petrified fright, "Did he kill the King?" he stammered, feeling his stomach beginning to turn over.

"No," hissed Luc, pushing past Ebenezer and hurrying away down the dark passageway towards the spiral staircase.

"Oh my God!" squealed Ebenezer, seeing Luc disappear into the darkness. "Wait, Luc, don't leave me here please." Without bothering to look through the grill at the chaos developing in the King's bedroom, Ebenezer turned and fled down the passageway after Luc.

Lord Chilworth suddenly appeared at John's side, a look of absolute horror stamped over his face.

"The King, John, how fares he?"

"He sleeps my lord," replied John. "He doesn't know anything about it. My guess is he has been drugged. How, I have not the slightest…" John didn't finish his sentence, his eyes expanding as the answer suddenly hit him. Dashing out of the bedroom, he stood on the landing, looking past the worried faces that had gathered outside the King's bedroom.

"Andrew!" he bellowed rushing to the top of the stairs. "Andrew!" he shouted down the stairwell, hoping to see his trusted valet hurrying up towards him. Several footmen standing around on the landing looked over in John's direction as he yelled out Andrew's name.

"Have you seen him?" asked John looking at one of them desperately.

"No, sir," he replied.

"Go to his room and tell him to get up here immediately," he instructed, watching the footman race down the stairs to the staff quarters.

Philemon and Sir Joshua came hurrying along the landing, Philemon doing up the buttons of his waistcoat.

"John, what's happened?" he asked. "The sound of two shots going off woke Jane and me with a start. Is it the King?"

"Yes, I'm afraid so," said John.

"Oh my God," said Sir Joshua. "Then your feelings were right, John. The assassins have struck."

"Not exactly," said John. "The King's unhurt. But Henry, his valet, lies in there dead, killed by the assassin. The assassin's dead too, shot by the two guards. Come with me, we'll see if we can identify him."

John led his two friends into the King's bedroom, Philemon and Sir Joshua astonished to see the King still soundly asleep.

"He's been drugged," said John, "and I'm sure I know who did it."

"Well, well," said Philemon, looking at the dead body lying next to the oak panel.

"It's Barold Raustin and he's dressed as a baker, but there's no sign of the Reverend Dunn. John, did you have any bread delivered late today?"

"Yes, that's it," said John, "they came in disguised as bakers. Oh, Andrew, how clever!"

John looked around as the footman who had gone to call Andrew rushed into the bedroom.

"Well?" he said looking at him impatiently.

"He's not there, sir. I looked in his room and his bed has not been slept in. There's no sign of him."

"As I thought," said John, shaking his head. "Just a minute," he said staring at the panel in front of him. "Now why didn't I think of that in the first place. Of course. It's only myself and Andrew who know about this!"

Philemon and Sir Joshua looked at John quizzically as he smoothed his hands over the panel, flicking at the grill with his fingers.

"After smuggling them in as bakers, Andrew must have shown them into the secret hideaway behind this panel where they waited until the King had fallen asleep. Then, he slipped a powerful sleeping draught into the King's nightcap when poor Henry was not looking. When the King was sound asleep, Barold then opened the panel and got into the bedroom to kill the King. Henry must have disturbed him and then Barold killed him, only to be shot down by the guards. The Reverend Dunn was likely hiding behind this panel too, whether alone or with someone. Come on, I know how he escaped."

John put his shoulder to the side of the panel and pushed, Philemon and Sir Joshua watching in awe as the panel slowly opened to show a small table and chairs up against the wall of a dark narrow-looking vestibule. Lord Chilworth and Sir Thomas Gage had seen John push the panel open and disappear into its dark recess followed by Philemon and Sir Joshua. With a quick dash across the bedroom, they tailed after them into the hideaway and then down the dark passage to where the spiral staircase dropped down to Saltram's dimly-lit wine cellar.

* * *

Andrew left the silver tray on a table in the kitchen and then hurrying down the corridor to the wine cellar, he opened the door and sidled into its dimly-lit interior. Squeezing past the gap at the end of the last wine rack, he stood at the bottom of the staircase looking up into the darkness and waiting for the sound of the first footstep. He imagined Barold cutting the throat of the King and then making his way back through the panel to join up with the other two for their escape down to the wine cellar. He prayed that Philippe and Robert would be waiting as planned with the horses. It would not be long now before he'd be sailing out of Plymouth harbour and en route to France. But where were they? Barold should have finished the deed by now, it'd been a good half hour since he'd knocked on the panel. He climbed up a few of the stairs listening intently for any sound that would indicate them coming. Everything sounded perfectly still and quiet.

The crack of the two pistol shots reverberating around the house made him jump with a start, the sudden feeling of dread causing him to grip the side rail of the staircase tightly. He strained to listen to any other sound coming from above, fighting off the temptation to race up and find out the source of the shots and why his three cohorts had not appeared. A feeling of nausea suddenly overwhelmed him as a babble of muffled voices seeping along the passageway overhead warned him that something had gone wrong with the plan.

He gripped the rail tighter, hearing Ebenezer call out for Luc to wait and not to leave him there. The sound of footsteps on the top stair made him rush back down to the bottom where he waited for Luc to appear from the darkness.

"Quick, Andre," yelled Luc arriving on the last stair, "everything's lost. Barold's dead and the King lives. We must get away now."

"But where's Ebenezer, is he coming?" asked Andrew.

"Yes, he's somewhere behind me. We cannot wait for him. Hurry now."

Andrew led Luc to the side delivery door of the wine cellar, the dim glow from the wall lantern affording them enough light to see their way. Behind him, Andrew could hear the loud footsteps of Ebenezer stumbling down the staircase as he called out for them to wait. Pulling the door key from his pocket, Andrew thrust it into the lock and as it clicked, he threw the door open for them to stagger out onto the rear basement yard.

"This way, Luc," he yelled, as he set off in the direction of the long driveway that would lead them out of Saltram's grounds.

Ebenezer got to the bottom of the spiral staircase and squeezing through the tight gap behind the last wine rack, he looked around the wine cellar for Luc and Andrew.

"The bastards have left me all alone," he wailed. "How am I going to get out of here? Luc, where are you?"

The banging of an open door in the night breeze caught his attention.

They must have fled through there, he thought as the sound of voices and loud footsteps above him warned he was being followed.

At the door he stopped, listening for any sign that his pursuers were in the wine cellar. They were not but the heavy sound of them descending the staircase made him bolt out of the door and slam it shut behind him.

"The driveway should be that way," he howled to himself, running in the same direction that Luc and Andrew had taken only minutes before. "I'll catch up with them, I simply have to."

Luc and Andrew tore up the slope that wound its way past Saltram's main entrance and on towards the long drive that led to the main gates. As they rounded the bend, Andrew grabbed Luc, pulling him back into the shadows.

"Two soldiers, Luc," he whispered, "over there in front of the entrance."

Luc squinted through the darkness seeing two of the King's cavalry guard walking up and down outside the main doors.

"If we skirt over there to those trees," whispered Andrew, "we can cut through the gardens where there's a wall that drops down onto the main carriage track. Philippe and Robert should be waiting with the horses in the lane not far down from there."

"Good," replied Luc. "Look, they're not looking this way, they're chatting. Come on."

Ebenezer raced along the path that wound its way towards Saltram's main entrance, and as he rounded a bend, he saw by the light of the moon, Luc and Andrew disappearing into a clump of trees. He was about to chase after them when he heard loud laughter coming from the main entrance. Hiding in the shadows, he watched as two heavily armed guards stood chatting and laughing outside the main doors. If he ran to the trees where he had seen Luc and Andrew disappearing, then there was a great chance the two guards would see him. On the other hand, if he were to stay where he was, then whoever was following not far behind would surely find him. He had no choice. Taking a deep breath, he took off towards the trees, running with an urgency of the hunted and not stopping until he was well through them and out of sight of the two soldiers.

Chapter 44

John led his search party down the spiral staircase, pleased to see that Lord Chilworth and Sir Thomas Gage had joined them. After the last of them had managed to squeeze through the gap at the bottom, they stopped to take stock of where Ebenezer and possibly Andrew could have gone.

"My guess is that Andrew is with Dunn," said John, "and likely the one named Luc Skorniere too."

"Yes," said Philemon nodding, "that name was mentioned by Betsy, when she said that Dunn wanted a face-to-face meeting with him in Plymouth. This Luc Skorniere is obviously a French spy running an espionage ring with Andrew, Barold and Dunn. We can be sure that the plot and the attempt to assassinate the King was planned by them. But how did they know the King would be staying with you John, here at Saltram, and on this very night?"

"There must've been a leak somewhere," said John. "This is why it's imperative we catch them before they leave the country. Sir Thomas, instruct the officer of the guard to make a search of the grounds with your men now. While they are searching, we'll ride hard to the Barbican, where I know there are a collection of French fishing vessels moored. One of them, I am sure, will certainly be theirs. They'll probably try to sail away before the coastguard knows anything about this. Lord Chilworth, can you delegate one of your party to ride to Plymouth harbour now and inform the coastguard to stop and search all vessels leaving the port? While you are doing that, gentlemen, we will organise the horses. The stables are on the other side of the courtyard, behind this wine cellar, just follow the slope down from the main entrance to the rear. We will be waiting for the two of you. Tell your men to make a thorough search of all the grounds. But please hurry, gentlemen."

Lord Chilworth and Sir Thomas Gage hastened away while John, Philemon and Sir Joshua let themselves out of the service door that only moments before had seen the exit of the three desperate assassins.

"The doors to the wine cellar are always locked," said John, closing the door behind him. "I noticed that the main door to the cellar was unlocked as Lord Chilworth and Sir Thomas left, as is this one. Andrew and I are the only ones in the house who possess a key. Now I'm positive Andrew is with them."

Luc and Andrew tore through the copse of trees, not stopping to see if the soldiers had seen them from Saltram's main entrance or whether they were following them. In a matter of seconds, they were out of the trees and running across a wide lawned area leading to the front of a row of thick bushes that shielded a large pond. Light from the moon glistened over the pond showing off a multitude of water lilies floating gracefully on its glass-like surface. Gulping for air, the two fugitives stopped by a picturesque wooden bridge that crossed over a section of the water.

"Over this bridge," gasped Andrew panting for breath, "is another copse of trees that leads to a hedge overlooking the main carriage track that runs directly into the city and the Barbican. A few yards down that track is the lane where Philippe and Robert should be waiting with the horses."

"Listen," said Luc, "they've started a search. It will not be long before they're out on the carriage track searching, and I doubt Philippe and Robert will hang around waiting for us. We won't have long, come on."

Ebenezer stopped for breath in front of a wide lawned area that led to rows of thick bushes on its far side. As he wheezed and gasped, he noticed the silhouettes of two figures on the far side of the lawn disappearing along a path that seemed to run through thickets of shrubbery.

"There they are!" he hissed. "Lucky I saw them. Andrew must know his way out from here. I'm on your heels, you French bastards."

Looking behind to check all was safe to cross the open lawn, he drew a long breath and bolted. Halfway across, he nearly pulled up in terror at the shouts of the soldiers in the copse behind him, bawling out that they had managed to find tracks of the fugitives. He knew the light from the moon would present him as an easy target, but if he were lucky, he would reach the safety of the bushes before the soldiers came bursting out of the thicket of trees.

Luc and Andrew raced over the little wooden bridge crashing into the dense copse that would lead them out to the hedge fronting the main carriage track. Not bothering to stop for air, they ran, jumping over tree trunks and ducking low-hanging branches until they were out of the trees and facing the high hedgerow that ran the length of Saltram's south-facing grounds.

"Come on," said Luc, "we're nearly there."

"The wall's behind that hedge, Luc," shouted Andrew, "we'll have to jump from it when we get there."

"No matter, let's go," yelled Luc.

The hedge was thickly knitted together with prickly barbs of briars and brambles, but the light from the moon showed a small gap where someone had obviously once squeezed himself through. As quick as a flash, Luc threw himself into the gap, quickly followed by his fellow countryman. They emerged on the other side cut and badly scratched, but they had made it.

Luc looked down at the drop from the top of the wall. It was a good twenty feet but ended on what looked like soft fresh grass. As they worked up the courage to jump, the noise of approaching horses froze them to where they were standing.

"Oh, *mon dieu!*" cried Luc, "After all that. We'll fight our way out, Andre."

"No, no, Luc," shouted Andrew, "look, it's Philippe and Robert."

Luc grinned as he looked down on Raymond's two crewmen sitting their mounts, each with two spare horses in tow behind them.

"We heard you crashing through the hedge," shouted up Philippe, "so we came to get you."

"Where are the other two?" asked Robert.

"Barold's dead," replied Luc, "everything's lost and the King lives. I will explain later. But now we must get to the boat. Move back a pace while we jump down."

Robert and Philippe steadied the horses as Luc and Andrew jumped. Landing expertly on the soft grass, they grasped the reins of a horse each and sprung up into the saddle.

"What about Ebenezer, Luc?" asked Andrew.

"Cut one of the horses free, Philippe," said Luc. "If he's lucky, he'll find it waiting here. Bring the other horse, Barold won't need it where he's gone!"

Philippe and Robert clicked their tongues and the five horses with four riders sped away down the track. Quietness descended along the stretch of carriage track where Luc and Andrew had jumped from the wall, broken only by the sound of a gentle munching as the horse that Philippe had left for Ebenezer, feasted on the clumps of soft fresh grass that grew along the bottom of Saltram's south-facing wall.

Ebenezer's luck was in, he had made it across the lawn and through the bushes to where a quaint wooden bridge crossed over a section of a wide pond. By the light of the moon, he made out a rough track running away from the bridge on its other side disappearing into a copse of trees. Scanning the area, he realised that this would have been the only logical route Luc and Andrew would've taken.

Andrew knows his way round here, he thought, *and he knows there's a way out of here through that copse of trees. It must've been the way they went.*

The sound of loud voices coming across the lawn warned of the urgency to get away and letting out a frightened whimper, he took off over the bridge, running hell for leather along the rough path and into the darkness of the copse of trees. Panting and holding his side to relieve the nagging pain of a stitch, he staggered out of the trees coming face-to-face with a long prickly hedge that seemed to run on forever into the darkness. He gazed up at the spiny thicket, knowing the only way out was through its thorny bulk.

Dropping his head, he barged into its spiky mass, crying out as the briars and brambles tore into his flesh. Bleeding and scratched from head to toe, he blundered on, tearing and pushing at the thistly menace until it gave way and he was out and within a foot of where a wall dropped down onto the public carriage track.

Gasping for breath, he stood still, listening for the voices of the soldiers pursuing him. There was nothing, no sound of footsteps crashing through the copse of trees or even a shout, but a strange chomping noise coming from below the wall made him prick up his ears and dropping down onto one knee, he grasped the top of the wall and peered over. His face suddenly split into a look of pure thankfulness, tears of gratitude filling his eyes. Wringing his hands in absolute relief, he looked down at the saddled horse Philippe had untied and left for him. Laughing with joy and wiping the tears from his eyes, he staggered to his feet.

"Well, at least they've left me a means of escape," he chuckled. "All I have to do now is to jump down. Ha, yes, easier said than done!"

The sound of his pursuers crashing out of the copse of trees, and a shout as one of them started to smash his way through the thorny barrier, swiftly spurred him on to make the decision. Clamping his eyes shut, he leapt off the wall.

He must have landed badly, as a searing pain shot through his ankle. He knew he had to get up quickly, the soldiers would be at the top of the wall at any moment. Crying out in agony, he forced himself up and with several hops made it over to where the horse quietly grazed. Grasping its reins, he slid his foot painfully into a stirrup, then swung himself up into the saddle. Clicking his tongue, he kicked his heels into the horse's flank and took off down the track in the direction of the Barbican, where he knew Raymond's fishing boat was moored and ready to sail.

John rode at the front of the search party as they pushed their horses into a trot down Saltram's long driveway. The light from the moon lit up the way ahead as the tall iron entrance gates loomed before them. Pulling his horse up, he quickly dismounted to open them. The sound of a horse's hooves thundering down the carriage track outside the gates suddenly startled the other horses into rearing up and biting at their bits to give chase. As John slid back the bolt and dragged the heavy gate back, the moonlight lit up the contorted face of Ebenezer, bent low in the saddle and squinting at them as his horse flashed past the gate.

"There he is," yelled Philemon, "let's be after him."

John pulled the gate open and giving an encouraging look towards the others, leapt back into his saddle, his horse bolting away in pursuit of the fleeing minister. The other four were quick to follow, spurring their horses into a gallop as Ebenezer, looking back over his shoulder and wailing in terror, hugged his horse's mane as it raced away and disappeared into the night.

Luc saw the lights of Raymond's sloop bobbing up and down as they cantered past the Duke of York Inn towards the wharf where the fishing vessel was moored and ready to depart. Raymond was standing on deck in the bow with Allain, his eye on the mooring rope which he would unhitch as soon as the others were safely on board. He had spied five horses but only four riders coming through the copse of trees and by the looks on the faces of the four riders, he knew immediately that something wasn't right.

"Leave the horses," shouted Luc, springing out of his saddle. "Come on, up the gangplank and we'll be away. Raymond, get ready to cast off."

Andrew and the two crewmen leapt out of their saddles and discarding their horses, raced up the gangplank to join Luc who was already on deck.

"Where is the other one?" asked Raymond. "The one who's the minister, the reverend."

"He won't be coming, Raymond," said Luc impatiently. "Cast off now. Barold's dead and the plan's sunk. The King lives and there's a search party not far behind us."

"But we can't just leave him here," said Raymond.

"Yes, we can," screamed Luc, "and I'm ordering you to cast off and leave now, Raymond. Now!"

Raymond nodded. "Allain, pull up the gangplank. Philippe, Robert, cast off. We're leaving now."

To anyone strolling along the Barbican at that time of the morning, they would have seen the twinkling lights of a fishing boat creeping out of Plymouth's old harbour for an early morning's fishing trip. Little would they have known that on board that fishing sloop were a dangerous nest of French spies, who but for the bravery of an English valet, would have been rejoicing at the death of the King of Great Britain and Ireland, and very likely fuelling plans for an imminent invasion.

In a darkened room at the top of a stone fortress overlooking Plymouth Sound, the night duty coastguard officer sat surveying the dark waters below him. Apart from a British Navy frigate leaving in the early hours, the traffic in and out of Plymouth Harbour that night had been light. Far below him, he followed the dim lights of a French fishing vessel, coasting out into the main channel and then gathering speed as a fresh wind caught its sails. As he watched the lights disappearing over the dark waters, the door to his room suddenly burst open. An officer of the military barracks stood with two armed dragoons, a serious looking cloaked civilian standing behind them.

"Sir," the officer barked, "an order from Sir Thomas Gage and the King's secretary Lord Chilworth. This gentleman has just ridden from Saltram House where the King has been residing before his address to the troops later this morning. He has given me news that there's been an assassination attempt on His Majesty. We believe the assassins will be attempting an escape by a fishing vessel, very likely a French one. All vessels leaving the harbour now must be stopped and searched. Is that clear, sir?"

The coast guard officer stared at the group standing in front of him and then turning to look out of his window at the dark waters below, shook his head in disbelief.

"Oh shit!" he muttered.

Ebenezer sat his mount under the shelter of the copse of trees that fronted part of the wharf on the Barbican where only moments before Raymond's sloop had cast off from its mooring. He stared at the five saddled horses grazing under the trees, knowing he had arrived too late. He looked out over the wharf, wide-eyed and aghast at the lights of a fishing sloop making its way towards the mouth of the harbour, its blue flag and three golden lilies fluttering over its wake. Tears welled up in his eyes at the realisation of Luc's abandoning of him and the dreadful recognition of his fortune disappearing before his eyes. He raised his fist in anger, shaking it violently at the departing boat while hollering out threats of retribution and revenge.

His ankle throbbed with pain and he knew at any moment John Parker and his search party would descend on the wharf looking for Raymond's sloop. He had seen them at the gates of Saltram as he'd raced past moments ago and was now certain that they'd found out he was connected to Luc's espionage ring and part of the assassination attempt. How, he had no idea.

Could Parker also know it was me who'd organised the smuggling ventures for Squire Maddock, he thought. *Ha, I doubt if he'll ever discover that.*

Scowling, he watched Raymond's sloop sail away out of the harbour then looking around to check he was still alone, a sudden thought occurred to him.

I need help and a place to hide away, I can't go back to Ashprington yet, it's the first place they'll look for me. Squire Maddock owes me, he has to help me. Molly will help if she's still there.

Grimacing with the pain in his ankle, he turned his horse out of the copse and headed down along the waterfront towards the Cat and Fiddle Inn. A sudden picture of Nancy welcoming him at the inn's door flashed into his mind.

Foolish girl, he thought, *sticking her nose into something that didn't concern her. She had to die, or she would have led us all to the gallows. Still, she was worth a shilling!*

About a stone's throw from the inn, he pulled up to check on a narrow carriage track that would lead him out of the Barbican and on across country fields towards Totnes and Dartington. Satisfied it was the right turning, he kicked his heels into the horse's flanks and with his ankle throbbing painfully, galloped away up the dark track. As the track widened onto open country, he gave his horse rein, happy to let it feel the openness around them. As they left the Barbican far behind, he settled himself forward in the saddle, rehearsing what he would say to the two people whom he was sure could help him the most.

* * *

John and the search party rode past the Duke of York Inn and then down through a copse of trees to stop on the waterfront overlooking the wharf and

Plymouth's old harbour. In front of them, numerous vessels bobbed up and down at their moorings, but as close as they looked, there was no sign of any lights shining from them or hints of any movement on board. A shuffling in the trees next to them made them swivel round as five horses suddenly emerged, chomping at the grass and looking as though they had been ridden hard.

"Well, looks like we've found the right place," said John. "Five horses, eh! That increases the numbers now. We thought we were looking for only three."

"Five horses abandoned, John, suggests they were in a hurry to leave," said Philemon. "My guess is that they dumped the horses here and boarded a vessel at that empty mooring, right in front of us over there."

"Which means they've scarpered. Sailed away, gentlemen," blubbered Sir Thomas Gage. "We've lost them, blast it!"

"Not necessarily so," said Sir Joshua, squinting along the waterfront. "Look, in the distance. The moon's showing up the silhouette of someone on horseback peering up at a turning."

All five peered into the distance, scrutinising their attention on a silhouette on horseback.

"That's him," said Philemon, "that's Dunn. He's missed the boat!"

As Philemon finished his sentence, they saw the figure suddenly dig his heels into the horse's flanks and disappear into the darkness of the turning.

"Come on, we have him," cried John, "at least we'll catch one of them. I guess he's on his way back to Ashprington, we'll catch him before he gets to the village."

Ebenezer raced across the country fields, watching the dawn slowly rise above the old oak and beech trees carpeting a good share of the land. Up ahead was a fork, one way leading to Totnes and the other to the village of Ashprington and its surrounding hamlets. He knew if he took the left fork, it would not be long before he'd come across a sign for Dartington and hence Darton Hall.

Sir Thomas Gage and Lord Chilworth had left the other three at the Barbican, returning to Saltram to prepare the King for his address to the troops but entrusting John, Philemon and Sir Joshua to continue their pursuit of the treacherous minister and to bring him back chained in irons. It was not long before they approached the fork that pointed one way to Totnes and the other to Ashprington. Galloping in the direction of the sign pointing to Ashprington, Philemon smiled, confident that Ebenezer was only a short length ahead of them and would very soon be cornered and shackled.

330

* * *

At the top of the winding hill that led to the Squire's hall, Ebenezer looked down at the River Dart, a picture of the skinny-dipping event with Molly, the Judge and Joy flashing before his eyes. With a grin and a shrug of his shoulders, he rode into the medieval courtyard, surprised to see it deserted of any life. From where he sat on his horse, he noticed all doors and windows tightly shut, no aromas of breakfast cooking nor the smell of baking bread wafting towards him. Dismounting, he tied the reins to an old wooden hitching post and hobbled over to the steps that led up to the main entrance. Taking one step at a time, he was reminded of Edmund Pickering arriving as Nero while he, dressed in the ridiculous toga the Squire had loaned him, played the part of Cicero. At the top of the steps, he hammered on the oak door, listening to its echo coming from inside. He waited and then banged his fist loudly on the door again and again. From inside, he heard the scurrying sound of footsteps followed by the grating of the small side door opening. The face of one of the Squire's servants, whom Ebenezer immediately recognised, peered from around the door.

"Yes?" he asked.

"Don't you recognise me, boy?" said Ebenezer, hearing the pleading tone in his voice.

"No," said the servant, "and we don't give to beggars. Now be on your way."

Ebenezer suddenly realised that still dressed in the now-ragged smock of a baker and the tight-fitting cap which was almost surely covered in the blood of his cuts and scratches, he must have certainly looked like a vagabond.

"I'm not a beggar," he said quietly, "I'm the Reverend Ebenezer Dunn of Ashprington. I've come to see Squire Maddock."

The servant obviously did not recognise him, but to get rid of him quickly, he told Ebenezer what he certainly did not want to hear.

"The Squire left here three days ago," he said. "He's gone overseas to stay with a cousin in Italy and I don't know when he'll be back. He left hurriedly after he had had a visit from someone in Ashprington by the name of Hilary. He has taken Molly and another girl with him. Now if you'd excuse me."

Ebenezer stood staring at him dumbstruck, the door slamming in his face to the sound of a bolt being hastily drawn across it.

"Oh my God, what am I going to do," he groaned. "I can't go to Elijah, Lucy wouldn't let me in, and anyway, I can't stay in Ashprington. But I need a change of clothes, some food and drink. I'll go back to the rectory and the church, and try to get in unseen, but then what?"

As he stumbled back down the steps to his horse, the words of someone who had suddenly appeared from a dark forest and saved his life rang in his ears.

"Should any of you fuckers be passin' through Paignton, or you need help, you'll find me in the Tor Bay Inn."

Well, I have no choice, he thought. *It'll be a long shot, but I've nothing to lose. Maybe Solomon can help me. There is only one way to find out. I will make my way there after I've sneaked into the rectory and changed clothes. I'll take the remaining bottles of wine from the church too.*

Wincing with the pain in his ankle, he slowly mounted his horse and with a last look at the desolate and empty Darton Hall, he spurred his horse out of the courtyard and headed down the hill in the direction of Ashprington, the church and its rectory.

Chapter 45

John and Philemon raced up the garden path of where they were sure they would find Ebenezer. Sir Joshua waited outside his house with the horses.

"Dunn, we know you're in there," shouted Philemon banging on the front door, "open the door now. There's no escape for you."

"Open the door or we'll break it down!" shouted John.

Silence filled the house and garden where John and Philemon stood listening and waiting.

"I'm not sure he's in there, John," said Philemon.

"Only one way to find out," said John, "two sturdy kicks should break it open."

The door gave way easily, the lock breaking away from its holding as soon as their kicks thudded into it. Philemon and John rushed inside.

"You take upstairs, Philemon, I'll look down here. Look under the beds and in every cupboard. If he is here, we'll find him."

The noise of John and Philemon shouting out for Ebenezer and the kicking down of his door had brought a small crowd up from the village to gather outside.

"Somethin' goin' on?" asked Rufus Mudd looking up at Sir Joshua, mounted and holding on to the two horses.

"Have you seen the Reverend Dunn?" asked Sir Joshua.

"Naw, not for a few days," came the reply. "Why you'm be askin'?" asked Rufus.

"John Parker, the Member of Parliament for hereabouts, has come to arrest him."

"Arrest the Reverend, for what?" yelled Lucy Hatch standing at the back of the crowd.

"Treason and the attempted assassination of His Majesty King George III," shouted John, as he and Philemon appeared from the garden gate.

"If any of you villagers here see or hear of Reverend Dunn, you must report to Captain Pownoll at Sharpham. I am John Parker, the Member of Parliament for Devon. I will be here for the rest of the day with my two colleagues. Captain Pownoll you know, and sitting his horse is Sir Joshua Reynolds. I have the power to make the arrest of the traitor. We will be searching the village and its surround. We will need helpers, so can I ask for a dozen of you to assist us in our search. Those willing please come forward and wait inside the rectory garden."

It did not take long for Rufus and a dozen male villagers to come forward. Looking aghast, Lucy hurried away to the Ashprington Inn to find Elijah.

Sir Joshua dismounted and securing the reins of the three horses to a railing outside the rectory, followed Philemon and John into the garden to brief those about to form a search party.

"The Reverend, a traitor and an assassin. I can't believe it!" said Elijah after hearing Lucy's report.

"That be what the gentleman said," said Lucy. "He be the Member of Parliament round here and has the power to arrest him. John Parker be his name."

"What, John Parker?" said Elijah, wide-eyed. "Us heard his name some time back when me and the Reverend visited Noah down in Stoke. Us also saw him down on Plymouth Hoe when they hanged poor Watt. Anyways, us was drinkin' Noah's ale in the church house when he told us that John Parker and a lord from thereabouts come in to the inn few days before. Yeah, he went on to tell us that he heard them talkin' that the King was goin' to stay down in John Parker's stately home in Plymouth the night before his addressin' the troops. Bliddy hell, the Reverend must have remembered all that and planned the assassination. Wonder who else be involved in all this treason? Bliddy hell, Lucy."

"Elijah, you'm doen owe the Reverend nuthin', so you'ms goin' to tell all of that to John Parker. He is over in the rectory garden now. Us'll come with you, come on, now."

John looked up from delegating search areas to his volunteers as Lucy and Elijah made their way into the rectory garden.

Introducing themselves, Elijah told him he had something of importance to tell him in connection with what Lucy had heard him informing the villagers about the Reverend Dunn.

John called over Philemon and Sir Joshua and taking Elijah to a quiet corner of the garden, they listened to his story.

"Well," said John after Elijah had come to the end, "now I know how they knew the King was coming to Saltram. It was my own fault. I'm not blaming your cousin, he was only socialising with you. He has nothing to do with what happened. I must be more careful with whom I'm talking next time."

"Now, what about Barold, John?" said Philemon.

Elijah suddenly went as white as a sheet as he heard Philemon mention Barold. Lucy's eyes widened in absolute shock.

"There was another traitor from this village," said John, looking at them seriously. "In fact, it was him who was caught in the act of attempting to kill the King."

John noticed the looks of utter surprise and amazement stamped over their faces.

"By the looks of you, you obviously knew him, Barold Raustin. He's dead, shot by two of the King's guards, trying to escape."

"Us only knew him by him comin' into the inn fairly regular. In fact, he was there nearly every evenin'," said Lucy.

"Did he have any close friends, anybody he regularly mixed with?" asked John looking into their faces.

"Only the regulars from the inn," answered Lucy, "doen know much about him part from that, do us, Elijah?"

"Naw, Lucy's right. He sat with the regular drinkers in the inn. The Reverend was one of them, as was poor Stephen. We heard about him t'other day. Shot down in Ditt'sum with a bunch of smugglers, us heard."

"You heard right," said John. "And those smugglers were his family. I suppose you've heard of Obadiah Tucker and his two sons, Elijah?"

"Ar, us's heard of them , but oi's never met them. Oi wouldn' know them if oi saw them," replied Elijah looking at Lucy.

"Mmm, is that so!" said John smiling at Philemon and Sir Joshua. "Now we will need to see Barold's wife, Hilary. Would you know if she is at home? We know where their cottage is."

"Her left the village yesterday," said Lucy. "Saw her leavin' crack of dawn. One-horse carriage picked her up, her and all her baggage. Doen know where her has gone, but her ain't here."

"We'll track her down," said John, "might take some time, but we'll find her."

"Is there anything else you can think of that may help in our search for the Reverend?" asked Philemon.

"Nuthin' as yet," replied Lucy, "but us'll let you know if we hear anythin', won't us, Elijah?"

"Ar, that us will," said Elijah, looking uncomfortable.

"Thank you for the information," said John. "You've really been most helpful."

They watched Lucy and Elijah leave the garden, waiting until they were well out of earshot.

"They looked very uncomfortable," said Sir Joshua, "especially when you mentioned the smuggling, John."

"Absolutely, but I'm sure they have nothing to do with Dunn and the spy ring. They were shocked when they heard Barold's name. But I put that down to them only knowing him as a regular drinker in their inn, we can't prove otherwise."

"It's smuggling, John. The village is full of it. I can feel it, and those inn keepers are deeply into it," said Philemon. "After everything that's happened, you can't believe that Dunn had nothing to do with the smuggling as well."

"I'm sure you're right, Philemon," said John. "I hate to admit it, but he really pulled the wool over my eyes. But that is another enquiry. First, we must catch the blackguard. Come on, our volunteers are waiting."

Lunch time in the Ashprington Inn was particularly busy, the conversation around the tables full of the action that had gone on at the rectory that morning and the breaking news that the Reverend Dunn was a traitor and was wanted for the attempted assassination of King George III. The chitchat became even more intense when news of Barold's involvement and of his being killed while trying to escape, flittered from table to table. Rufus sat staring at his empty cider mug, deep in thought while Elijah sat opposite him listening to the gossip being tossed around the inn.

"You'm could've knocked me over with a feather!" said Rufus. "The Reverend of all people. Him standin' up there at the altar every Sunday tellin' us how to behave and to be careful of what us said around the village in case any of they garlic eaters be around and listenin'. And now Barold! Bliddy hell, makes you'm wonder whom you can trust!"

"Ar, that it does, Rufus," said Elijah. "I suppose you'm be wantin' a refill in that mug."

"Ar, proper job, Elijah," replied Rufus.

Lucy suddenly called out to Elijah as he was getting up to refill Rufus' cider mug. "Cider barrel's finished, Elijah, can you get another barrel from stock room out in the yard? Hurry it up, customers gettin' thirsty."

Elijah nodded towards Lucy, hastening out into the yard where the door to the stock room stood shut and firmly locked. Fumbling around in his pocket for the key, a gentle hiss from behind made him turn around abruptly. Scanning the yard, he heard it again, "Pssst, pssst, Elijah, over here behind the empty barrels," a voice called.

"Bliddy hell, oi recognise that voice," muttered Elijah, hurrying over to where a dozen empty barrels were stacked.

"Reverend, what the hell you'm doin' here?!" said Elijah looking down at the dishevelled figure of Ebenezer crouching behind the barrels. "Doen you'm know that half the village be out lookin' for you. Captain Pownoll and John Parker be organisin' the searches, they'm got a friend with them too. You'm lucky 'tis nearly lunch time as most of they what be lookin' for you be in the inn."

"Elijah, I need help," wailed Ebenezer. "I've injured my ankle and it's throbbing badly. I also need some food and drink and a change of clothes. I cannot get into the rectory as there are three farm labourers guarding it. The church is also being guarded. They must be expecting me to return here. I am going to try and get to Paignton, to the Tor Bay Inn where Solomon Metcalf spends most of his days. You remember him, don't you?"

"Ar, that I do," replied Elijah. "But why do you want to find him?"

"Because when he left us that night after the Elberry Cove mishap, he told us that if we ever needed his help, then we should look him up in the Tor Bay Inn. I'm desperate, Elijah, I think he can be the only one who can help me. He lives his life outside of the law and as I'm now on the run, so to speak, he may look on my plight favourably."

"But oi can't help you, Reverend. Lucy would turn you in should her know you'm be out here hidin' and talkin' to me."

"But, Elijah, please, you've got to help me get away."

Elijah thought for a moment.

"Stay here, Reverend, us'll get you a pasty and some cider. But then you must be away. Wait here behind these barrels, us'll be back sharpish."

Ebenezer pushed himself further back behind the barrels, peeping through a gap at Elijah as he unlocked the stock room and came out carrying a barrel of cider which he promptly took inside the inn. He reappeared with a flagon and a large hot crusty pasty, which Ebenezer devoured like a starving animal, gulping mouthfuls of cider while stuffing his mouth with the delicious delicacy.

"Oi can't get you'm any change of clothes, Reverend," said Elijah looking at Ebenezer's appearance. "But if you'm take off that ridiculous baker's cap, you'm might look less like a beggar or someone on the run. How did you get all that blood over it and the smock too?"

"That's another story," replied Ebenezer with his mouth full. "Now, how am I going to get out of here?"

"Oi've had a thought, Reverend," said Elijah. "You'm can't go near the rectory or the church so's you'm goin' to have to go across the fields to the woods by the River Dart what flows past Sharpham. Drop down to the river when you'm gets to the woods and about a hundred yards along that track, there be an inlet. In front of the inlet be a load of bushes and a giant trunk of an old oak. Now, behind that trunk there be an old rowin' boat, two oars be in it too. Oi knows this as oi sometimes use it for a bit of illegal fishin' for the inn. You'm take that boat, Reverend, and row down to Stoke. Leave the boat where we moored up in Stephen's boat when us visited Noah and then hide away til' it be dark, then cross the fields to Paignton. If you be careful, you'm can do it. Don't go to the Church House Inn, Noah won't help you, he will turn you'm in for the reward that'll be on your head soon. If you'm go now, there be a good chance of gettin' to the river without bein' seen. Behind the yard here be a gate leading to the fields. Come on, go now, Reverend, and good luck to you."

"Thank you, Elijah," sighed Ebenezer, getting up slowly and wincing with the pain in his ankle.

Elijah watched him hobble off down the yard, stopping at the end to look back over his shoulder, summoning up a smile. He nodded and with a wave of his hand, he disappeared around the corner.

* * *

Philemon put down his knife and fork and gazing out of his dining room window at the great sweep of fields sloping down to the banks of the River Dart, he looked across at his two close friends.

"If he's not in the village, he must've taken the turning to Totnes."

"But he's surely going to try to return to the village soon. I'm certain he'll take the chance," said Sir Joshua sipping at the glass of claret Philemon had poured with their lunches. "He'll need a change of clothes at least."

"We've got half the village out looking for him," said John. "There are roadblocks in and out of the village and even up to here at Sharpham. If he comes back here, we'll get him."

"But what if he's already here," said Sir Joshua, "and we've missed him."

"If he is, where would he go?" replied Philemon. "We've set lookouts outside the rectory and the church. He would not dare enter the inn, so where would he go? No, he will try to get into the rectory, of that I'm sure. After luncheon, we will resume the search, we'll get him."

A gentle knock on the dining room door interrupted their conversation.

"Ah, Betsy," said Philemon, "what can we do for you?"

"Excuse me please, gentlemen," she said smiling at young Jane hovering by her side. "I was wonderin', sir, bein' such a lovely day, would it be alright for me and young Jane to pick some flowers down by the river?"

"Why yes of course, Betsy. We will be here for another hour or so before resuming the search. As you know, half the village are out looking for the treacherous priest. We will be joining them later. Please, go ahead and have a nice time. Come, Jane, give your Papa a big kiss."

From the dining room window, Philemon watched Betsy cradling a wicker basket as she ambled along next to Jane over the neatly-cut lawn, then skipping ahead, Jane disappeared down the pathway followed by Betsy calling out to her to slow down and wait.

Ebenezer limped across the field, coming upon a wooden stile that overlooked a rough path winding its way into the trees and down to the track that Elijah had told him ran alongside the river. Flinching with the pain in his ankle, he struggled over the stile and looking behind to make sure he was not being followed, set off down the path towards the track and the sound of the river below.

Halfway down the path, he stopped to listen to the sound of a multitude of forest birds chirping out harmoniously through the trees around him. The sweet-sounding melody of a woodlark serenading from somewhere afar drifted between the trees and looking up at a branch, he recognised the yellow-lemon breast of a wood warbler trilling out its high-pitched metallic ditty. Hobbling on, he marvelled at the rows of pretty dog roses weaving in between the forest greenery, their large pink and white petals glorifying the woods in summer while the sweet scent of honeysuckle, twining around the forest shrubs and trees, indulged him with an abundance of their heady aromas.

It was not long before he came across the trunk of the giant oak lying in front a thicket of bushes behind which lay the inlet and hopefully, the boat. Looking over to the where the giant lay on its side, he stood wondering how he could manage to climb over it, when the sound of female voices singing a well-known lullaby wended along the path. The sprain in his ankle thwarted him from making a quick dash for cover and as Betsy and young Jane Pownoll came around the bend, he froze.

Betsy's eyes widened in shock as she recognised the tousled figure standing beside the tree trunk.

"You," she screeched, dropping the wicker basket. "You'm devil priest, trying to escape from what you'm did. Us all knows you'm be a traitor along with that builder, Barold. Oi knew before anyone, and it was me who told Master Parker and Captain Pownoll. Oi heard you in the church planning with that traitor Barold. You'm goin' to hang, you'm devil, yes, and us'll be there on Plymouth Hoe to see the devil himself take you straight down to hell. You'm be goin' there, Reverend, not oi."

Pushing young Jane behind her, she flew down the path at him, her fingers outstretched like an eagle's talons, ready to claw at his eyes and flesh.

"Go, Jane," she yelled, "go and get your Papa and his friends."

Seeing her coming at him like a crazed animal, Ebenezer let out a wail of terror, turning to see where he could run. A sudden searing pain shot through his ankle as his legs buckled beneath him and in a second, Betsy was on him, punching and clawing at his face.

"Get off me, you wicked old cow, you can't do this to me!" he screamed.

"Ha," yelled Betsy, spitting and slapping him around his face, "maybe I'll save the hangman the job and do you'm in meself, you'm bliddy devil."

As Ebenezer flailed under Betsy's clawing and slapping, his right hand touched a length of wood that had splintered off the giant tree trunk. Clasping it, he brought it up and smashed it against the side of Betsy's head. Betsy dropped off him in an instant, lying at the side of the tree trunk in a pool of blood.

Struggling up, he grasped the side of the tree trunk levering himself to his feet. Looking down at Betsy, he snarled at her unconscious form. "You stupid old bitch," he yelled, "why did you have to come along this path? You stupid meddling old hag, now look at you."

Folding his arms as far as they would go around the tree trunk, he managed to pull himself up onto it, screaming out in agony as his ankle seared with pain. Wriggling across the giant trunk, he dropped down on the other side and barging through the bushes came out onto the stony inlet. There nestling among the pebbles was the rowing boat.

Young Jane raced across the lawn that only a short time ago had seen her and Betsy on their way down to the riverbank.

"Papa," she shrieked, "Papa, Papa, come quickly!"

"My God, it's Jane," shouted Philemon springing out of his chair and running to the front door.

"Papa!" cried Jane, throwing herself into her father's arms.

"What is it, Jane? Tell me," demanded Philemon.

"Papa, that horrible man," stammered Jane gasping for breath, "the Reverend who looks like a silly old clown. We saw him in the woods. Betsy ran at him and told me to go and get you. Papa, come now, quickly."

"John, Joshua, there are two muskets in the cupboard at the bottom of the staircase, powder and balls next to them. We'll prime them down at the scene if we have to."

John and Sir Joshua rushed into the house and in seconds were back with the weapons.

"Come on, let us go. Jane, show us where the horrible man is."

They raced across the lawn, young Jane directing them down the pathway and into the woods. Holding her tightly, Philemon sprinted round the bend where the giant oak tree trunk lay, John and Joshua fast on his heels.

"Oh my God, it's Betsy," he shouted, putting Jane down and hurrying over to where the unconscious Betsy lay.

"She's still breathing, Philemon," said John bending over her face, "although she's lost a lot of blood, she's not bleeding much now. We need to get her back into the house and call for a doctor."

"Yes, of course," said Philemon, "but where's Dunn? He could not be far away. Joshua, prime the muskets, I will get over this tree trunk and skirt about behind those bushes, the river's flowing right behind, so maybe he's trying to cross it. I'll yell if I see him."

Ebenezer pulled the rowing boat a fraction away from where it had been standing.

"Blast!" he muttered. "It's heavy, it obviously needs two men to do this."

He worked out that by wobbling and then pulling it, it moved further and with a concerted effort, he managed to drag it down to the water's edge. One final push and the boat gently floated out onto the water. Holding onto the bow, he heaved himself over its side, managing to get himself in. The two oars lay under the seat and picking them up, he fitted them into the oarlocks.

Controlling the fearful panic rising in him as he heard Philemon's voice shouting out on the other side of the bushes, he slowly let the oars dip into the water and manoeuvring one of them forward, he felt the boat slowly turn around. Sitting facing the stern and the inlet, he dipped both oars and pulled. The boat slowly slid away and repeating the procedure, he felt himself coasting away from the riverbank towards the middle of the river.

"John, Joshua," yelled Philemon as he stumbled out of the bushes onto the pebbly inlet. "Quickly, finish priming those muskets as fast as you can. He's getting away, he's in an old rowing boat out on the river."

John and Sir Joshua burst onto the inlet the muskets primed and loaded.

"Look, out there. He's obviously going to try to row away downriver."

"Philemon, take this," said Sir Joshua handing him the musket, and stepping back to allow John and Philemon a clear aim at the fugitive.

"Make it count, John," yelled Philemon, "we can't let him get away."

"That I will," replied John, levelling the musket to his shoulder and taking aim.

The rowing boat had reached the middle stream of the Dart and the current was beginning to drag it sideways downriver. Ebenezer began to struggle with the oars, desperately trying to turn the boat in the right direction when the sound of the muskets being fired startled him into terror-stricken panic. Dropping the oars, he heard the whizzing sound of the two musket balls zipping across the river towards him. The slam of the two balls thudding into the side of the rowing boat spun it round drastically, and as he looked over his shoulder to see where the current was taking him, he screamed out in sheer terror.

Philemon, John and Sir Joshua watched open-mouthed as Ebenezer's boat spun out of control, the current dragging it further away from the middle of the river. The two oars, snatched out of their oarlocks, disappeared over the side as the boat hurtled towards a huge jagged rock-like boulder rising out of the water near the far side bank.

The current hurled the rowing boat at the rock, smashing it against its scabrous surface like a frenzied monster, bits of wood flying everywhere across the river while Ebenezer, thrown high into the air with arms and legs flailing, plummeted back down to within inches of the rock, disappearing under the fast-flowing water.

Within seconds, there was calm, debris floating over the river and drifting down the river with the current. Half of the boat lay upturned on the rock, the bow having fastened itself to a jagged spear-like point. There was no sign of Ebenezer.

"My goodness!" uttered John, staring at the debris floating in the water.

"There's no sign of him," said Sir Joshua peering downriver.

"There's no way he could've survived that," said Philemon. "He's drowned. The current will have taken his body way downriver. We will send out a search party to find it. John, can you inform the appropriate people of his death. When we recover his body, it'll be buried quickly and without any fuss."

"Yes, I'll make sure the authorities are informed," said John. "So, gentlemen, that's the end to all of that!"

"Come, we must make sure Betsy sees the doctor," said Philemon. "We'll carry her up to the house and I'll send Wilf to fetch him."

Young Jane was waiting next to Betsy, who had woken from her unconsciousness, still groggy and sore.

"Come on, Betsy," said Philemon, "we're going to carry you up to the house and wait for the doctor."

"Did he get away?" asked Betsy. "That devil priest."

Philemon picked her up in his arms, carrying her gently back up the path.

"Don't you worry about him, Betsy," he said, "it's all over. I will tell you all about it when we're in the house. By the way," he said looking over his shoulder at John and Sir Joshua, "I wonder how the King's address went."

* * *

Dusk was beginning to fall over the River Dart. Fragments of debris from the rowing boat floated randomly over the water, while other splintered segments jostled their way up against both sides of the riverbanks. On a reed-covered inlet on the opposite bank to Sharpham Manor, Ebenezer coughed up a stream of river water, spewing it out onto the grimy stretch of mud where he lay. His head throbbed from being knocked unconscious when he had hit the water; apart from that, there was little he remembered. He flexed his fingers and wriggled his toes, pleased that he could feel them – he was alive.

Pulling himself up, he struggled to his feet, wondering which side of the Dart he had ended up on. Peering up the river, he saw a jetty on the other side of the bank that led away from a riverside boathouse. His eyes travelled up through the trees behind the boathouse to where the dwindling sun was reflecting on what he guessed had to be the windows of Sharpham Manor. The current had not taken him that far, he thought.

With Sharpham Manor on the other side of the river, the woods and fields behind him had to be pointing in the direction of Stoke Gabriel, and hence on to Paignton. He knew he had to get away from the river, search parties would be out looking for him soon. Somehow, he would have to look presentable enough to avoid drawing attention to himself. How, he did not know.

Wading through the reeds, he stumbled up onto the riverbank and seeing a fallen tree in front of the riverside woods, staggered over to seat himself on its thick trunk. Asking for help from anyone in or near Ashprington was unthinkable, he would hang if he tried. He would have to forage for food around the countryside and somehow find a change of clothing. But first, he needed shelter and somewhere to dry out and keep warm. Breathing in sharply, he struggled off the tree trunk and with his ankle still throbbing, he limped away towards the dark confines of the riverside forest where he'd find his way through and then on towards Stoke Gabriel, a straight line from where he was. He would look for refuge, anywhere beyond what was now for him the hostile communities of the village of Ashprington and the riverside hamlets that fringed the River Dart.

Stopping, he turned and gazed across at the span of green and claret coloured fields that sloped down to the ancient oak and beech trees guarding the river. His eyes soaked up the magnificence of the fields and meadows stretching far back within the acres of Sharpham Estate, their richness radiating in the now setting sun. Listening to the sound of the river coursing its way towards the sea, he turned back around and with a desperate sigh, hobbled away from the setting that he had once thought of as home.

High up on a branch of a spindly pine tree on the opposite side of the river, the glowing yellow eyes of a bird of prey bored down on the water below, x-raying a shoal of wild brown river trout as they rode the current past the riverside jetty of Sharpham Manor. Calmly, the osprey opened its hooked black bill and rising effortlessly from the branch, dropped down to scoop a good-sized member of the shoal cleanly from the water. Clutching the trout firmly in its talons, it rose from the river and with its wings bent and bowed downwards, it arrowed up the River Dart to skim the foliage at Ham Point and on over the village of Ashprington to its stick nest high up in the riverside trees.